AMIDST A PROPHECY
SORCERER'S DOOR – BOOK II

by

Steve Graziani

Grazarts Publishing

Printed in the United States of America

First Printing, 2015

ISBN 978-0-9961375-3-9

Grazarts Publishing
1839 Blake Ave, Loft 12
Los Angeles, CA, 90039

www.grazarts.com

Cover Art by Steve Graziani

IN MEMORY OF
Donald E. Washburn

Prelude

Peter and Devon Capwell came from the stars across the Universe to the Sphere for other reasons than to be part of a prophecy... they simply came to survive.

Long ago, five species were placed on the Sphere and separated by virtually impenetrable walls. Left hidden in each of the five lands was the Sorcerer's Door, a spell not bound by walls. Also left, a Prophecy that someday two round-ears would come and topple those walls. The Prophecy did not say if this would be good or bad... just that it would be.

Now Peter and Devon are caught in the Prophecy... on opposite sides...

Chapter One

I f Grimicks could smile... and it's hard to tell with an animal that's a cross between a large frog and a jackrabbit... the two frolicking in the deep blue grass would at least be grinning. These two are just pups, only a foot and a half tall, still small enough to be hidden in the deeper grassy patches.

They pop up now and then, get bearings on each other, and then disappear in the wave of blue, only to pop up again in a few seconds, and yards away. They're playing a game of Grimick tag.

Grimicks, being rather vain creatures, can't resist stopping when their play drifts down close to Spirin's western wall. They stand as high as they can on their back legs and peer curiously at their reflections in the wall.

From a distance the wall almost imperceptibly blends with the real landscape of Spirin. It's a mirror membrane that stretches as high and wide as one can see, and it makes Spirin seem like it goes on forever... Nothing could be further from the truth. While at one time the wall protected the Land of Spirin, though few thought about it in that way, a recent series of events now makes it seem more like the massive wall imprisons the land.

Abruptly the self-obsessed Grimicks stop ogling themselves in the mirror, spin around and speed into the brush.

Peter Capwell, now nineteen, floats over the ridge and down towards the wall on his hoverboard. As he comes up on the wall, Peter glances over at the two Grimick heads taking a peek. They duck down and scurry away, undulating the grass. Not that Peter is known for mistreating Grimicks, but he has no great fondness for them ever since his girlfriend, Shan, turned him into a six foot Grimick a while back... it is an experience not easily forgotten.

It's been two years since this Earther accidently tumbled out into Spirin, and only three moons since Peter narrowly escaped a battle beyond the wall that now stands before him. Once he viewed the wall with reverence; now he looks upon it with measured concern. Beyond that wall is the Land of Goreipor, a land of leather-clad soldiers who thrive on war.

Peter and Shan had to face off against some of those soldiers... and against Peter's kid brother, Devon, who went to that land in search of power.

He does his best to shake the unpleasant memory.

He shifts his thoughts to the reflection he sees of a cave dug into a tier of rocks not far from the wall. This is what he had come for in the first place... not to remember battles lost. Peter turns away from the wall, with a small uncontrollable shiver and heads for the cave... Devon's cave.

Cobwebs quickly claimed the interior of Devon's boy-cave after he left. The cave is a sanctuary strongly resembling the survivalist cave he once had back on Earth. Peter brushes the webbing away as he enters. A small glow globe floats slightly ahead of him to light the way, causing the shadows to dance about the room. Once inside he conjures a couple of larger light globes that drift up high and illuminate the whole cave.

It's pretty much as Peter remembers it. He has only been there once, but it reminds him of the cave Devon holed up in on Earth... the same cave in which Peter had partied back before this adventure began... the same cave in which Devon had to survive when the area where they both lived turned into a quarantine zone from which no one escaped alive.

Peter tries to get a handle on what happened... on what he might have done differently. It's a useless exercise, but he can't shake the guilty thoughts racing around in his head. He thinks on how small things from the past irreparably shape the future, but we usually don't know to what degree until it's already done.

He kicks a homemade bunk. A cloudy plume of dust drifts up reminding him of when he, Shan and Ramie first got back to Earth to discover the ash-covered wasteland that was once his home in Oregon. Three thousand square miles were laid waste by a meteor sent by the Lord of Goreipor, a dark land just beyond the wall.

Lost in thought, he takes a seat on the edge of the bunk.

He notices a piece a paper on the floor, almost obscured in the dirt. He moves it with the tip of his shoe and realizes it's a folded photograph. Peter picks up and unfolds the photo – it's of him and Devon next to his dirt bike... from a lifetime ago... back before their worlds changed.

Staring at the image of a younger, perkier Devon brings back so many memories... most of a boy that needed his older brother... far from the situation now. Back then Devon's only concerns were school, chess, a little skateboarding and impressing his older brother. Life's twists ended up repainting a much darker Devon.

Peter has to remember that some of those twists were his fault... not intentional, but still his fault. When he accidently fell through the Sorcerer's Door he left Devon to grow up far too fast... in a violent wasteland that did not nurture the weak. Without guidance Devon mistook violence for strength... and when they were reunited, before Peter could teach his kid brother the difference, Devon jumped the wall to Goreipor in search of power... carrying his violence with him.

Peter folds the photo of lighter days and slides it into his pocket. He stands and starts towards the cave's entrance but before he gets more than a couple feet he stops at a workbench. Like everything else, the bench is cobwebbed, but a glint off a piece of metal catches his eye. Brushing it off, Peter realizes it's an unfinished razor disc. Devon had fabricated a number of them to use as weapons. At a very intense point before Devon jumped the wall, Peter even thought his brother might use one of those discs against him.

A familiar female voice yells in from outside the cave, "Are you going to linger in there all day?"

It's Shan... Peter welcomes her breaking into his thoughts since they're getting him no closer to understanding the whys of the past. With one last glance at the disc he holds, he tosses it back on the workbench. Dust drifts up as it clangs down.

As Peter emerges from the cave, he finds Shan leaning up against an outcropping of rocks. Shan is the budding beauty that Peter almost landed on when he first fell through the Sorcerer's Door a mere two years ago. She has blossomed. Not only is she a striking young woman, but she's also the only person in Spirin whom Peter would trust with having his back in a dicey situation... he knows how much that trust has cost her.

He doesn't bother asking why she doesn't come in.

He knows the cave is an unpleasant reminder to Shan of her loss of innocence about what men are capable of doing to each other. Even though Devon fought at their side then, the battle on the plateau of Goreipor was a horrific window into what she, herself, is capable of doing.

In one manner or another Devon is responsible for introducing Shan to the darkness of men... she wants nothing to do with him... or his cave.

Finally Peter asks, "You been waiting long?"

With a slight chuckle, Shan says, "You know me better than that... I don't wait long for anyone... even you. Now on the other hand, Gran-D has tugged for both of us, and he's not that good at waiting."

"I know... I know," Peter says, trying not to be short with her; he has felt the tug, too. How could he not feel it here on Spirin where everything is done by sorcery, including their version of person-to-person phone calls? Tugs by Gran-D, the Grand Master in Spirin, usually add complications. Peter's musing over Devon has his head reeling already... he's not anxious to hear of more complexities.

He just nods to Shan in agreement that they should go. But even before leaving, his attention is once again drawn towards the massive mirror wall, as if he can sense Devon staring at him from that other land – so close and yet so far away. Perhaps even laughing from that distance.

Chapter Two

Devon stands on a battlement near the drawbridge of Lord Kildemar's dark fortress in Goreipor. He stares towards the East and the unseen land of Spirin, where he knows his brother must be looking back. Devon's not laughing.

It took a long time to reunite with his brother. When Peter came back to Earth and rescued him, he thought at long last they were together again, as they belonged... brain and brawn. Naturally Devon knew he was the brains side of the equation. If Peter only understood the power the two of them could have together, they would still be united. This loss saddens him.

"You abandoned me!" comes a voice from behind Devon.

Without any sense of urgency Devon turns to Ramie Dee, Shan's kid brother, and smiles, "Stop your whining... you seem to still be in one piece."

"No thanks to you... Some witch is bossing me around."

"Maybe that witch is protecting you... just as I have been. You ever think of it in that way?" Devon says.

With self-righteous puffing, Ramie grumbles, "The way I think of it is that you needed me to get you here... and now I'm stuck taking orders from a whole new set of older people."

"Un-puff yourself, it doesn't suit you... And, by the way, don't you think I could have figured out how to use the pendant on my own? You're here because I figured that after you settle down and accept what is happening, I could use a valuable ally." Devon knows what effect this will have.

Ramie tries to hide it but it's clear he likes even the slightest hint of his being important; his whole demeanor eases.

"Have you used any of your powers yet?" Devon asks, trying to sound as nonchalant as possible.

Ramie meekly says, "I'm scared to."

"See... You have better instincts than you know," Devon says, knowing a little praise goes a long way with Ramie. "I suggest you don't, at least for now."

While Ramie is both soaking up the attention, and pondering what he means, Devon adds, "It might be important to both of us if you'd keep track of that witch... I think her name is Racinda." Devon well knows Witch Racinda's name, and that his request has more weight than he wants to let on. No use having Ramie thinking on it too much.

To save face Ramie has to add a touch of rebellion, even if he knows the answer in advance, "And if I do, you going to send me home?" It comes off with a slight tone that he's not really all that anxious to leave.

With a laugh, "Not yet... but it would go a long ways towards me keeping you alive while you're by my side."

Ramie really can't tell if he's joking or not. Before he can think of a way to not feel confused, Devon cuts off his thoughts by casually pointing over Ramie's shoulder. Ramie turns to see Captain Pirus marching down the battlement with two of his personal guards in tow.

Ramie wants to feel included... but not that much, at least not for now. Ramie's only a troublemaker on an amateur scale... he knows he's out of his depth here. With a quick nod to Devon, he turns tail and rushes away from the approaching soldiers. He tries not to look scared. Devon is glad Ramie lacks bravery; it makes him easier to control.

A smile leaks out of Pirus as he arrives. "Where's the little one going in such a hurry?"

Devon brushes it off with, "Who knows? ... I think away from your weapons."

Captain Pirus, being the soldier who played along when Devon allowed Shan and Peter to escape, has something on Devon... just as he knows the boy has something on him. Devon's brashness and early display of strategy struck a favorable note in Captain Pirus. For now he is willing to play along... but then, nothing is written in stone.

"You tell him not to use his powers yet?" Pirus asks.

From the look on Devon's face, Pirus knows it is an unnecessary question. He likes seeing the boy staying on his game, but the game is just starting.

Devon changes the subject with a gesture at the two guards who have hung back, "Are they here for me?" He says this with a tone of levity, having recognized the two as among Captain Pirus' personal guards there at the battle on the plateau, though they remained below. His deal with Captain Pirus spared his personal guards, even if the Captain was not fully aware of it.

"You know they're not. We have an audience with Lord Kildemar. He doesn't like being kept waiting. I brought them along just for show... don't think Kildemar quite trusts you yet," Pirus says with a hard to read smile.

"That doesn't worry me. Did he consider my suggestion yet?" Devon asks. He can't imagine his suggestion would not be considered, but he figures it's polite to ask.

"I suspect that is what the audience is about." With a slight laugh he adds, "Either he's considered it, or he wants me to take your head." With this, he gestures for his soldiers to lead the way.

Devon is more than anxious to get on with it since the first stage of his plan has to precede the next. Like fishing, he needs to know he's set the hook before the play can begin.

As Devon falls in beside Pirus, the Captain says, "Have to admit it was a pretty gutsy proposal in a land of 'kill first... think later'."

All Devon responds with is, "Change is coming."

As the two head off, Pirus' two guards dutifully fall in behind.

Ramie creeps down a stone hallway lit only by wall-mounted torches. The flickering light forms ominous shadows created by silhouettes of armor mounted along the hall's walls.

From what little Ramie knows of armor, which is nothing, he finds these mounted testaments to war somewhat strange. The pieces are far from what he would imagine a person would want to display. They are badly dinged from wear; metal torn, chainmail ripped, rust or brown discoloration splotching all over... hardly display quality. Then it suddenly dawns on him... these were taken from the defeated! The tears are real, same with the brown stains. Now the shadows created by the grotesque collection take on a new, darker feel.

Ramie shudders.

He starts to back out of the hallway as quietly as possible, making sure to stay in the middle so as to not arouse the ghosts of the shadows. Unexpectedly, he backs into something in the middle of the hallway... nothing should be there. A look of shock comes over him as he reaches back and feels something leathery.

Ramie jumps forward, holds his breath and spins around. It is exactly what Ramie was hoping it would not be... a soldier.

"What are you? And, what are you doing here?" the soldier coarsely demands.

Ramie stutters out, "I'm... I'm a guest... of the witch."

It must mean something; for the briefest moment Ramie detects a hint of fear wash over the soldier's face. It is only momentary, his scowl returns quickly.

"I know nothing of any... guest... what is a guest? Whatever you are, you do not belong here!" he says as he takes one loud step towards Ramie.

Ramie isn't really sure he saw fear in the soldier's face at the mention of the witch, but being the mischievous runt that he's always been he can't resist trying to play the angle. "You mean someone under the protection of Witch... uh..." For a moment he struggles to remember her name. "Witch... uh... Racinda... Someone under the protection of Witch Racinda is not free to roam around the stone... whatever it is?"

The soldier may have shown a hint of fear before, but now he senses he's being played and his irritation is unmistakable. With one hand now firmly placed on his sword he takes a louder stomp towards Ramie. "It's a fortress... for soldiers... and you don't belong here, whatever you are."

Ramie inches back, figuring he's overplayed his hand.

From behind the soldier comes a woman's voice, "Do we have a problem here, sergeant?"

Now the fear in the soldier's face is crystal clear.

Witch Racinda's position of power is unmistakable, being the dark Lord's personal witch and, for that matter, the only person up till now who has magical powers in Goreipor. He's seen her stop a man's heart with the slightest gesture of her staff. Granted, that was at the request of Lord Kildemar, but the sergeant isn't about to guess what she does on her own time.

He spins and comes to attention. "I did not know he spoke the truth... I meant him no harm."

"Be off with you... I will deal with my... guest," Racinda says, with a wave of her hand.

The sergeant gives her a quick bow and then rushes away.

Witch Racinda stands out amongst the hard, cold Goreiporians partially because she doesn't look like she's on the verge of killing someone, but more due to her slightly softer skin and the curl to the bottom of her ears. It's the same type of curl that those who inhabit Spirin have. Granted, she doesn't look like she'll kill, but her black gown frames the cold sternness of her pale skin.

Ramie looks pleased with himself till he looks up at Racinda's glare. He backs away a step.

"I thought I suggested you not wander around for a while," she says.

The first thought that crosses Ramie's mind is that she used the word *suggested*... but he's not home in Spirin and playing on words may not be the wisest idea at present. If he can't wheedle out of it maybe the best thing would be the truth. He says, "I was looking for Devon and got lost." Well, at least a half-truth.

"And did you find him?" she responds.

Even half-truths become complicated. "Um... well... yeah, but when I did, some big guys with weapons came along... I didn't get much chance to talk to him." It's clear he's struggling with what to say.

Seeing this, she eases her glare. "I suggest you follow me back to the safety of my wing of the fortress for now... but soon we'll have to discuss your round-eared friend."

"But... " Ramie starts to protest.

She cuts him off with, "Not now... first you need to figure out whom to trust."

Devon kidnapped him into this scary land, but might still be his friend... The witch is from Spirin, but must have done something horrible to end up here... then, she just might be keeping him safe! Ramie knows he's going to end up with a whopping headache tonight.

How much Ramie longs for the simplicity of getting yelled at by Shan, or even his father, Kalish... how safe that would all feel right now. He thinks that if he ever gets home he'll stay out of trouble. Finally... a thought that causes him a welcome laugh.

Chapter Three

Peter and Shan float over a hill on their hoverboards. In the distance lies the Dees' home. A couple of years ago, a house shaped like a tall brightly colored pyramid supporting a wide yellow umbrella-style roof might have seemed strange to Peter. Nowadays, a simple cubical home would look out of place. The yard of glowing flowers is surrounded by a lime-green picket fence.

If Peter were to give it a second thought, he would probably say the Dees' home is tame by Spirinese standards.

As they come to the picket fence, both kids go to ground and, with a snap of their fingers, their hoverboards disappear.

Just then Atta Dee rushes out of the house and straight towards the fence gate by the kids. As she reaches them she energetically blurts out, "I'm off to see Cassandra, she says she can sense Ramie from beyond the wall."

Shan shakes her head. "Mom, she's a crackpot... All she can sense is how much attention you'll give her if she says something like that."

Atta puts on her motherly look, "Shan, I wish you wouldn't use those Earther terms like *crackpot*... they're so tasteless." Then, to Peter, "I blame you for teaching her those words." Getting no response from Shan, she breaks down, "OK... she is a bit... odd, but I can't just sit here doing nothing."

"So you're going to listen to nonsense?" Shan says with a hint of exhaustion.

Calmly Atta answers, "No, I'm going to listen to a well-meaning woman about what she thinks she hears because it's important to her... and that makes me feel good."

Shan is caught off guard by her mother again... she has little valid response other than to smile her youth.

Atta Dee is the matriarch of the family; quietly, and in her motherly fashion, she shapes the flow of life for the Dees. Most of the time with smiles and gentle suggestions... when she's not smiling, all back away to listen. That is, for all but her father, Gran-D... she has yet to come close to taming him.

With a smile she starts to head on her way, but she turns and says, "By the way, Gran-D is looking for you."

"We already felt him," says Peter.

Then Atta's off to make someone happy.

Just as Shan and Peter move towards the house, but before they reach the porch, Kalish Dee, Shan's father, comes out.

After a glance around he asks, "Your mother off to Cassandra's?"

He's a bear of a man with gentle eyes. For a living he uses his sorcerer's skills to build most any- and everything. In Spirin there is no money, just skills that the people happily trade with each other.

Shan sheepishly offers, "Yeah, she's gone off to help someone... I should have known."

"Not to worry child, she's sneaky in that way. I'm off to fix the Healer's porch... Peter, you really need to stop needing to be patched up." Off on his way now to do his chores, he says, "By the way, Gran-D is looking for you."

Shan and Peter say in unison, "We already felt him."

Without another word, Kalish turns and heads away.

Shan and Peter glance at each other, take a deep breath and head inside in search of Gran-D.

The kids enter the living room. Their slow movement shows they're not that anxious to hear whatever new twist they're sure Gran-D is about to spring on them. He's been mysteriously absent for the past few days, which makes them even more suspicious.

Gran-D is sitting in his chair by the fireplace with a look that's less than his normal mischievous smile. This tells Peter and Shan they were right. He quietly gestures for the two to take a seat... even more ominous.

Gran-D has always had a knack for seeing what's going on in others' heads. "Quit dragging your feet... we do have something to talk about... and, yes, you're probably not going to like it," he says. When Gran-D is not playfully talking in puzzles to ease the kids to the point, he can be pretty direct.

"OK, it sounds serious so cut to the chase," Shan says before Peter has a chance to.

"A message was sent to the Council from beyond the wall by someone named Lord Kildemar. They plan on coming through the wall and meeting with the Council," Gran-D says in a matter-of- fact tone.

Peter is the first to jump up, clearly upset. "When did all this happen? Why didn't you tell us about it?"

Gran-D calmly says, "Perhaps because of the way you're acting right now... The Council voted to delay mentioning it to you and Shan till we had a chance to consider the matter. If it makes any difference, I did not agree with them."

Shan chimes in, "You've gone against the Council many times... why not now?"

"Child, because age taught me to not to do the same thing every time... it loses its potency. It wouldn't have mattered anyway... the communication wasn't in the form of a request. They sent a written message through the wall in a tone that strongly implied they were not even expecting a response," he says.

Peter immediately wonders if Devon was able to hide the existence of the remaining pendant; if so, there would be no way Spirin could answer anyway. It's something Devon would do; he always likes to keep information as a weapon, a side effect of so many years of chess strategy. Then again, from the little he and Shan were exposed to those beyond the wall, they didn't seem like the type of beings who *asked* in the first place. Peter is clearly agitated by the prospect of them coming to Spirin.

Trying to bring him back on track, asks, "So, what is the Council's stance on this *visit?*"

"They're mixed... but you know this idea of outsiders is all vary alien to them," Gran-D says apologetically.

"You mean they're frightened," snaps Peter.

"They want to see it as a possible alternative to their worst fears." Gran-D knows Peter is right... they're frightened.

Peter comes back, "Just like the Prophecy, they want to bury their heads in the sand and hope everything works out on its own... it won't. They haven't seen the people who live beyond that wall."

Getting keyed up, Shan adds, "And Devon can't be trusted!" She takes a breath and tries to bring it back down, "Did they say when they would be coming? Are they going to bring Ramie back with them?"

"When... soon... about Ramie, I don't know," says Gran-D. What he's not saying is that he does know when.

Peter appears lost in thought for a few seconds, then, "Devon's going to be with them... and he wants the remaining pendant, no matter what he says. He either told them about the key and they want it... or he didn't, and he wants it for himself."

"The pendant is safely hidden away," Gran-D assures him. What he doesn't tell Peter is that he hid the pendant as a condition of Master Imton's bringing it out of hiding in the first place to get Shan and Peter to Goreipor. He had to swear a Sorcerer's Oath that he would never disclose its whereabouts to the round-ear, Peter, without the full Council's approval. This was the cost of sending the two kids after his kidnapped grandson, Ramie.

"Until they scare the other Masters," Shan points out.

Gran-D smiles at Shan and says, "That is one of those times of potency when I went against the Council... they don't know where I hid it. Only Master Carringer and I know. He was the other Master who protested against allowing them to address the Council. But what can we do, pretend we're not home?"

Trying to get past his anger, on the matter Peter asks, "Are Shan and I invited to this pow-wow?"

Gran-D's not sure what *pow-wow* literally means but he gets the gist of it. "That hasn't been determined yet, but I promise to push for it, especially if we discover Devon will be with them."

Shan mumbles, "That rat," and uncharacteristically spits in the fireplace.

After a quick laugh, Gran-D says, "Shan, consider all sides of it... if Devon is among them, then that will probably mean that Ramie is still safe. If he is not with them, then we have to be concerned about both of them and their safety." Gran-D tries to see as much as positively as he can, though it is a stretch. He adds, "Who knows? Maybe they will bring Ramie back as a sign of good will. All we can do is wait."

"This is not going to be about good will," Peter says with little doubt.

Clearly wanting to wrap it up, Gran-D says, "As with everything else, only time will tell."

Having gotten the most recent bad news from Gran-D, Peter heads down towards the kids' favorite log by the Graveyard of Spells to try to shake off the prospect of the pending Goreiporian visit. Shan is by his side.

Shan struggles to find something positive about the situation, "I don't know... we didn't really meet any of their leaders, only their soldiers... and it wasn't much of a conversation, with all the fighting. After all, they haven't had a way to cross over before now... maybe they do mean to talk of peace."

"Have you forgotten the arrow in my chest... they clearly had a way to get someone over before Devon stole the pendants," Peter says. Then, more heatedly, he adds, "No, Devon's behind this move somehow... and it's not for the good."

She thinks on it for a brief second, "You're right... I'm going to wring the neck of that brother of yours! Now... I hope he dares show his face."

Even though she didn't say it in a joking tone, it brings a smile to Peter. With a light-hearted lilt, he says, "What happened to that girl who... on rare occasions... only took out her frustrations on me... like turning me into a Grimick?"

The look on Shan's face shows she finds his comments less than funny. "What happened to her... was your brother."

"You mean... my world and its ways, don't you?" he says, with less levity in his voice.

Shan backs down, "No... The same kind of darkness exists beyond that wall. It's just that your brother is bringing it to us. Who knows what's behind the other walls of our land."

Peter's quiet for a minute as the reach the log. It's the same log Devon split in half with his razor discs... the moment when

Peter knew there was the split was final between them. The log was stitched together by Peter, but it never will be as it had been. Peter takes a seat on the log and stares up at the Graveyard of Spells, once the resting place of the spell that set the events of the last couple of years into motion. He remains quiet for the longest time.

Shan knows something is churning in his head so she simply takes a seat beside him and lets him churn.

Finally she's had enough silence, "OK... what's going on in that head of yours?"

"The other walls," he says, still staring off.

"What?"

Peter turns to her, "You're right... we don't know what's beyond the other walls. There may be beings that can help... they may even have powers greater than we have in Spirin... and maybe they're not as naïve."

"You mean powers that they may know how to use for defense, not like here." After saying this, she realizes how snippy it came out; she also knows how right it came out. When it comes to defending their land all the power that the people of Spirin possess as sorcerers is useless if they are not prepared, or willing, to defend themselves.

Peter's look says he knows exactly what she's thinking. He knows the people of Spirin should not be faulted for their innocence; it is just their stubbornness over opening their eyes that frustrates him. It's not even the people of Spirin... it's the Council that doesn't inform them. He finally says, "I'm sorry to have to suggest it, but they can learn. Unfortunately, it may require them to see why they need to learn."

Chapter Four

Master Carringer, the youngest of the seven Masters and the only one undignified enough to enjoy using a hoverboard, cuts a wake across a field of blue grass near his home. It's late morning and the afternoon promises to be taxing so he's trying to let off tension while he can.

Carringer is also the only Master, or outside Shan and Peter, the only one still in Spirin, to have had any dealings with those beyond the wall. Those dealings were not pleasant... he almost lost his life to Goreiporian soldiers.

As he whips over the crest of a hill, Peter and Shan sweep in on their boards. They converge on him from both flanks... a friendly ambush.

All three bring their boards to ground.

"And it's nice to see you, too... what's with the ambush? Or, should I say what are you two after?" Carringer says. He knows they've heard of the meeting.

Peter remembers the first time he met Master Carringer when he auditioned to be trained by the Masters so long ago... he appeared to Peter as a six-foot orange lizard. Some of the other Masters have a hard time tolerating Carringer's antics but he is the head Spell Master, and the primary spell creator. It's a position that requires a youthful imagination so they tolerate his style... with a degree of grumbling.

Shan says, "We were hoping that you'd give us a little more information about this get together with those from beyond the... you know. Gran-D only... "

He interjects, "And you figured I was the only one who might be swayed by your smile." Before she can respond, he goes on, "It's not exactly a get-together when you're informed *there 'will be a meeting'*. We could try not being home but who knows the consequences of that."

"So they set a time for when they're coming?" Peter asks.

Master Carringer now looks a bit uncomfortable with being put on the spot. "Gran-D didn't tell you because he wants to protect you... you know, you as part of the Prophecy...."

"I'm so sick of that damn Prophecy stuff," Peter snaps.

Carringer continues, "But other's on the Council are afraid, what with your history with Devon and your experiences beyond the wall, that you'd mess things up. If they could exclude me they would. Some are holding onto the idea that this is an *friendship*-type meeting."

In an irritated tone, Peter says, "This has nothing to do with friendship or olive branches... and you know that... you've been beyond that wall. It's a strategic move on Spirin... plain and simple!"

"Peter and I think Devon is behind this," Shan adds.

Carringer protests, "We don't even know if Devon is with them. For that matter, as hard as it sounds, we don't even know if Devon is still alive."

"Trust me... he is... and he's somehow orchestrating this. They sent someone to kill me... twice. They're into show-of-force, not strategy, and even if you don't know it, strategy is more dangerous than force in the long run." Peter truly believes what he is saying.

Carringer counters, "So what are you two going to do, be an army of two barging in to strike them down? Maybe the Council is right not want you there."

"We just want to be the ears of reason, not coming from a position of fear and only hearing what the Council hopes to hear," Shan says.

Peter is quick to add, "... even if it's not what's being said. Look, I know my brother and how he thinks... and whether you believe it or not, knowing his mind will help us figure out what's actually being said. We should be there to hear it so we can be at least advisory voices after the meeting."

"Gran-D doesn't trust them... I don't trust them... and I think by now you know Imton is not of Spirin, so he's not the trusting type, by nature. I think we have some balance within the Council to deal with this. I can't invite you to this meeting," says Carringer with a sense of finality.

Then he conjures his hoverboard and mounts it. Just as he's about to take off, he pauses and looks back at Shan and Peter. "If you use one of those new mini-spy globes that are harder to detect at the meeting that's 'not' happening today, I can't do anything about it." He pushes off.

Peter yells after him, "Is the meeting *not happening* at Master Melick's?"

Master Carringer does not answer as he swoops away, but he shoots a mini-starburst that pops high in the air above him as an answer.

Carringer is gone but Peter and Shan have gotten what they came for. All there is to do now is wait, so they head for their special log.

"So what are we going to actually do?" Shan says as they sit next to each other, back against the log.

"Exactly what Carringer told us *not* to do," Peter answers.

"If Devon is there, won't he know it?" she asks.

"The mini-globe is something Carringer and I conjured up since we got back, just in case it were ever needed... I don't think Devon will detect it, at least not right off. We don't need to be there, we just need to hear the tone of it," Peter assures her.

"Like Master Carringer said, he may not even be there. I hope he is for Ramie's sake... I even hope Ramie is," Shan says wishfully.

Peter puts his arm around her. "Don't hold high hopes for that. Ramie is a pawn right now."

Having become even more proficient with chess than Peter, Shan knows what he says is probably right. As Ramie's sister she hates that he's right.

Peter senses her torment. "Don't you know what this meeting means? It means they are stalling... no matter what they say."

Shan looks a bit puzzled.

Peter continues, "They're afraid of us, or I should say, Devon knows to be afraid of us. If they had the power they would not waste time talking."

"You mean those soldiers we fought on the plateau fear us... are you kidding?" Shan is not following his logic yet.

"You mean the soldiers we defeated, don't you? Did you see any magic, any sorcery, on that plateau? We have the power, even if we don't know it." Peter says this as if he were convinced of it... at least he hopes he is.

Shan lets out a little laugh, "Can you imagine my mom defending us on that dark plateau?"

"We have to use what time we can," Peter says. Then he laughs, "Teaching Atta to handle a sword is sort of a comical vision."

An echoing voice comes out of nowhere off in the distance, "He's right about that part... she would be a sight."

Peter immediately recognizes the voice as Devon's even if Shan can't place it right off from the echo. Peter identifies the words, not the sound.

A swirl of smoke drifts down into some bright colored bushes about ten yards away. After a couple seconds Devon walks out of the bushes. He wears his razor disc belt and carries a lance.

Before Peter can react, Shan is up on her feet charging at Devon, regardless of his weaponry. Before Devon can react, she slaps him across the face. The sound of her slap echoes... so much for magic when a good old-fashioned belt will do.

Devon rubs his face and just as Shan is about to strike again, he raises a hand, "I give you that one, but back off now." When it appears she's not listening, he holds the hand out. Her next swing is stopped by an invisible force field. He backs away from her, and says to Peter, "Call her off... before she gets hurt."

By this time Peter is on his feet. With a slight chuckle he says, "Shan, let's hear what he has to say before you beat him up too much."

Shan glares at Devon, "Where's my brother?"

"I'm afraid Ramie couldn't make it this trip, but trust me, he's alive and healthy," Devon says, knowing this will not do.

"Trust you? Bull!" she snaps. But she backs away.

Devon smiles, "Now, if you're through attacking me, may I talk with my brother privately?"

Shan looks to Peter, who nods that it might be best.

She turns back to Devon and points to the bushes he came from, "I'll be just over there... one wrong move and I'll be on you in a flash... understand."

"I'm shaking in my boots," he says, with a wink.

She doesn't care for the wink but she backs away, never taking her eyes off Devon.

Devon turns his attention to Peter, "I created a minor difficulty for myself by skipping out on my handlers to talk to you before our historic meeting... at least they think they're my handlers." There's a twitch to Peter's face that Devon catches, "Oh... they didn't invite you to the meeting... did they?"

Peter tries not to show Devon he's right. "What did you come to say? Get it out before I sic Shan on you again."

"I just wanted to give you another chance to be on the winning side... for old time's sake," says Devon.

"Are your friends going to mention *winning and losing sides* to the Council, or are they just going to straight-out lie?" Peter studies Devon's face, knowing he didn't get him alone just to offer him another chance to change sides... something Devon wouldn't expect him to do. "Do you think getting me alone will get you the other pendant?"

"No, not this time. I don't think you have it anyway... Gran-D has probably squirreled it away somewhere. He's a crafty old guy."

Devon, in turn, watches every twitch of Peter's face, looking for any information he can glean. He smiles, "The truth is that we really don't want to get into a conflict with Spirin. You can thank me for that."

"Bull," is all Peter says.

"It's true. I have a whole world to try and take control of over there... and they are concerned about your powers of sorcery. I convinced them that if we reassure you that we will not mess with Spirin, you would keep to your world."

"And what about Ramie?" Peter says.

"I know you're not going to believe it, but Ramie doesn't want to come back. I offered to bring him this time, even if just for a visit, but he was worried the family wouldn't let him come back. He and I have powers over there... and he likes it," Devon says, trying not to let his lie show through.

"And the other lands?" Peter says this to get a reaction more than words.

"Goreipor is plenty for me. Right now they think I serve them, and it's going to take some time for me to turn that around." Devon says this with as much sincerity he can muster. Then he adds, "By the way, you wouldn't consider trading that other pendant for Ramie, would you? He likes it there, but with the right incentive I can be pretty persuasive."

Now it's Peter that smiles, "Nah, I think we'll keep a hold of it till I come to get him... and you."

"Well, I guess there's not much else to say for now... If I get a chance I'll swing by after the meeting to tell you what happened, considering you won't be there." Devon is trying to dig his spurs in a bit. He never figured he'd get the pendant, but he has gotten some of what he is after.

Peter nods, "Tell Ramie I'll see him soon... and tell this to Lord Kildemar, I think that's his name... that I send my regards. See, I'm not as far out of the loop as you think." Peter also feels he's gained as much as he can from this encounter, perhaps even more than Devon is aware.

As a final gesture, Devon leans his lance against the tree. "Brother, when you come, you might as well have a weapon."

He turns and makes a pretentious bow to Shan. He then turns into a wisp of smoke that shoots up into the lavender sky.

Shan picks up a rock and throws it at the wisp, knowing it will have no effect... it just makes her feel better. Once he's gone Shan walks back over to Peter, still keeping an eye on the sky in case Devon returns.

"I would have turned him into a Grimick, except I like Grimicks too much." She turns to Peter, "So what was that all about?"

"Feeling each other out," is all he says. After she glares at him a little harder, he adds, "He's going after the other worlds before us."

Later that afternoon, Shan and Peter are in the woods some distance from Master Melick's cottage. Neither is watching the cottage. Instead they watch a floating spy globe hovering above them. It's the receiver for the mini-globe that they have conjured within the cottage. Traditionally spy-globes don't require a sending element but Peter has gathered from Carringer's *non-suggestion* that a regular globe wouldn't work. For a people that don't embrace defensive thinking, he suspects they're getting awfully suspicious.

After the images of those gathered in the cottage disappear, Peter takes a deep breath, snaps his fingers and the globe pops.

Now the two turn their attention to the actual cottage. The door opens and Master Melick is the first to exit, followed by Devon, Captain Pirus, Taligarr, the dark lord's eldest son, and a couple Goreiporian soldiers. Melick nods to Taligarr, which gets little response, and then those from beyond the wall move off to the west towards their home.

Gran-D and Master Carringer exit and immediately turns their gaze directly towards where Peter and Shan are hiding.

Before Peter and Shan can retreat, Gran-D disappears and instantly reappears directly behind them.

"So what did you two think of the meeting you were not invited to?" It's not clear if he's upset or not. Peter starts to say something, but Gran-D holds up a finger.

"It's been a long day. Tomorrow I want both of you to meet with the Council." Then he disappears as abruptly as he arrived.

Sheepishly, Shan says, "Do you think he's mad?"

"No... I think he totally counted on us watching. He just couldn't tell us to do it. We've been had by Carringer and the old man... again." Peter has gotten used to being manipulated, even if he's never gotten to liking it. This time, though, he does see the logic to it... *plausible deniability*.

Chapter Five

The grand hall of Lord Kildemar's fortress is filled with its usual entourage of upper level soldiers and inner circle courtesans... along with a fair-sized contingent of armed guards that go hand in hand with the nature of a suspicious ruler.

Fresh back from their excursion to Spirin, Captain Pirus and Devon stand before Kildemar's throne. His son, Taligarr, leans in towards his father and whispers something in his ear.

After Taligarr is finished, Lord Kildemar looks up at Captain Pirus, "I understand that the foreigner separated from the group and you've not rebuked him."

Devon speaks up, "I... "

Kildemar quickly cuts him off. "Silence! I was not addressing you."

Captain Pirus, a professional soldier known for respecting, but not fearing Kildemar, appears unflustered by the accusation. He calmly composes his words, "Within the enemy camp, I don't reprimand my soldiers unless it serves a strategic purpose... it did not. And, with all due respect, ask your son to make his accusations out loud, like a man."

Many in the court wouldn't dare phrase their responses in this manner, but Captain Pirus has proven his worth many times over. Not to look too lenient, Lord Kildemar stares hard at Pirus for a couple of seconds before responding. Others wait to see if the response will be harsh... Pirus is unconcerned.

Lord Kildemar finally says, "Careful, Captain, your straight talk is a privilege, not a right."

Pirus knows this is for the sake of the court. "When I cross the line, I welcome you telling me so."

"When you cross the line I will not have to say it, you will feel my wrath. That said, what of this trip by young Devon?" Kildemar asks.

Pirus nods to Devon, then says, "He chose to do it on his own, true... but when he explained the departure to me it made sense... and, more importantly, it served you."

Captain Pirus speaks his mind, but he's learned how to phrase things so as to keep his head.

"He separated to confront his brother, the other round ear." Pirus pauses here, knowing there will be some flack coming. He also knows it's better to face it straight on.

"The brother whom you professed to have killed?" Kildemar watches the Captain carefully now.

"Yes, sire... I placed a poisoned arrow in the middle of his chest... and, I don't miss," Pirus says without a flinch. Dodging or making excuses would be more damning now.

Devon steps forward without permission and speaks up, "If I may, the people beyond the wall have powers few in your world do, and that includes healing." He's sure that being timid is not the way to win Kildemar's respect, but he doesn't want to push it, so, after that, he steps back.

Lord Kildemar knows Pirus wouldn't dare lie to him and sets aside the erroneous kill for the moment. He addresses Devon, "Your mouth is already open... tell me what you learned from your brother... and why I'm hearing about his being alive only now."

Devon takes a breath, he knows he has to play this right. He decides to go for the hard punch right up front. "Peter, my brother, knows we will be scouting the other lands."

Kildemar sits back on his throne. "Did he tell you this?"

"I've played games of strategy with him too long not to be able to read between the lines. As for why I didn't bring him up before, I wanted to see what I could learn from him that would be of use to you," Devon says, and then pauses for a reaction.

"I will decide what's of use and what's important to me... do you understand that? From now on, I expect to know your plans before I allow them to be mine," Lord Kildemar says coarsely.

"Yes, sire," responds Devon, with an appropriate bow. He hates the bowing part, but it's prudent for now.

Kildemar thinks on the matter a few moments. "If this brother of yours is so, intuitive, perhaps I should send Captain Pirus to finish the job he was supposed to have completed already... to kill this Peter."

Devon doesn't want to fall into the category of the hordes of *yes men* Kildemar has around him... and if harm were to come to Peter, it should only come from him. The trick is to control events without looking like doing so.

"To judge from our meeting with their foolish Council, they want to believe in peace even beyond logic... Is it not better that you support them in this illusion? If you choose to stage another attempt on Peter, you may destroy your well-crafted illusion. You can always kill my brother later." Again, Devon pauses and waits for a response.

Wanting to make clear he's in charge, Kildemar gruffly says, "I'll think on it." Carefully watching Devon's reactions to the threat to his brother's fate, Kildemar adds, "You have something else to say?"

"I would like to scout the other lands as soon as you allow it." Devon doesn't want to push too hard.

"Are you afraid they will use another pendant to mount their own exploration?" Again Kildemar pauses to read the boy. "I'm no fool. You would not have had to judge your brother's intent if the people of that land were locked in. There is another pendant... isn't there?"

Devon's sure that Pirus did not give away the secret of allowing Peter and Shan to escape with a pendant; otherwise, his head would be on the block. Maybe the lord knows something he doesn't, and it would be foolish to challenge him.

He settles on, "There may be. All I was aware of were the two, and I brought them to you... but I was not fully trusted while I was in their world. I would not be surprised at their deceit."

"The question is... whether I should trust you in my world," Kildemar says.

Taligarr, who has been quiet till now but was offended by Devon's earlier remark against him, says, "Why take a chance on this boy not of our world? If we must explore these other worlds, I can do so with soldiers."

Kildemar glares up at Taligarr. He is not sure which he hates more... the hint of challenge from his court, or from his sons. He can easily strike down those of his court... but, though he's not above it, striking down a son is touchier... especially his eldest son, Taligarr.

He decides to be generous, "I'll think on that as well."

That evening Peter stands at the entrance arch of the Graveyard of Spells staring into the forest of thin red stone columns floating in a sea of green mist. He has sneaked out on his own to the one place he understands the least to search for answers... and he doesn't quite know why.

He feels that somehow the Graveyard's green misty fingers have had a hand in more than anyone has been aware. Long ago the Graveyard led Ramie to the forbidden spell that resulted in Peter coming across the Universe. When Peter came home from Earth with the badly wounded Devon, he tried to discard the gun he brought, and the Graveyard, in its own magical way, had him keep the weapon. It's as if the mist within its gates were orchestrating the Prophecy even more than Gran-D.

There are answers in there... he's just not sure how, or what, to ask. Without a clue, he steps into the Graveyard in the hope that answers would somehow come.

Slowly he walks forward, trusting something will reveal itself. The green mist swirls around Peter's feet as he goes, but that's just the motion created by his movement, nothing more... at least, he guesses it's nothing more.

The stone columns he passes are tall headstones for outlawed spells. The spells in the Graveyard aren't necessarily broken... many have been banished because they were deemed too dangerous... or, perhaps, just irrelevant. Peter has often wondered what might exist in the Graveyard of Spells that would be useful weapons for Spirin's defense.

He continues deeper into the forest, reading the names on the different columns as he goes: *'Cold Lightning', 'River of Birds',* and *'Cave of Darkness'*. Each one flames his imagination.

Peter reaches down and brushes his hand through the mist... nothing. The green mist that has so often appeared to have a personality is nothing more than simple fog tonight.

Frustrated Peter throws his hands in the air, "OK... You want to play stupid, I give up!"

He spins around and starts back towards the entrance arch with an angry gait, half hoping his show of temper will spur some reaction... with no idea if playing psychological games with fog will work. As he approaches the exit he decides... probably not... and it feels stupid.

Almost at the gate, Peter turns and stares back into the Graveyard, at a loss to what didn't happen. Nothing again. He lets out a sigh and gives up. His shoulders slump as he turns to walk out. Suddenly a thick finger of mist rises from the groundcover. It spirals up around him like a corkscrew, constantly spinning.

Peter remains still as it spins around him. Unlike so long ago, when the mist formed into a cocoon to hold him, he is not being restrained and it doesn't close up around him. It almost seems as if it were scanning Peter, somehow looking for what he wants. Peter remains quiet, allowing it to look... partially because he's not actually sure what he wants to say.

After a minute of probing, as abruptly as it formed, the corkscrew melds back down into the groundcover. Once it is completely dissolved, another straight finger of green mist rises up high in front of Peter.

Atop the finger a thin, delicate strand of smoke rises and floats lightly in the air. Below it, at the top of the finger, a six-inch globe of mist forms and the strand of smoke merges down into the globe.

Peter struggles to interpret what the mist is saying but it's like playing charades in a foreign language.

Now a one-foot cube of mist forms below the floating globe. Just as before, the globe merges down into the cube. An even larger cube forms below the existing cube, and once again the upper form blends into the one below.

Peter is becoming more than a little frustrated by the repeating process, but continues to watch patiently... it must be saying something... just what it is, exasperates him.

By now, the forms have collapsed down to the level of Peter's chest. He half expects yet another cube to form below the last, but, instead of a geometric form, an organic manifestation takes shape. It's almost like a 3-D image of rough terrain. There's something vaguely familiar about it. The last cube dissolves down into this new image.

Maybe the significance of the show put on for him will sink in later but it's beyond his grasp right now. All he knows is that there must be a reason for it. Intuitively, Peter raises his hand, holds his palm directly out at the foggy sculpture and fans his palm from left to right scanning the green mist.

Then he steps back and in a rather confused tone says, "Thanks... I think."

The image before him dissolves down into the ground cover and there's a brief bubbly burp of green smoke. It's clear it has finished talking.

Chapter Six

It's such a beautiful day with all the Sphere's multiple suns shining that Peter and Shan almost hate to ruin it by meeting with the Council. They both know they will most likely be listening to fear-driven logic... even if they are listened to at all. Change is frightening, but denial is dangerous, and they know the Council leans towards denial far too often.

Peter hasn't told Shan about his visit to the Graveyard of Spells the night before, partially because he hasn't quite figured out what it all meant. He's not sure how it will come into play but he's confident it will. The one thing he is sure about is what his next move should be; whether he will be able to do it is another question altogether.

Before they reach Master Melick's cottage, Peter says, "You ready for this?"

"You mean am I ready for them to believe Devon is not a lying little rat... no," Shan responds.

"I wish you wouldn't mince your words, just say what you think," Peter says with a slight poke and smile at her.

With a bit more understanding in her tone, "I can't really blame them... I don't want them to have to do, or see, things I've already had to. They simply don't understand how one person can harm another... it's never been part of their world."

"Somehow I can't help feeling that I brought all of this about," Peter says. He struggles with this more often than he wishes to admit.

She tries to console him, "As Gran-D would say it, the Prophecy was meant to be or it wasn't. Nothing you've done has intentionally been meant to bring harm to Spirin."

"And yet... here we are," says Peter, unconvinced. The thought still nags at him. He's glad to see that they're at Master Melick's cottage. "Well... let's go see what they think they heard."

All seven Masters are gathered inside Melick's living room. They're seated in a quarter circle, much like when Peter was first brought before them a little over a year ago. The only difference is that Gran-D isn't off in the shadows; now, being Grand Master Dar, he is perched on the center seat.

Peter once again feels like he's standing before the Supreme Court of sorcerers, but this time he has Shan beside him. The other big difference is that he's not there for their approval this time. He's intent on getting some answers, even if they don't know it yet... and probably on saying some things they won't want to hear.

Gran-D is the head Master but Master Melick, being more statesmanlike, tends to be monitor, especially since it's his home. Melick is the first to speak, "Peter... and Shan... Master Dar insists that we relate yesterday's events to you for your thoughts on the matter."

Master Sashaw, definitely the most lawyerly-looking of the lot, gets to his feet in an overly dramatic way. "I want to object one more time to bringing these kids in. This is Council business... it's not meant for students."

Master Haring is a dwarf who resembles a short Viking, and has a temperament to match. He grumbles, "Sashaw, would you plant it... we've all heard your objections." Then he turns to Peter, but addresses the rest, "The kids went head to head with these *neighbors* and, I don't know about the rest of you, but I'd like their opinion." With a glance back at Sashaw, "It's not like they have a vote, so settle your feathers."

Sashaw puffs up like he's about to mount a rebuttal.

"Would you two hush up and let them know what was said yesterday?" This comes from Master Warnig, the only woman Master on the Council, and usually to-the-point as opposed to posturing.

Peter glances at Gran-D, who, he knows, is well aware of the bug he and Shan planted. He sees no outward sign that would lead him to believe Gran-D has told the Council. Then he realizes that it doesn't matter; it's not for Gran-D to expose it, it's on him.

"You don't have to tell us what took place. I placed a mini-spy globe in the room."

Gran-D appears pleased by Peter's words; so does Carringer. Both knew Peter would own up to his actions, even if others did help manipulate him into acting.

"You what?!" spouts Master Imton. He's the one Master not originally from Spirin, or for that matter, even the Sphere... though this is taboo to discuss... that long ago he came from Earth. He's also the most mistrustful of the round ears, Earthers, because he remembers the violence they're capable of.

Gran-D is about to come to Peter's defense, but Peter holds up his hand and continues, "I'm not going to apologize. Shan and I know more about defending ourselves than any of you... and I know more about my brother. Until yesterday none of you had even seen these creatures from beyond the wall."

He is aware that Carringer has, but as far as he knows that's not common knowledge and it's not for him to make it so.

"We should have been included in the meeting... and I made sure we were."

A few in the room huff and puff but, before they can object, Peter continues, "You call them *neighbors*... they're not neighbors, they're the enemy. They didn't demand an audience to borrow a cup of sugar."

It's clear the reference slips past half the room.

Sashaw gets to his feet yet again, "I'm with Imton... I object that the boy dared to spy on us."

Haring shakes his head, "Sashaw... quit popping up like a Grimick in the bush! It's already been done, so now let the boy finish, for geffen sake."

Master Melick wants to keep a handle on the meeting. "We'll deal with the consequences of Peter's actions later. As for now, I'd like to know what he and Shan think as well."

Sashaw starts to pop up again but glances at Master Haring's scowl and speaks from his chair, "We've already made an agreement."

Shan snaps, "With the people who stole Ramie?"

"Ramie was taken by his brother," says Imton, pointing at Peter. "For that matter, we don't even know if Ramie was taken... or if he chose to go in the first place. These Earthers are at the root of everything that has happened here."

Master Imton left Earth long ago because many with dark needs sought the sorcery he had been taught. He stole the pendant from the master sorcerer he trained under to escape. Neither of them knew where the pendant originally came from. And, at the time, Imton had no idea of where he was escaping to... all he knew is that the pendant would take him away. Now he sees himself as Spirinese and he can't help having a core mistrust of aliens from Earth, including Peter.

Peter can't completely read the faces in the room. It feels like he has some support, but he's not sure how much. He says, "Can't you see Devon's influence is behind all this. He knows we could be dangerous so they made this false promise that if we don't venture into their world they will leave us alone."

"And what's wrong with that?" asks Master Warnig.

"It's a lie," Peter responds. "He is going to see if more powers can be gathered from the other lands before Goreipor makes a move on us."

Peter can feel the skepticism in the room... even from Gran-D to some degree.

Up until now Gran-D has remained quiet. Now he finally says, "Peter, what are you asking us to do?"

"Let me explore the other lands of the Sphere," says Peter. "I will try to do what I know my brother is doing... try to find allies for us... if others are out there."

Sashaw is quick to jump on this, "And if these people beyond the wall are so bad, you want to chance opening our doors to others... never!"

"If I were given the means to explore, no one need know," Peter argues.

"You mean... if we gave you the pendant?" Imton snaps.

Though not as heated, Master Melick's tone is just as skeptical, "Peter, if you were discovered, wouldn't that be considered an act of what you call war?"

Peter responds, "There's a saying on Earth... If you don't know you're already at war, you've already lost."

Even Shan knows they simply don't understand. What Peter has yet to accept is that the people of Spirin have no concept of war... even the Masters only speak of it as an abstract concept.

"You propose to jeopardize out remaining pendant? Your brother taking the other pendants is the reason we're in this mess... and now you want to take the last one," huffs Master Imton.

The remaining pendant is the one he brought from Earth, and it's a sore subject that Peter was allowed to use it in the first place.

Carringer is the only master in the room that truly appears to be on the fence. He has had first-hand experience with the soldiers of Goreipor and he lives with the fact that his parents were killed across the wall... even if they had chosen to venture there.

Gran-D can see that they are at an impasse. "We'll take your suggestion under advisement, Peter."

"What's your answer? This cannot be sat on," Peter snaps impatiently.

"Like I said, we will let you know... after we've discussed it," Gran-D insists.

Peter glances around the room, then curtly says, "So... I think I already have your answer."

Shan can also see this is going nowhere. She places a hand on Peter's arm, "Let's go."

Peter angrily spins and storms out. Shan nods to the Masters, but from her eyes it's clear it's only out of formality... not respect. Then she turns and follows Peter.

After the kids leave the other maters turn to Gran-D, now as Grand Master Dar. Sashaw is of course the first to speak, "You're not considering the boy's reckless request, are you, Dar?"

"Out of respect for what Peter and Shan have gone through, I told them we would discuss the matter... before I tell them no." Gran-D is not the head of the Council because he cannot read a room. He also knows when to be transparent, and when not.

"And the pendant? Is it safe?" Imton demands. The look he gives Gran-D says it's more a matter between the two of them than for the Council as a whole.

Gran-D solemnly nods, "It's safe." He is more than aware that his old friend will hold him to his word about the hiding of the pendant, regardless of what the Council decides... as if the decision was ever in the air.

Lord Kildemar runs his metal-clawed hand across a flattened map of the Sphere carved into his war table. He and his two sons, Taligarr and Janick, are the only ones in the fortress' massive war room. The claw makes a steady scratching sound as it moves over the table.

Janick, the younger son, paces impatiently while Taligarr calmly watches their father think.

The war room's stone walls are decorated with the tattered flags of the many warlords Kildemar has defeated to become the ruler of Goreipor. For all the flags captured, Lord Kildemar still feels like there is much he does not rule... and, in his mind, anything he doesn't rule is a potential threat. This is further aggravated by the fact that there are few in Goreipor left to conquer... he misses the simplicity of war.

The map embedded in the war table only has geographic details of Goreipor; the other five lands are blank, displaying only their names. One of these lands is but a sliver called the Portal that lies in the north and touches all the other lands. Outside of the Portal, the rest of the lands are about the same size.

The absence of terrain details is not a surprise since, as long as anyone could remember, the impenetrable mirror walls have separated all the lands. The reemergence of the Sorcerer's Door that enables the crossing of these borders has changed all of this. For some, it means the thrill of conquest, for others it means greed. Lord Kildemar represents both.

Janick, tired of the silence, abruptly says, "You're not going to let that boy who isn't even from here have his way, are you, father? If it were up to me, I'd have his head today." Janick, unlike his brother, is more about blind action than the subtleties of command.

Immediately, Taligarr gives his younger brother a harsh glare. He knows Janick often opens his mouth without thinking.

The glare was not quick enough. The crash of Lord Kildemar's metal claw slamming onto the war table echoes over the room. The clawed hand is a mere fraction of what it cost Kildemar to build his empire and a constant reminder to him that any sign of stupidity or weakness can be fatal... he can't, and won't, brook it in his sons.

He yells at Janick, "You set aside your prejudices and learn to use whatever weapons you find... if they don't serve you well, you simply destroy them before they can be used by others... How many times do I have to tell you this?" After a brief moment, "If you had asked me that question, in that tone, in the presence of others... you would be wearing another scar!"

Taligarr shakes his head... well aware that was coming.

Janick shows enough wisdom to not compound it by arguing.

A loud bang sounds on the room's massive double doors.

Kildemar orders Janick, "Show them in... That would be the boy that isn't from here. Mind your tongue if you wish to keep it."

Lord Kildemar is feared enough that he has no need for door locks and a simple yell would bring in the arrivals, but he wants to rub his son's nose in it, perhaps to teach him... perhaps just to show him his place.

Janick opens the doors and Devon, followed by Captain Pirus, enters. Pirus knows, and Devon is learning, to let Lord Kildemar start the dialogue. They walk to the war table and wait quietly.

For impact, Lord Kildemar waits a few seconds, then looks up at Devon. "I've decided to allow you to serve me. I want you to do as you suggested and feel out the other lands."

Devon unwisely is quick to speak, "Then I'll be off... "

Kildemar slams his fist on the table again. "I'm not finished!" he yells.

Janick lets out a slight laugh that gets him another harsh glare from his father.

Kildemar continues, "If you think I am about to send you off with one of my pendants, you've sorely underestimated me. You are to go along on this expedition for a few reasons... to demonstrate how your powers serve me, to use those powers to protect the mission, and, finally, to display the illusion that we are lenient with other races. My son, Taligarr, will be in charge. Janick will go along to learn... and Captain Pirus, along with his guards, will go to remind you of your place."

Janick holds his tongue at the remark about learning; he considers himself the fiercest of warriors... others might just consider him bloodthirsty... few would ever say so.

Devon has little concern about the perceived hierarchy since he eventually plans to dethrone Kildemar's clan anyway. He bows, "As you command, my liege."

Captain Pirus, knowing a bit more about Devon, smiles at this false kowtowing... he keeps the smile wisely small.

Chapter Seven

Peter and Shan swoop down near the Graveyard of Spells. A flock of silver birds that have been playing tag around the kids fly off as they get close to the Graveyard.

The two go to ground.

"Why are we here, not down by our log?" asks Shan, glancing at the Graveyard.

Peter just stares at it. "I don't know... hell, I have no idea what the Graveyard is about or what it tries to say."

Other than it keeping her out long ago, Shan has yet to have much interaction with the green mist in the Graveyard, so viewing it as something with anything to say is still a bit unusual to her. She trusts that if Peter has heard it, it must be trying to communicate in some way... or his imagination is in overdrive.

"What did it try to say?" she asks.

"It seemed like some kind of a puzzle... parts going into other parts... or at least that's what it appeared to be."

Peter focuses on playing out the sequence from the other night in his head. Something clicks.

"I think I know what it might be."

Shan perks up, "What?"

"The pendant," Peter says as though a treasure chest has opened.

"The pendant is back inside the Graveyard?" she asks.

"No, but the Graveyard is trying to tell me where it is. I just can't make it out," Peter says.

Shan's enthusiasm is evident. "So tell me exactly what it showed you."

"The first part makes sense. It's in a globe that's in a box, or a room, that's in another box, or larger room. The last part is what puzzles me... where the box or room is. I can show you that part, maybe it'll make sense to you."

Peter holds out his hand, palm forward, and an image of the final part, a 3-D image of rough terrain forms in front of them. It remains floating there even after Peter lowers his hand.

Shan walks around the image, studying it, trying to test her memory with its shapes... after all, she has lived in Spirin much longer than Peter.

"Anything?" Peter asks impatiently.

Shan holds up her hand for him to keep quiet. She continues to circle, racking her brain at every angle.

Suddenly she stops.

"You know what this looks like?" It's a rhetorical question. She continues, "Gran-D took me on a trip to the north of Spirin long ago. It was to see a rare bird that only lives in the rock formations up there. It was even rarer because in all our land we have little fear, even of creatures, but this bird was different."

"In what way?" Peter asks... hooked on what she's saying.

She looks at him as if she fully understands, "It protects those rock formations... aggressively if needed. Most Spirinese would stay well clear of the area."

Peter knows she's right; all he asks, "How aggressively?"

Two thin wisps of colored smoke curl through the open sky as they shoot high over the Spirin landscape. The way they intertwine almost looks like they are at play on their way north.

They quit squirreling around the sky and start flying parallel to each other.

A voice from one of the lines of smoke shouts over the rush of the wind, "So... we're going to steal the pendant... if the bird doesn't get us, and then go to the other lands against the Council's decision? That the plan?" It's Shan's voice.

The other line of smoke, Peter, shouts back, "Let's just get the pendant first and then decide what we're doing."

The first line of smoke is suspiciously quiet at this evasion.

Two streams, one green and the other purple, jet down to a blue field. They deposit Shan and Peter. Off in the distance is a single crimson mountain with a very jagged profile. It's seems to be made up of many stalagmite-like columns. The mountain is a sharp contrast to the general softness of most of Spirin.

Peter immediately regenerates the 3-D image he recorded from the Graveyard. He intently looks back and forth between the model and the mountain. Now he's sure that Shan has found the key to the puzzle.

Shan is not so intent on comparing the two... something else is on her mind. Finally she says, "Why did you avoid the question of what we're going to do if we get the pendant?"

"Because I don't actually know what we're going to do... can we please just deal with one step at a time?" Peter says defensively.

She knows he's avoiding the discussion, but decides to leave it at that... for the moment. She's not happy about letting him off the hook.

Having dodged the bullet for now, Peter goes back to comparing the model to the reality. Like enlarging an image on a computer pad, he holds out his hands and spreads them apart... the image enlarges. There is more detail to it than he would expect from something generated by mist. Peter leans in and focuses on one spot. It gets Shan's reluctant attention.

He points to the spot that has his interest, "Doesn't that look like an arch? Like a fabricated arch, versus natural?"

Shan is interested, but her focus is on a different spot on the model, a little higher than the place Peter is pointing to. She points and says, "Doesn't that look a bit like a bird's nest?"

Peter looks at where she's pointing. "How big is that bird Gran-D took you to see?"

Shan gives him a concerned glance, "And it can become invisible."

As Shan and Peter near the base of the rocks, Peter asks her, "You have the staying invisible spell down, right?"

"Most of the time" she responds.

This reminds Peter of when he first started training, and how grating it was to Master Melick when Peter said *'most of the time'* he could control floating. Now he understands the Master's frustration.

About a half hour later, deeper in the folds of the mountain, the sounds of crumbling rocks and climbing fill the air. An invisible foot kicks a toehold in a crevice in the soft rocks. An equally invisible source says, "Shan, how you doing?"

Below that voice, Shan's voice says, "Fine... if you'd stop kicking dirt in my face."

"I can't see your face," says Peter. "What was that bird Gran-D showed you called?"

Climbing sounds continue. Shan sounds a little winded, "I think he called it a Koridor."

He sounds just as winded as her. "Maybe it's extinct now."

Suddenly a big chunk of rock just above and to the right of where Peter doesn't appear explodes and tumbles down.

Shan's voice yells, "I think you just pissed off something that you think is no longer alive."

Peter flickers into visibility as he generates his protective shield. The shield is large enough to cover both him and Shan, but it takes too much of his energy to hold and be invisible at the same time. Shan figures there's no use hiding if he's visible and she appears as well. Being visible also makes it easier for her to be protected by the shield.

Another chunk of rock explodes outward and the shrapnel bounces off the shield. Where it exploded, just for a brief second, Peter sees what looks like a giant gold beak striking sparks on the rocks.

He yells down to Shan, "How big did you say this thing is?"

"I think it's gotten bigger," she yells back.

The two of them squeeze close together and back into a crevice in the cliff. Peter struggles to make sure the shield remains aimed at where he thinks the Koridor is.

Now seeing its adversary, the Koridor slowly becomes visible. Perhaps it wants to instill fear in its adversary... perhaps it just has a sense of fair play. Either way, it's quite a sight to see. The Koridor must be at least twelve feet high. It has bright crimson wings with silver and black accents and, as Peter thought he saw, a gold beak. Its talons are gold as well. If it weren't attacking them, the bird would be quite striking to admire.

The talons strike hard against Peter's shield, hard enough that it's difficult for him to hold the barrier steady.

"Gran-D didn't happen to tell you anything about handling this big bird... did he?" Peter yells.

"Only that it is a little egocentric," she yells back.

"Great... so you're suggesting we try therapy?" Peter sarcastically comes back, all the while trying to fend off talon strikes.

Something must have dawned on Shan. She yells, "Wait here!"

Peter glances briefly as if to say, '*Where the hell am I going,*' but as he does, she fades away into invisibility. He doesn't have much time to be concerned because the Koridor switches tactics from using its talons to striking at the shield with its beak. The strikes are much harder; it takes all Peter's effort to ward off the increasing impacts.

After a couple of minutes the strikes change from hard hits to light taps and they appear to be falling shy of hitting the shield. It couldn't have happened at a better time because Peter's shield is starting to flicker. Though Peter is a bit confused, the change is a welcome relief.

Shan reappears behind Peter and taps his shoulder. When Peter turns to her, she says, "I know you call me a tomboy... but occasionally a girl has to conjure a mirror... I just made a slightly larger one."

Peter, dumbfounded, turns back to the Koridor and, true enough... it seems to be admiring something rather than attacking. Apparently Shan's mirror is see-through from their side.

From the other side of the mirror, the Koridor is quite impressed by its newfound friend, a handsome bird that now stands before it. They tilt their heads this way and that in unison... both pleased with what they see. The two intruders are a distant memory for the Koridor. It has a new friend... itself.

Peter's engrossed in watching the Koridor watch itself.

Shan tugs on his shoulder and says, "I think it's going to be preoccupied for a while... shall we get moving?"

As they start to move off, Peter remarks, "Therapy."

With the Koridor preoccupied with itself, Peter and Shan quickly make it to the arch Peter saw on the model. He was right, it's manmade not formed by nature. The arch leads to a cave in the mountain.

At the entrance to the cave Shan asks, with a slight touch of sarcasm in her voice, "The green stuff didn't happen to tell you where to go from here... did it?"

Peter loves Shan, but at times she can be exasperating. "No, it didn't. I assume we just go in... Unless you have another suggestion."

She just smiles, and then gestures for him to lead the way.

As he slowly proceeds, Peter remains alert. He doesn't anticipate traps like in some Indiana Jones movie, that wouldn't fit the nature of Spirin, but something dawns on him. He asks, "Did Gran-D ever say what that overgrown chicken was protecting?"

Shan thinks a second... What would the only dangerous creature in the land be protecting? For that matter, why would it even be there? She gives up and shrugs, "I guess we can ask him when we get back."

"That might not be the best idea... considering we're stealing the pendant. Asking about its guard may tip our hand," says Peter, a touch too condescending.

Shan sticks out her tongue at him, since his remark is unworthy of a response. She figures eventually they will find out what it was guarding and dismisses the matter for now.

They continue on... carefully.

As the cave goes deeper, Peter notices unlit torches on the walls. He takes one and with a snap of his fingers a spark brings it to life... now they have light.

A little farther into the cave they come to a set of massive metal double doors. The doors are completely covered with cobwebs, except for some bare patches on the bar-type handle, meaning someone has used it recently. There are also arcing swing marks in the dirt of the cave floor.

Shan walks up to the surface of the doors and brushes away some of the webbing to reveal symbols cast in its trim... the characters are not Spirinese. She brushes away more, trying to make sense of it.

Peter's a bit more interested in the goal at hand than ancient symbols. He tells her, "Stand back and I'll break it open."

As Peter looks like he's about to cast a spell, Shan simply takes hold of the door's handle with both hands and lifts. It's heavy but, with a little effort, it squeaks up. Then she pulls and the door opens.

She turns to Peter, "Simple is better."

He stares at her for a split second and moves past her with the torch. She gives him a satisfied smile and follows.

What they find inside is a surprise to both of them. It's a long, wide hallway that, for the most part, is encased in a transparent, greenish material, somewhat like being filled with resin. The first half dozen yards of the encasing material has been carved out, leaving access to two doors, one on each side of the hall.

Peter can see through the wavering image of the resin-like material that there are other doors farther down the hallway. They tickle his interest, but that is not the mission today.

They try one of the two accessible doors and it opens with little effort. Shan and Peter glance at each other before heading in, silently confirming they have each other's back.

Once in the room, they find little. It's a small room with a large stone block with nothing on it in the center. Shan notices a slightly discolored rectangular blank shape on the wall, as if long ago something might have been there, but the wall is now evenly covered with cobwebbing.

No pendant... or box that would hold one.

One down... now Peter and Shan move back into the hallway and to the other door. This one is locked. Shan knows Peter's been anxious to break a lock so she backs away and gestures for him to get it out of his system.

She was right. Peter plays up the dramatics as he casts a relatively simple spell at the door. Grinding metal parts are immediately heard inside the door's lock. A second later the door pops open about an inch. Peter looks pleased with himself.

Shan just shrugs and quips, "Satisfied?"

As Peter marches to the door, it's clear he is.

Inside they find another large stone block positioned as in the other room, but a box sits atop this one. The box is locked and Peter gets the satisfaction of using his spell one more time.

When they lift the top a small globe floats up... within the globe is the pendant. Peter reaches out and the globe pops, dropping the pendant into his welcoming hand.

After leaving the room that surrendered the pendant, Peter glances back at all the encased doors, wondering what they might be hiding. From the writing they have seen, clearly it's something ancient.

Shan can see his itch. She takes his arm and quietly says, "Some other day."

Gran-D is mid-conversation with Master Melick. What they're discussing is too quiet to hear, but it's clear something distracts Gran-D. He looks up and glances around... a small smile flashes across his lips.

Melick is confused but knows Gran-D must sense something, "What's going on Dar?"

Gran-D brushes off the incident with, "Nothing... just a thought." He knows it's much more.

As Peter and Shan swoop away from the northern mountain, the two glance down to see the Koridor turning to the side to get a better view of its tail feathers in the mirror. They both laugh just before going into hyper-drive and turning into streams of smoke.

Chapter Eight

Now bored out of his mind and fairly sure he's not going to be killed, Ramie is doing what he does best... whatever he's not supposed to be doing. Right now he is supposed to be studying lessons about Goreipor that Witch Racinda feels will aid in his survival. What he is doing is walking the top edge of the battlement wall like a tightrope.

He hears one of the fortress' heavy exterior doors slam and loses his balance. Just as Ramie is about to go over the edge, he uses his powers to right himself. It doesn't dawn on him that a non-sorcerer would notice such skills... it just comes natural, and he easily forgets he's been told not to display what comes natural.

"I've a mind to send you flying off that wall myself," Witch Racinda says.

Another voice comes from the shadow of a guardhouse, "I have to agree with her." Devon steps out into the light.

By the look on Racinda's face it's evident that she feels ambushed... and she doesn't like it. The look on Ramie's face says he doesn't like getting caught by either of them, so obviously he hasn't set it up.

Ramie still hasn't figured out whom he should trust... and whom he should fear. For now he jumps down from the wall and backs away from them both.

"Madame Racinda, we have yet to have a chance to talk," says Devon, trying to sound sincere and open.

Witch Racinda doesn't make any effort at sounding either, "That's OK, you can call me a witch... I could care less."

"But you're not a witch... you're a sorceress from Spirin... aren't you?" Devon says in a polite tone that sounds like a catty challenge.

Ramie stands off at a slight distance. It's true he doesn't know whom to trust, but what is frustrating to him is that neither of them is paying him any attention.

"What counts is that I have the ear of Lord Kildemar... where I am from is unimportant." Clearly she doesn't sound as if she's going to warm to Devon any time soon. She figures he's looking to worm his way into the inner circle; he will have to offer something substantial before she's that interested in listening.

As if Devon could read her thoughts, he says, "I'm new here, and if there is anything I can do for you, please feel free to ask at any time. I'm not trying to mess with your position in the court... you have a sweet deal."

"Forget the kissing up... what do you want here?" she says flatly.

"All I want is to use my skills to serve Lord Kildemar," Devon says, well aware that this does not fool her.

"Did you know Kildemar has a room of heads? That's right... he collects them from people that pretend to serve him," Witch Racinda coldly says and winks, as though she fully expects to see his decorating that room someday.

Ramie walks in between them, "I thought you both were here to get mad at me." He would rather be in trouble than ignored.

Witch Racinda actually appreciates Ramie breaking in since the conversation with Devon is at an impasse... but she's not about to show it to Ramie. "I thought I told you not to use your powers unless I was present."

"So... I should have fallen?" Ramie says.

"You shouldn't have been on the ledge in the first place," she responds.

Devon knows he's not getting any further with Racinda, for the moment, so he turns to Ramie, "You'd be smart to listen to her. I only stopped by to say I'd be gone for a while."

Ramie, with a slightly panicked tone, "And you're leaving me here?"

Devon nods to Racinda, "You're in good hands."

He turns to go and Racinda calls after him, "Make sure you don't visit the head room."

Devon just keeps walking.

Deciding he has little choice, Ramie turns to Racinda, "When am I going to get to use my powers? It feels so strange doing everything... so... abnormally. This is as bad as being on Earth."

She says, "Patience, my boy... there'll come a time when your powers will serve both of us." With this she nods for him to follow, turns and walks away.

Ramie lets out a breath of exhaustion, but follows.

Shan and Peter are unusually quiet on the trip back from the northern mountains. She knows he is keeping something from her... he knows it, as well. Neither are in the mood for an argument.

But now approaching home, Shan figures it's better to get whatever it is out in the open before they run into Gran-D. Peter's less concerned about arguing with her than he is about Gran-D sensing they've stolen the pendant. They land near the log to gather their thoughts.

"Are we going home for dinner... or are we going to hash out what we've not been talking about?" Shan finally says.

Peter thinks on it a moment and blurts out, "I'm going to jump to the other lands alone... OK, is that what you wanted to hear?"

Shan half expected this was churning around in Peter's head. She encountered it about Earth and then about going after Ramie, but she figured after fighting side by side on the plateau in Goreipor he would be past the '*I have to protect you*' mentality... maybe not. Then again, maybe it's something else.

If Peter has learned anything about Shan, it's that she doesn't fight fair.

Shan studies him a second, and then says, "OK... Give me your reasons, and then I'll tell you whether you're going to win this argument or not."

Peter thinks, '*She cheats... and worst of all, it usually works.*' He's hard pressed to remember the arguments he's won. He braces himself for yet another non-winnable argument.

He says, "As soon as I jump the wall, I'll be going directly against the Council's... even Gran-D's, orders. If something goes wrong, or even if I get back OK, you may be the only sane voice the Council will listen to."

"You'll have to do better than that," Shan responds.

Peter knows his next point will be a little touchier. "The Council won't prepare for the worse. If it comes to war, you will have to train and lead the young of Spirin. You're the only one that knows what... it might take to survive."

"You mean to kill," Shan says with a bit of pain.

"Yes," Peter says quietly.

Shan turns and walks a short distance away... thinking.

Peter watches, trying to guess what's going on in her head.

After a minute she proclaims, "You win the argument."

Funny, for some reason, Peter doesn't feel like he wins, even when he wins with Shan.

As the two arrive home, hoping no one is the wiser about their trip, Gran-D meets them at the front door. Peter figures they are already busted, but Gran-D only gives them a mischievous smile and holds the door open for them to enter. This silent courtesy makes Peter and Shan even surer they've been busted... *'Why do spiders play with flies?'* crosses Peter's mind?

When they enter, they find Kalish and Atta readying to leave. All Kalish drolly says is, "Mother and I are having dinner over with the Healer... aren't we lucky?" This makes Shan and Peter even more suspicious since Kalish has no great love of the Healer. He finds her too flamboyant... and independent.

But what tells them they are being set up for something is when they come into the dining room and find Master Carringer sitting at the table. He gets up as Shan approaches.

Peter isn't interested in waiting to get blindsided. He turns to Gran-D, "OK... what's this all about?"

Gran-D smiles and addresses Carringer, "How is it that youth doesn't see the strategic value of vagueness?"

Carringer shrugs, but Peter mockingly, answers, "Maybe because *youth* likes straight answers. We want to know what's really going on."

With a wave at the table, Gran-D says, "OK, have a seat and we will tell you what's *not* going on... that's the best I can offer."

Master Carringer pulls out Shan's chair... Peter and Shan, frustrated, take their seats reluctantly.

Shan starts to say something but Gran-D holds up a hand to stop her. He waves in the direction of the kitchen. A tray floats in, a little wobbly. Everyone watches as it drifts off course, a few holding their breath wondering if it will run into the wall. Finally it redirects itself and safely lands in the center of the table. All but Gran-D relax... he knew it would make it... or was pretty sure it would.

The tray is filled with sandwiches and bits of fruit.

The niceties done, Shan turns to Gran-D, anxious to get to the point, "If this is about where we went today... "

Gran-D cuts her off and in a slow tone says, "No... We would prefer not knowing where you were today."

Master Carringer grins at Gran-D's dance.

The old man continues, "I'm sure you knew where the Council was leaning on your suggestion." After Peter nods, "Well, it's official, you're not to take any actions that might irritate the relationship with Goreipor."

"'*Irritate the relationship*'... It's not a relationship... they told you what to do, and now you're doing it!" snaps Shan.

Master Carringer politely says, "Shan, let him finish."

"The Council is frightened that Goreipor, having two pendants, will be monitoring us to see no irrational preparations for defense take place." He pauses a moment, "So they must not see irrational preparations."

Peter gives this double-talk an irritated glare, but remains quiet as Gran-D continues.

"Since Carringer and I went against the Council back when you went to Earth, we have to officially walk a tighter line and support the Council's vote now," says Gran-D.

Carringer inserts, "Or we can be of little use to you... we can even be voted off the Council."

"If you visited a bird today, we don't want to know. If you try to set up some form of defensive training for our young, we do not want to know. If you need help with anything we don't know about, please let us know. Any questions?" Gran-D pauses for their reaction.

Shan and Peter glance at each other. Peter shrugs.

"Is this *non-speak* the language of aging?" Shan asks.

"There's a time to speak up... age lets you appreciate timing. Trust me, girl, you do what youth does quietly, and when the time comes, the voices will be there," Gran-D assures her.

Shan shakes her head; Gran-D is being as he's always been... filled with puzzles. Peter sees it with a different slant... the old man is being as manipulative as always. As far as he can tell, Gran-D is saying he will support them as long as they take the blame.

Even Carringer tires of double-speak and changes tone when he addresses Peter, "If you're going to other lands, I should be at your side."

Gran-D glares at him, knowing this will not do, but Peter speaks first, "If I were going to do that, I would have to do it alone. Shan will need you more here. She needs the Spell Master to know what is usable." He glances at Gran-D and adds, with an obligatory tone, "But... of course I'm not going anywhere... satisfied?"

Gran-D shakes his head in disapproving surrender.

After a casual dinner of vague non-plans and non-discussed details, Peter and Gran-D stand in the living room by the window. It's the same window they stood by the night Peter was a frightened boy who had just landed in a world across the Universe from his own. They both stared out at the stars, as they are doing right now.

Gran-D asks, "Remember, back then, I asked you what you saw in those stars, and you said how small they made you feel?"

"Yeah... and you said some kids looking up at those stars will become world changers... I still don't feel like a world changer," says Peter, not taking his eyes off the sky.

"No, it's kids like your brother who feel they have to change worlds who don't... it's someone like you who doesn't need to see himself that way who often makes the most difference," Gran-D responds.

Peter knows Gran-D has promised Imton that he would not disclose where the pendant was hidden. He knows it must have hurt to be a party to breaking that promise.

He's quiet for a second, then looks over at Gran-D, "And what about those who think they have to be behind all those changes, at any cost?"

Gran-D remains quiet.

Chapter Nine

Devon stands near the western wall of Goreipor at dawn, looks at the entourage he has been saddled with, and shakes his head. He especially notes Taligarr, who has the Sorcerer's Door pendant around his neck.

Devon is armed with his razor disc belt that he brought from Spirin, and a new lance he fabricated after giving Peter his old one. It crosses his mind that his new lance may have to meet his old one.

Captain Pirus steps up behind Devon and quietly suggests, "I would hide my disappointment about not being in charge a little better if I were you."

The group to travel, by Lord Kildemar's command, is Taligarr, Janick, Captain Pirus, along with four of his soldiers, and Devon. What Devon is unaware of is that Taligarr and Janick don't plan for the group to be quite as large by the time they return. They don't like how quickly Devon has gained favor with their father and would happily welcome an excuse to come back light one round-ear.

Devon learned how to operate the pendant from Ramie, and in turn had to teach it to Taligarr. He knows his powers are a strong carrot for a warlord with a larger vision, but a threat to his shortsighted sons. When Taligarr glares in his direction, Devon puts on his best subservient smile. He tries not to let it show that he could probably eliminate all of them with ease.

In his best leadership voice Taligarr announces, "Captain, have your men at the ready."

Captain Pirus thinks to himself, '*Does he even know what he means*,' and acknowledges the command with a nod.

Taligarr dials the pendant and swoosh... the whirlpool of white light forms in front of him. He backs away uncontrollably. Bracing himself, he points to Pirus, "Have your men go through first."

Captain Pirus smiles at the lad's hesitance, "As you wish, Commander."

Taligarr and Janick have both been dubbed Commanders for this mission. Of course Taligarr is Commander slightly above his younger brother, Janick.

To Captain Pirus they are both inexperienced lads from whom he finds it irritating to take orders. He is confident of whom his men will follow in a pinch. What worries him is that Janick's tendency to violence could get his men hurt.

The four guards step through the portal, one at a time. Taligarr and Janick listen to see if they hear screams... none. They try not to show their fear as they step forward.

Captain Pirus lets out a laugh and walks into the light, followed by Devon who is just as casual about it. The last to go through the door are the two brothers.

Even a hardened soldier like Captain Pirus is caught off guard by the vista that stands before him. He's so focused on the landscape that he doesn't even glance to see Taligarr and Janick tumble out of the light behind him.

Both Lord Kildemar's sons go sprawling as they arrive. As each gets up he is as speechless as those who arrived before them. All eight men stand on a plateau staring, none knowing exactly what to say for the longest time.

What they look out upon is a dense blood-crimson jungle with plumes of reddish-orange steam drifting up. Off in the northern distance, fingers of lightning strike down from a dark reddish tinted sky. Off in the other direction are cliffs flanking a volcano that spits up a black cloud, and oozes bright red lava.

A four-foot long, jet-black centipede with massive razor sharp pincers crawls out of the undergrowth near Captain Pirus. Barely taking his eyes off the vista, Pirus quickly unsheathes his sword and impales the centipede. The screech from the skewered creature sets off a cascade of howls and screams from deep in the jungle. It's like a thousand creatures celebrating the kill.

The eight continue to stare silently out on this land that makes even Goreipor feel inviting. If an overall initial impact of a land could be condensed into a smell, the land of Cretorn would smell of pure death.

Peter hates last minute goodbyes because they drag out too long, and, once the decision to go has been made, they serve little purpose. Shan, uninvited, hitched a ride to Earth at their last *goodbye*. Peter has little concern about that this time since they each have a purpose that lies in different directions.

Unlike Gran-D, Carringer is not as comfortable with all the politicking and deception; maybe it's the age difference... maybe it's just that he would rather jump into the adventure himself. Either way, he's there along with Shan to see Peter off without Gran-D's knowledge.

"Are you going to do one land at a time and come back between each?" Shan asks. She's hoping Peter will not be absent long, but suspects she's wrong.

"I'm going to play it on the fly," is all Peter can say.

"You know that if you do that you're more likely to come upon Devon... and the men he'll probably be traveling with?" she says, this being her real fear.

Peter senses her fear and takes hold of her shoulders, "I can sense my brother's presence, and I promise to avoid him... for now. OK?" He adds, "You have a major task yourself, don't waste time worrying about me."

"I should be going with you," says Carringer.

Peter laughs, "You mean, you wish you were going with me."

Peter glances at the eastern wall of Spirin, and then towards Shan and Carringer, "Look, as Ramie would say it... this is all getting icky. It's time for me to go."

He gets one last hug from Shan and she backs away.

Peter dials in the pendant and the whirlpool doorway flashes up in front of him. He grabs his pack and the lance Devon gave him. Then, with one final nod to Shan and Carringer, he jumps through the Sorcerer's Door.

Peter falls out of the door into the land of Acculas. He lands on a hillside partially covered by full blooming trees. Here is the peacefulness he has come to know in Spirin, but in a completely different color range. Where Spirin is predominantly blues and purples, oranges and yellows overwhelm Acculas... Not the kind of hard orange that reeks of danger in Cretorn, but an orange of richness.

He gets up, dusts himself off and surveys the world he must explore. It hasn't crossed his mind till now, but Peter wonders if the magical phenomenon of being able to understand all languages exists all over the Sphere. It would be a shame to find potential allies and not be able to communicate... or worse, miscommunicate. Then he remembers being able to understand the violent language of the attacking soldiers on the plateau of Goreipor... he decides it will be all right.

After seeing no movement of any sort while scanning around, his next concern is... '*Will he find anyone to understand?*' Peter suddenly feels incredibly alone. The only solution for this lonely feeling is to get busy and start looking for someone. He shakes off his fears, picks up his lance and moves out... no time to waste.

An hour into his walk across Acculas, Peter has still seen no sign of animal life... even wildlife. He considers using a hoverboard; if it worked fine on Earth, it's bound to work here. Then he reminds himself that he's not using it for the same reason he didn't initially allow Ramie to use it on Earth... to avoid exposing skills that might frighten. He knows most people's initial response to fear of the unknown is violence.

He keeps walking.

As Peter crests a hill, he thinks he hears the faint sound of growling somewhere in the distance. He can't see anything but he takes a lower profile and heads in the direction of the sound.

The growl sounds get louder and it dawns on Peter that he's not exactly looking for something that growls. The lack of finding any animal life so far makes it worth exploring. As the sounds get closer so does he... to the ground.

The growls are coming from more than one source... a fight between animals? It seems to be coming from just over the next ridge. A thicket of yellow bushes stands on the ridge from where he can view whatever is going on safely. As he nears the thicket he gets down in a crawl... a slow crawl at that, since these animals might have finely tuned hearing. He's not concerned with smell... the breeze is drifting towards him.

Once at the thicket, Peter gently pulls some brush to the side. Below him are a number of large cats... really large cats! They remind Peter of pictures he had once seen of saber tooth tigers with very intimidating tusks. Instead of their coats being brown, each of these cats has a distinctly different pattern of bright colors. There are a total of three cats below. The largest one is colored like the landscape, orange and yellow stripes. Another is a mixture of green and purple, and the last, green and orange. Even Peter knows that on Earth species usually have a common color scheme... but this isn't Earth.

The one thing that is consistent with what Peter would expect of a pride of cats is that one has a dead animal, resembling a purple deer, by the neck. The cat drags the deer into the center of the clearing. What's unusual is that the other cats calmly watch instead of trying to claim a share of the prize. The growling seems more like communicating than aggression. Peter finds their behavior fascinating.

Suddenly there's a low guttural growl from directly behind Peter... he freezes. He has a momentary instinct to reach for the lance lying nearby. It's only a momentary instinct, and he wisely decides against it.

The low growl slowly morphs into a guttural voice that's hard to understand, "Join the pride, boy..." The tone rises towards clarity, "... or I'll kill you where you lie."

Peter snaps around to find himself face to face with a blue-orange spotted saber tooth tiger.

"Down below... now, boy," growls the tiger.

Peter staggers to his feet, never taking his eyes off the cat. Since his adversary does not attack, Peter backs slowly down the embankment, the cat matching him step for step.

Seeing Peter back down into the clearing, the other three cats fan out into a half circle. None of them show any sign of aggression, they just growl among themselves.

Once in the clearing Peter glances down at the dead deer, and gazes over the four cats, wondering if that would be his fate... to be dinner. He decides that if they were going to kill him, he'd know by now... and none of them would have needed to talk.

Mustering up all the bravery he can manage, Peter starts, "I would..." He stops when he realizes that his voice is squeaking from fear and clears his throat, "I would like to speak with your leader."

There's a guttural chuckle from the pride. Peter's not sure what bewilders him more, that he's trying to talk to some kind of cat or that they're laughing at him.

Almost like they can read his mind, their chuckles grow to bolder laughs. The tiger who has captured Peter says, "If you want to speak with our leader, you will have to ride one of us."

Peter takes a deep breath. They haven't attacked yet, so in for a penny, in for a pound... "Which one do I have to ride?"

Now Peter has no doubt that the growls are laughter.

A different growl, deep enough to shake the grass, comes from atop the ridge. Peter spins to see a tri-colored tiger at least half again larger than the others. There's a proud majesty to this one, and his glistening blue, orange and yellow coat is perfectly groomed.

From behind, in unison, the four other tigers say, "Him."

The largest tiger by far slowly swaggers down to the clearing, his every move artistically deliberate. It doesn't take much for Peter to guess who the leader is.

A funny thing crosses his mind... if these tigers are suitable allies, how will he introduce them to the people of Spirin. It's funny since he's not sure he'll survive the ride anyway.

The pride splits apart as the large tiger enters the clearing. It comes directly up to Peter and places its face inches away from his... then waits. Peter stands his ground, trying not to break their eye contact.

The tiger backs up, "A brave lad." Then he says, "I am Prince Jarium... I hear you want to talk, boy. Then climb that rock and mount me, if you dare. We'll see how brave you are."

One of the other tigers growls, "When you fall off, you become ours."

This puts a different slant on the ride. Peter wonders how anxious he is to make friends. He's well aware that if he were to back out now his fate would be sealed anyway so he climbs the boulder.

Prince Jarium positions himself for Peter to slide onto his back. Once Peter is on, Jarium starts slowly up towards the ridge. Peter doesn't know what to expect so he holds on tightly, with both his hands and legs.

On the ridge Jarium suddenly rears up like a stallion. It takes all Peter's effort to hold on. Jarium turns back to the pride below and yells, "Prepare to move our kill. I'll make short work of our intruder."

Then, like a rocket, Jarium takes off down the other side of the ridge. Peter holds on for dear life. He can hear the roars of approval from the pride diminish as they get farther away from the clearing. Jarium may be large but he's sleek and extremely agile; it takes all of Peter's effort to remain on his back.

As the sound of the pride fades and they are far out of sight, Jarium slows to a prance and then to a causal pace. His tone also becomes more casual, "So, boy, where do you come from? You're not of my land."

Peter, now twenty, tires of people calling him '*boy*' but he's not about to argue the matter with a seven-foot high saber tooth tiger... And, this isn't exactly a person. Who knows how old this tiger is? Perhaps he's even a Gran-D of Acculas.

"I come from beyond your western wall," Peter says.

Prince Jarium stops and bows down for Peter to dismount, and then turns to him, "If you were not here, I'd say that is impossible... but you are, so that would be a waste of effort. Now tell me how and why you are here."

Peter says, "It's a matter of a Prophecy."

Jarium tilts his massive head for a moment, studying Peter. He says, "That sounds like a matter for my father, Chief Adair."

Peter feels like he's making progress. He nods and then asks, "Is he larger than you?"

Jarium laughs, "You will not have to ride him."

Jarium kneels down, which Peter takes to mean mount up, so he does. As they start, Jarium says, "We must get back to the pride; it will take us a day to reach my village."

The team from Goreipor has spent the night on the bluff where they landed, per Taligarr's orders. A few of Pirus' soldiers have been allowed to do short-range reconnaissance, but that's all, per Taligarr's orders.

It's morning and Captain Pirus stands at the edge of the bluff, looking out at the crimson jungle. He has no high regard for Taligarr or Janick; they are not soldiers in his opinion... and they are sure not Lord Kildemar. He grows tired of his time being wasted.

Janick comes up and asks, "See any movement yet, Captain?"

Captain Pirus ignores his question, turns and walks directly to Taligarr, "Taligarr, we are here to scout this world... we can't do it from the safety of this mound."

Taligarr has his priorities a little off, "That's Commander... if you don't mind, Captain."

Devon is off on the sideline. He watches how Pirus handles this. Unknown to Lord Kildemar's two sons, Devon has seen more action in the quarantined zone on Earth than they've ever seen in their world.

Pirus lets out a breath, "Listen, pup, we're in the field, not the fortress. I'd look foolish addressing you two as Commander number one and Commander number two, so Taligarr and Janick is what I'll use until you earn different." He lets the shock of his words sink in for just a second and adds, "We'll be moving inland now... with your permission... Taligarr."

Not waiting for his permission, Pirus turns to his troops, "Gear up... we're on the move."

Janick scurries over to his brother, "You gonna take that from him?"

Taligarr is still a bit red-faced, but he's better at holding his temper than his brother. "Give it time, he'll get his," is all he says. Unlike Janick, Taligarr is the calculating schemer.

Devon walks by the two brothers and comments as he goes, "Listen to him and we might all stay alive." He continues on past them before either can voice a reply.

Chapter Ten

Captain Pirus' team has to hack their way through the dense jungle, made especially hard going by a myriad of bright red thorn-covered vines that entwine their path. The canopy almost blacks out any resemblance of daylight, impeding progress even further.

At a slightly more open spot, where at least some sky can be seen, Pirus calls a break. Taligarr and Janick have been complaining for a while, but the Captain rests when his men need it... after all, they are doing all the hacking.

Taligarr comes up, "Captain, chopping our way through a jungle is a waste of time... this horrid land has no one."

Pirus doesn't look at him, but says, "A shame... just as we're coming to a path of some kind."

"And how would you know that?" snaps Taligarr.

Pirus casually points to the reddish sky where a few birds of prey are hovering.

"Birds feed on paths." After saying this, without waiting for a response, he walks over to his men. "Ten minutes, boys. Easy on the water till we find a refill source."

Devon stays quiet as he watches all these interactions. One thing he has learned from chess is to know the board, and be patient. He could probably make clearing their path easier with some spell but he prefers to keep the range of his skills to himself... no doubt they will eventually be needed.

Once the break is over and after about ten more minutes of chopping their way through the jungle, Captain Pirus is proven right... they break through to a trail of some sort. It's not a wide trail and, judging by its undergrowth, it isn't used that much... but it is a trail.

Of course, Taligarr and Janick are far from being satisfied. Janick comes up to Pirus, "This doesn't tell us anything... it's no more than an animal trail."

While Janick is spouting at Pirus, Devon looks at a tree along the trail. He walks over to them with a section of vine in his hand and holds it out.

"Animals don't use blades," Devon says.

He hands the vine to Janick... it has a cleanly cut end. It's not clear how long ago it was cut, but they certainly didn't cut it. Janick holds it out to Taligarr and throws it to the ground.

Captain Pirus says nothing, but gives Devon a nod of approval before he signals the group to keep moving.

As they trudge forward, Devon comes up to Pirus' side and asks, "Aren't you at all worried about the kickback from how you're treating the two *commanders?*" It's said more to get a better read of Pirus' style than to sound critical.

Pirus smiles, "Depends on whether this mission of yours pays off... Kildemar is more about results than education... that is, unless he's disappointed."

More time passes. The narrow path the group follows spills out into a wider trail. The groundcover here is more trampled; it's clearly a trail that has gotten more use. Even Taligarr and Janick can't dispute signs that more than animals use it.

As they round the next bend the signs of non-animals become gruesomely clear. One of Pirus' soldiers points up into the trees. The emaciated remains of what appear to be humans hang from them like ominous decorations. Even gorier... below the bodies are piles of what must have been their internal organs rotting in the sun.

Taligarr, staring at the half-dozen or so bodies, says, "We don't need whoever or whatever lives here."

Janick nods his agreement.

Captain Pirus doesn't seem to be moved... he's seen worse.

In a strikingly cold tone Devon speaks up, "If they can be controlled, they may be exactly what we want."

Even Pirus gives him an odd stare. The signs of violence do not throw him, but he prefers disciplined troops to savages. Keeping an open mind, he finally says, "These may not be the only creatures in this world."

Taligarr snaps, "How would you know that?"

Devon volunteers, "We don't know what this is. Some warlords on Earth used to impale their enemies along the borders of their lands to ward off invasions... you don't put up scarecrows if there's no one to scare away. There are clearly multiple sides here."

Pirus, having seen what there is to see, continues down the trail. "Let's try to find the more evolved savages here... and the sooner the better. This place is food for dark dreams."

Peter is still riding Jarium when the two arrive back on the ridge overlooking the clearing. He looks down at the clearing and sees four men, each a different shade of darkness... orangish-brown, bluish-brown, and more. They are busy strapping the pride's deer on long carrying-poles.

Before Peter can say anything there's a screech from above.

Peter looks up and a gorgeous bird, the size of a large condor but much more colorful, swoops down towards him and Jarium. With the bird diving directly at them, Peter tries to duck to the side in preparation for the attack, but falls off Jarium instead. Even on the ground Peter holds up his hands in defense.

Just as it is upon them, the bird flares its brightly colored wings... and transforms into an equally beautiful woman. The transformation is perfectly timed to allow her to softly land on Prince Jarium's back.

Jarium looks down at Peter and says, in his coarse tiger voice, "Let me introduce you to my wife, Topolina."

Feeling both confused and a bit foolish, Peter gets to his feet, dusts himself off, and bows to Princess Topolina.

She nods and says, "He has excellent manners... I think I already like him."

She knows having manners when they are expected has to be much easier than showing them when you're stunned by events, as she's sure Peter is.

"What is your name, young man?"

Peter is grateful that he's at least graduated from *boy* to *young man*. He smiles and answers, "Peter, ma'am."

"Please call me Topolina, Peter," she responds.

Peter looks back down at the clearing and realizes that everyone must have dual physical appearances... if not more. He glances at Jarium and asks, "When do you change?"

"Someone has to be on guard during the long walk home. Not all animals in our land are also people, and some are truly dangerous," Jarium answers.

Princess Topolina stands up on Jarium's back and, with the balance of a ballerina, springs into the air. As soon as her feet are clear she morphs into her bird-self.

She does a barrel roll and swooping back down yells, "I'll fly ahead and tell your father we will have company." She does another graceful barrel roll, adding, "Very nice to meet you, Peter."

She soars away towards the west.

Shan sits thinking on the front porch. She knows what she has to do in large broad-stroke terms... the small points bewilder her.

The screen door squeaks as Gran-D comes out and takes a seat beside her. They have the house to themselves since Kalish and Atta have left early to do errands. He remains quiet for the longest time, knowing she's wrestling with something.

He finally says, "The big picture is sometimes clearer than the little one... Am I getting close?"

Shan looks at him with a touch of suspicion... so many times he's been able to do that to her yet, to the best of her knowledge, sorcerers, even powerful ones, haven't mastered reading thoughts. She just stares at him... no words.

"It's so large that it's hard to know where to start. That's not mind reading... just experience," he answers her thoughts.

"Where would you start?" she asks.

"With those whom you understand the most... the youth," he offers.

Shan has already crossed that bridge in her head, but it doesn't resolve her dilemma. "I sort of figured that part out... but how do I train people, even kids, to fight when they have never even heard of fighting?"

"You don't start by teaching them to fight... you start by teaching them to defend themselves. Unfortunately, one will lead to the other," Gran-D says, with a degree of sadness.

With equal sadness, Shan says, "What will happen then?"

"I don't know child. If the prophecy is true, it doesn't say we will like it... or what the costs are." He adds, "I think, with your guidance, most will learn well how to use their new way of having to think."

Gran-D gets up and starts to leave, but he turns around to conclude on a more upbeat note, "Start with that boy Yadar... he's always thought you were cute."

Sarcastically, Shan responds, "Thanks, old man."

Chapter Eleven

Pirus' team, and it's truly his team, continues on the larger trail they have found. His four soldiers are on a mission, as they have been so many times before... Taligarr and Janick are ambling on, and Devon seems to be operating a little on his own. Everyone still performs within Captain Pirus' brackets of acceptability... but they haven't seen action yet.

One soldier is on point; two soldiers are flanking well back and one pulls drag. Taligarr and Janick walk mid-forward, making too much noise for Pirus' taste.

Suddenly Captain Pirus' senses are tweaked. He moves up to Taligarr and his brother.

He quietly says, "Slip back and keep quiet." It's clear he's not asking.

Pirus gives a hand signal to his two flanking men. They tighten and drop to their knees. Just then the point man comes back to him and the drag man closes in. Corporal Garr, his point man, quietly tells him something and Pirus signals all to stay put. He starts to move forward with Garr.

Devon joins him. He answers Pirus' disapproving look saying, "You may need my powers."

Captain Pirus is not a big fan of hocus-pocus but doesn't want to waste waist time with arguing. He nods to Devon to come along. When Taligarr starts to get up, Pirus gives him a hard glare... Taligarr is smart enough to squat back down.

Devon and Pirus follow Corporal Garr cautiously.

"What's up?" Devon whispers.

"The corporal may have found something up ahead... he doesn't know what to make of it. We're taking a look."

With this, Pirus bows an arrow. Taking Pirus' lead, Devon readies his lance... naturally, his weapon is backed by sorcery, making it more than what meets the eye.

As the three emerge from the trail into a clearing, Devon can hardly believe his eyes; it's like some ancient photograph in a history book. A gigantic half pyramid, at least a hundred feet high, extends out from a red rock cliff. Wide stairs rise up the pyramid's face, like those on the Inca pyramids... only much cruder.

Corporal Garr silently directs their attention off to the distant left of the pyramid's base. There's a row of what appear to be animal pens, with what, at this distance, look like men in them. The men are lying about, unaware of the Goreiporian team.

Captain Pirus is more focused on the many cave-like holes in the rock cliff than the pens. The men in the pens are a known entity... what concerns him is the unknown. He glimpses a movement at one of the holes and signals Devon and the Corporal to concentrate on the cliff.

The trio catches further glimpses of movement in the dark cave mouths, but whatever is in the caves hasn't made any overt actions.

From behind, Pirus suddenly hears a very loud whisper, "Captain, what is happening?" It's Taligarr.

He and Janick, having tired of being back on the trail, have advanced. Two of the other three soldiers closely flank them. The rear guard has remained in his place, lest unknown forces attack them from behind.

Pirus glares at his sergeant, but the sergeant's shrug and headshake tells him they have little choice but to protect the *commanders* and advance with them... stupid or not.

With a disapproving look, Pirus tells Taligarr and Janick, "Stand your ground and keep quiet."

They don't like it but Pirus doesn't wait for an answer. He returns his attention to the cliffs... still no action.

Devon taps Captain Pirus' shoulder and points to something on the other side of the pyramid's base... a massive pile of bones. Some are bleached, but others are clearly fresh and smeared with stained blood.

Pirus whispers, "Whatever is up in those caves may be the more evolved ones."

Despite Pirus' orders, Taligarr moves up closer and says, "Captain, let's get out of here... we don't need them, whatever these creatures are."

Regardless of their reasons, Pirus is aware that if they were to start backing away it would surely invite an attack... the more primitive the enemy, the more they will immediately react to an overt action. Even the team's hesitation is causing more movement within the caves.

The jewel in the middle of the pendant that hangs around Taligarr's neck begins to glow, as if trying to say something. In the intensity of the moment, no one seems to pay attention... except Devon.

When Taligarr realizes Pirus is not backing down, he unshoulders his bow. The loose hanging pendant is in the way and he simply tucks it into his shirt... almost unheard.

Devon senses something is about to happen, and, without worrying about being loud, yells, "Everyone, close on me."

Pirus isn't sure what Devon sees, but yells out, "Now."

The whole team moves quickly towards Devon, while Devon holds up his staff. Abruptly arrows come flying out of the many holes in the cliff. They shower down on the team, but Devon has created a protective shield that deflects all within a twelve-foot radius around him.

None of his team is harmed... more importantly, those in the caves see this.

Before another barrage can rain down on them, Devon points his staff at a cave halfway up the cliff. A ball of energy shoots from the staff and the rocks around the cave explode.

There's an uneasy silence from the caves. The team waits to see what comes next.

Janick loudly whispers, "Hit them again."

"Keep your place," Pirus snaps at him.

Movement from behind him makes Pirus spin around, but it's only his rear guard joining the group after hearing the explosion. Pirus nods and refocuses on the caves.

A bow is thrown out of one of the lower caves. After a couple of seconds a Neanderthal-looking being inches out. No others appear near any of the openings. The man kneels to the ground in an obvious show of submission.

Pirus looks over at Devon, "What now, kid?"

Before Devon can respond, Taligarr starts to get up. Captain Pirus grabs his arm with one hand and forces Taligarr back down to his knees.

Seeing this, Janick moves towards Pirus but the sergeant's blade at his throat quickly convinces him to stay put. In the heat of an encounter, the sergeant has little concern for egos... his leader is his Captain, no one else.

After this little drama within the ranks, Devon stands up. He doesn't move forward since his shield may be needed if there's another volley of arrows. He yells to the man, "Who is your leader?"

The cowering man looks up, "The strongest."

Another man, just as Neanderthal as the first, exits a cave. He pushes a smaller man in front of him, using him as a shield.

"I lead them," he declares.

Devon glances over at Pirus, who nods for him to continue.

With lightning speed, Devon whips a razor disc off his belt and sends it flying. The disc flies past the shield-man by inches and embeds in the self-proclaimed leader. He topples to the ground, quivers a moment and dies.

Devon looks at the man who first came out, a strong-looking specimen, and says, "You are now the leader."

Captain Pirus gives Devon a puzzled look but, when Taligarr stands as if to take the lead, he snaps, "Don't interfere."

It's not that Pirus is endorsing either of them... he just knows that if there appears to be confusion over who's giving orders, it makes the team look weak. The question of who's in charge can wait till after the current situation is settled.

"We do this all the time on Earth... install puppet leaders," Devon says, assuring Pirus that he knows what he's doing.

He figures this one has the sense to see an overwhelming force, the smarts to act first and, now, a slim allegiance to the one who has just given him power. Whether he can hold on to that lead is up to him.

This action establishes Devon's willingness to topple anyone who opposes him. Devon's well aware that such a tactic would not work with a more advanced group... but he's gambling it will here.

"What is your name?" Devon demands.

The man stands up, and, trying to show no fear, says, "Rahl."

"You know as soon as we leave, they might eat *Rahl*," Captain Pirus quietly says.

"Then we'll make another Rahl," Devon quietly responds.

Rahl points to Devon's staff, "Where did you get the lightning that comes from your stick?"

"That's not for you to know... you just need to know that we all have lightning sticks."

Devon tries to keep it as simple as he can, doubting they will understand more... also not wanting them to understand more. To make his point he levels his lance at Rahl, raises the point and fires off another energy bolt. It explodes high up the wall.

Rahl drops to the ground again. There's a frightened buzz from within the caves.

Devon demands, "Who are those in the pens?"

Staying on the ground this time, Rahl lifts his head and quickly says, "They are nothing... from a small tribe... we are stronger."

"NO! We are the strongest!" Devon snaps.

Devon points up to the sky, figuring he might as well play this little charade to the hilt.

"We have chosen you as leader. Now we will go away, but not for long. When we come back you will have gathered all the tribes to fight for us."

Still on the ground, Rahl asks, "Fight what?"

Using a bit of sorcery to magnify his voice, Devon bellows, "Silence!" Then, dropping the volume, "You will do as we say or all your people, all your tribes, will be destroyed by lightning." To accent this, he points at the sky again.

By this time many of Rahl's people are at the edge of the caves... they all look up at the sky in fear. A bolt of lightning cracks from the clouds and strikes down in the nearby jungle. They immediately pull back into the darkness of the caves.

Captain Pirus does his best to hold a stern face, though he feels like cracking up. Even Taligarr and Janick look a little impressed by Devon's performance, but it's not enough to appease Janick's violent appetite. Not bothering to whisper, he says, "Kill a few more so they won't forget."

Pirus snaps, "Sergeant, if he opens his mouth again, gag him." Then he turns back to Devon, "How are we ending this?"

"Have everyone circle tight around me... everyone touching," Devon says.

As Captain Pirus has his men do so, Devon turns back to Rahl, "Remember our commands... we go now."

With this, and the whole team tight around him, Devon sets off an explosion of dense purple smoke masking everything within a ten-foot radius. The purple smoke clears slowly. When it does, Devon and his entire party are gone.

A buzz of awe and fear spreads quickly among Rahl's people.

The team materializes about a couple of miles from the clearing with the pyramid.

Devon is more than drained... blood trickles from his nose and, a couple of moments later, he staggers. Pirus steadies him until he gets his bearings.

Concerned, Pirus says, "You OK?"

Devon nods... but, for the first time, he realizes that his powers have their limits. He's not about to say so, but this is a disturbing discovery.

As quickly as he can, he attempts to regain his composure so the chink in his armor will not be too evident... he knows illusion is often more real than truth.

Neither Taligarr nor his brother care how Devon feels. But Taligarr takes note for later use.

Janick is the first naysayer: "What happens when they find out we are not from the stars? And why did you stop me from demanding we show more force?"

"I don't care who steps up first, but in a confrontation you don't change lead in midstream. You and your brother can spout all the orders you want behind the lines... but not in the heat of a confrontation... do you understand?" Getting no response from Janick, Pirus repeats, "Do you understand?"

Trying to break the tension and to show he's fully recovered, Devon says, "Once superstitions and tales take root, they are hard to separate from the truth. This is a word-of-mouth world... by the time we need them we will be unchallengeable. No more violence was needed. Remember, we have to look both strong and magnanimous."

Devon starts to turn away, but stops, "And... I am from the stars."

Though not as disdainful as his brother, Taligarr says, "It was an entertaining performance, but we have no need of people like this. They are stupid savages."

Devon's first inclination is to say, '*and you aren't*,' but he holds this thought. Instead he says, "Your father will have need of them. If any of the realms we encounter have strength... and we know Spirin has the potential... then we need pawns to be sacrificed. Trust me, they will be of use."

Having more concern for the moment at hand, Captain Pirus says, "Your illusion won't hold if we get spotted, so I suggest we get well away from here."

"Tribes don't range far. If we're going to plant the seeds of fear, I suggest we give Cretorn a few more stops before moving on. When rumors from one area meet the same rumors from another they explode," Devon explains.

"I don't like staying in this land," Janick grumbles.

To ease the tension between him and the lord's sons, Captain Pirus states, "I agree, but I don't want to come back soon. If we are going to seed this land, it's better we do it now and have done with it. What do you think, Taligarr?"

It's amazing what being asked can change in a person... Taligarr thinks on the matter a second, and then, "I don't agree with the boy about needing these savages, but if we're going to do it, let's get it over with."

Devon gives a slight, silent nod to Pirus as if to say, "Well played." But he has other reasons for remaining a bit longer... reasons he doesn't plan on sharing.

Chapter Twelve

The massive trees they've passed throughout the trip to Prince Jarium's village have fascinated Peter. Many are like gigantic brightly colored oaks. Jarium has told him along the way that the trees are home to many of his people. But nothing prepares Peter for what he sees as they crest the final hill leading to Jarium's village.

A grove of trees the size of a small city stretches out before them... as wide as he can see and at least a hundred feet high. Even from a distance Peter can see the trees are honeycombed with dwellings. The combination of yellow, purple and blue leaves with equally colorful structures creates a giant kaleidoscope.

Prince Jarium can see the awe in Peter's eyes, and says, "My humble village awaits."

As Peter turns towards him, Jarium transforms from a noble saber tooth tiger to a noble young man. His complexion is a royal bluish-brown; his bearing is that of a leader, strong and proudly upright. Now Peter knows why he was the largest tiger in the pride.

Prince Jarium, his men and Peter casually walk under the umbrella of the massive tree city. People of many colors, some as animals and some in human form, wave and say *hi*... Jarium is gracious to all, a true leader, or at least future leader.

Peter glances at the sole deer the men have on the carrying poles, and then back at the city.

Little escapes Jarium's attention. "We were not on a hunting trip for the city. The deer was injured. If we do have to kill, it would be an insult to the animal not to fully use its body. Most of our diet is fruits and vegetables."

Considering that they would be classified as both hunter and prey, this isn't a surprise. Though he wouldn't say it, Peter has to remind himself that only man hunts for sport, and as far as he could see, the people of Acculas are neither solely men or solely animal... maybe they're the best of both.

The other thing that crosses his mind, and he's not proud of it, is that, thankfully, these people are not pacifist and that may be useful... Does he have too much of Gran-D in him?

Peter brings his head back to the purpose of the trip. He asks, "When do I get to meet your father?"

Amidst greeting people along their path, Jarium responds, "Tonight at the festival."

"Is it some special occasion?" Peter asks.

"Not really, just a good night to have a festival," Jarium casually answers. "Before the festival you must rest up, it's been a long trip. We will celebrate this deer's life tonight."

Peter is growing to like these people more by the minute. That doesn't mean he knows that they will be willing to go to war... but there seems to be clear nobility in them.

They come to a wide tree limb that arches all the way down to the ground. One set of stairs bridges the limb and another goes up the center like the veins of an arm.

Peter glances at the limb that reaches down to the ground and remembers something he was told long ago on Earth: "*When a tree bends over and touches the ground, it's a portal to another dimension.*" He thinks, '*Funny what you remember...*' especially since he's come through so many dimensions since then. He steps onto the limb and follows Jarium upwards.

Later that evening, after a good rest, Peter is escorted into the Big House, a massive room where many of the tribal leaders and their families often gather to celebrate... almost anything.

The Big House has about a three-story ceiling and, to the best Peter can reckon, it's about the size of a football field... all floating somewhere up in a giant tree. The structure is made of raw beams carved to represent animals and painted in a myriad of bright colors. The outer walls are supported by hundreds of these totem poles.

Peter looks up and sees laughing children sitting on beams along with a variety of animals. He wonders if all the animals are people as well. It would seem odd in a land like this for people to have pets, so he assumes they must all probably have dual selves.

Tables surround a large open area in the middle of the hall, and fire bowls on high posts surround the tables. A young maiden leads him to what appears to be the head table where he finds Prince Jarium and Princess Topolina already enjoying the festivities. Jarium gets up and waves for Peter to take a seat at his side.

As Peter does, his eyes keep darting all over the massive hall... so much to see.

Jarium laughs, "More elaborate than a tiger's den, true?"

When Peter left on this journey he expected to find new worlds, but he didn't expect them to be so exciting. He looks at Jarium and just says, "Much more."

"You must tell me of the tigers of your Earth that you think I resemble," asks Jarium.

"Unfortunately, they're extinct," Peter responds.

"Ah, in that case, never mind," Jarium says with a smile.

The room is almost a deafening buzz of chatter. A horn sounds and all ceases in anticipation of something. Drums begin, slowly at first and then they pick up the beat. Peter looks over to Jarium and Topolina, but they wave his eyes back towards the center of the room. They seem to be taking delight in seeing Peter's fascination.

All of a sudden dancers stream in from the many entrances to the hall. Other instruments join the sounds of the drums. An elaborate, energetic ballet bursts across the center stage area. Dancers turn into birds and other animals; at the same time birds and other animals turn into dancers. All builds into a frantic, artistic spinning to the beat of the music.

The spectacle goes on for a half hour... without a boring second in it. After it reaches a finale, the crowd in the room roars with delight.

Peter is on his feet applauding. For a boy who has been shuffled around foster homes in small towns of the Northwest, this is the biggest live show he's ever seen... outside of something like a Super Bowl halftime on television. He never knew how much energy comes from the real thing. Spirin has magic, but, being a laid back community, is shy of spectacles like this. This is more than an adventure... it's an eye opener.

Jarium is happy his guest is so pleased... it's a good omen that honors his house.

When Peter finally sits back down, a little out of breath, he smiles at his host and says, "That was great."

After the festivities fall back to a normal pace, Peter asks, "Where is your father?"

"He and the other chieftains are meeting in the small hall before joining us," Jarium answers.

"About me?" Peter asks.

Topolina laughs and says, "I'm sure you will be mentioned since no one has ever come from beyond the walls, but they have other business to discuss... like all old men do."

Jarium adds, "They will not talk much of you till they have heard your words."

This pleases Peter. For people to listen before they speak is refreshing. Then he feels a bit guilty about asking if he was their primary topic in the first place.

Jarium sees this and pats Peter on the back, "Don't worry, my father will join us shortly... then you can speak your mind."

The festivities around the Big House momentarily tone down as the chieftains enter the hall. The chieftain leading the procession is Chief Adair, Jarium's father. One at a time, the other chieftains split off and take seats with their families at the tables leading up to the head table.

To the best Peter can tell, Chief Adair seems to be about sixty years old. His age wrinkles suggest he has smiled much of his life; they don't have that dragged down look of people who find life disappointing.

As Adair approaches his place at the head table, Jarium and Topolina stand out of respect... Peter is quick to do the same.

Adair pauses to take a long look at Peter, and then waves for all to sit down. To Peter, "So you're the lad who came through the wall... and from what my son tells me, you come from even farther away."

"Yes sir, from a place called Earth, somewhere way out there amongst the stars," Peter gestures upwards.

Chief Adair looks up and says, "We have a legend of someone coming from way out there." His tone is not exactly uplifting.

"May I ask what your legend says?" Peter asks politely.

Adair seems distant, "It is... cloudy." Seeing this is far from what Peter was hoping to hear, he adds, "My guess is you will find that a prophecy, a legend, a story exists in each land you visit. Each may have different details, but some similarity... change is always predicted... unfortunately, rarely welcomed."

Though Peter wouldn't, as a guest, say it out loud, he thinks, 'This old man is as bad as Gran-D.' He thinks, *Enough with the vagueness,*' and starts off, "There's a land named Goreipor that can jump the walls. They are dangerous, dark people who want to rule all... "

Chief Adair holds up his hand to interrupt Peter, "And who leads these people?"

Peter has no idea how he would know, and technically it's not yet true, but he knows to mislead the old man based on semantics would be unwise. "My brother will eventually become their leader."

"As I said, I believe you will find legends in all the lands... and, again, often they are very close to each other. Ours speaks of a dark brother as well," Chief Adair says.

"Then you know why I am here," Peter declares with the hope of putting the talk back on solid '*what are we going to do grounds*'.

Jarium and Topolina listen to this conversation carefully, but do not interrupt with their opinions. They know their father does not talk in concrete terms until much thought is given to a matter. That is the way in Acculas.

"You are here because you wish to talk of war." Adair shifts in his seat and stares into Peter's eyes, "War is not a small change... We swim in change all around us. Often it moves slowly and is hard to notice... but sometimes it comes hard. Our legend talks of one of those hard changes."

Not wanting to offend, but tiring of puzzles, Peter says, "What exactly does that mean?"

"That is why I said our legend is cloudy... one dark brother, one light... it is hard to tell who wins. My experience is that clouds block out the sun, not the other way around." Seeing his metaphors are frustrating Peter, Adair says, "I have to decide how dark your brother will make you before I can talk of the lives of my people. This is not a decision I make over dinner."

It is not exactly what Peter is hoping to hear, but at least it tells him that the real matter at hand is going to be considered. "If there is more that you need from me to make your decision, please ask."

"Time... is what I need." Then lightening his tone, "You will stay with us for a while... to give us both... time."

Peter realizes that in his fervor to find allies he has been willing to make an alliance without taking the time to know whom he was trying to align with. This is not questioning his choice of friends, but how unwise he must look to Chief Adair. No wonder the leader of Acculas wants... time.

Chapter Thirteen

The fire crackles on the last night the team is spending in Cretorn. They've planted the seeds of fear in three other locations with the hope that like a virus it would spread across this scary land. Taligarr and Janick wanted to jump immediately but Captain Pirus didn't want to land in a new world after dark. His strategies have kept them whole - no casualties thus far — so the *commanders* reluctantly agree.

Taligarr and Janick have stepped away from the team to speak privately. Neither is happy that, in spite of being put in charge by their father, Pirus has been running the show. It's even worse that the alien, Devon, counsels him.

"You know what my answer is?" Janick says, partially unsheathes his sword.

Taligarr puts a hand on his brother's shoulder, "There will be plenty of time for that before this trip is over. His magic can still be of use for now. Try to think like our father."

"He said if the boy tries to take control, bring back his head," Janick grumbles. "As far as I'm concerned we should bring back Pirus' head as well."

With a smile at his brother's anger, Taligarr says, "I agree. He has much to answer for, little brother, but we have to be wise about this. We will let our father mete out our vengeance."

Taligarr knows well the guards are Pirus' personal troops and there would be little chance of ridding themselves of the Captain. Though he won't admit it, he also knows the Captain has much more experience in the field than either he or his brother. He even knows they need Devon's magical powers, but he's not about to argue that point with his brother.

Sitting by the fire, Devon leans over to Pirus, "Think they are out there in the dark trying to figure out how to take our heads?" His smile says it's of little actual concern.

"Let them plot and grumble... they're not the type to take action with their own hands." But Pirus adds, "If we go back without them, no matter why, we're both dead."

"Speak for yourself, kemo sabe."

The reference to Earth terms goes right over Pirus' head, but why shouldn't it? Pirus is not from Earth.

Devon goes on, "Look, if we don't even pretend to listen to them we may be dead anyway... you know Kildemar better than I do."

Devon feels invincible, partly because of his powers and partly because of his youth, but letting Pirus think they are sharing the boat will keep him closer as an ally. Captain Pirus prefers soldiering to diplomacy.

"So what are you suggesting we do?"

"Work in a way that makes them feel like they're in charge; people on Earth do it all the time. Let them make unimportant decisions," Devon suggests.

"In the field, there are very few unimportant decisions," Pirus answers purely as a soldier.

Devon smiles, "Then make them feel like they're making the important ones... it doesn't have to be more than an illusion."

Pirus thinks on it for a moment and says, "Devon, you're scary. I'm glad I'm just s soldier." After a moment he adds, "Careful what games you play with me, boy."

The conversation ends as they see Taligarr and Janick come back into the camp area.

Pirus looks up to them and says, "If you feel we've finished here, we can move on to the other world in the morning."

Taligarr, a bit surprised by Pirus' tone, just nods and says, "Yeah... Captain, I think we should."

Devon gives Pirus a knowing smile.

Late that night Devon slips away from the camp. Once he's sure he has not been observed, he vanishes in a stream of smoke that whisks upwards.

He rockets over the jungles of Cretorn. From his point of view, the deep red terrain below is as black as the night. Against that blackness, he sees the glow of large fires approaching on the horizon.

As he gets closer, he can see the flicker of the fires in the red rock walls where they discovered the caves. Devon rises high, and then vertically flies down the cliffs, directly above the pyramid nested against the mountain.

He slows as he gets to the pinnacle of the pyramid. Carved into the stone wall atop of it is a large eye... and in the center of that eye is the jewel of Cretorn... that Devon knows as the Sorcerer's Door pendant.

Yadar takes turns with his friend, Creb, popping up the side of a wall on their hoverboards to see how far they can go before having to flip back down. They're in an old stone barn long been unused.

Yadar is a seventeen year old from the village of Klavedar, the largest village in Spirin. He used to have a crush on Shan until she cold-shouldered him too often. Then, once Peter showed up, Yadar learned what it was like to get punched in the

nose, a very alien thing in the land of Spirin. Wisely, he inter-
preted this to be a signal to end his crush on Shan.

Once Shan was chosen to study sorcery under the Masters
she lost track of the kids she knew from the village... as they
did of her.

Creb whips up the wall to almost eight feet before his feet
start to separate from the board and he has to come back down
to the floor. He enthusiastically yells, "Got ya! Beat that."

Not responding, Yadar appears a little distracted.

Creb says impatiently, "What are we doing here anyway... why
all the secrecy?"

"Shan Dee asked me to come and she said it was OK to
bring you, but for some reason she wanted me to keep it quiet,"
Yadar says. Kids have a funny way of remembering things so he
adds, "She was all hot over me a long time ago, so I said yeah. I
don't know what it's about."

With some irritation, Creb says, "So why drag me along?"

"Like I said, she was all hot for me and I figured if you were
here, it wouldn't get uncomfortable," Yadar says with an egotis-
tic grin.

"Hey, isn't she the girl that the Council was trying to turn
into some hot shot sorcerer... along with that round ear?" Creb
says with a little more interest.

"Yeah, I guess so... she pretty much quit coming around the
village about a year ago," Yadar replies.

They hear the outer door open.

"That must be her now." Yadar looks towards the door.

Creb shakes his head, "Finally... maybe we'll find out what
we're doing here... and get it over with."

Shan enters to find both boys leaning up against the wall trying to put on their best cool, impatient look. She smiles at this
façade, knowing they probably have nothing else to do anyway.

Before she can say a thing, Creb irritably says, "Please don't tell me I'm out here because you want to see Yadar."

Shan's answers this with a long booming laugh. It looks like Yadar doesn't appreciate the joke so she settles down and says, "What kind of rumors are you hearing in the village?"

Yadar, still a little hurt by how funny she found the idea of wanting to see him, snaps, "You sent me a tug to catch up on village gossip?"

"No... To see if anything more serious than gossip is circulating," she says in a sincere manner.

Wanting to go, Creb pokes Yadar. Yadar stares at Shan, trying to figure out what she might be up to. They haven't seen each other in a while, and she's been involved in some heavier sorcery then he's ever been privy to... this alone is enough reason to be curious. Now she seems seriously concerned about something, and it sparks his interest.

He brushes Creb back and takes a seat on a stone bench. "We've been hearing that someone was able to get through the wall that no one's supposed to be able to. I think people are wondering if it was your Peter... or that brother of his."

"Oggy said he saw some real strange men here a few days back, but we figured he was just being Oggy," Creb chimes in.

Yadar shakes his head, "Oggy thinks he sees things all the time... in his case, it doesn't mean they're there."

Shan knows Oggy probably did see someone... the men from Goreipor. There's no use in beating around the bush if she's going to get anything started.

"Look, what I'm about to tell you has to be strictly for the people we choose to get involved... is that understood?"

Suddenly Shan now has their full attention because being included in an exclusive group always appeals to teenage boys.

Plus... there's not a lot of intrigue in Spirin, so even a little bit is enticing. They both readily nod *yes*.

All she says to lock them in is, "We have to prepare to defend ourselves and Spirin."

Creb and Yadar ask in unison, "From who?"

"An army that exists beyond the wall. I can't go into all the details right now, but dark times are coming and the Council is closing their eyes... it's up to us," Shan says, knowing how weird this must sound to them.

"They're old... OK, what do we need to do?" Yadar asks eagerly. In part, he doesn't want to know all the details yet to avoid being frightened off.

"Feel out young Spirinese that you think would be willing to learn new ways... and be willing to keep it quiet," Shan says, hoping she has chosen well.

"You mean... troublemakers that don't mind getting into more trouble?" Yadar says glibly.

Though this doesn't sound great, Shan realizes that is what she will need, at least at this early stage... a bunch of misfits. She grimaces as she says, "Exactly."

It's daytime and the morning is long past. The members of the Goreiporian team are more than anxious to get out of Cretorn. It's a foreboding and unpleasant land... all the way down to its smell. The problem is that not all in the party want to jump in the same direction. Taligarr and Janick want to go home, while Devon gently pushes towards heading to the next land.

A map of the Sphere is spread out on the ground. Devon points to the borders, "We haven't tried jumping multiple borders at one time. Here we are right next to this land called Capulia." He indicates their location on the map.

"Your father knows someone from Spirin may guess what we're doing... so time is important. I say we need to keep moving forward."

Of course Devon knows the Sorcerer's Door is not restricted in such a manner... he used it to come from Earth, much farther than two borders. It doesn't serve his purpose to let on too much.

With a childish-sounding arrogance, Janick snaps, "But... you're not in charge."

Captain Pirus, who would just as soon stay out of the politics of the matter, takes a deep breath and points to a spot on the map called the *Portal.*

"The farther we go, the farther we are from home base. If we go here first, and it's friendly territory, we can use it as our hub... it touches all the lands. That way we will never be more than one extra jump from home." He tries to say this in a tone that would sound like he's asking Taligarr's permission. Might as well create the illusion the boy needs... as long as he keeps sound military control, he could care less about illusions.

Taligarr likes the tone... he thinks that maybe everyone, except this alien boy, is starting to recognize his leadership. He scratches his chin and says, "You have a point, Captain. I've decided we will explore this Portal next."

Taligarr is pleased with himself and his decision-making... and, at least, Devon doesn't get his own way.

Though he tries to keep it out of his tone, a slight touch of condescension slips in when Pirus says, "OK, it's decided, Commander Taligarr... perhaps we need to get moving towards the other border."

Chief Adair has made it clear that he, and the other chieftains have to consider Peter's request for an alliance. In the meantime, Peter might as well get to know the people of Accu-las. Peter realizes that it's more about them watching him... he can hardly blame them. What he brings with him means monu-mental change. Peter knows it will probably be the same in each new land he ventures into.

A day has passed and Peter has taken the advice to get a feel for the people of Acculas. They fascinate him... almost as much as the sorcerers of Spirin... in some ways more. They're all a combination of animal and human, and the nature of their ani-mal identities tends to show in their human personality.

In addition to wanting to get a sense of these people, he's the first to admit that he also wants to get a sense of their useful-ness in a fight... of course he'll only admit this to himself.

Prince Jarium has shown Peter around earlier in the day, but his duties have pulled him away. He suspects Jarium's duties might be related to him. Peter has chosen to continue wander-ing on his own.

Clearly Peter's not from Acculas, and most of the people know of his arrival, but none seem to see him as a threat. Maybe a few see him as a curiosity, but even that is not enough to make him feel uncomfortable. He remembers how out-of-place he was made to feel when he first arrived in Spirin... this is nowhere near that bad.... but Peter was part of the problem in Spirin. Anyway, everyone is friendly here... so far.

The village he explores is woven into the trees high above the ground, connected by a mixed fusion of tree limbs and suspen-sion bridges.

Peter already knows, from Jarium that, unless at festival or for self-defense, people appear within the village limits as peo-ple... not their animal counterparts. There are official excep-tions to this rule, but these have not been explained to him.

As Peter crosses a suspension bridge, a kindly looking woman passes him and politely bows, with a slight giggle. After the woman passes, Peter turns and sees a fox running on an adjacent suspension bridge. A parrot is riding the fox. At the end of the bridge, they whip around and start back down the bridge Peter is on.

When the two near Peter, they transform quickly into kids and run past him. Peter smiles at the thought that among the exceptions to the rules about appearance are kids... all worlds are a bit alike when it comes to kids breaking rules.

Though Peter has a good feeling about these people, he is not yet willing to demonstrate any of his powers. He knows his initial decisions sometimes are wrong and has started to appreciate the value of pausing before acting.

A little further into Peter's exploration, he sees a large hub structure in one of the connecting trees. It's different... more isolated than other parts of the village. The suspension bridges leading into it from all sides are suspiciously absent of people. The rest of the village has been buzzing with activity... but not here.

It sparks Peter's curiosity, and he chances taking one of the bridges towards this isolated hub. Halfway across, Peter sees men exiting the structure over a distant bridge... They seem to be carrying a load that appears to be a large cache of weapons.

Peter has half a mind to use his powers to become invisible to get a closer look, but before he does a giant bird swoops down. Landing directly in front of Peter, it morphs into a stout man. He doesn't share the warm smiles of most of the people Peter has met thus far. He has a military bearing.

The man snaps, "This area is off limits."

Peter, trying not to show the interest he actually has, says, "Sorry, I didn't know. Just wandering around... guess I'll wander somewhere else."

The man's scowl suggests he agrees. Peter backs away a few steps.

"Well... I'll be going... now."

The silent glare he gets says to go about doing so. Peter turns and leaves, but he knows there's something hidden back there that he will need to find out about... another time.

Almost off the suspension bridge, Peter glances over his shoulder... the stone-faced guard is still planted on the bridge. Peter gives him a smile and continues on.

All of a sudden Peter staggers, as if hit by something. He grabs the rails of the bridge to avoid tumbling off. A vision overwhelms his head... Devon! The images of Devon in Peter's mind overlay all other thoughts in his head... Peter stumbles about, trying to keep his balance.

Holding the railing as tightly as he can for stability, Peter tries to focus on the vision. He's had visions of Devon in dreams that he couldn't explain, but he's fully awake now... this can't be mistaken for a dream. Now he wonders if the dreams were actually dreams.

There's no sound to the vision and the edges are out of focus. He sees Devon standing near a mirrored wall... reflected in the wall are blood crimson jungles. In the hazy periphery of the image there are other men, but Peter can't make out who they are or how many.

Suddenly a man comes up to Devon and into focus... it's Captain Pirus. Peter doesn't know who Pirus is but for some reason he seems vaguely familiar... there's something about his face. Then Peter remembers that when he, Shan and Devon fought the Goreiporian soldiers on the plateau and he was wounded, just before he passed out, there was one last soldier on the plateau. He held a bow that was aimed at the kids... it is this man.

The vision disappears as abruptly as it came on. Peter collapses on the bridge, almost unconscious. Even the stone-faced guard on the bridge knows something's wrong and rushes to Peter.

"You OK, boy?" he says, helping Peter to his feet.

When Peter catches his breath he looks at the guard, "I'm fine, just got dizzy... probably from the height... thanks."

Once Peter is on his feet, the guard says, "Got to be careful about that... now, if you're OK... get off my bridge."

Peter takes this to mean, 'OK or not.' He just nods and, a bit wobbly, moves away. With his head clearing, Peter tries to reconstruct his vision. He now knows for sure that Devon is visiting other lands, just as he is and, unlike himself, his brother is not alone.

He also knows the visions are not dreams; maybe the connection that has allowed the two brothers to sense each other is evolving. The problem is that he has no idea what brings the visions on, and, they take their toll on him physically. If only he could learn to control the visions, they might be of some practical use... and be worth the strain.

One last thought crosses Peter's mind... if the soldier in his vision is the same one as on the plateau, how is it that he and Devon are now working together? Peter still wants to hold onto a sliver of hope that Devon hasn't fully become his enemy... albeit a very tiny sliver.

Chapter Fourteen

A flash... and the swirl of light that is the Sorcerer's Door appear. A second later a soldier is spit out... followed by another, and another. After a couple of minutes the whole team from Goreipor is through the door.

Most of the men pull themselves together from the landing while Devon stands looking up at the impressive skyscraper of a rock mountain in front of him.

The Portal, on the maps, is somewhat round, discounting for a slightly jagged perimeter. The maps that Devon has seen showed no terrain details but, now here, Devon suspects the column-like mountain is the Portal's dead center... somehow he knows it's the essence of the Portal.

Captain Pirus, after checking on his men, comes to Devon's side. He looks up, lets out a sigh and says, "It would have been easier if the door dropped us on top of that. How about you using that bubble of yours to take a look before we waste time climbing all the way up there?"

Devon is positive, even without seeing the top of the mountain, that there must be something important up there. But, Pirus is right; it's best to take a look first. He's also right about it looking like a long climb.

Taligarr and Janick have joined them. "Doesn't look like this land supports any people... at all," Taligarr says.

"We're going to look and see what's up there," Pirus says.

Devon conjures a spy globe that floats up in front of them. The image within it quickly comes into focus and starts to fly up the mountain face. They all watch intently.

From what appears to be about halfway up the mountain, the image in the spy globe starts flickering. Suddenly it turns to snow.

"What happened?" Taligarr snaps. "The boy wonder's powers disappearing?" He's less concerned with the image in the globe than the opportunity to take a dig at Devon. Devon knows such a stupid remark doesn't deserve an answer, but, at the same time, may be accidently on the nose.

He tells Pirus, "I'm going to take a run at it." Before either Taligarr or Janick can object, which they usually do, Devon disappears into a wisp of smoke shooting upward.

As he flies up, Devon feels like his powers are flickering just as the image in the globe did. The big difference is that if he stalls, for him, unlike the non-physical image, it's a long way down. As a precaution, he shifts his flight path over next to the cliff.

His move to the cliff is just in time. Devon's powers give out and at the last moment he frantically grabs for rocks to avoid falling. His fingers scrape on the surface trying to gain some purchase as he slides downwards. Finally his right hand takes hold of a crevice in the rock. He finds himself hanging precariously on the face of the cliff, a narrow ledge just a few feet below his feet. Carefully he drops to the ledge. When he looks down he sees he's less than half way up the rocky pillar.

This might deter others, but it convinces Devon that he is right... whatever is atop this mountain is truly important. He's positive that his power failing on the mountain is not an accident.

Now feeling a little more stable, he realizes he's on a climbable ledge that is a path spiraling upwards. Leaning over the edge, Devon yells down hoping they'll hear him, "Looks like we do this one on foot."

Devon wants to see what lies atop the mountain before the others, so he sets off up the ledge on his own.

A while later the team reaches the top of the mountain to find Devon standing on a ledge overlooking a flat recess, somewhat like a crater of a volcano, but only half a dozen feet deep. Nestled in the large flat area is an open temple. It's made up of a gigantic, slightly raised circular dome-like altar stone, surrounded by five evenly-spaced small marble buildings.

The altar stone is about fifty feet across... and strongly resembles the Sorcerer's Door pendant sculpted in marble. It's hard to tell because a couple of inches of dust or ash cover everything.

As Taligarr walks up next to Devon, he asks, "What's this all about?"

Devon holds out a hand, "Let me see the pendant." Seeing Taligarr hesitate, then he says, "Come on... it's not going to work up here anyway."

Reluctantly, Taligarr takes the pendant from his neck, and hands it to Devon. Devon climbs down the outer rim into the crater.

While this is going on, Captain Pirus is doing what he does best, scouting the terrain to get his defensive bearings. From what he sees from the upper rim of the mountain, he estimates the Portal to only be about ten to fifteen miles in diameter. It's hard to truly judge distances since the Portal is surrounded full circle by faceted mirror walls. They're disorienting, like being in a funhouse... with all the walls having distorted reflections of the pillar-like mountain in the center.

After determining the breadth of the land they're dealing with, Captain Pirus climbs down and joins Devon in the temple area. It only takes a couple of seconds before he sees the same thing that is fascinating Devon. Pirus quietly says, "That what I think it... "

"It is," Devon cuts him off, holding out the small pendant. "Big question... what does it mean?"

Devon has already kicked away some of the dust to determine the surface of the circle is indeed etched somewhat like the pendant, but there are distinct differences. The altar stone only has one outer ring of symbols instead of two. Having seen no clear break lines, the ring doesn't appear to be movable. And, there are only six symbols instead of the seven on the actual pendant.

Taligarr and Janick come up to join the two. Glancing out on the circular altar, Taligarr says, "Looks like we have found something of importance after all... if it weren't thousands of years old." From his tone, it's clear he doesn't see the significance of the Portal.

Devon is pleased by his shortsightedness.

"I thought we were looking for people," Janick says impatiently. "Unless I'm wrong, there haven't been any people here in a long, long... long time."

Trying to distract their interest from the altar, Devon says, "Generations... I would suspect... guess we wasted a climb."

Even Pirus is unaware of how much Devon would prefer to pass on this location. Turning to Sergeant Rooter, he says, "Sergeant, take a couple men and reconnoiter those buildings." From what they've seen, he doesn't expect them to find anything, but he's a thorough soldier.

Taligarr asks, "Any idea why your powers don't work here?"

"Nope... guess it's just a dead land," Devon responds, hoping no more is read into it than that. His big concern is that Taligarr will find this enough reason to have an excuse to go back to Goreipor and reevaluate things.

Pirus has already started to read Devon better than Devon would want. He says, "We haven't finished seeing what's here... don't start looking at the downside yet."

Devon snaps a suspicious glance at Pirus. Lucky guess... or is he that intuitive? Either way, he doesn't like being read so easily; he'll have to watch the signals he's sending out.

Taligarr glances around, "It's clear there's nothing here. Down below will at least make a good jump hub."

This concerns Devon but he tries not to show it.

"I think we should jump home and update father about how useless this trip has been so far," says Janick.

Pirus snaps a look at Devon, aware this is at least part of what he is concerned about. Then he addresses Taligarr, "And tell your father you didn't manage to find anything but a few savages and some ruins? I don't think that was the mission he sent you on, but maybe I'm wrong."

Pirus looks over to Devon with an invisible wink. He may like the straightforwardness of being a soldier, but he's capable of politics if those tactics are needed. The Captain is keeping his options open when it comes to Devon. Knowing what other beings might be on the planet serves him as well as Devon.

Janick is quick to say, "Tali... let's go home. We can try again later. All we've found are inferiors... or nothing."

"You always underestimate the fury of our father," Taligarr tells Janick in a tone that says he's already made a decision. "We keep going... at least till we have something to go home with."

Taligarr would rather continue on an expedition he doesn't care for than face his father with nothing.

"But...," protests Janick.

"But, nothing... we go forward!" snaps Taligarr.

With one problem solved, Devon still has to figure out how to keep the Portal from being a strategic hub. He wants as little focus on this place as possible... there are secrets here he needs to keep to himself until he discovers how they may play into his strategy.

Pirus and the others have drifted off to watch the soldiers clear the buildings. Devon takes the moment to further inspect the altar. He proceeds to the center of the altar where there appears to be a circular mound of dirt. The dust he finds there is different; it's crystalized, as if intense heat has passed through it.

Devon takes the end of his lance and taps the layer of solidified dust... it cracks away like a crust. When he clears a few chunks away it exposes a giant clear jewel, just as the pendant has in its center, only six feet in diameter. If diamonds are the currency in any of the lands, this is a king's ransom. But Devon knows it's more valuable than a diamond.

He stands in the middle of the altar and looks around at the five buildings, then at the short round pedestals just outside the ring of symbols, and he tries to make sense of it all. The ancients of whom he has heard rumors supposedly placed five races in five lands... what was meant for this small fragment of land? Why were no people placed here? If there were, where are they?

The most logical conclusion he comes up with is that in some way the Portal is a control room. This theory is not something he has any interest in sharing with the rest... even Captain Pirus.

Having seen all there has been to see atop its peak, the group carefully descends the narrow path down the mountain of the Portal. As they travel, ideas rush around in Devon's mind of how to give this entire land a wide berth. He knows he can tell them that he can probably use the door to jump multiple walls, since he already knows he can, but that doesn't negate the Portal as a strategic hub for possibly staging troops. There has been no sign of water... That might work against the location, but that's not enough.

Just past half way down in their descent, Devon knows he has his powers back... he can feel the surge of power in his bones. There's no use making a point of it to his companions.

He notices the common fracture lines in the rock formations all around him and has an idea. He's used energy globes to make a show of creating explosions, but with a little finesse he could probably be subtler.

Without attracting attention, he flips a mini-charge at a fissure in the rock... it cracks slightly, causing little real effect. No one notices. They keep moving downwards.

He tries again, with a little more punch. This time there's a clear sound of a fracture... still natural enough not to appear artificially created. A few small pieces of rock break off and fall downwards.

This does catch some attention.

Captain Pirus warns, "Everyone, watch your step... our mountain isn't completely stable."

After another couple of minutes have passed, Devon repeats it, this time with even a dash more punch. There's a loud crack to the right of the group, but this time a substantial fissure of rock breaks away and tumbles down. As it goes, it naturally snowballs by breaking away the ledges it hits. Everyone hugs the shaking cliff walls. By the time the rocks reach the bottom, they've become a small avalanche of boulders.

The trick is to do this without taking out the path the team needs to climb the mountain. After the billowing cloud of dust disperses, the team can see they still have a path.

Devon does it one more time before they reach the narrow section of flat land at the base of the mountain... just for good measure.

When the team finally gets off the mountain they can see the fresh boulders, many of which could have crushed a man.

Captain Pirus peers up at the mountain. "Sergeant, get everyone near the wall and away from this rock." He gives Devon a suspicious glance and adds, "So much for this being a hub... it's too unstable to risk it."

Chapter Fifteen

Peter is on a street-wide limb. He sits on a small vine-like limb that serves as a bench. From the look on his face he still seems drained by his experience with the vision of his brother.

Most people who pass by give him no more than a polite nod, but a young girl sees that he's out of sorts. She comes over to him and holds out a piece of fruit that Peter doesn't recognize... but it does look succulent.

She smiles, inches it closer and simply says, "Energy."

Peter returns her smile, accepts the fruit and takes a big bite of it. It's so ripe that juice runs down Peter's chin.

The girl laughs.

Peter manages to swallow the large bite he has taken and says, "Thank you."

She nods with a smile, and gestures for him to keep eating.

Before taking another bite... and it is refreshing... Peter says, "If you don't mind my asking, what are you... when you're not... you know, you?"

In a land where everyone is naturally something else it's not a question that she would ever hear, but she takes no offense to it. She lets out another glowing grin... and gives him a wolf pup's howl. At least, that's what it sounds like to Peter.

Peter laughs... not at her, but with her... and asks, "What's your name?"

He must have hit a bashful nerve because she giggles and skitters away. She looks over her shoulder and says, "Leep."

"Well, thank you for the fruit, Leep," Peter replies before she's out of range.

Prince Jarium has silently been watching this encounter from a limb slightly above Peter. He hops off the limb and softly lands like a cat near Peter.

A slightly startled Peter, "I know you're a cat... but do you have to show up like that?"

Jarium smiles. "I see you've been making friends," he says, gesturing toward Leep retreating in the distance.

With a glance Peter says, "Oh, you mean the young wolf."

"What's a wolf?

It hasn't dawned on Peter that his Earth references to animals have little relevance to the Sphere. Even when he had referred to Jarium as a saber toothed tiger, it didn't register that Jarium was too polite to question it.

Jarium can see it's troubling Peter and proceeds to say, "We call her other self a *leeger*." After a moment he adds, "And, I and my men would be called *torens*."

Faulting himself for his ignorant assumptions, Peter just nods that he understands. He holds up the piece of fruit Leep has given him, now half-eaten.

Jarium notes, "A *cruet*... but we're not offended by your not knowing our names for things... just call it bright orange fruit... and if I'm a tiger to you, that is perfectly fine with me." His smile tells Peter he is being sincere. Jarium adds, "The fruit is known for the energy it brings."

It must be true since Peter looks more composed and focused than just a few moments ago.

"How has your exploration of my village been going?" Jarium asks.

Peter takes a second, "It's been very open, but I did come to... "

"I heard," Jarium says, cutting Peter off. "Our citadel is off limits to all except for our version of a police force." Seeing Peter eyeing him suspiciously, he continues, "You find that disturbing? Young Peter, you already know more about us than we do about you. You have come to suggest that we get involved in your war, but show us nothing of what you bring to it."

Prince Jarium has a point. So far, Peter knows the people of Acculas can transform into animals... some of them, very formidable creatures. He also knows their tribes are not totally incapable of defending themselves, and they have police... perhaps even an army.

But he has yet to reveal anything of the defensive forces that Spirin could bring to the conflict... because he's not really sure as yet of what they are.

Peter nods that he understands. Though he's not prepared to lay out all the potential Spirinese powers, he realizes that some hint at the strength of his hand would be a fair return gesture of good faith.

Peter glances upwards and suddenly he morphs into a stream of smoke. The thread of smoke shoots up through the tree looming above and around them. Weaving in and out of the limbs for effect, he makes sure the stream of smoke is more visible than it would usually be. Just as abruptly, Peter reappears next to Jarium.

The Prince is duly impressed. "You move faster than my wife, Topolina... and invisible to the eye that doesn't know what to look for."

Peter thought this display would knock Jarium's socks off, but he appears to take it in stride. It's as if Peter's simply shown a new weapon to someone who handles weapons all the time.

Jarium's last few words even strike Peter as what an adversary might say. He's glad he didn't become fully invisible... at least for now. He thinks perhaps he's being too suspicious, but the stakes are high enough to be overly cautious. Peter truly hopes he will eventually be able to share more of his secrets with Jarium.

Sensing Peter's turmoil, Jarium says, "We have no current wars... have had none in some time. But, unfortunately, my people have had to defend themselves. That is the reason we value our peace... so much so that we would be hesitant to make hasty decisions over such a matter, as I think you're hoping."

Though he would like to counter that logic, Peter cannot. It dawns on him that making such unsupported requests of the chieftains may have only been displaying to them his own youth and inexperience... not exactly something, or someone, that a leader could trust.

Now another old thought flashes through Peter's head... that the people of Spirin have never had to earn their peace. He knows that's why they don't understand its value... and why they lack the willingness to defend it. His greatest fear is that the people of Acculas, and any other land he visits, will see this as well.

Jarium grins and says, "For such a young man, you think too much. Relax, and let us get to know you... trust me, your actions speak on your behalf."

Peter takes a breath; he realizes Jarium's right.

He wonders what has happened to that boy that didn't want anything to be more complicated than fixing motorcycles... and an occasional party up at the cave with his friends.

Peter curses Gran-D, and prophecies, under his breath.

Chapter Sixteen

Yadar, Creb and a number of their friends fool around at the base of a rock formation far from the village of Klavedar... actually, far from any of their homes. Shan has chosen this distant place for privacy. The only down side... since the kids don't have her flying skills, it's a long trek for them on hoverboards.

Creb, a continual grumbler, grumbles, "OK, Yadar, where's this ex-girlfriend of yours?"

"She'll be here... you have anything better to do?" responds Yadar as he whips past him on his board.

The group is mostly boys and a couple of stubborn girls who have caught wind of the training and have insisted upon being included. They're a raggedy bunch that, thus far, doesn't seem to be taking the gathering very seriously... but Shan has yet to arrive. And, as Yadar has said, most don't have anything better to do.

Shan is not far away. She's watching the group from a nearby bluff. Many of the kids know Shan, to differing degrees, from growing up around Klavedar. She wrestles with how to reintroduce herself to them. She must admit she has become distant from them since Peter's arrival... even more distant since beginning advanced sorcerer's training.

Lisha, one of the headstrong girls who wouldn't be left behind, stands by the rock wall as Creb does his best to impress her. He whips his hoverboard as high up the face of the wall as he can before losing control and flipping back down. As he passes Lisha, he does his best not to look like he's trying to impress her. She gives his efforts a shrug... trying not to look like she's impressed. They're being kids.

Shan watches their childish antics and comments to herself, "What have I gotten myself into?"

Just as Creb starts another run at the wall, a bolt of energy slams into the wall and sets off an explosion. It's far enough away not to harm anyone, but close enough to get their attention. Sheer terror rushes over the kids' faces... the kids of Spirin have never seen an explosion before. Even the *coolest* of them is overwhelmed.

As the shock fades, they turn to see Shan in a stern stance on the adjacent bluff. She has a firm grip on the lance she holds up beside her. As much as Shan dislikes going near Devon's old cave, she has retrieved a few props from the cave that she feels might be useful... the lance is one of them.

She knows she now has their attention... the question is, how is she going to explain war to the clueless?

The swirl of the Sorcerer's Door spits out the team from Goreipor, one at a time. To their surprise they plunge directly into a sea. Panic erupts among them since Goreipor has only limited bodies of water; at least half the men can't swim, and all are weighed down with armor and weaponry.

Devon's quick to yell over their cries, "Get rid of your weapons... everyone!"

Those who can swim try to keep those who can't afloat. It's contrary to all their training as soldiers to discard their weapons, even in the face of being dragged down to death by them.

Captain Pirus, who can swim, tries to help others and screams a command, "As Devon says... lose your weapons!"

Taligarr and Janick, both born to privilege and able to swim, make little attempt to help those thrashing about around them.

Devon manages to get a bobbing glimpse through the waves of an island about two hundred yards off. Not sure if it will work, Devon conjures up his protective half-shield hoping it will serve as a boat. Adjusting his sorcery-focus, the shield seems to work and he enlarges it. Unlike his normal shield, he makes this one visible.

"Move towards the shield!" he yells. Devon knows he could easily jettison himself out of the water and to safety, but losing his team would not do... He even must try to save Kildemar's two obnoxious sons.

Unwilling to lose his weapon, one of Pirus' privates disappears under the waves. Pirus sees this and, after helping another man on to Devon's shield, he swims to where the private went under. He takes a deep breath and dives down.

Devon would help but he has to maintain the shield. Most of the men now hold onto the edge of his makeshift life raft.

Captain Pirus breaches the surface and gasps to refill his lungs. He glances around and dives again.

Now safely holding onto the shield, Taligarr and Janick have no interest in helping Pirus find the drowning man; after all, they see it's just a private.

The longest time passes and Pirus doesn't surface... Devon starts to worry that he's lost his best ally to the water. Then, all of a sudden, the Captain breaks the surface. He coughs as he tries to suck air into his empty lungs.

The Captain's eyes tell Devon the fate of the young private.

Pirus has lost many men but it never gets easy. He shakes it off for the moment and swims over to join the rest. Only then, taking a head count, does he realize that a corporal is gone as well. The anguish shows on his face. Devon sees this but there's nothing that can be done.

He shifts his focus to the moment at hand and yells, "There's land over there." Pointing, "We can get there if we stroke together."

Indifferent to the loss of the soldiers, Janick snaps, "Let's get going before we all drown."

Captain Pirus glares at him and holds back the urge to drown both Kildemar's sons. He knows if he were to kill Janick, he would have to kill Taligarr as well. Pirus doesn't like emotions to slip into his decision-making, so he hopes they keep their tongues to themselves till he can regain his composure... if they don't, so be it.

Taligarr sees the anger in Pirus' eyes and takes hold of Janick's shoulder, "Row... and stay quiet."

More than an hour later Pirus and the other survivors lie, well worn, on the pink sands of an island's beach.

Devon lifts his head long enough to glance over at Taligarr to see if he still wears the pendant... the mission can afford to lose a spoiled son, but not that pendant.

After a breather to recover from the ordeal, Captain Pirus gets up and surveys the beach they are stranded on. Pirus can't change the loss of his men, but it's especially hard losing one as young as the private. All he can do is pull things back together and move the remainder of his team forward. He'll come to terms with the loss in the privacy of his mind, as he has done with so many soldiers who have fallen before.

Observing the Captain's demeanor, Devon begins to suspect his character is subtly contradictory to the coldness of most inhabitants of Goreipor... and reminds himself that Pirus has to keep more on guard than most. Perhaps this is the reason he is slightly open to the changes Devon has covertly suggested.

Pirus makes an eyeball inventory of the men and what equipment they have left... not much. A few of the men, including Pirus, still have knives... but swords, lances and bows are all at the bottom of the sea. Even Devon has lost his trusty razor discs.

Sergeant Rooter comes up to his Captain. They glance at each other. Having been through many battles together, they speak without words. As Devon staggers towards them, the sergeant hands Pirus a soggy torn hat, "Captain, found this in the water... it belonged to Private Gee. He was a good lad." Nothing more needs be said so the Sergeant walks away. Glancing at the hat, Pirus stuffs it in his vest.

Devon steps up beside Pirus. The two of them silently scan the horizon that shows many small islands off in the distance... they are now in the land of Capulia. Unfortunately, they are there with little means of defending themselves... or impressing anyone with their military prowess.

Glancing around to make sure their remarks will be private, Devon asks Pirus, "How long before the two *Commanders* start whining to go home?"

Still watching the horizon, Pirus responds, "They may have a point. We're virtually unarmed and without supplies."

Devon reminds himself of the value of picking your battles, and that Pirus does have a point, yet he wants to delay the retreat a bit: "If we go back to get re-outfitted, wouldn't it be to our advantage to know what we're gearing up to encounter?"

"You plan on doing a lot of swimming?" Pirus says glibly.

Devon insists, "Now that we're out of the water and not thrashing about, I can try to jump us together as a group. It takes a lot out of me but as long as I can rest between jumps..."

He's cut off by Pirus, "To where? We have no reconnaissance, and blindly hopping island to island doesn't resemble a plan to me."

Even if Devon planned it Pirus' wording could not have come out better. "I think I have a solution to that," says Devon.

Looking like a drowned rat, Taligarr stumbles up to them. "Captain, prepare to retreat home."

Taligarr is not experienced enough to know there are certain catch words that are not the wisest to use with a soldier... *retreat* is one of them. A retreat might be called for but calling it so too early tends to set a soldier's heels in.

Before an argument can ensue, Devon conjures up a spy globe to float in mid-air in front of the three of them. Wanting to keep his cards close, Devon is cautious about how many tricks he lets out of his bag, but now is the time for one. He says, "Why don't we just take a look around first."

"It can't hurt to get some sense of the lay of the land before we make any moves," Pirus suggests... not letting it sound like an order, even if it is.

Lacking a valid argument, Taligarr shrugs and says, "So what's that thing do?"

Back in Spirin, a spy globe is used like a stealth *tug* when it is directed at a person's signature; here Devon has to use it more like a roving drone. To show how it works Devon sends the image feed high above the beach. The image they see within the globe is of them. To further impress them Devon zooms the image in on himself, Pirus and Taligarr... their images fill the globe.

Taligarr quickly tires of Devon's advanced skills and snaps, "If you're going to take a look around... get about to doing so."

Devon likes irritating Taligarr and Janick, but just up to the edge. He nods with a glint in his eye, and the image in the globe takes off.

As they watch, the image zooms over a crystal-clear water-filled landscape, mottled with brightly colored islands. Most of the islands they see rush past are small and have no apparent dwellings, but it's an alien land and they are not quite sure what they are looking for. Perhaps the people, if any, live in caves like those of Cretorn.

Suddenly Devon slows the image over a dark red spot that sharply contrasts to the water. When he zooms in they see it's a ship with crimson sails. He keeps tightening on the ship until they can see the sailors. Both the ship and its crew remind Devon of Vikings, or an alien version of Vikings... the same, but different. The red sails are giant triangles that look more like they would belong on a Nile barge than a Norse ship. The men themselves are armed like Vikings.

Panicking, Taligarr blurts out in a loud whisper, "They'll see us if you get any closer!"

Devon holds back his laugh, "There's nothing to see... it's magic. They have no idea they are even being watched." He adds, "And, you don't have to whisper."

This gets a slight chuckle from Pirus and a harsh glare from Taligarr.

He tells Devon, "My father will want this tool."

"My sorcery is not like a tool you can steal... it takes my talents."

Even as Devon says this he knows it's possibly not true. He came from Earth and was able to learn these skills in Spirin. Perhaps it's the nurture or nature question in a whole new form. Maybe round ears are destined, as indicated in the Prophecy, to become powerful sorcerers, but it may be in the nature of Spirin to bestow the magic on anyone who spends time there.

Devon sincerely hopes not... the mixture of the soldiers of Goreipor and sorcery even scares him... What about the savages of Cretorn with magic wands? This is so far-fetched that Devon laughs and decides that it's his destiny... not everyone's.

After they've ogled the ship long enough for Captain Pirus to assess its strength, Devon moves the image in the spy globe farther on. The ship must be going somewhere so he flies the sensor in that direction. Before long, islands start becoming a little denser, as though heading for more land.

Being the first to notice, Pirus points off to the left of the image. In the distance is what appears to be a seriously larger landmass, perhaps a continent. To Devon, "Take us there."

By now Janick has joined them. He immediately sees the globe as a weapon. "Can you carry things in this bubble of yours?" he asks.

Knowing where Janick is going with this, Devon says, "I'll think on it." He wants it clear that his *toys* are completely dependent upon his existence.

"Get back to the moment," demands Taligarr.

Knowing where he wants the image to go allows Devon to get it there quickly... the view rockets over the water. In a matter of seconds their view approaches a large, populated harbor.

Moored in the harbor are many ships of varying sizes. An ancient-looking city skirts the harbor. Behind the buildings connected with the workings of the harbor, a high stone defensive wall borders most of the city. The image flies over the wall.

A dense city exists within the walls. Again, Devon gets the feeling of a Viking world, based on what he's read and drawings he's seen... yet it's different. Most of the structures are of heavy logs, no doubt carved from the massive forests on the hills beyond the city. One thing it has in common with Spirin is the people's liking of bright colors.

Captain Pirus has seen enough. He turns from the image and says, "These are not savages in caves whom I wish to approach with just a few knives and a little magic."

Before he continues, Pirus decides to play the diplomacy card, "Taligarr, I would suggest we jump back to Goreipor and re-equip ourselves."

It's clear from Taligarr's face that he appreciates the matter being put to him... even if he knows it's not exactly a suggestion. "A sound plan, Captain."

"My little magic is enough to handle whatever we come up against," says Devon, obviously not pleased.

Gloating, Janick says, "Boy, you will go where we choose."

"It's settled," Pirus says definitively. To Devon, "I don't want to go anywhere with only one person having weapons... even your kind of weapons... and we're short two men."

Devon tries to protest, "We can steal the feeble weapons you use."

Devon's wording is unwise. Pirus raises his voice directly at him, "The matter is settled."

Both Taligarr and Janick crack a smile.

Their smile does not last long as Pirus walks up to Taligarr and coldly jams the lost private's hat in the noble son's fancy vest. Then he turns away.

Janick starts to say something but Taligarr's arm stops him. As for Taligarr, he is wise enough not to say a word.

Chapter Seventeen

Peter sits at the head table in the Big House for yet another night of festivities in Acculas. Wine and laughter flow freely. Princess Topolina is at the table, but Jarium, his father and the other chieftains are not present.

Leaning over to Topolina, Peter speaks loudly over the festivities, "Is there a festival every night?"

She laughs and says, "The other nights were just dinner... tonight's a festival."

"What are we celebrating?" Peter asks.

She shrugs and just says, "Life... that's what all festivals are about." She doesn't bother trying to explain some ancient excuse for the celebration. She respects her people's history, but she also respects that their festivals are more about celebrating life today than ancient events. If Peter is around long enough, explaining history will be important... but not tonight.

Instead of history lessons, Topolina refills Peter's glass.

Peter is a little perplexed by her simple answer. Back on Earth people needed excuses... they little understood ancient history but they spouted a lot about it. Maybe these people truly live for the moment; he hasn't been around long enough to know the truth of that.

Prince Jarium finally shows up, but instead of taking a seat he taps Peter on the shoulder, "Your presence is requested in the Small House." He leans down and gives Topolina a kiss before leading Peter to the Small House.

From the previous night, Peter knows that the Small House is where the chieftains gather prior to the main festivities. Since there seem to be festivals all the time, maybe it's just their version of a brandy room... how much tribal business can there be to require meeting every night? He reminds himself that his arrival surely requires extra meetings.

Prince Jarium leads Peter into the Small House where Chief Adair and a dozen other chieftains sit around a large round table. Chief Adair gestures for him to have a seat.

Not well-versed in diplomacy, Peter barely settles in his seat before he asks, "So have you come to a decision?"

Most of the chieftains around the table laugh.

With a smile, Chief Adair says, "It's good to know youth is the same beyond the wall... maybe the same everywhere... impatient."

Peter immediately realizes he should keep quiet and listen before he puts his foot in his mouth again. Jarium takes a seat beside him and lightly slaps Peter on the back to ease his embarrassment... he's been there himself.

"We've thought on your presence here, and as I have said, our legends are not clear. They may not even have anything to do with you... but they may," Adair says calmly.

Any other old person talking in double-talk would exasperate Peter but he's wise enough to hold his peace while Adair continues... after all, it's his house. He's not sure what to expect... either detailed questions about the conflict he has come to tell them of or, as in Spirin, denial of their needs... he gets neither.

"Out there in the Big House, my people laugh and enjoy the now because we have fought wars and my people know how precious the moment is," Adair says slowly, watching Peter's reactions carefully. "This is why I will not commit my people to your war... for now."

Before Peter can try to mount a rebuttal, he continues, "But... I will not say no. What I will do is send my son with you to these other lands we know nothing of. He will gather knowledge... of you... of them... of the chance to not have a war." With this Chief Adair gets up and smiles, "Now... we go to the festival."

Peter is a bit stunned. He has expected to have to plead his case, or at least have some debate on the matter. He hasn't expected such a short, simple answer. As he tries to think of what to say to get them to reshape their decision, the chieftains file out, interested in hearing no more.

Jarium stands up and waits for Peter to do the same. In a resigned tone, "Well, young Peter, I guess we go off on an adventure together... but not tonight... tonight we party." He turns and walks away.

With little choice, Peter gets up and follows Prince Jarium towards the Big House. As he goes he realizes the chieftains gave him the only answer that makes sense, considering what they were presented with. At least he has gotten the possibility of support.

Dinner is just finishing up at the Dees' home. Master Carringer leans back in his chair and pats his stomach. With a big satisfied grin he says, "Atta, that was truly a fine meal."

"Master Carringer, you're always welcome here... and skinny as you are, you should take me up on it more often," Atta remarks as she starts to gather up the dishes... sorceress- style... The plates float towards the kitchen.

"How often do I have to tell you to call me Carringer?"

"You're a Master... and that's what I'm going to call you... unless I'm angry," she responds.

Kalish admonishes, "Atta, leave the poor man alone." He pats his much more rotund belly. "Not everyone can have a fine physique like mine."

Shan laughs.

Kalish gives her a funny scowl and turns to Gran-D, "You have any idea when Peter might come back?"

Gran-D puts on a serious look, "He went off on his own... how should I know when he will come back? All I know is that the Council is pretty upset by his actions." Trying to sound totally innocent of the matter, "I don't know what got into the boy."

Shan struggles to hold back a comment.

Kalish stares right through the old man, "Of course you don't know where he went... but I hope you make sure the boy gets back well, and soon... we are already missing one son."

Gran-D knows his façade doesn't hold up well around home. He gives Kalish a nod that says he's aware he's been warned.

Carringer watches this, knowing it's not his place to say anything, but aware they're not putting anything over on him.

Kalish gets up and starts to help Atta clear the table, but he does it the old-fashioned way... by hand. As he passes by Master Carringer, he says, "You too." The family puts up with Gran-D's little façade of not being Grand Master Dar, but little truth escapes this household.

Shan, though, knows her parents are not aware of everything, and she feels guilty about it. With the absence of Ramie, she fears telling them that she's formed an underground resistance group would be too much for them... at least for now.

About this time Carringer would be joining Gran-D in the living room for a touch of the jug the old man, not so secretly, hides in the bookcase. As they start to go in that direction, Gran-D gestures for Shan to join them.

She assumes it's not to share in his jug. But if he didn't invite her to follow them, she would have anyway since she has something on her mind.

As Gran-D digs out the jug, Shan steps up to Carringer, "Master Carringer, may I ask a favor of you?"

Taking Shan's sleeve and leading her towards the window, "Certainly, how can I be of service?"

Gran-D pretends to be preoccupied; since he will learn everything anyway, he might as well feign ignorance.

Shan glances around to make sure her parents are still in the kitchen, and then quietly says, "That thing that I'm not actually doing... I'm having some problems not doing it."

After another glance at the kitchen door, "Peter only showed me some things that are defensive... and I figured, maybe you would know some other things... you know, being the Spell Master."

The truth is that learning to be defensive, in that way, would be new to anyone in Spirin... even Master Carringer. He thinks on it for a second, then, "I'll dig around and come up with something. Otherwise, how's that thing you're not doing going?"

Shan lets out an exhausted sigh, "They're kids!"

Gran-D walks up to the whispering duo, "You know, neither of you would make very good spies."

With a little protest Peter allows Jarium to refill his glass yet again. He wonders how long the celebration will go on... and how long he can remain upright.

Jarium slaps Peter on the back and loudly proclaims, "Now, you're in for some fun." Jarium gets to his feet and, with some effort, helps pull Peter up. Then he waves to the hall and yells, "Clear the pegs!"

A loud cheer roars from all in the hall.

Peter, slightly blurry-eyed, wonders what's up as many men pull back massive panels from the floor. Below the panels is a mud pit filled with posts extending up about three feet above the mud. The eighteen-inch diameter posts are spaced all around, about five feet between each.

A man hops onto a post and then half jumps, half long-steps from post to post around the pit as the crowd cheers. Another man jumps out onto a post on the opposite side of the pit as a challenge to the one already in the ring.

From what Peter gathers, the object of the game is simple... you chase each other around the ring till one man topples the other into the mud. How much encouragement one contestant gives the other to fall is open to debate.

As the two playing the game leap from post to post, people in the surrounding crowd toss each a long pole... clearly the competition is being cranked up a notch.

Both players handle the poles with amazing agility. When they get within striking distance, they swing the poles at one another. It's apparent neither is trying to harm the other with direct body hits; it's more a matter of knocking the other off balance. One man manages to jump to a post behind the other. With a jab, not hard, of his pole, the other player tumbles into the mud.

The crowd cheers the victory.

Once the bout is over, Jarium slaps Peter on the back and gestures towards the pit.

Peter staggers back, "No way!"

Jarium jumps out and precariously lands on a post. He waves for Peter to join him, "Come on... you wanted to know our ways... come out and play... I'll even let you use the magic you speak of." Then he adds, "And we don't have to use poles."

To taunt him further, Jarium struts around the posts in the pit. The crowd goes crazy for their Prince.

Peter can see he's not going to get out of this, and what sobriety he has left knows the chieftains are also watching. He takes a deep breath and leaps for a post, half expecting to fall flat in the mud well before the game starts. To his surprise he actually lands on the post. After some serious swaying back and forth, he even steadies himself.

Jarium, across the pit, bows to him. Peter bows back, and everyone, including Chief Adair, claps with approval.

The game progresses with the two half-drunk players wobbling with each leap. Peter ignores Jarium's offer and plays it straight... no magic. They get close to each other a couple times but both manage to keep their footing. Finally, at one point, they cross paths a little too close. Peter topples into the mud... Jarium barely rights himself before following.

Peter lifts his head, wipes the mud from his face and laughs out loud... beaten fair and square. The crowd applauds his gamesmanship.

Prince Jarium reaches out and a woman hands him a goblet of wine. He squats down on the post closest to Peter and extends the goblet. Peter accepts the goblet and, as he struggles to his feet in the mud, he toasts the victor.

When Jarium reaches out to help Peter back up on a post he doesn't appear quite as drunk as he lets on. With a wink the Prince says, "Show'em something, Peter."

At first Peter is a bit puzzled by this, but when Jarium gestures at the post and then retreats to a separate one, he knows he's being challenged to a second bout. If he's correct, this bout is more about strategy and making impressions than a simple game.

Peter climbs up on the post and nods to Jarium. The crowd is more than happy to see another round... their cheers show it.

The two players bow to each other.

But before this match starts, the two are tossed poles. Peter almost falls off the post catching his. Jarium spins his pole above his head briefly like a helicopter blade, and then he nods with another wink to Peter.

They dance around the post, occasionally clipping poles.

Jarium advances a post closer, and, with a sly nod, he starts a swing at Peter. Peter jumps towards the swing but disappears in midair. Jarium's pole hits nothing.

A gasp comes over the whole hall.

As for Peter, he finds it hard enough to land on a post when he can see his feet... being a little drunk and invisible is a whole new level of struggle. Barely stabilizing on the post, Peter becomes visible once again.

From the look on Jarium's face, it's clear that Peter read his lead well. The crowd, still caught up by the surprise of Peter's abilities, slowly builds its applause.

Jarium nods to Peter to go one more time. It's not about the game any longer... it's a show.

Peter takes the cue and leaps for another log. Again, in midair he becomes invisible. This time the audience is ready for him and a loud cheer rises. But, this time the marriage of drink and invisibility proves too much and there's a sudden splash and mud goes flying. Slowly Peter reappears neck deep in the pit... but smiling.

Prince Jarium jumps down into the mud and helps Peter to his feet, and then holds Peter's hand high in triumph.

Most express approval, even though Chief Adair seems a more reserved about it. He has a look that says he knew what his son was up to... but is not quite sure it was the wisest choice. Powers they have never encountered give him some pause.

Jarium can see this mixed emotion in his father... it seemed like a good idea at the time.

Peter glances over at Jarium. He wonders if exposing his skills was a wise idea... only time will tell.

Chapter Eighteen

Captain Pirus and Devon stand in the empty Grand Hall of the Lord Kildemar's fortress. They both still wear the gear they wore in the field... neither is armed. Before them are the closed doors that lead into Kildemar's war room. A guard mans the doors... not one of Pirus' guards. Another two stand behind them. It feels all too much like house arrest to Pirus, though it's not formally so... to his knowledge.

Pirus and Devon glance at each other, knowing this could go either way... good or bad. Naturally, Devon has no intention of going quietly; he only hopes that if it comes to that, he can save Pirus as well.

The massive doors open with a hollow echo, ominously beckoning them.

As the two enter they find Lord Kildemar, flanked by Taligarr and Janick. His sons are now in fancier court dress rather than their field gear. They're back under the protective umbrella of the dark lord. Who knows what version of the expedition they have told their father?

Captain Pirus doesn't take the smirk on Janick's face as a good sign, but he knows from experience not to assume anything. Once inside the room he comes to attention, as the professional soldier he is. Devon is a little slacker about his stance, but has the good sense to silently leave the opening move to Kildemar.

Lord Kildemar is well aware of the value of a dramatic pause on his troop's nerves, but knows this tactic has little effect on Pirus... so he doesn't drag it out too long.

"My sons say your venture was a failure, in which I lost two of my soldiers... What do you think Captain?" asks Kildemar.

It's evident by the looks on Taligarr and Janick's faces that they were hoping for their father to come down more decisively on their side. Now they're not so sure... Janick's smirk fades.

Pirus shows no sign of fear, "We scouted one land... "

"Savages," Janick snaps.

Lord Kildemar's harsh glare at his youngest son quiets him.

The Captain continues, "As I was saying, we scouted one land and found a primitive force that, in my opinion, could be utilized in a limited manner."

Devon interjects, "Pawns."

Kildemar angrily snaps, "I was not addressing you... yet."

Devon nods quietly.

"The other land of Capulia seems to have potentially more sophisticated forces, as I'm sure your sons mentioned... the land where I lost two of your soldiers."

Pirus knows both the duty, and the value, of taking responsibility. To lay blame would defeat any trust he has built up with Kildemar... and it would be contrary to his training.

"In my opinion as a soldier, regardless of what we found in those two lands, the exploration should continue. Whether we forge alliances or just determine the strengths of our enemies, we need to know the field."

He can see Lord Kildemar understands his words... even if there have been few enemies left in Goreipor, he is a soldier.

Kildemar leans forward, "What about the third land you went to? My sons saw no more there than ancient rocks. Is that all you saw?"

Kildemar has no illusions about his sons, they do not yet think like soldiers.

Pirus can almost hear Devon's urgent, but silent whisper in the back of his mind. He knows Devon wants to downplay the Portal. He's not sure why... but he has his hunches.

"It's a dead end as far as I can tell. I thought it would make a good hub, but without water and given the unstable nature of the mountain... I see little value in it," Pirus says.

It is clear Devon is itching to speak.

"You have something to add?" Kildemar asks him.

"I think the door will work past multiple walls... I came from Earth, and that's farther away than any of these lands," says Devon, hoping Kildemar won't see anything more in it.

"And you see nothing in this Portal?" asks Kildemar, with a suspicious tone.

Devon knows he walks a fine line here. If he completely discounts the place, and it becomes needed, it will appear he has his own agenda. On the other hand, he gains nothing and perhaps loses more if someone like Racinda figures it out before him... he has to remain vital.

"At the moment, I see no importance in it, but I can't speak for the future. There are no forces there to contend with, and like the captain said... it's a bit unstable," says Devon. This is the best he can do; the next move is Kildemar's.

"I already told you, it's no more than a speck that no one has seen in ages. Why are you asking this boy?" Janick blurts out without being asked.

The dark lord turns to him and gruffly says, "I've already heard your account... including your account of how the two men were lost. If I wish to ask you more, I will."

"But...," Janick starts to say.

Rage comes over Kildemar's face as he pivots and backhands his son. "That's the second time you've challenged my words... don't let there be a third!"

Janick staggers back from the blow. His hand, white-knuckled, grasps at his sword's handle... but he cowers at Kildemar's glare.

Taligarr is quick to step between the father he knows would not hesitate to even strike down one of his own, and his brother. The anger in Kildemar's eyes eases slightly and his muscles relax, shy of striking again.

"Leave me, all but the Captain... we have strategies to discuss," Kildemar finally announces.

"And my voice?" interjects Devon. He's not sure this is wise, but he doesn't want his council to be simply dismissed.

Kildemar, without even looking at Devon, "If I have questions of you, I will ask them at another time. Your powers were of use on the mission, and, though my sons urge me to take your head, I see value in you. You would best be advised to keep your peace, and your head, for now."

Louder, he announces once more, "All but Pirus... out!"

At times Shan feels like she's trying to wrangle an elementary school; the recruits she has are more about playing than learning. Despite her every effort to explain the idea of defending against violence, the idea of violence itself doesn't sink in enough for them to take the training seriously. She can't exactly kill one as an example, though it's crossed her mind more than once.

She can hardly fault them... When Peter tried to explain it to her long ago it was like hearing a foreign language. There is something about violence that has to be experienced to fully grasp, at least to grasp enough to be willing to do what is needed to counter it. Outside of Yadar, no one here has ever seen a person been hit, and Yadar was on the receiving end.

As little regard for Devon as she has, she knows he'd put a few in grave danger to get the idea across to the others. She's grateful not to be that desperate yet. This still leaves her with the dilemma of how she's going to train them.

As Shan comes around an outcropping she sees Yadar charge against another boy, Doget, who is charging just as fast at him. The two are carrying flickering shields Shan had taught them to make. Like charging bulls, they hit in the center. Both bounce back onto their rumps, and break up laughing. The surrounding kids whoop and howl.

Shan curses Peter under her breath... what was he doing telling her she could teach kids. She knows part of the problem is that she would rather be out on the adventure of discovering new lands... not babysitting!

Tucking in her head, Shan turns and walks away.

A couple of minutes later sudden screams burst from back in the ravine... not sounds of playing, but of fright. Shan spins and runs back to where the kids are training. Reaching the top of the bluff, she's stunned to see a leather-clad Goreiporian soldier charging her wards.

The soldier swings a lance that loudly impacts Yadar's invisible shield, sending the boy hard to the ground. Instead of finishing him, the warrior swings on Doget... with the same results. He continues charging down the ravine as kids run in sheer terror.

Figuring out where he came from is the least of Shan's concerns right now... saving kids is her first concern. Shan takes a stance atop the bluff. She knows how to send an energy globe, but her accuracy worries her... she has had little time to practice her aim.

With both kids and warrior mixed in the fray, the only way Shan can get a clean shot is to spread everyone out. She levels her lance and fires a globe slightly ahead of the melee. It explodes far enough away not to harm the kids, but close enough to make them scatter.

It works... she now has a clean shot at the soldier. Just as she's about to take it, he throws his lance away and frantically waves his arms over his head... hardly what she would expect from a Goreiporian soldier. Shan, unsure of what is happening, lowers the tip of her lance for a moment.

As he continues to wave his hands wildly, the illusion of a Goreiporian soldier morphs into Master Carringer.

Shan collapses on her backside and shakes her head in puzzlement. At first she's grateful she didn't fire, but this is quickly replaced by anger. She wishes that she had placed the globe close enough to scare him... as much as he scared her.

By the time Carringer makes it up to the bluff, Shan has settled down to just wanting to slap him... master or not. As she starts to open her mouth, he simply gestures at the kids below. Even though Carringer has tipped his hand, many of the kids are silent, still overcome with looks of shock.

For kids who have never encountered physical aggression, apparently Master Carringer's ruse has served its purpose... and, with a Devon-style solution, none needed to be hurt. The question still remains... will it result in her young recruits taking training seriously?

"Am I forgiven?" says Carringer with a smile. "I assumed from the other night you needed some outside motivation."

Shan is still a bit upset, "But why didn't you tell me?"

"Thought it might take some of the edge off the impact," Carringer explains.

"What it almost took off... was your head! I almost did that," she blurts out.

Carringer just now notices Shan's hands are shaking. Realizing the folly of his actions, he takes her by the shoulders, "Shan, I'm so sorry."

She lets out a breath, "No. You're an idiot... Sir."

He takes this to mean he's off the hook. Now all he has to do is come up with a few more tricks to help Shan train this motley crew... and tell her about them in advance.

Chapter Nineteen

An arrow rockets towards Ramie; at the last moment it freezes in midair and drops to the ground. Another comes flying in and Ramie reacts a little more slowly. The arrow freezes a bit closer to him this time.

Ramie waves his hands in the air, calling for a cease-fire.

Rupert, Witch Racinda's non-magically-skilled assistant, looks over at her, but she nods for him to fire again. He unleashes another arrow.

Panicked, Ramie does manage to stop it, but it's clear that he's on the verge of seeking cover in the gorge where this is playing out.

Witch Racinda shakes her head and tells Rupert, "Enough." With a stern glare, she waves at Ramie, "Come here, boy."

Grumbling under his breath, Ramie takes his sweet time coming to her. He has never liked lessons of any kind, but ones that send sharp arrows at his head are a new low on his list.

When he reaches Racinda, Ramie is about to say something, but she puts her finger to her lips, "Before you complain about being out here again, I can teach you spells that serve our masters at the fortress... but teaching you self-defense skills has to take place in private."

"I thought you said I was safe," he complains.

"Under my wing, you are, for now... Your young friend, Devon, is putting things into play that may change all that. I'm not sure, but I sense change is in the wind. Do you want to be able to defend yourself... or not?"

She says this with hopes that Ramie will get more behind the training, but also with the resolve that she's going to train him, whether he likes it or not. Ramie truly hasn't registered the significance of being one of only three people in Goreipor who has sorcery skills.

Ramie looks up and sheepishly nods his agreement. She seems pleased, but when he glances over at Rupert, he can sense a deep-seated resentment... maybe because he's replaced Rupert in her thoughts.

Peter's eyes can see the impression of light, punctuated by dashes of shadows through their closed lids. His stomach bounces up and down, and reverberates through every inch of his body. His nose smells clean fur and his ears echo with the sounds of the countryside, which would normally be pleasant. All of this is disorienting. He knows if he were to open his eyes it would make sense... he also knows that if he were to opens his eyes, the enormous hangover he has will slam down like a sledgehammer.

A coarse voice says, "Why prolong it, boy? It's time to wake... come face the day."

Peter recognizes it as Jarium's voice, in his other body... the friend that got him so drunk the night before. Jarium's words are not enough to entice Peter into opening his eyes and facing the inevitable. Then, he catches a drifting whiff of perfume... just enough motivation to finally brave the sunlight.

He opens his eyes.

Big mistake. What he sees is the ground bouncing up and down at him and back and forth. Peter finally realizes he's draped over the back of the tiger Jarium, like goods on a pack animal. He twists his head far enough to see Princess Topolina riding behind him, no doubt to stop him from falling off. She gives him a warm look.

Trying not to speak too loudly, Peter says, "Stop, please."

Jarium's booming laugh is not appreciated, but the end of his bouncy gait is. Peter does his best to scoot off Jarium's back and land on his feet. The drop is too far and his legs are too wobbly... he lands on his rump.

Jarium laughs again. Peter hears Topolina slap the tiger's back and chide, "Jar... be kind."

Peter grumbles, "Listen to your wife."

After a half hour breather from their trip, Peter has managed to adjust to the sunlight. The echoes in his head soften somewhat.

"Seems like a sorcerer who can do feats like becoming invisible could overcome a little hangover," Jarium jokes.

"I don't think I've ever drunk that much before... and, for your information, it's not a *little* hangover," responds Peter. "Trust me, if there's a spell for hangovers, I'll find it."

Peter glances around, "Where are we?" They clearly aren't in the village and the terrain isn't any he has yet passed through in his short stay in Acculas. This landscape is more mountainous.

Still a tiger, Jarium replies, "On our way to the eastern border of my land. We're off on that adventure you wanted."

Topolina has gone off to scout, in her bird self, while Peter tries to get his bearings. Upon her return, she swoops down and flares her wings. Just as she touches ground, Topolina transforms back to a woman.

Not trying to be too obvious, Peter gestures to Topolina as she lands. "Is your wife seeing us off?" He's hoping that is the case; being teamed up with Jarium wasn't in his plans, but seems necessary... adding yet another is pushing it.

His gesture was not as hidden as he hoped. Topolina walks up to the two of them, "My dear husband doesn't wish to tell you he has little choice in the matter. He's not about to go off on an adventure of a lifetime and leave me sitting around watching the home fire."

A slight, low guttural growl escapes Jarium.

"Was that a growl I heard, Jar?" scolds Topolina.

"No, dear, just a moan of acceptance." He follows this with a little laugh... a hint, perhaps, that this is not the first argument with her that he's lost.

Peter laughs, even though it doesn't sit well with his hangover. He says, "I know the feeling... I have a girlfriend back in Spirin."

Topolina, sounding quite serious, "There are things you two can't do, that I can."

Looking away, Jarium grumbles, "Like winning an argument."

Ignoring this Topolina adds, "You two men need the balance I provide... and you need someone watching your back."

Peter feels like he's hearing an echo of Shan, and, in truth, he wishes she were by his side on this trip. He wanted to keep her safe. He knew she had necessary duties to carry out in Spirin but, nonetheless, he misses her. New friends are one thing, but tried and true ones are hard to do without. Not knowing how long he's going to be gone also weighs heavily on him.

Topolina, as if she can read his thoughts, offers, "A sister cannot replace a girlfriend, but trust I'll have your back as well, young Peter."

Her seeming to read his mind reminds Peter of Shan as well.

Changing the subject, Jarium shakes his mane and says to Peter, "We should get going if you're up to it now."

"You know, I could get us to the wall much quicker... that is, if you go back to your human self." Peter is obviously referring to being able to magically transport them.

Jarium pauses for a second and says, "Who knows what we'll encounter in those other lands... maybe it's best we take the time to get to know each other a little more. Slower, I think is better. And, if we are to be gone long, I want to take in my land a bit more."

Peter can't argue with any of these points.

Devon and Captain Pirus have been summoned to Lord Kildemar's war room. As with any other summons by Kildemar, they never know what to expect.

As they walk through the hollow hallway, Devon asks, "You think Kildemar will send the same group out again?"

"If he sends anyone... I have no idea." Then he adds, "May I remind you, within the fortress it would be wise to say '*Lord Kildemar*'... these halls have ears."

Pirus probably knows more than he lets on but he has learned, as a soldier, to play his opinions close. When it's needed he will speculate, but the meeting is just down the hall and what is to happen will reveal itself soon enough.

Devon senses this and regrets he asked in the first place.

The massive double doors to the war room open; Captain Pirus and Devon enter to find Lord Kildemar, Witch Racinda and the lord's two sons already present.

Neither Taligarr nor Janick are smiling, which Devon immediately takes as a good sign. Of course he doesn't say a thing about it, but sometimes words are unnecessary... Janick glares at him as if he's throwing knives.

Lord Kildemar hasn't looked up yet. He keeps staring at the outline of lands on the war table's map.

After a long minute of silence in the room, Taligarr quietly says to his father, "All are here, father."

Kildemar's teeth can almost be heard grinding, but he has more leniency with his eldest son, "Someday you need to learn the value of a dramatic pause."

He finally looks up at the others and steps away from the table, "Captain, good to see again. My sons see no advantage in this excursion into the other lands. They think we should conquer one land at a time since we have control of the pendant."

He walks back to the table and glances down at the map once again. "They have a valid point but, as usual, limited vision." He pauses to see if his sons are stupid enough to object, and is glad to hear nothing.

"Lieutenant Devon here suggests that his brother is exploring the other lands with another pendant. If this is true the can of worms has been opened."

Janick injects, "We didn't see any sign that anyone else is out there."

Taligarr shakes his head at his brother's unwise words, suspecting their father will react badly.

Kildemar takes a deep breath and lets it slide, for now. He continues, "It doesn't matter if it's true or not. I believe there are other pendants out there and, once change begins, they will have a nasty habit of surfacing. That is enough reason to move first, and, as the Captain well knows, not knowing the strength of all your enemies is a fatal flaw."

Devon, trying to read what's being said, does his best not to appear smug... that could also be a fatal flaw.

Lord Kildemar is actually explaining more of his thinking than he usually does... he catches himself.

"The exploration of the other lands will resume."

Taligarr chances a suggestion, assuming that as long as it doesn't challenge his father's decisions he's on relatively safe ground. "Father, what of establishing outposts as we go?"

Kildemar truly wants his sons to grow... as long as they remember their place. He knows both his sons have lobbied for outposts, perhaps for their own sense of safety. He has made a decision on the matter long before this meeting but it has a better impact to appear as if he's thinking about Taligarr's suggestion.

After a couple moments, "It would be good to have a line of communication but I want no outposts. Outposts are fractions of my forces that, if overcome, will give my enemies a sense of power."

"But... " Janick starts to say.

Kildemar slams his steel hand on the table; it echoes throughout the room. "There will be no outposts!"

After he's sure Janick will say no more, he adds, "But we will set up a line of communication."

All, including Captain Pirus, are curious how he wants to set such a thing up. Pirus knows Kildemar clearly would not jeopardize his remaining pendant by giving it to his troops, even one of his trusted generals. He doesn't even trust his sons to have both pendants... the pendants are too powerful a key to not hold one himself.

Lord Kildemar can see his Captain's gears turning. "Captain, my witch will solve the problem that you're vexing over. She will find me a way to send and receive messages without risking my key."

Neither Taligarr nor Janick can hide their disappointment. Each has thought they might be chosen to set up a forward base. This would be an ideal assignment, to be a player without boots on the ground... and, to control the extra key.

Witch Racinda is not surprised by the declaration... it's a move that his father would have made. What concerns her is that his father would have given her leeway to find a solution; she has no such illusion about Kildemar. All that taken into account, the one thing she's sure of is that it would be a waste of time to protest.

Witch Racinda simply nods to Kildemar... truly with no idea if she can do it or not.

"And for the expedition, my liege?" Pirus says.

Kildemar stares a second at each of his sons, then, "Both my sons still need more field experience; they will go with you as before... with one difference... you will command. Perhaps you will not lose men quite so quickly."

Captain Pirus is a savvy soldier who would not have accused the ruler's sons, so it's clear Kildemar read between the lines of Pirus' earlier mission report.

Kildemar continues, "You will replace your men... of your choosing, of course. Lieutenants Devon's skills come into play so he will be under your command as well."

Devon nods; it's playing out better than he expected.

Taligarr and Janick are not happy about any of this, but simply nod to their father's command.

"It is settled. Now, leave me to talk with my witch," Kildemar declares. There is no more to be said.

Before leaving, Devon quietly passes by and asks Witch Racinda, "How's my little friend Ramie doing?"

Coldly she answers, "Do you really care?"

Devon figures he will not get a straight answer from her and drops the issue. He also figures he will eventually have to come to terms with this Witch... he's not about to let her stand in the way of his plans.

All have left the war room except Lord Kildemar and Witch Racinda. Kildemar stares at Racinda for the longest time.

She finally says, "Your dramatic pauses have little effect on me, my lord."

Sometimes Racinda's brazenness infuriates Kildemar, at other times it amuses him... this time it is the latter. "Poking at me will not relieve you of the task you're charged with."

"You know that for me to create what you ask I will need your pendant?" she responds.

"You will have it by day... along with my guards. I wouldn't want you to think of using it to leave us," he slyly tells her.

Racinda notes with sadness, "To go where? I've done too many things for you and your father for me to ever belong any-where else."

He stares at her, "Perhaps." After another second he adds, "That boy, Ramie, I think, that you've taken a liking to... if you fail me or even consider misusing my pendant I will slit his throat... and no *defensive* training you do with the boy out of my sight will save him."

Racinda is well aware this is not an idle threat.

Chapter Twenty

Peter lifts his head up to see Peter.

He glances around and sees neither Jarium nor Topolina. For just a fraction of a second, before he's completely awake, he wonders if they exist... or were the past days just a dream. Fleeting moments like this make him question if the past two years have been a dream... then he wakes.

Shaking the sleep out of his eyes, he remembers that they camped by the mirrored wall between Acculas and Capulia... one last night in a land he knows to be peaceful. Now he, Prince Jarium and Princess Topolina are set to jump to the next unknown land.

There's a distant growl on the hillside behind him and instead of turning around Peter looks at the reflection in the mirrored wall. The saber toothed tiger he knows as Jarium comes over the ridge, galloping at full speed. Swooping beside him is the beautiful Topolina. The way they move appears like two very different animals playing. The tiger veers off to the south and she banks with him. Then they veer back towards Peter in unison.

As they get closer he can hear the two laughing. Even closer, they both transform into their human selves... still roaring with laughter.

Peter grins and says, "Thought maybe you two wised up and had second thoughts."

"Not likely, young Peter. You've come from a world in the stars and seen other lands. We've been locked behind these walls all our lives, and, as for me, I'm been aching to see beyond them forever," Jarium says with enthusiasm.

Topolina's smile says she's of the same mind.

Peter is glad to see the two of them on two legs. He hopes this is the way they plan to go through the door since a saber-tooth tiger may not have the best initial handshake.

He ventures to say, "Nice to see you back with us... I mean that you're not going through as... you know."

To Jarium and Topolina being animal or human makes little difference; in their world everyone is a bit of both. For outside his land, Jarium sees the logic a bit differently: "You were able to bring your magic through the first wall... who knows what we'll be able to do beyond this one. I figured I'd have more flexibility in this form... and, OK, I do look a bit friendlier."

With a slight snicker, Topolina adds, "I don't mind remaining a bird." She gestures at Jarium, "But who wants a hairy beast around... especially when he gets wet."

"OK, you got me... I hope you don't take it wrong, but I do think we're better going through as humans," Peter admits.

"Of course you would," says Jarium, a touch irately.

Topolina playfully slaps him on the shoulder, "Give the boy a break; our ways are probably as strange to him as his disappearing is to us. We can argue animal prejudices at some other time."

Jarium knows his wife is right, but he mutters, "It's not as if I were a hyena."

Her stern look tells him to hush up.

Peter turns the corner in his thinking... he's now glad she's along for the ride. She brings balance to the team.

"As someone I hope you meet someday would say... if we're gonna go, I guess we better get going," Peter says as he backs away from the wall and takes his pendant in hand.

Both Topolina and Jarium step up beside him. As tough as they are, they can't help but look a little nervous. They've spent their entire life in one world, and now are about to go where no one they know has ever gone before.

Sensing this, Peter says, "Don't worry, I do this all the time."

Enough talk... Peter dials in the symbols and, as many times before, swoosh, the swirling pool of light forms in front of them. He has done it so many times by now that it doesn't even make him flinch, but his companions back away a few steps from this strange light.

Jarium and Topolina glance at each other and back at the swirling pool with some hesitation. Peter starts to move to the door, figuring that will get things going. Before he does, Topolina gives Jarium a quick kiss and then dives into the light. Jarium shrugs to Peter and follows her.

One glance back at the land he's just discovered, wondering if the next will be as friendly, and Peter jumps through.

Peter falls out of the light and splashes down into water.

Unlike Devon's crew, they land in rolling surf. A dozen yards away is the pink sandy beach of an island that Jarium and Topolina are already making for.

Peter stands up, waist deep in the water, and slowly turns around surveying yet another strange new land.

Devon stares out at the black rocky landscape of Goreipor from its fortress' battlement. He's more than anxious to get back on his quest to discover the new lands... and control them. His fist constantly taps on the rock wall as though he's listening to the beat of music in his head... probably more like the rhythm of his ambition.

From behind him, Captain Pirus casually says, "Your impatience is showing."

Spinning around, Devon says, "You have Kildemar's ear... what is holding us up?"

"Do I need to remind you again, it's 'Lord' Kildemar within the fortress? Only a fool has his plans disrupted over such a casual mistake; don't let your ego be his weapon."

Getting back to Devon's question, "He will not release us till his witch finishes devising a way to send messages without jeopardizing either pendant. While she works with one, he won't release the other."

Not much for the false etiquette of the court, Devon thinks what he calls Kildemar is of little importance. Perhaps too little, because Pirus is right... arrogance should not handicap his game. But Pirus is more concerned about a name than about deceit... he makes details vague as well. Maybe that is because the Captain is still keeping his options open... Devon would, in his place.

There's the creak from a turret door fifty feet away from where the two talk. They go silent, waiting to see who emerges.

It's Ramie wandering around against Racinda's advice, as he often does. From the look on his face, he's surprised to have come on Devon. At first Ramie energetically starts towards Devon, but slows as Pirus comes more into view.

Pirus lets out a little chuckle, "I think I frighten your little friend."

"Many things do. But, he may be useful in the future, so it would be good to ease that fear," responds Devon.

Pirus turns to head away, "I'll leave the hand-holding to you... I have other things to attend to." With this, he's off.

Once Pirus retreats, Ramie picks up the pace.

As he approaches, Devon says, "You even look like you're happy to see me."

Ramie hates the fact that he can't hide his inability to hold a grudge, after all it's Devon who landed him here. Putting on his sternest face, which isn't very convincing, he responds, "Not really... but I *only* know three people here, a witch, her assistant who doesn't like me... and you."

"We'll have to do something about that," Devon says.

"Why?" asks Ramie.

Now Devon puts on his best sincere façade: "Because someday you're going to be very important here... you just don't know it yet."

He knows what buttons to push in Ramie, and, as expected, he sees a leak of a smile from the boy.

Ramie catches this and wipes it off his face. "I don't trust you."

"That's good kid, keep it up, it will keep you safe. But, it's not me you shouldn't trust," he says. "For now, that's OK, but here's what I need you to do, even if you don't trust me."

Once again, he's sparked Ramie's interest, as he can tell by the boy's slight lean forward. He thinks how easy it is to read him. Devon gives it a second before continuing, "You need to learn as much as you can from the witch."

The last thing Ramie wanted to hear... study!

"The key to playing a game is to know your opponent," Devon confides, with confidence that he knows how Ramie thinks.

Ramie, trying to sound like a player, says, "I think I'd be of more use if you took me on these trips I hear you've been taking."

"Sorry kid, they wouldn't allow both of us to be gone at the same time," he says as if they are equally important.

Ramie snaps, "So, I'm a hostage?"

Sounding like he's sharing a secret, Devon leans in, "We're letting them think so... it's all part of my plan. Believe me, you're safer here anyway." This is probably the only true thing Devon's said so far.

"Now, I need you to get back to your quarters, we don't want them to see us together too much."

"But... " Ramie starts to say.

Devon glances all around, as if there's intrigue afoot. "But nothing... get going before we're seen."

Ramie, not knowing how to counter, quickly walks away, glancing everywhere as he goes. He's pretty sure he's being played... but it's better than being ignored.

Once Ramie is gone, Devon chuckles to himself.

Topolina comes out of the island foliage carrying fruit in her arms, announcing, "No people, but there's good food."

With a nod up at Topolina, Jarium says, "That's my wife, she has her common sense priorities."

"More useful than you two sitting on a beach, staring out at the water," she counters.

Peter gets up, "She's got a point. I can generate a spy globe so we can get an idea of where we are."

Just as he's about to conjure up his spy globe, Jarium tugs on Peter's pant leg and points off into the distance. The mast of a ship flying deep red sails is coming around the point.

Jarium jumps up and takes Peter's arm, "Till we know what we're dealing with, I'd suggest we retreat into the jungle." Peter seems to resist at first, so he adds, "I'm the hunter among us... it's better we see who, how many and what their weapons are before we decide how to approach them... I suspect not all are as kind as my people."

Peter bows to more experience, even though he knows he may have better defenses than Jarium is aware. Whatever they do, it is better that their first encounter not be an adversarial one. It is better to know who and how to approach, but eventually someone will have to stick out their hand.

He joins Jarium and Topolina as they slip into the foliage.

From what the three can see, the sailors on the ship have not caught sight of them leaving the beach. As the ship sails closer into the cove, sails start lowering.

It's a fair-sized ship and, to the best of his ability, Peter can make out about two dozen men in the crew... he has no idea how many might be below deck. Though Peter is far from being an expert on ships, he does make out what appears to be large weapons on the ship's deck.

He points at the ship and whispers, "They're armed. I think those are catapults on the deck." In truth, Peter's not actually sure since he has only seen catapults in movies... and he thinks he remembers seeing one in a comic book once.

Since they don't have mechanized-based weapons in Acculas, the word *catapults* doesn't register with Jarium... but he well understands *armed*. For that matter, they don't have sailing ships in Acculas... but Jarium is a quick study.

He looks at the catapults and responds, "I take it you mean large weapons, and by the looks of them they must throw stones. My guess is that ship travels by wind, and since they're lowering their cloth, they're stopping."

Now well into the cove and all the sheets down, the ship drops an anchor from its bow, the chain rattling as it feeds out.

Peter says, "From those catapults, I'd have to say you were right about choosing our time to approach them. We haven't seen any sign of life on the island so my guess is they're coming ashore for supplies."

Jarium and Topolina have both pulled their bows from the packs they brought along and are stringing them. Jarium nods to Topolina, then tells Peter, "We'll slip back into the forest till we find a better moment to reveal ourselves. Killing anyone is not a great welcoming card."

Peter's guess is played out as they see longboats being lowered over the side. Quietly, the three withdraw into the denseness of the jungle.

Chapter Twenty-One

A regiment of Goreiporian soldiers on horseback stands in the fortress' courtyard. Captain Pirus, Devon and the lord's two sons are amongthem. Six of the soldiers are Pirus' guards and the rest are escorts who will return with the horses after Pirus' team jumps the wall.

Devon has already said the pendant would work from farther distances. Lord Kildemar, assuming the pendant's jump back would return to its origin, prefers not having his fortress being a landing zone. He's ordered all jumps be made from near the wall; in this way anyone who arrives would be exposed for at least a half day.

Lord Kildemar stands on the battlement peering at his forces. He loves his delay periods so he lets the horses restlessly tap the ground with their hooves. Pirus is used to this tactic so he calmly waits for Kildemar's signal.

Having received his due, Lord Kildemar yells down, "Find me mercenaries worthy of my employ."

Captain Pirus nods to Kildemar's command and he moves the column out to the beat of the fortress drummers. Pirus is happy to get away from all this ritual, and to the task at hand. The field has always been more home to him than the trappings of the court.

Well within the tree line, Peter and his friends catch glimpses of the ship's sailors on the beach. A dozen men have come ashore. A few are armed with longbows, but most of the men are armed with swords or knives since they are only on the island to forage for supplies. All appear to be a cross between pirates and Vikings.

Topolina quietly says, "I should approach them."

Jarium clearly doesn't care for this idea, but he knows from experience not to dismiss her ideas offhandedly.

"OK... why should you approach them?"

She gives him a *duh* grin, "Because... they're men."

Peter looks at the two of them and shrugs, "Actually, it's not a bad idea. All we have to do is get their attention long enough so they don't shoot first."

Raising his voice a little louder than he should, Jarium exclaims, "It's a horrible idea."

Topolina admonishes, "It's a horrible idea? Because it's horrible idea or because I'm your wife?"

Jarium hates arguments that he already thinks he's going to lose, and he's not about to give up on this one quite yet. He snaps, "Both... We have no idea what kind of men these are."

Peter offers, "What if I can protect her?"

"And how are you going to do that?" counters Jarium.

"I have a few magic tricks up my sleeve."

Peter knows he can protect all three of them, but if they all go it might be seen as a show of force. He's also pretty sure he has enough sorcery in his back pocket to overcome the twelve sailors... and again that would send the wrong message.

What does concern Peter is what kind of men are these inhabitants of Capulia? All he knows thus far is that they are seafarers who are heavily armed... perhaps they're no better than those of the land of Goreipor.

Jarium is resigned to losing the argument, so he says, "We'll all three go together."

Before Peter has a chance to object, Topolina definitively asserts, "No... We won't. If they don't play nice, Peter and I may need you to come and rescue us... maybe even the other you."

He's lost the argument... and just shrugs acceptance.

Peter leans into him and whispers, "I know the feeling."

A few of the sailors have remained on the beach near the tree line while the others are out foraging for water and fruit in different directions.

Yarlick is an elderly master mate who seems to be a jovial-looking character. He sits in the sand, leaning up against the bow of the beached longboat, relishing the sun.

Two of his men are having a friendly game of *battle-ax*. Standing by palm trees that are about twenty feet apart, they take turns hurling massive battle-axes at the opponent's tree.

Yarlick lets out a booming laugh and yells out, "You two play like old men... in my day we held palm leaves in my teeth."

One of the sailors dismisses the old man with a wave of his hand... just before an ax flies past... close enough for him to feel the displaced air. The ax solidly embeds into the palm next to him with a force that would split a man.

Yarlick suddenly perks up as a beautiful dark-skinned maiden emerges from the jungle about fifty yards down the beach. He only grabs his bow after he sees Peter following her out.

He yells at the other two sailors, "You two stop playing and stand to."

Rising to his feet, he bows an arrow, but doesn't take aim. The other two, seeing what Yarlick is looking at, rush to the longboat and grab their bows.

Topolina and Peter advance cautiously, knowing Jarium is watching hidden in the jungle.

The sailors, now all armed, move towards Peter and Topolina. With all their bows trained, Yarlick tells his men, "Unless they do anything, take it easy... it would be a shame to hurt such a fine lass." Then he focuses on the strangers, "Where, pray tell, did you two youngsters come from?"

Once again Peter is a bit irritated by people referring to him as a youngster... but that's a battle for another time. He yells back, "We mean you no harm."

As too often happens when men have readied weapons, the slightest misunderstood twitch can cause irreversible actions. As Peter raises a hand, the youngest sailor inadvertently lets fly an arrow. It ricochets off the invisible protective shield Peter has already created around himself and Topolina. Even though the arrow causes no harm, Topolina still jerks back. The young sailor is also a bit shocked, not knowing how his arrow didn't hit its mark.

His shock ends abruptly when Yarlick slaps his head and yells, "I told you not to fire!" He looks back at Topolina, "You have any weapons?"

Peter is relieved that the little-understood universal translator works here as it has so far elsewhere on the Sphere.

He steps ahead of Topolina and without any sudden movement calmly says, "We're not here to hurt anyone, we just want to talk."

He figures saying *take me to your leader* would sound too corny even though they wouldn't get the reference.

Yarlick, who is only holding his bow at the half ready, now lowers it and nods for Peter and Topolina to advance. As the two get closer, Yarlick addresses Topolina, "Marooned... are you, lass?"

She gives him a warm smile, "You might say so... We have another still in the trees, may he come out?"

"As pretty as you?" Yarlick says with a gleam in his eye.

"Hardly," responds Topolina. She lets out a whistle.

A couple of seconds later Jarium emerges from the brush. He joins the others. Even as a human, Jarium is far more formidable in stature than Peter and probably would have caused more uneasiness if he had come out earlier. Wisely, Jarium has broken down their bows and now only carries their packs.

Yarlick, to Topolina, "He's a big one... good he waited."

By this time the commotion has brought the foraging sailors back to the beach. Yarlick is quick to wave at them to stand down.

He smiles at Topolina, "I guess you just got rescued... and, we'll take the other two for ballast."

When the team from Kildemar's fortress reaches the western wall, they find a small encampment already set up. Captain Pirus immediately sees Witch Racinda. He suspects she's there with the new communication system she has come up with. Kildemar has said nothing about it, but Pirus knows the mission wouldn't have been given the go without it.

Racinda and Pirus haven't dealt directly very much, but of course they know each other. Pirus dismounts and walks to her. "You have something for me?" he asks.

Before she answers, she sees Taligarr and Janick rushing over.

"Sorry, Captain, Lord Kildemar instructed me to give it directly to his eldest son... in private.' She shrugs, "Don't shoot the messenger... we're both under his thumb."

"Captain, I have private business with my father's witch," Taligarr says as soon as he reaches them. He has an air of arrogance since he's being favored over the captain.

With a nod, Captain Pirus turns to leave. He glances at both of them and says, "Finish your business quickly, we have a trip to make." Then he walks away.

Pirus understands Kildemar's style of dividing up powers so no one feels like they have that much... he doesn't like this game. He has clearly been given command of the expedition, and yet the communication set up is given to Taligarr. He sees little logic in this, but it would do no good to protest... and he's not about to give Taligarr the satisfaction.

Glancing around to see no one is near except Janick, Taligarr turns to Racinda, "OK, what do you have for me?"

Witch Racinda, not playing at being so covert, simply holds up a tiny silver globe, about the size of a large marble. She twists it and the ball divides in half. A small piece of parchment is inside.

"It's not complicated... write your message on the slip, put it in the sphere and toss the sphere up in the air... it will find its way to your father."

"How do I get a message back?" Taligarr whispers.

A smirk comes on Racinda's face, and without bothering to whisper, she says, "If your father chooses to answer you, the sphere will return to its sender. I'm not going to waste my time explaining how it works... it's far beyond you."

There's no love lost between Kildemar's kids and Racinda. Taligarr knows any disdain he shows will be ignored, so he doesn't bother.

Janick asks, "What if my brother is dead?"

This gets a harsh look from Taligarr.

"Like I said, the sphere returns to its sender." She glances at Taligarr, "So don't die."

With this, she takes a half dozen little spheres from a bag, drops them in a little leather pouch and tosses the pouch to Taligarr.

Devon comes up to Pirus, "What are those two up to?"

"Playing spy," he responds. He turns to Kildemar's sons in the distance and yells, "Anytime the royal sons are finished playing, we have a mission to get to."

If looks could kill, the glares Taligarr and Janick throw toward Pirus would do so.

Witch Racinda tosses caution to the wind and laughs.

Chapter Twenty-Two

S han has another get together with her resistance forces, using the term loosely. She has to admit Carringer's stunt has partially aroused the kids' attention, but so far she has limited tools with which to teach them. They've learned to make protective shields and to generate spy globes. Both are useful, but purely defensive.

She's been hesitant to teach them the few offensive weapons that she knows, like firing energy globes... they're still kids, and still playing too much to use lethal tools. She tells herself it's for their safety, but she really knows that the next step will rob them of their innocence... the dilemma Shan inevitably will have to come to terms with.

Right now they practice with their protective shields and using sticks as swords. They have no idea what it's like to draw blood or even see it drawn, but they try to take the training seriously.

As Shan watches the kids practice from her bluff perch, Master Carringer materializes next to her, giving her a start.

"Wish you wouldn't do that," she snaps, adding, "I thought you were the hoverboard type anyway."

"Not when I'm supposed to be doing this in secret... and, it's too far," he responds.

Shan nods, thinking now that it was a stupid question.

"There are no stupid questions, child. You have a lot on your mind," Carringer says as if reading hers. Before Shan can obsess on if he is, he jumps to the point, "I dug up a few of the spells from the Graveyard... well, I didn't actually dig them up because you know they aren't... ah... "

Shan is used to Carringer occasionally being a bit scattered so she cuts him off, "I understand. You think they might be usable?"

Sounding a little offended, Carringer says defensively, "Of course they're usable... I invented them... at least most of them... But I'm just not sure what they can be used for."

Realizing she should be grateful for any help she can get, Shan smiles and says, "I guess we can try them out, and then figure out how they can be used."

Captain Pirus is the last to tumble out of the door into the land of Acculas. They have landed on a ridge deep in the mountains... a far sight from the rolling plains where Peter emerged. Upon rising he sees Devon is off on a ridge already scrutinizing the distant land. He has chosen to save revisiting Capulia, the land of water, for another trip.

Pirus, being a military man, is concerned first with his team, "Everyone make it through OK?"

Beyond a few scraps and scratches from landing on a mountainside, all seem to be in fair shape, except Janick.

Janick rubs a scrape that bleeds through his pants and when he tries to stand falls to the ground. Among hardened soldiers he doesn't want to complain, but for the wrong reason... not from the strength of a soldier who knows his condition must be accurately assessed, but out of vanity.

Captain Pirus comes up to him and says, "Have the corporal take a look at that before it gets infected."

"It's fine," protests Janick.

Pirus snaps, "I didn't ask you... do it."

Pirus doesn't care much for him, but he knows what's best for a mission... allowing an injury to fester slows everyone down. Turning to Corporal Opper, who's not far away, he says, "See to him." Then he moves on to check on the rest.

After a double check, Pirus goes up to the ridge where Devon stands. "What do you see out there?"

"Just a whole lot of land, but I'm sure there are people somewhere," responds Devon, not taking his eyes off the horizon. Then, even though he doesn't truly care, Devon looks over and asks, "Everyone OK?"

Pirus glances down at the corporal who is looking after Janick, "We might have a minor hiccup."

A couple of minutes later Corporal Opper finishes up with Janick and heads to Pirus. "The leg's not broken, but he has a bad sprain. Combined with the gash, if he moves on it, we might be looking at an infection."

Having been on a number of campaigns with Opper, Pirus trusts his assessment. He asks, "So what do you need?"

"A day. I can treat the cut so there's less chance of infection, and the sprain will be much better. A day now, or a number of days later... your call, Captain," says Opper.

"You have your day," answers Pirus.

Taligarr shows up. "What's going on with my brother?"

"He has a minor sprain... we're standing down for a day," Pirus answers.

Taligarr says, "Why not just send him back? My father was very clear about our mission. Go in heavy and get whomever we find to submit. With the Earther's magic, this should be easy."

Even though Pirus has been put in charge of the campaign, he's very aware he walks a fine line with Kildemar's sons along. Kildemar's style, and instructions are much as Taligarr says...

How heavy-handed and bloody they will be is the question. He also knows Taligarr has a means of communicating with Goreipor.

Devon has been listening to this and sees an opportunity to serve his own purposes. He tells Pirus, "I can use the day to do some scouting."

Taligarr insists, "No. As I said, send my brother home so we can move on."

The down day is something that serves Devon so he's not about to lose it that easily. He says, "He got the sprain tumbling out of the door... you really want to throw him through the door again?"

Without waiting for Taligarr's reaction, Pirus yells out to his sergeant, "Sergeant, set camp for the night." He turns to Devon, "We stay together... including you."

"Sorry, Captain, I need a little breathing room." With this Devon disappears into a wisp of smoke and streaks away.

Taligarr is livid, "Where did he go?"

Captain Pirus knows there's no use getting upset about something he can't control. He takes a deep breath and shrugs, "Scouting... I think. If you can pull off some magic, you're welcome to go after him." He walks away before Taligarr can say more.

Devon is only visible as a purple stream of smoke weaving its way through the skies over the land of Acculas. He flies over orchards of giant trees that pepper rolling plains. Outside of animals here and there, he sees no people yet.

Far below is a shorter, denser canopy of trees that seems to be rooted in orange fog. It appears to Devon to be some form of Acculasian swampland.

All he wants to do is reach the people of this land before Lord Kildemar's heavy-handed sons. Devon's not shy of violence, but he fears to use it blindly as Janick would; it could ruin any alliances that might be formed. He also wants the advantage of the people seeing his face as the first to breach the walls that cannot be breached... it would give him a psychological edge.

Out of the blue, literally, a giant bat-like creature dives in and attacks the stream of smoke that is Devon. It's as though it's attacking empty airspace, but his invisibility doesn't throw off the sonar a bat uses.

Caught completely off guard by a sharp claw tearing into his shoulder, Devon loses the focus that enables him to control his sorcery... he materializes as be begins to fall. His flailing about is enough to ward off the bat, but he's not out of harm's way... Devon plummets downwards towards the dense swampland.

A crisp breeze fills the sails on the Capulian ship. The sailors know how to turn the sheets to catch all of it and they make good time over the waves... Peter just wonders to where they're making good time.

Prince Jarium sits on the deck, occasionally taking a nervous glance over the rail. Topolina watches this with a mixture of concern and amusement.

Seeing this, Peter steps over to her and asks, "What's up with Jarium? He's missing his easy going bravado."

"Cats don't like water, and this is a whole lot of water... he'll be OK. Down the road I'll tease him over this, but trust me, now is not the time to say anything," Topolina responds.

Peter shakes his head, "You women have no mercy. When Shan wants to get at me she turns me into a Grimick." She looks puzzled and Peter adds, "It's sort of a big hairy frog."

With a little laugh, "I think I like this Shan already."

"Figures," Peter grumbles.

"I take it she can do magic too?" asks Topolina.

"She's from Spirin, a land where everyone can do some sorcery. Of course some are more skilled than others... she's very good... I'm the newcomer to it all."

"And yet you're the one on the quest to find allies among my people to save a land that's not your home... this seems strange." She says this while watching Peter carefully, trying to get a read on him, and his true motivations.

Peter just stares over the rail, out at the rolling ocean. "For the longest time I didn't have much of a home back on Earth, and my only family was my kid brother. I've come to believe home and family are where you find it."

"That the kid brother who is now your enemy?" she asks.

Peter turns back to her. "Devon was a good kid left in a bad situation too long. That's the reason I'm responsible."

Sounding sincere, she asks, "I take it you were the one to leave him there... Did you choose to do that?"

"I'm not sure I've had a choice in much of anything for a long time," Peter says, a little distantly.

"Of course you have... what you have to remember is that your brother has had choices too," she assures him.

Yarlick, the master mate, comes up to the two of them, glancing at Jarium on the way. With a nod in Jarium's direction, "What's up with the young lad?"

Someone from the land of Capulia, where seventy-five percent of the surface area is water, is not used to seeing seasickness.

Topolina replies, "He's just a bit woozy... he'll get over it."

Yarlick doesn't make a big deal of it. Turning his attention back to Topolina, "We're making good time and should be dropping anchor in about a day."

Peter turns to him, "Yarlick, outside of barely acknowledging us, how come your Captain Varner hasn't met with us?"

Yarlick tries to choose his words well, "The Captain's a very formal man... in a special situation. He felt it best, mind you, in his formal way... that you limit your talk... to little." With a broad grin he adds, "Aren't I fine company fer the three of ya?"

"You mean he doesn't trust us?" Peter says flatly.

"Ain't quite like that... but he has to be... formal about it. He'll be taking you before the king himself, I suspect... when the time's right," Yarlick says. His tone and expression say, *'Accept it, that's the way of it.'*

Both Peter and Topolina nod that they understand, even if they don't. They know Yarlick is between a rock and a hard place; pressing him further would serve no purpose and make him needlessly uncomfortable.

Jarium quickly leans over the railing to take care of business... again.

Chapter Twenty-Three

Master Melick's home is abuzz with discontent over the unknown. Nothing can rile a group of people used to being in charge more than suspecting they're not. Even the hint of it beckons their fears.

As Gran-D enters he immediately senses all the discontent and he adopts his Grand Master Dar demeanor, even if that's not far from his normal nature... it's just louder. "What are all you old birds cackling about?"

"Dar, this is no time for your levity. No one has seen Peter in some time," says Master Warnig.

Master Sashaw picks it up, "There are rumors that he did exactly what he was told not to... that he went over the wall. Do you know about this?"

"The rumors... or... the facts?" Gran-D glibly asks.

Master Melick, trying not to sound as recriminating, "Do you have any idea where the boy has gone?"

Imton is the one Master not to skirt the matter, "You're the only one who knew where the pendant was hidden... did you give it to Peter?"

"No," says Gran-D.

He doesn't like lying to his friend. Technically he isn't, but that's a fine line. Until he discovers what Peter's trip reveals it serves no purpose for him to lose control of the Council... and admitting he had a direct hand in this would do just that. "Peter's a very resourceful sorcerer... so I can't be sure he didn't locate it on his own."

"And, you didn't tell him?" Imton presses.

"I didn't tell him... I can't guarantee he didn't figure it out on his own." Gran-D stands by this technicality. He doesn't like it, but he sees it as trying to protect Spirin.

Imton knows the old man's tendency for using half-truths to stay the course he feels best, so he asks straight forward, "Has Peter gone off beyond the walls?"

Gran-D is aware everyone in the room is hanging on his answer; vagueness will serve little, but that's the territory he has to remain in.

He says, "If he has, you know as well as I do he is doing it to help Spirin."

"You mean... in his opinion," snaps Master Sashaw.

As one of Peter's few supporters in the room, Master Carringer says, "At least he's not sitting on his hands."

"So, we finally get an answer... he has," grumbles Sashaw.

"There's also a rumor that Shan is trying to train some of the kids from the village. Do you know if that's true?" Master Warnig aims this directly at Gran-D.

Gran-D smiles, "Rumors abound today."

"It's a valid question, Dar," says Melick.

If Gran-D stays in full denial over everything, it will further destroy what credibility he still has left. "I am aware that she's trying to teach a few kids to defend themselves... it's just a few of the malcontents in the village, and adds up to nothing." He adds, "If Peter did go beyond the wall, he probably set her to that task just to keep her from insisting on going with him."

Sashaw seems exceptionally nervous, "And if that welcoming committee from Goreipor comes back and discovers she is making our people aggressive, what do you think they will do to us?"

In his nervousness he fiddles with something buried in his pocket.

Master Melick tries to take the middle road, "Can't you discourage her?"

Gran-D smiles at him, "No offense meant, but it's clear you've never raised kids. Attempting to discourage them is the worst kind of encouragement."

Master Warnig, who has raised a family and runs the floating library that kids come to, smiles at this truth.

Sashaw is persistent, "Like I said, what happens when those beyond the wall find out?"

He doesn't realize his nervous fiddling with something in his pocket has partially emerged. Down by his leg, Sashaw neurotically turns a tiny sphere around between his fingers. Becoming aware of it, he quickly shoves it back in his pocket. It doesn't appear anyone has taken notice.

"And how would they find out that little discretion anyway? Like I advise, leave it be and it will just fade away when the kids tire of it." Gran-D says this in the sincere hope that the opposite will happen; all he's trying to do is buy time. He can't help giving a quick glance over at Carringer.

Warnig suggests, "I agree with Master Dar... the chances they will come back are slim, and their discovering Shan's small efforts are slimmer. If we leave them alone, and whatever they're learning is useless, they'll lose interest."

Master Imton, clearly upset with Gran-D's excuses, "We're getting off track... what do we do about Peter's use of the pendant? He's going around the Sphere telling whomever he finds that we should be at war."

"If he has gone... then what do you propose doing about it? It's out of our hands at the moment." Gran-D says this knowing everyone suspects he knows more about it than he lets on.

The one Master who has said little thus far is Master Haring, the short, gruff drill sergeant of a man. When some in the room look to him, he seems hesitant, then says, "I'm truly not sure we shouldn't be looking at this from different angles. All we have is their word they won't bother us... what if we're wrong?"

The room grows uncomfortably quiet.

Devon comes to at the edge of a swamp. Orange fog drifts all around him as he sits up. He rubs the shoulder that has a gash from the bat's claw. Apparently it is a minor wound; it's no longer bleeding. After a second he looks around and tries to piece together what has happened since his plummet down from the sky.

Fragmented glimpses come back to him. He remembers trying to catch himself in midair but failing. How did his fall get broken? He can't put his finger on it. As his head clears, he remembers trying to create a protective globe and also failing. And finally, he sees an enormous splash. The globe must have been formed sufficiently to diminish the hard impact and he must have landed in the water.

But, how did he get to the edge of the swamp? How long has he been unconscious?

Devon decides there are too many questions to pull from the fog in his head. He stands up, determined to get back on track. He can only push his independence from the group a day... maybe a day and a half... so he's wasting time on this ground.

He concentrates to bring his sorcery into play and shoot back up into the sky... Nothing happens.

There's a commotion at the other end of the ravine where Shan's kids train. She has just arrived for the day and heads over to see what it's about, before her misfits get into more trouble.

Her little group stands, all with hands on hips, facing a small brigade of new kids from the village... not the malcontents. The best Shan can quickly judge is that there are around two-dozen new faces.

Yadar is all huffed up as he says, "We don't need you."

Shan steps in, "Have you been missing the point of my training? This might end up in a war... we need everyone who is willing to train." Turning to the new kids, she adds, "And can keep their mouths shut about the training, at least for now."

The new arrivals nod energetically. Shan wonders if they have any real idea why they are here... other than to get in on something they feel they've been left out of.

She asks, "Any of you know what we're doing here, or what's beyond our walls?"

Roland, an older member of the group, steps from the line, "We know. Our parents have been gossiping about it, pretending it's nothing... They sound scared." Roland then stares at Yadar, and his hoverboarding crew, "We're here in spite of them, not because of them."

It's pretty clear there is no love lost between the two groups of kids.

Shan hates to admit it, but she sees some advantage in a little healthy competitive dislike... maybe it will bring out more aggression in them. It makes her a little uncomfortable that she's beginning to feel better suited for this task than she originally thought... it's a cold feeling.

Peter stands alone at the rail of the ship watching distant islands as they pass. All of a sudden he staggers and appears disoriented. Silent images rush through his head of Devon wandering, lost in something like orange fog somewhere.

As suddenly as the images have come, they disappear.

Peter stumbles back.

A passing sailor rushes up to help steady Peter and sets him down on a deck-hole cover. He asks, "You OK, young man?"

After recovering his focus and balance, Peter responds, "I'm fine... just a little dizzy... thank you."

This is the third image of Devon that Peter has been struck by. The first he dismissed as a dream and the second was on the suspension bridge in Acculas. Now, beyond any doubt, he's certain that their mutual psychic connection is evolving. He still has a big question... will it be something that he can eventually control? The other big question... Are images coming to Devon in the same way... and, has he figured out how to control them?

Devon tries to generate a protection globe to test his abilities... still nothing!

Perhaps it is Devon's preoccupation with figuring out why his powers aren't working, or perhaps the swamp settling after the sudden intrusion of an outsider... but he now hears the silent swamp coming alive. The distant sounds of wildlife come from every direction.

Devon notices footprints in the mud around where he has awoken. They are of less concern to him than his loss of power. But when he hears the ferocious growl of a lion he decides the prints require more attention... they are a mixture of both animal and human. Perhaps the human ones will give him an idea of where to escape... if necessary.

The breaking of a twig behind him makes Devon turn abruptly. Just as he does he gets the briefest glimpse of a fist coming at him... then all goes black!

Chapter Twenty-Four

With the kids all gathered a good distance behind him, Master Carringer holds out a token and generates a spell named *'Cold Breath'*. Abruptly, a thick sheet of ice blankets the ravine in front of him.

Yadar is the first to react, "Cool!"

He runs and jumps on the half-pipe sheet of ice. He surfs up one side before losing his footing and tumbling. He slips down the ice face, sliding well along the pipe. Once again he yells, "Real cool!"

Shaking her head, Shan glares over at Carringer, "All we needed is something else for them to play on."

Carringer shrugs and responds in his defense, "I hardly remember what half these spells do. I bring them out of mothballs... you're the one who has to figure out if they're of any defensive use."

Shan turns back just as a bunch of other kids take Yadar's lead and dive onto the giant frozen slip-and-slide. She shakes her head in bewilderment.

Roland steps up beside her and points out, "A wall of ice could have some use, don't you think?"

She glances at him and then looks back at the spell's result. Shan realizes that she will have to be flexible in how she thinks about the tools they find... everything might be adaptable... it's just up to them to bring their imagination into play. She nods with a smile, as the kids continue to frolic on the slide.

Carringer says, "I'll dig out some more old spells."

Peter stands at the bow of the ship as it approaches a large island. He catches a glimpse of ships in the outer harbor and suspects there's a major port just around the point. The ship's large mainsheet is being pulled in.

Topolina joins him at the bow and, while Peter looks off in the distance, she seems to notice something much closer.

"Peter, your pendant is glowing," says Topolina.

He glances down at the pendant hanging from his neck... she's right. The center jewel pulsates a faint white glow. Peter takes the pendant from his neck and peers closer at it. Examining it, Peter inadvertently holds the pendant closer to the ship's railing... the glow becomes brighter. Seeing this, he holds it out over the water and it becomes even brighter.

Peter isn't sure of the reason the pendant seems to be speaking to him, but it is. Instinctively he takes note of island landmarks in a way one would triangulate a location... he sets those points to memory and puts the pendant back around his neck. He knows there's something important about this event; he's just not sure what.

About twenty minutes later, the ship slowly sails around the point and into the port of Realia, a major city of Capulia.

Peter again glances at the pendant, but the glow is gone.

As the ship rounds the point, Peter lets go of thoughts of the pendant. Before him lies a massive port harboring many sizes of sailing ships... from war ships like the one under his feet, to merchant ships and fishing boats of all shapes.

The dock and wharf-side businesses are buzzing with activity, from ships, loading and unloading, and fish vendors, to people milling about their daily duties. To the right of the dock, an open-air market bustles up against the high stone defensive wall surrounding the main city.

Peter can't see much of the lower city through the wall's large gates, but above it he sees the turrets of a castle deep within the city.

Yarlick steps up behind Peter and lets out a little chuckle, "What did you expect, grass huts?"

Peter would never say so, but that is what he has halfway expected. The only cities he's seen on this world are the village of Klavedar and Jarium's massive tree village. Both have many people, but they are a far sight from the size of cities Peter has been used to seeing on Earth. Even if Realia is a medieval-looking city, far different from a place like Seattle, it must still house many thousands of people. It's an alien version of Tortuga.

Peter glances back to the bridge of the ship. Captain Varner stands beside a signalman, who's busy using flags to talk with someone atop the city's perimeter wall. After a few more moments of hand flags whipping around, the signalman speaks to Varner and the Captain nods.

This is too far away for Peter to hear, but he's pretty sure it's about his presence. When Captain Varner looks up and begins heading directly for him, Peter is positive.

When Captain Varner reaches him, he says, "Now... I can introduce you to the people of my land." He turns to Yarlick, "Master Yarlick, take these people into custody."

Peter, surprised by the words, spins around to see armed guards have quietly moved into position.

Overcoming these guards would not really be a problem for Peter, but it would defeat the whole purpose of being here. He hopes Topolina and Jarium will understand this.

Jarium tenses at the situation but Topolina gently squeezes his arm... he doesn't like it but he finally drops the pack that holds their weapons.

Captain Pirus stands on a ledge looking out at the rolling land of Acculas wondering where Devon is off to. Quietly Taligarr comes up behind him, as if trying to sneak up on him.

Before he gets close, Pirus, without turning, says, "What can I do for you, Taligarr?"

With a slight laugh, Taligarr responds, "My father said you have eyes in the back of your head... apparently he's right."

"You best remember that... Now, like I said, what can I do for you?" Pirus doesn't sound like he's much in the mood for small talk.

Taligarr cuts to the chase, "Where's that trusted little friend of yours? It's been a day."

Pirus' mood extends to not wanting to answer senseless questions. "Go check on your brother and get ready to move out."

Before Taligarr can respond one way or another, Pirus turns to him. His eyes make it clear, even to Taligarr, that it's no time to dance with him. Taligarr leaves.

Pirus turns back to the vista and mumbles silently, "Where are you, kid?"

Devon wakes to a hazy, spinning vision of faces staring down at him. As his eyes focus, the numerous faces blend into only one. He's not even sure of that since this single human face seems to be attached to an animal's body. Devon shuts his eyes.

Someone kicks his foot.

This is a nightmare that's not going away, so Devon tries to sit up... he suddenly realizes that his hands are tied behind his back. This wakes him quickly; he squirms and struggles against his restraints to no avail. His fingers can tell that his belt of new razor discs is no longer at his side. When he does manage to roll to half-sit up, a hoof pushes him back down.

A voice comes from behind him, "Who are you and what are you doing in our swamp?"

Devon twists around and sees another creature who is part man and what appears to be part goat... he has the arms, shoulders and head of a man, combined with the body and four legs of a goat. Beside him is a woman who is part woman and part black leopard.

Being the only people he's seen in Acculas, Devon assumes these are the beings he came to meet. It crosses his mind that this may only be slightly better than Cretorn.

Another creature walks into his vision. This one is a mix of man and horse. He asks, "He tell you where he's from yet?"

Before anyone can answer, Devon speaks up, "My name is Devon, and I've come to meet your people."

There are laughs from those Devon can see and from many he can't. As he manages to lift his head slightly, he can see a slew of creatures around the swamp clearing. All are varying mixtures of humans and animals.

The half-horse, half-man, after he stops laughing, says, "Well, young Devon, I'm Siros. I'm the king of my land's very best prison. Now... what are *you* really doing in my prison?"

Devon vaguely remembers not being able to use his powers, but he tries nonetheless... they're gone, at least for now. Having no recourse he doesn't see any advantage in mincing words.

"I was flying over your land and got struck by something, and I fell into this swamp. I woke up... and here I am. What do you mean... a prison?"

"You were flying over... as a bird?" Siros asks.

"Something like that," Devon responds, not interested in getting into details.

"How is it you have not changed into your two selves?" Siros says this with a tone of honest bewilderment.

"I am not a bird; I'm just a human. What do you mean by *my two selves*?" It's now Devon who's puzzled.

A murmur sweeps through the others around the clearing. It's as if they're hearing something that astounds all of them. Siros glances around at the others and loudly pronounces, "Nonsense!"

He looks back at Devon, "If you value your life, speak the truth. We all have two beings... how is it that you did not merge when you fell into the mist?"

"I come from beyond the walls of your land... I don't know what you're talking about?"

Disregarding the two-beings issue, something else clicks in Devon's mind: "Is this mist what keeps you imprisoned here?" Having been locked in a quarantined zone on Earth for over a year, there's something very familiar to Devon about this.

Typically, being in prison, information would be a valued commodity, but this new arrival has Siros' attention.

"The mist forces our two selves into the same body, stripping us of truly being either... it strips us of the power to jump between them, it brands us as outcasts... and it keeps us locked here," Siros says. He says this as though he believes Devon's claim to not be from this land... as though he really wants to explain the horror of this prison.

This is the first thing that truly makes sense to Devon... the mist strips them of their powers. Now... his powers are gone. Are they gone forever? After all this, has he come full circle back to being imprisoned in another version of a quarantine zone?

Chapter Twenty-Five

Captain Varner leads the way as a group of armed sailors escort Peter, Topolina and Jarium through the narrow streets of Realia. The streets are like canyons paved with cobblestones; along the sides are doors leading into every kind of business from artisans' shops to bars. As the group passes, townsfolk mumble with curiosity.

The three visitors are not prodded or pushed, but they are bound. If their powers existed here, Topolina could fly away and Jarium could turn into a ferocious beast and probably run away... but where would they go? As for Peter, he could easily escape, but he has no interest in doing so... as long as they're not seriously threatened.

Peter is aware that this is a mission that he's passionate about, but Topolina and Jarium are only along for the ride because Jarium's father gave them the task... he suspects they're not prepared to become prisoners far away from home.

He leans in towards them, "I used some powers they're not used to. If I were them, I'd bind us as well. It's just a safety precaution for taking us to their leader." He listens for an understanding response... none comes quickly.

In a situation resembling captivity far more than safety, Jarium says nothing. Seeing her husband's stubbornness, Topolina finally says, "I hope you're right."

Reaching the steps leading up to the castle entrance, Peter says, "See, they wouldn't be taking us into a castle if they meant us harm."

Unfortunately, rather than being led up these stairs, the three are veered to the left and onto a smaller staircase... that leads down, not up.

Jarium breaks his silence, "Their chieftains must prefer the dark."

Lacking a comeback, and wise enough to keep it to himself if he had one, Peter says nothing. He hopes he's not wrong about these people. Having initiated this adventure he feels responsible for his two ride-along friends.

They continue farther down the stairs into darkness.

Pirus' men have broken camp and are ready to move out, but Taligarr and Janick are off in a huddle some distance away. Even from a distance, Captain Pirus can see Taligarr release a small sphere that arcs away in the direction of the wall.

The Sergeant comes to Pirus, as if he has something to say.

Pirus, looking over Sergeant Rooter's shoulder at Taligarr, says quietly, "I saw it."

"Just thought you oughta know," Sergeant Rooter says, and then heads away.

The sergeant's glad it's only his duty to report, not analyze. As far as he's concerned, soldiering should be kept as simple as possible... follow orders and keep your men alive. He does his best not to let the fact that the two *princes* were partially to blame for losing two men influence his duty... at times that is hard to set aside.

After Taligarr and Janick break their not so secret huddle, they come up to Pirus standing on the ridge.

"So where's the boy witch?" Taligarr demands.

Pirus glances right and left as if to silently say, '*If he were here, you'd see him.*' Then he gestures at Janick's leg, "How's the ankle?"

"I can walk," is all Janick says.

"Then Devon can catch up with us when he gets back. Grab your gear, the mission is still a go." Eying Taligarr's pouch with the communication spheres, Pirus adds, "Unless you've heard any different."

He's more interested in letting Taligarr know he knows that is his answer.

Taligarr's face says he gets the point. To change the subject he says, "I don't trust that kid being out on his own."

"I'm not suggesting that you trust him. I'm saying he's not here and we are moving out."

After Pirus says this he doesn't wait for a response; he just signals Sergeant Rooter to get moving.

With no Devon to send out a spy globe to reconnoiter the land, Pirus' team just heads straight inland from the wall. They have no idea when they might encounter the people of Acculas... or if there are any people. Silent, Pirus is pretty sure there are... and that is why Devon hasn't returned.

A couple of hours into their march inland, Pirus' team has yet to see any sign of life outside of a few large birds that circle high above. If he didn't know better, Pirus would suspect the birds have been dogging the team.

They've had to call more rest stops than usual due to Janick's ankle. His leg is holding up and there's no sign of infection but the team is making slow time.

Just as they approach a stand of trees, nine horses come galloping out past them. Initially, they seem spooked, but about a hundred yards away, they settle down in a meadow.

"Sergeant, see if you can round them up. Consider them confiscated property."

Pirus says this knowing that if the horses are wild, there may be little chance of getting close. Worse, if they are not wild, how will the locals take to them being horse thieves? But, since his team is making unacceptable progress on foot... he'll cross that bridge when he comes to it.

The Sergeant takes the two men he knows have the most experience with horses and they cautiously approach the small herd of fine-looking ponies. They move ever so slowly; they don't seem to be spooking any of the horses. They remain grazing as if they're already broken.

Pirus watches from a distance and observes two things... there must be people close by, and he may very well have to answer for stealing horses.

Taligarr steps up beside Pirus. As if reading his mind, he says, "We're not here to make friends, Captain... we take what we want."

Taligarr's words make Pirus almost want to spook the horses himself, but they can use the transportation.

Sergeant Rooter manages to isolate what he feels is the lead stallion and gently places a rope around its neck. He must have chosen well because as he walks the horse back to the team, the rest of the herd casually follows.

It strikes Captain Pirus odd that there are the same number of horses as there are men in his team, an unusual coincidence... he doesn't much like coincidences. But a horse is a horse, and it's better than being on foot.

When the sergeant arrives leading the small herd, each man chooses a horse. Sergeant Rooter brings the lead over to Captain Pirus. All of the men, including Taligarr and Janick, are adept riders, though they are not used to riding bareback. It doesn't seem to matter. The horses seem very willing to being mounted, especially considering that the soldiers are in full armor.

Once all are mounted Pirus orders, "Corporal, take point."

He does and the rest head out in single file, following him down the trail.

About a half hour into their ride, everything seems to be going just fine. The private assigned to be riding drag trots up near Captain Pirus; he appears a bit confused.

Pirus snaps, "Private, why are you out of formation?"

The private nods towards his horse as he tries to pull on its mane; the horse speeds up instead of responding to command.

Suddenly all the horses seem to be taking their own lead, rebelling against the efforts of their riders. All gallop forward towards a stand of trees.

With great effort, Pirus succeeds in muscling his mount slightly to the side of the trail... just enough that when he manages to dive off, he doesn't get trampled by the other horses. He tumbles into deep grass and rolls away as quickly as possible.

The rest of the riders, completely unable to control the horses, are carried forward. The horse Pirus was on pulls up on its own and circles back in search of its missing rider.

Crouching low, Pirus crawls through the high grass at an amazing speed for his size. Realizing the horse is returning, he drops into a dirt crevice and pulls a loose log over himself... motionless, he remains silent.

The horse prances around the deep meadow and then, not finding Pirus, gallops off after the now distant group of horses and riders.

None of the men are in control of their horses as they gallop under a dense canopy of trees. Many men would do as Pirus had, but now several more horses join the the herd, creating a rumbling stampede. One private tries, only to be crushed by the horses following, which have little chance of avoiding him.

Sergeant Rooter sees the loss of the private but can do nothing in the midst of this seeming chaos. He yells, "Everyone, stay mounted!"

A few minutes more into this crazy ride and suddenly the horses carrying the remaining men slow down, and the horses trailing behind branch off. Clear of the danger, each man jumps away as the opportunity avails itself. As each horse becomes rider-less, it speeds away.

Now in a clearing, all the dismounted men find themselves shaken but, for the most part, intact. All of the horses have galloped well away.

Abruptly, heavy cargo-style nets drop from the trees above... snaring the entire team in their mesh.

Once Pirus is sure the horse, or whatever it is, is not circling back he makes for high ground to figure out where his men are... now he could really use Devon's help.

Chapter Twenty-Six

The inhabitants of the swamp have removed Devon's restraints... after all, why worry about keeping a prisoner in a prison.

He has no way of proving that he's from beyond the walls that all believe are impenetrable. The same mist that chains the creatures here have stripped away his powers as a sorcerer. He has no idea if he will ever get them back. The only thing that backs his claims is the fact that he is not a half-animal. Unfortunately, in this prison, Devon's razor discs have value... they have not been returned to him.

Siros and the other creatures in this zone remain fairly stand-offish towards Devon. For some reason Siros finds Devon an interesting curiosity... maybe he has nothing else to do.

Overall, this zone appears less deadly than the quarantine zone on Earth was... but Devon has no intention of being here a second longer than necessary.

Devon's found out that, not unlike the quarantined zone he escaped from on Earth, deadly towers surround this zone, apparently killing anyone who tries to escape. The next thing he must do is observe the edge of this zone in order to formulate a plan. Siros has agreed to take him to the edge of the zone, but no further.

On their way, Devon asks what he's been hesitant to ask up to this point, "Why are you all locked in here?"

"We lost," is all Siros says.

Devon wants to push it, but Siros moves ahead, apparently not interested in explaining. For the moment, Devon decides to leave it be. After all, he doesn't plan on being here long enough to care... and he needs Siros' help.

What he does file away is that these are dissidents who might be useful at a later time. The people caught in the zone back on Earth were initially innocent, but, over time, they became resourceful fighters... those few that managed to survive.

The swampland varies in density as they travel towards its outer edge, but everywhere they go is the orange fog. Devon suspects this is what somehow nullifies magical powers. He imagines the implications of that if the fog could be harnessed and used on the people of Spirin... something else Devon files away for his potential arsenal. For now, he has to figure out how to get back in the game.

Siros, being half-horse, intentionally walks slower so Devon can keep up. As they proceed, he says, "I don't know what you expect to find. Those who tried to get out were struck down only a short distance outside... they died with their two selves still merged. Their shape-changing abilities didn't come back just because they escaped the fog."

Devon is not about to have his hopes dashed without exploring every possibility; he can't... he's gone through too much to surrender easily. What he is sure of is that no one inside will volunteer to test the containment... if he wants to escape, he's going to have to figure it out by himself.

With the persistent orange fog, it's a bit hard to determine exactly where they are. This is even true for Siros, a long-time resident... he seems to keep looking around to get his bearings. As his glancing around increases, Devon figures they must be getting close to the perimeter of the zone. When Siros starts speaking in a softer tone, he's sure of it.

Abruptly Siros stops and sniffs at the air and glances all around. "This is as far as I go... you're on your own from here. The edge of our prison is just ahead."

If Devon still had his powers he'd force Siros to keep going... even to the point of having him test the defenses... but if he did have his powers, he wouldn't be here at all.

All Devon can say is, "Will you wait here for me?"

Having exhausted all hope of escaping, Siros can't see what the boy is planning to do. He says, "You'll either be back shortly... or dead. I'll remain here till the second sun is almost down."

As Devon starts to leave, he turns back to Siros, "You said *'you lost,'* as a reason for being in here. What does that mean?"

"What can I tell you, one side wins, one side loses... we're prisoners of war." He glances at the sky, "Your time's short... Once the sun is down, fire lights the flat zone."

By Devon's guess, this means the kill zone. He doesn't have time for history lessons. He nods his thanks and moves on alone, hoping he will never see Siros again... or, at least, until he can use him.

Alone, Devon approaches the outer edge of the quarantined zone in about fifteen minutes. He can see why Siros wanted to remain solidly inside the zone. As he gets closer to the perimeter, he sees the dense trees that offer cover, giving way to lower foliage.

Once he gets close enough to see the distant guard towers Siros warned of, he sees the outer edge of the fog that defines the zone undulating. It ebbs and flows like the tide... so much so that one could be well within it one second and twenty yards out of the safe area the next. What is clear is that beyond the flow of the fog is a killing zone.

He has gotten so used to having his powers that Devon finds it awkward to function without them. He would normally send out a globe to determine what's on the outer edge of the killing zone... relying simply on his vision is irritating... and dangerous. He can see, at this distance, there are large wooden towers spaced about a hundred yards apart. He can't see who or what mans them.

Something that's not inescapable is the evidence of no one getting out. About fifty yards into the killing zone lie the skeletal remains of those who have tried. Hundreds of arrows, some rotting away with age, are embedded in and all around the skeletons. Whoever mans those towers may not have weapons comparable to those of Earth, but they seem just as effective.

An eerie silence floats over the whole area.

His heart drops as he sees the skeletons appear to be composed of merged human and animal bones. This reinforces what Siros had said... the power to change did not come back just because they managed to get clear of the fog.

Will his powers react differently, or, if he goes for it, will he be added to the killing zone's bone yard?

Taligarr is one of the last to come to. When he sits up, he sees they are in a large metal cage. From what little he recollects, they all fell in a clearing. With consciousness returning, he sees the cage is in the middle of a compound, enclosed by a tall log wall with guard towers at the corners.

Sergeant Rooter walks over to him. "You OK, sir?"

"What happened?" Taligarr asks.

"We got ourselves good and trapped. All I remember is that after the nets came down, I saw a giant bird fly in carrying some kind of vase. It spilled something high over us... and everything went to black."

The sergeant offers Taligarr a tin cup of water. The arrogance of the son of a lord slips back in as his head clears, "We all got trapped... except your Captain."

The Sergeant's tone chills, "That's a good thing... someone's going have to get us out of this mess. I don't suspect that's going to be you, sir."

With this, the Sergeant turns and rejoins his men before he says more than he should. As the Sergeant walks away, he reminds himself that just because a man wears a uniform it doesn't mean he knows what it stands for.

As soon as the Sergeant is gone, Janick shuffles over to his brother. He quickly says, "Shoot off one of those spheres so our father can send in troops."

Taligarr feels for his pouch, but it's gone. He looks out through the bars and sees the team's equipment heaped near the compound wall... the pouch is there, along with all their weapons.

He says, "Even if I had one, I wouldn't send it."

"Why not?" demands Janick.

"Someday you will get to know our loving father... and you will stop being slapped by him. To send a rescue party, he'd have to use his only pendant... and he's not going to do that for us."

Taligarr gets up, trying to appear more together. "I wouldn't. Anyway, if we yell for help this early, you think he'll ever put us in charge of anything again?"

"He didn't put us in charge," snaps Janick. But even he knows his brother speaks the truth about their father using the remaining pendant. He asks, "What happened to that coward of a Captain?"

Taligarr glances over at the Sergeant and back to Janick in a stern whisper, "Keep your voice down, the lower ranks are loyal to him... not to us."

"I'll have their heads if they're not," Janick whispers.

"Not just now, little brother. Right now, we need them," Taligarr warns.

Devon kneels near the edge of the swamp zone, watching the pattern of the fog roll out and back in. He keeps count, trying to establish a timing pattern. He also watches the uneven edge of the fog bank to determine what segments extend out the furthest and withdraw the most.

He glances over his shoulder, realizing almost two hours have passed. The second sun is almost touching the horizon and Siros is probably heading back into the swamp. This doesn't really bother him; if he were stuck in another quarantine zone, he would rather be on his own anyway. That's how he survived on Earth... having to only watch out for number one.

The descending sun works for him because he needs the dim lighting of dusk.

Along with the towers he has seen there are many torch stands. Devon assumes that is what Siros meant by *'fire lights the flat zone,'* though he can't imagine those torches covering the entire kill zone. Still, it's better to move before they light up.

When the wave of the mist slowly breathes out, Devon moves forward to a position just about midrange of its cycle. He kneels low as he counts under his breath, timing its movement.

The next time the fog breathes in, he will be exposed in the kill zone, but only a little. Since he won't be moving, he won't be an obvious target. If he were seen at all, even the longest launch of an arrow would have little chance of finding its mark. Most of the dead lie farther out, as if they tried to make a swift run for freedom... unsuccessfully.

Devon still needs to find out something before his next move. He waits.

Dusk arrives. When the layer of thick orange fog recedes, Devon is exposed about three yards out in the hundred-yard deep killing zone, but momentarily free of the fog. He remains still for what feels like the longest time, waiting to see if arrows rain down on him... they don't.

Making sure to move slowly, Devon glances back at the fog; it's at its recessed limit and starts towards him again.

Waiting as long as he can before the fog reaches him, Devon finally attempts to conjure a protective globe. The outer edges of the globe start to lightly flicker... it's trying to come into existence. Devon strains to hold it together, but the soft touch of the fog chills his back and the globe dissolves.

Devon sits back as the fog engulfs and drifts out beyond him. A smile comes over his face... he's now reasonably sure he can get his powers back. The big question is, since he will have to go out beyond the rolling fog's range, can he get his powers back before the arrows find their mark?

Hidden back in the swamp, Siros watches the boy at the edge of his prison kingdom. If the boy dies, so be it, but if he is on to something, it could show a means of winning freedom.

Sergeant Rooter gets to his feet when he sees a human Acculasian come through the gates and towards the cage. Even though Taligarr and Janick are present, the sergeant sees himself as ranking first among the true military... his men are his responsibility. Taligarr sees it differently and moves forward, shoving the sergeant out of the way.

Before their captor even reaches the cage, he announces, "My name is Taligarr, son of Lord Kildemar, ruler of Goreipor..."

"As if I care," the man says, cutting him off. Somehow the man senses who has the bearing of being in charge, and says to Sergeant Rooter, "One of your men escaped. Where will he go?"

"Don't know what you're talking about... actually, I think about twenty of our men escaped... no, probably more like thirty," Sergeant Rooter says defiantly with a broad grin.

The man gives him a knowing nod and starts to turn.

Taligarr isn't willing to leave it with being dismissed so high-handedly, "I am the leader of this expedition, I demand to speak with your superiors."

He continues to turn and move away as if he's heard nothing.

Sergeant Rooter doesn't expect an answer but yells out anyway, "How'd you know we were here?"

Walking out through the gates, the man says, "One of your thirty men told us."

Captain Pirus sees birds flying high above. Since the horses acted with the precision of soldiers, he has to assume the birds are enemy troops as well. He doesn't waste time worrying about the nature of the inhabitants; he's only interested in assessing the opposition.

The sun is almost down and until he can use the cloak of darkness, he's limited to moving stealthily under the cover of the low-lying brush. Waiting is not an option... his duty is to track his captured team.

The sun has almost fully set. Devon knows dusk is the ideal time, but that time has come and almost gone. He figures that the torches near the distant archer towers can only light so much.

Having timed the ebb and flow of the fog, Devon watches its fingers drift out to its farthest point. There has always been a long pause before it begins retracting so he quickly moves as far out into the kill zone as the fog allows.

Motionlessly, he waits to be uncovered. Since he's still a long way from the towers and torches, Devon hopes to remain undiscovered until the fog's effect on his powers wears off.

Just as the fog bank leaves him exposed, he sees the torch stands by the towers light up. He is right... though they put off a lot of light, their glow doesn't reach him.

All of a sudden a finger of fire races down each of the torch stands. When it reaches the ground, it ignites flammable trenches... fingers of glowing fire shoot across the kill zone like the spokes of a tire. As they burn, the entire kill zone becomes illuminated... the torches were just there to trigger this ribbon version of security lighting.

With the light rushing towards him, Devon doesn't have all the time he has expected to let the effects of the fog wear off. Either he tries now, or he has to run for the cover of the swamp. A lot of open field stands between him and the swamp.

He decides to go for broke. Devon attempts to conjure his shield... it flickers with a little more strength than before.

Arrows from two of the guard towers take to the air in a high arch. He hears the first volley streaming through air just before their sharp thuds find the ground around him.

No doubt having estimated his range better, the archers release another volley. He abandons creating a shield and concentrates further. A moment before this round of arrows rains down on him, Devon disappears into a swirl of smoke... and shoots skyward.

Siros, sitting at the edge of the swamp, stares at the space where Devon once was.

Chapter Twenty-Seven

Peter, Topolina and Jarium don't sit in the main hall of the castle of Realia; they sit in its dungeon. This is hardly where the three of them have expected to be at the end of their long voyage. Yarlick, who had been so friendly when inviting them aboard from that beach, had given them no hint.

Even Peter grows a little more resentful as the hours tick by. Jarium seems as upset with Peter as he does with his captors. The only one of the three who doesn't seem too shaken by it all is Topolina.

She turns to the two who have such sour faces, "And neither of you would temporarily detain someone who has invaded your land?"

Sounding indignant, Jarium gestures towards Peter and says, "We didn't lock him away."

"Tell me you didn't have him followed every moment till the chieftains said to stop," she snaps at him.

"Topolina!" Jarium says, not believing she said that.

Peter glances around at the food their captors have delivered to the cell... and the absence of implements of torture. He has to admit they're not exactly being mistreated.

"At least they're not spying on me," he says.

"Are you two going to set your pouting aside till we find out what's actually happening?" Topolina chides.

Peter and Jarium look at each other with expressions of surrender... before Topolina resorts to grabbing them both by their ears.

The dungeon door creaks open and Captain Varner comes in. Up till now he has maintained a very neutral and distant position... now, he smiles. Without much to judge it by, Peter is not sure what brings a smile to the man... good or bad news.

Captain Varner says, "Now... I can officially welcome you to Capulia." He adds, "I'm to take you to quarters where you can rest up."

"I'm not interested in resting up... I want my freedom," says Prince Jarium irately.

"By your own admission, you came to our world. You need to understand this is a serious event for my people, and you must give our leaders time to gather and arrange an official audience for you," Varner calmly says.

Neither Peter nor Jarium can really fault this logic.

With a little more experience at being the new kid in town, Peter speaks as calmly as possible, "Do you have any idea how long we will be your *guests* before meeting your leaders?"

"The king is out on a hunt. A messenger has been dispatched and his party should be back on the morrow. Till then you we will make you comfortable as our guests," answers Varner.

All three realize that what is meant by guests... is prisoners, only in nicer surroundings than the dungeon.

Gently slapping the other two on the back, Topolina says, "I prefer a comfortable bed, if you don't mind," and she merrily walks past Captain Varner.

Varner notes, "Once the king's party returns, we shall have a feast."

Peter holds his head, remembering the state he was in after the last *festival*, "Another feast?"

Under the cover of darkness, Pirus does the best he can to track his team. He still doesn't chance coming out in open... the birds tracking him could be nocturnal. It's slow-going.

He has already found where the men had lost their horses, or whatever those creatures were. From the ruffled brush, drag marks and wagon tracks, he knows his men were loaded unconscious onto a wagon and carted off. Just as important, there were human tracks other than those of his men where they were snared and netted. Now, he follows the wagon tracks... and something more than animals.

Devon, extremely happy to have gotten his powers back, zips all over as a thin stream of smoke, weaving in and out of the trees. He makes sure to zip close to the ground, figuring whatever attacked him before is still out there. Since it seemed to locate him with sonar, as bats do, the darkness is not sufficient defense.

It's night and he's been gone for almost two days. Even though he wanted to approach the people of Acculas on his own, Devon knows he can't abandon the support of Goreipor and has to search for Pirus and the others.

He follows the direct path inland from the wall that he figures Pirus would take. Flying, even in his erratic pattern, Devon covers much more ground than the troops would and he's surprised he hasn't crossed the squad's path yet. He would use his spy globe but it's night and, in truth, he's still enjoying his freedom to fly.

Purely by luck he passes over a clearing where he sees a reflection. When he goes to ground Devon finds the reflection comes from the light of the moon glinting off a sole knife blade... it's a Goreiporian blade.

Soldiers don't *accidently* lose knives; he knows something is amiss. Looking around, he sees some action has taken place in the clearing and he discovers the same wagon tracks as Pirus has.

It's time to get smarter than fly randomly. He knows whatever is in the towers guarding the zone is defensive in nature. He has to accept the idea that, at least, they have been captured... maybe worse. Luckily there are no signs of blood.

Even though it's dark, Devon sends out a spy globe to scout in the direction of the tracks At least the bright moonlit night offers some visibility.

After a short while, the globe detects the glow of firelight in the distance and Devon sends the feed there. It comes in low over a square compound surrounded by log walls. Since the feed is undetectable he has no concern about sending it in close.

The caged Goreiporians have no idea that Devon is watching; more importantly, neither does the enemy. First he gets a good look at those captured. Captain Pirus is not among them, meaning he has either eluded capture or is dead. From what Devon knows of Pirus, he thinks it's the former.

Now he has the feed drift up towards the guard towers that sit atop each corner of the enclosure. Two men stand in one guard tower. Beside their complexion being bluish-brown, they're no more alien than regular humans... not half-animal, half-human like Siros. They're armed with medieval weapons; swords and bows... nothing that Devon can't overcome.

The question facing Devon is whether he wants to mount a rescue of these men, or go in search of Captain Pirus... if he is still alive. It's not a hard question... the men in the cage are expendable, even Taligarr and Janick... Pirus plays into Devon's future plans. He realizes saving Lord Kildemar's sons might be a more important than he cares to admit, but they can wait for the moment... they're not going anywhere.

The spy globe does an ever-expanding search pattern around the compound where the men are being held. Devon is positive Pirus is searching for his men and, knowing him, he should be close if physically capable.

Devon gets lucky; it doesn't take long for the image in the globe to show Pirus. Staying low for cover, Pirus has to stick to making short dashes. All Devon has done is have the feed search for movement.

Now Devon needs to physically catch up with the globe feed.

When Devon first started conjuring spy globes this would have been a harder task; he would have had to see landmarks to determine their location. Over time, however, he has adjusted the spell to perceive vibrations from the feed-point... somewhat like a tracking device.

Pirus has tracked his men to a position from where he can see distant torchlight reflected by the canopy of trees. He hasn't gotten close enough to actually see the compound yet, but knowing something is close has slowed his pace.

It's second nature for Pirus to reconnoiter an entire area as he proceeds, but that doesn't prepare him for Devon's means of arrival. Startled, Pirus draws his blade and spins into a protective stance as a silent hair-thin strand of smoke drifts down... and deposits Devon in front of him. A split second after Devon materializes, the blade's point has already come to rest against his throat.

Pirus whispers, "Never come on me in your magic way again."

Unruffled, Devon raises his finger and gently pushes the blade away from his neck.

"Figures... you'd be the one not caught," says Devon.

Pirus stands down and Devon points toward the compound, "They're down the road a bit, well locked up."

He generates a smaller spy globe that replays what Devon has seen earlier.

"So how's your bag of tricks going to help?" Pirus asks.

"Jumping fewer men back in Cretorn just about did me in... Not going to try it that way again," says Devon.

"Four towers... two guards per tower... maybe a few we haven't seen... that something you can handle?" asks Pirus.

Devon thinks about the zone and says, "I suspect the beings here can shift back and forth between being men and animals. They're going to have quick reactions."

"I guessed as much. It could make it a bit more difficult, unless you strike all of them at the same time. Like I said, what's in your bag of tricks?"

Pirus doesn't appear thrown by the adversary's capabilities. He hasn't seen an actual transformation but all the evidence has already led him to that conclusion.

"We're here to win hearts and minds... a large body count may not fare well on that front," Devon responds.

Looking toward the compound, Pirus says, "Kildemar's sons may see it differently."

"I know. That said, blood is not always best," Devon says.

Dead serious, but flexible, Pirus says, "I'm not leaving my men... not even those two. Give me an alternative."

Devon thinks for a moment, "I got an idea... We need to move in closer."

After a second glance at Devon, Pirus asks, "What happened to your razors?"

"It's a long story," is all Devon answers.

Pirus shrugs; he's not in the mood for a long story anyway.

A short while later Devon and Pirus are close enough to the compound to see the log walls. Pirus keeps glancing up at the trees above.

He says, "I think one of the animals they can change into is a bird. I saw large birds dogging us before the ambush." He thinks a second longer, and adds, "If they can change, does that mean they can do the things you can... I mean, witches?"

He can tell that the idea troubles Pirus... it should. Devon has told Kildemar that Spirin could be their strongest enemy if they realized the use of all their powers. Spirin is totally non-violent, but this land shows signs of military, strategy, mass imprisonment and who knows what else. The idea that they possess powers akin to those of Spirin would trouble anyone.

From his experiences near the kill zone, Devon guesses, "They use ancient bows and arrows. I think it's their nature to be animal and human, it's not a magical skill."

Sounding a bit insulted, Pirus says, "We use the same weapons. What's ancient about them?"

Devon sometimes forgets that his memories of Earth are not shared. The last thing he wants to explain is a modern weapon. He blows it off with, "Just meant they don't have my skills."

Pirus is no fool; he can tell Devon is hiding something, but now's not the time to get into it. He refocuses on the issue at hand. "So, what do you want me to do?"

Having noticed Pirus' persistent glances up into the trees, looking for birds, Devon thinks how best to approach this.

He smiles, "I'm going to borrow a trick of my brother's... of course combined with one of my own. You have to get in and bust open the cage."

"What's the signal?" Pirus asks this with a sound of simple trust. He hopes Devon understands that trust comes with consequences... if his men don't survive, his weight will be thrown on Devon's shoulders.

"You'll know," is all Devon says.

Captain Pirus waits inside the tree line close to the wooden compound. When he had jumped from the horse earlier, he lost some of his gear; he is only armed with his sword and a knife, which he's proficient at throwing.

He quietly waits for some form of signal.

Devon sits high in the canopy of trees over the compound. He's invisible. He watches the limbs below, looking to home in on any bird that might be the enemy in disguise... a hard task even for Devon. When a very large and unusual looking bird flies in and lands on a limb just above the cage area, Devon realizes he has been giving all the tiny birds he had been scoping out a bum rap. Now he knows what to look for... a creature with the arrogant bearing of a human.

Discovering an enemy bird in the tree that can fly for reinforcements too soon causes him to rethink plans slightly. Harming the bird would mess with the farther-reaching plans he's coming up with on the fly... but the bird can't be alerted too soon either.

When Devon was experimenting with weapons in the cave he built in Spirin, he played around with potion spells he learned from Master Warnig. One of the potions he tested out with the help of an unwitting Grimick was a sleeping aid. Devon simply weaponized it... any specific effect forced upon someone is in itself a weapon.

The nice thing about some spells is that they don't require carrying along a lot of hardware... for the most part they're in your mind.

Focusing on one guard tower at a time, Devon sets his plan into motion. He floats a small invisible sphere out well over each tower; within each sphere is his potion. The little spheres flicker slightly, but not enough to be noticed. Even the bird keeping watch from a limb well below him sees nothing to raise an alarm.

It dawns on Devon that he doesn't even need Pirus to pull this off. An internal warning quickly follows telling him not to let his ego get too big... even if he feels he doesn't need allies, it is necessary to make them think he does. He knows Pirus is waiting to do his part.

Before Devon can place the last sphere over the bird below him, it takes flight. It doesn't appear to be alarmed... just an ill-timed stretching of its wings. Devon watches as it flaps away into the forest. His plan is already in motion so he sets aside his concern over the unknown.

He simultaneously pops all the spheres above the towers. The sedative in the spell has been adjusted to not take effect immediately... but it does.

The last thing to put into play is confusion, just in case the bird is hovering. Borrowing from Peter's playbook, Devon explodes a cloud of purple smoke that cascades down over the whole compound.

A 'noticeable signal' is an understatement. Pirus, seeing this massive cloud, moves out, zigzagging for the compound gates. He simply trusts Devon has neutralized the towers.

Pirus quickly breaks the lock and releases his men. Under the cover of the purple cloud, they make their way out of the compound. Since he doesn't know that the guards are all out, Pirus drives his men hard to the tree line.

In case he misjudged the sleeping spell, and as a safeguard, Devon generates a protective globe to cover the men's escape.

Almost immediately, he realizes this is one step too much... vertigo strikes him. He almost slips from the limb, but catches himself.

After a few seconds regaining his composure, Devon disappears into a stream of smoke and shoots away.

Chapter Twenty-Eight

Topolina stands by a castle window staring out at the night sky. Two moons are reflected in the tranquil harbor. The stone room where she stands is warmly enhanced by ornate tapestries and artistically carved furniture. A fire crackles in a massive stone hearth along one of the walls. The room has all the comforts of a sophisticated society.

Jarium comes up from behind and gently puts his arms around her. He remains quiet.

Without turning she quietly says, "You quit pouting yet?"

His gentle squeeze tells her he has. He says, "OK, I don't like being locked up... but I guess we would do just about the same if our chieftains were on a hunting trip. At least it's good company to be locked up with."

"Oh, you mean Peter?" she says jokingly.

In answer to her question, Jarium turns Topolina around and gives her a long kiss.

As Devon flies invisibly through the trees, he glimpses the large bird from the compound settle on a high limb for only a moment and then fly away again. Below are Pirus' men; the timing meets with Devon's approval.

He joins the group as a wisp of smoke, but quickly transforms into his human form... making a point of not being too close to anyone. After his experience with Pirus, Devon realizes it can be disconcerting to have someone instantly appear in their face.

How quickly Taligarr forgets he has just been rescued. He rushes up to Devon and snaps, "Where did you go off to?"

Pirus walks up and loudly whispers, "Keep your voices down or I'll gag the two of you. In case you didn't notice, he just saved your ass."

"Don't worry, we have time... the guards back there will be out for hours," Devon says with a slightly shaky voice.

Without warning, he staggers back and Captain Pirus catches him as he falls. Devon has passed out. Between losing his powers in the swamp and his recent efforts, Devon's magical powers have been drained.

A couple of hours later Devon comes to. The first thing that comes into focus is Pirus' face looking down on him.

"Thought we lost you, kid," Pirus says with a slight smile.

"How long have I been out?" Devon asks.

"A few hours... longer than I wanted to stay here," says Pirus, glancing around the surrounding forest.

Devon sits up and immediately notices that fewer men are in the group. He asks, "Where is everyone?"

Pirus appears frustrated by the question. He says, "We lost one man in their ambush, and Janick took off with a few of my men without a word. I'm going to skin him... "

He cuts himself off as Janick and two of his men come through the trees... they are spattered with blood. Pirus jumps to his feet and storms towards Janick. Devon remains seated, still trying to clear his head.

"Where have you been?" demands Pirus.

"Tying up some loose ends," says Janick. An infuriating grin is on his face.

Immediately, Pirus knows what they've done. Though he's no stranger to killing, slaughtering sleeping men is unacceptable to Pirus... even by Goreiporian standards. He also sees that they have lost another soldier to the enemy... his anger, though, is more about chain of command than sorrow or ethics.

The two soldiers left who had gone with Janick were replacements for the men lost on the last mission, so they're not his regulars.

Pirus addresses them, "Who gave you permission to break ranks for this action?"

They both nod at Janick and Corporal Leigh says, "Commander Janick's orders, sir."

The other soldier is a private. He says passionately, "Sir... they took one of our own... We were due payback."

Pirus realizes he's walking a fine line here... even with his own men who were friends of the downed soldier.

He says, "Killing sleeping soldiers is not payback, but that's another point. This mission is under my command, regardless of insignias. You break from my ranks without permission again and I'll have your heads... understand?"

He turns his gaze to Janick, "And if you take action without informing me again, I'll do the same to you."

"Devon's powers assisted us, but those men know we don't have his powers... they had to die," Taligarr says with self-righteous arrogance.

Janick may have taken the action, but now Pirus suspects Taligarr was behind it. Devon joins the group and notices the blood on the men.

"What happened?" he asks.

"They killed the guards back in the compound," says Pirus matter-of-factly. After all, what's done is done.

"You killed helpless men? You've messed up my plans!" Devon says in a tone clearly not appropriate to his rank.

"How dare you?" snaps Taligarr. "You are here to serve my father and this mission... not to make the plans."

Now Pirus turns to Devon, "What plans?"

They may be conspiring with each other to some degree, but Pirus doesn't like being blind-sided by anyone.

Devon immediately realizes he misspoke. Controlling outcomes is one thing... arrogantly declaring them as '*his plans*' is something else altogether. All he can do is carefully back-step.

He says, "Once I knew we had to get the men out, I saw it as a way to show our power without blood."

Knowing Devon is not saying everything, Pirus asks, "How would they know?"

"One of them was a bird in the tree, and it flew away before anything was done," Devon admits. Devon says this suspecting that Captain Pirus would know it's a lie.

The boot private who took part in the action spouts, "Well... we still got our revenge." Drawing a glare from Pirus, he backs away.

"What you did is kill eight men for nothing," Devon says.

Janick yells at Devon, "Where do you get the... "

Pirus cuts him off, "Enough! Everyone... What's done is done... we need to clear out of here... Now."

Too late...

Abruptly all discussion ends with the sound of hoof beats out in the woods... a whole lot of them.

Pirus' men quickly arm themselves. Being soldiers, they manage to grab much of their equipment in the midst of hectic preparation for defense.

The hoof beats stop about a hundred yards away, but sounds of movements can still be heard.

Pirus' team gets into position and braces for a battle.

Suddenly, Devon steps out in front, "We shouldn't do this."

This even surprises Pirus.

Devon goes on, "Have you forgotten our mission? We've shown our capabilities with the escape from their compound. But thanks to your senseless killing, you've shown our threat... sustaining casualties will only show our weaknesses." Devon is sure of his strategic move. He's prepared, if needed, to restrict even his own team.

He adds, "We are here to find allies for a bigger fight... if we haven't alienated them already."

Pirus' soldiers silently glance at Captain Pirus. They are warriors, and prepared to make a stand, even though they are sure the attacking forces will be greater than the eight at the compound.

"You're suggesting we simply get captured again?" says Taligarr... trying not to sound like he would prefer capture to death in a hopeless defense. He has been in battles, but only ones heavily weighted in favor of his father's troops.

Devon decides to play to Taligarr's vanity, "If you let me, I will make sure it's something less dramatic, sire."

The sounds of men moving in the woods get closer. Pirus looks at his men and at Devon.

After a second he says, "Stand down... no action without my command."

He can see some of his men, including Sergeant Rooter, grip their weapons tighter... ready... itching for a fight.

"I said, stand down... and that means you too, Sergeant." This time Pirus does not bother keeping his voice down.

"You heard Captain Pirus, stand at the ready, but no one engage without orders," Rooter barks.

The men bring their weapons to their sides and Devon turns to face whatever comes out of the forest.

Captain Pirus steps up to him and says quietly, "Hope you know what you're doing. Next time you have one of these little surprises, I'd appreciate knowing in advance."

Equally quietly, Devon says, "I was planning on their forces catching up with us... how else could we make contact? I didn't plan on it being after a slaughter."

Pirus glances at Devon and sees blood trickling from his nose.

"You OK, kid?"

Devon wipes the blood away, "Fine."

They all wait for what comes out of the trees next.

A knock sounds on a heavy adjoining chamber door.

Topolina, sure she's more amiable than Jarium, goes and opens the door. After a second, she gestures for Peter to come in.

"I'm glad to see they gave you the nicer room," Peter says, trying to keep things light.

"Yeah... we have the fancier jail cell," Jarium grumbles.

"Peter can come in here and you can have his room if you don't hush up," Topolina scolds.

Peter muffles his slight laugh... not very well; it earns a glare from Jarium. Avoiding his look, Peter walks to the large window and glances out at the night.

"You have a great view," he says. "You know that if we're going to approach these people, we have to play nice, don't you?" The comment is clearly meant for Jarium.

"And you remember that we are on two different missions?" says Jarium. "You are looking to start a war... we're here to watch, and decide if we want anything to do with you."

"Would you two stop, already?" Topolina snaps. "We're here as guests... uninvited ones, may I remind both of you." Staring directly at Jarium, "You and I have always wanted to see beyond the walls... this is an adventure. That's what you need to remember."

Just then there is a knock on the main chamber door. Without waiting for an answer, a key unlatches the lock, and the door creaks open. A young woman pushes a wooden meal cart into the room. It's loaded with a feast of fruits, vegetables and breads, along with some wine. She gives a smile and then leaves. They hear the door locked behind her.

Topolina walks over, picks up what looks like a blue apple, and takes a big bite.

Chewing, she says, "I don't know how much of this torture I can take."

Neither Peter nor Jarium can hold back their laughter.

Warriors of Acculas slowly walk out of the woods, far more than Pirus' now eight-man squad could handle in a straight up fight. They all have their weapons trained on the smaller group, ready to get at it.

Devon walks forward, Pirus at his side. Clearly Taligarr and Janick aren't ready to join them, which doesn't bother either Devon or Pirus.

As they move forward, Pirus quietly asks, "What now?"

"A touch of showmanship, if it's not too late," Devon says and gestures for Pirus to hold back.

From anyone else, Pirus would ignore the suggestion... but from Devon, with his hocus-pocus, he heeds the warning.

Before stepping away, he says, "Don't push it with these guys, they've been bloodied."

Devon nods, sincerely hoping he knows what he's doing.

An Acculasian warrior, apparently in authority, steps forward and draws his bow.

He yells, "Stop where you stand!"

Devon doesn't. He assumes whatever action he takes could rattle nerves, so gently with one hand he raises an invisible shield.

Then he says, "We wish to be brought before your leaders."

This receives cold silence.

Devon waves at a tall tree off to his right. The base of the tree explodes. As Devon has expected, the Acculasian force steps back and releases a wave of arrows at his group. The volley hits the invisible shield making crackling noises like a string of small firecrackers. The arrows fall harmlessly to the ground... to the dismay of the Acculasian warriors.

The tree topples over, forming a straight low barrier between Devon and the warriors. As soon as the tree hits the ground, Devon wills it to burst into flames. As he expects, the half-animal side of the warriors of Acculas rear away from the wall of flames.

As a final flair, Devon generates a separate protection globe around himself. He levitates up and floats directly over the flames of the burning tree. The flames seem to form a nest beneath the seven-foot round sphere... and Devon.

These tricks, however, push Devon's powers to their limit. Blood starts to drip from his nose again as he weakens. Unsure how much longer he can put on this show, Devon sees their ranks break and retreat into the forest.

Still Devon needs one last trick. As the lead warrior begins to follow his retreating troops, Devon topples a smaller tree right on top of him. He hopes the trunk doesn't hurt the man too much... his being alive is part of Devon's plan.

Having drained his powers, Devon's protection globe starts to flicker. Pirus knows that's a bad sign. Before Devon completely loses the globe and falls into the flames, Pirus dives up into the air to knock Devon to the ground away from the flames.

"Might have been easier to fight," Pirus says with a sigh.

Clearly drained, Devon says, "Wouldn't serve the same purpose... rumors are more powerful." Pointing at the downed warrior, "See if the he's Ok."

"Let me guess, you're using him as a messenger," says Pirus, hitting Devon's intentions on the nose.

Devon smiles. He's glad to see someone understands his strategies.

Chapter Twenty-Nine

The suns are up over Capulia and Peter's having breakfast with Topolina and Jarium in their chambers. The tensions between Peter and Jarium have subsided. Jarium writes it off as being part animal; he's not accustomed to being caged... even in the most gilded of cages. Topolina is not so affected by it, but maybe that's because if she has a mind to, she could transform and fly out the window. Truth is, she doesn't see their treatment as being that unreasonable... she takes another sip of her juice.

There's a knock on the door and, as before, they hear the lock being undone. This is a sound that grates especially hard on Jarium.

When the door opens, Captain Varner comes in and says, "The king has returned. You'll have an audience with him at the evening feast. Just thought you would want to know."

Having delivered his message, he turns to leave.

"Thought a ship's captain would have gone back to his ship by now," Peter says.

He glances back, saying, "I'm also the king's brother-in- law... you'll probably see more of me than you expect. I brought you to the castle... you're my responsibility." With that, he leaves.

Not hearing the lock reset, Jarium rushes to the door. He opens it and looks back at Peter and Topolina. Neither of them looks like they're anxious to go anywhere.

"We came here to meet them, and now we're invited to the feast to do exactly that... Is it worth pushing things before we need to?" Peter asks.

"I don't know about you two, but I'm still having breakfast," says Topolina, with her usual smile.

Jarium lets out a little sigh and closes the door.

By now Shan has set up quite a little camp out by the ravine where she trains the ever-growing number of kids. A few of them, like Yadar, who come from less involved families, have even started staying in a tent camp near the site.

Carringer has also been sneaking away more often to join the group. On the bluff overlooking the ravine, he has set up a large tent of his own for working on spells. The interior of his tent is starting to look like his home, cluttered and chaotic, with books and charts all over.

Kyra, a tomboyish girl of sixteen, is a relatively new recruit. Shan took a liking to her right off the bat... probably because she sees a lot of herself in the girl. Kyra comes into Carringer's tent carrying a small boulder on her shoulder. She drops it on a large table with a loud bang.

Carringer is quick to say, "Child, you should have asked for help with that."

He gets a harsh glare from Kyra, who considers herself quite capable.

"Or not," Carringer adds.

Kyra lets out a sigh, "You're a kook, aren't you?"

"Probably... Now, where were we?" he says in puzzlement.

Kyra sighs again, and points at the rock.

"Oh, yes, I remember," says Carringer.

He rummages through a pile of spell tokens and comes up with one that looks like a cross between a wand and a silver chisel. To anyone else his pile would appear to be cluttered; somehow, to Carringer, it all makes sense... that is, when he can remember what he's doing.

Master Carringer holds the token about a foot above the boulder Kyra has delivered. He closes his eyes and squeezes the token. Shan and the couple of other kids in the tent hold their ears. Nothing happens.

Carringer looks befuddled. Then he perks up and says, "Oh, yes... I know what I forgot to remember."

Both Shan and Kyra shake their heads.

Once again Carringer holds the token above the rock and squeezes. A tiny bolt of lightning spits out of the token and strikes the stone. With a loud crack, the stone splits in half. Carringer looks very pleased with himself.

"Very nice," comes from a voice behind them.

All turn to see Gran-D standing at the entrance of the tent. He smiles, "I'm not welcome here?"

"Of course you are, Dar... It's just rare to see you here. For that matter, have you ever been here?" asks Carringer in his usual absentminded manner.

"Have to keep up appearances and, with you out here as much as you are, I have to be around to cover your tail. You know I have all your backs," says Gran-D.

"Gran-D, it's great to see you, you know that," Shan says.

"So... how about showing me some of the tools you've come up with, old friend," Gran-D asks Carringer.

"All I come up with are the seeds, it's the kids who make them into tools," Carringer responds.

Gran-D, Carringer and Shan stand on the bluff overlooking the ravine. A lot has changed since Shan first brought Yadar and a few of his friends out here. Off to the far right are a bunch of kids practicing combat with wooden lances.

Gran-D points at them, "I thought we were learning how to use our gifts to defend ourselves?"

"Trust me, they need to learn to defend themselves from the ground up... I've had to use those hand-to-hand skills," says Shan with regret in her voice. "Learning close fighting teaches them what it means to fight. If I showed them how to use spells from a distance, they would never understand the cause, and the consequences, of what they're doing. Peter told me that on Earth fighting became more like video games, and some lost track of what they were physically doing to each other... it became too remote... too easy."

Gran-D has no idea what a video game is, but he gets her point. He sees that what Shan says is needed, and he trusts her... after all, she's the only one beside Peter and Devon who has ever really had to fight. He still can't help regretting the need to rob the kids of their youth.

Sensing the old man's turmoil, Carringer brings things back to the moment by pointing off to the far left of the ravine, "They're working with a few new spells... well, they're not actually new... they're sort of... revised."

"I get the point." Gran-D says to his friend with a smile.

In the ravine, Creb runs full force towards Yadar. Suddenly Yadar lifts up a staff that spews a long stream of red dust. As the dust hits Creb, the boy freezes in his tracks and swiftly turns to stone. After three seconds the human statue effect wears off, Creb shakes the dust from his head and continues charging forward.

"Well... it's a little short-lived," Carringer says in the spell's defense.

"So if you get it worked out, we'll have human-sized statues of soldiers all over our land?" asks Gran-D in a rather tongue-in-cheek manner.

Carringer glances down at Creb and imagines thousands of Creb statues everywhere. He says with a wince, "You have a point."

Shan muffles her giggle at the thought.

Moving away from the subject of statues, Shan points to a narrow ramp atop the other side of the ravine.

"Peter told me of a weapon they have beyond the wall that throws large stones."

"For what reason... oh, I see," Gran-D says, realizing it takes a shift in Spirin thinking to see things in terms of war. It's a shift he finds disturbing.

Two kids near the ramp roll, with some effort, a fairly round boulder up onto the chute and rest it against a wedge.

Carringer yells down to a boy in the ravine, "Ready?"

The boy nods energetically and Carringer waves to the two by the ramp. One pulls the wedge from in front of the boulder and it builds up speed as it rolls down the ramp. At the bottom it flies out of the chute towards the waiting boy.

The boy, holding a staff with two hands, raises it high with a sweeping motion as though painting the sky. A giant rectangular spider web forms in midair about ten yards in front of him. The web catches the boulder, taking most of the momentum out of it. The elastic strands that encase the rock stretch downward until it lies harmlessly motionless on the ground.

"I adapted another version of the spell that slices the rock into a hundred pieces... but we decided the pieces could still do harm," Carringer says energetically.

Gran-D looks at the ravine in dismay, "Why in Spirin would you have created such a spell in the first place?"

The question honestly puzzles Master Carringer.

After a moment of thought he shrugs, shakes his head and says innocently, "Because I could."

Carringer has often been more intrigued by the challenge of creating something than the reason for making it.

Shaking off his puzzlement over such a bizarre question, Carringer points to yet another spell all set up for testing.

A straw scarecrow stands in the ravine. Carringer has dressed it in black cloth to represent a soldier from the other side of the wall. He has even given it a mock lance to make it more intimidating... but it still looks like a scarecrow.

Roland steps out from below the ravine's overhang into the sunlight. He carries what appears to be a whip. It's clearly not for whipping the mock enemy figure since the scarecrow is too far away. Roland glances up at Carringer to get the go ahead.

Master Carringer nods.

Roland lashes the whip through the air with a great roundhouse swing and there's a loud snap. A visible ribbon of energy shoots from the end of the whip and races towards the scarecrow. Reaching its target, the ribbon slices the figure diagonally... the upper half topples to the ground, leaving what would be half a man just standing there.

Gran-D stands on the bluff speechless. The novelties of the other spell tests are wiped away by the harsh reality of this one. Staring at the halved man for the longest moment, he begins to have a hideous sense of what war might mean.

As if she knows what is racing through her grandfather's mind, Shan steps up and takes his hand.

She says nothing.

Chapter Thirty

Having used his spy globe to locate the main village of Acculas, Devon sets about transporting the team, two at a time, to a location close to it. Captain Pirus insists that he do it in such a manner as to avoid depleting his powers as he had done before. He even insists on reasonable breathing periods between transportation runs.

Finally arriving at the spot with the last two men, Devon won't admit it but he's glad Pirus required it done this way. He battles the idea that he is limited in any way; Pirus is not handicapped with such a youthful ego.

As Devon materializes, he hears Taligarr already running his mouth, "Who is in charge of this mission? He sends the only captive we have back with a message. My father... "

Pirus cuts him off by simply turning and going to check on his last arriving troops.

"How dare you!" huffs Taligarr.

Captain Pirus spins around and snaps, "If you challenge my command again, I will pack you and your kid brother off to your father... and trust me, he's a seasoned soldier who will honor my decision."

Pirus is not at all sure Kildemar will understand or not, but he's just about had enough of these two loose versions of soldiers... especially after the massacre.

Even Taligarr knows when to pull his fangs in. He walks away, trying not to appear to be pouting.

"You're playing with fire with those two, you know that?" Devon quietly says to Pirus.

Pirus isn't that happy with Devon either. He's a soldier who believes in a few less surprises than the boy wizard comes up with. Ever since he backed Devon's small deception on the plateau, Pirus has felt he has to keep his options open with this young magician; at times, he debates the wisdom of this.

The advantage of being a soldier is the illusion of not having to be caught up in the intrigue, but Pirus well knows it's only an illusion.

In the distance the team sees Ariet, the city-size tree village of Acculas. This massive vision even impresses Taligarr and Janick.

The unsaid question is: Will the people of this land talk after Devon's display of powers, or will they immediately try to kill in revenge for Janick's display of brutality?

Devon realizes he can't keep doing things solo or he will find himself without the muscle to carry out his plans. After a couple alliances have been built he may have more flexibility. He's pretty sure about Pirus, but now he has to start playing to Taligarr... and even Janick. If he continues to make enemies of them, he will have little leverage once back in Kildemar's court.

He goes to Taligarr, "With your approval, I could take point as we approach the city... as your emissary... in case they don't accept your message."

He's offering to be point man in a possible minefield... to someone who won't want to take the risk himself.

Taligarr takes a moment to think about it, "Only till we determine their intentions. In no manner are you to speak for Lord Kildemar. I represent our land... do you understand that?"

"Perfectly, sire," Devon answers.

A couple of giant birds fly overhead and then immediately set course for the city.

Pirus, amused by Devon's kowtowing, steps up to them and says, "We've been spotted. I suggest we give them a slight window of time for their powers-that-be to reflect. There's no need to encounter the hotter reactions of the lower ranks." Pirus knows their common soldiers will be hungry for blood after losing their own… at least, his men would be.

Taligarr nods his agreement to this strategy and retreats toward his brother.

"See you're trying to kiss up to the royals," Pirus tells Devon, more to make Devon aware that little passes his notice, than as a criticism.

"Can't kill'em," Devon glibly says.

Sometimes this boy's brazenness even bewilders Captain Pirus. He says, "Don't you worry such foolish comments around me could cost you your head?"

"I can't work in a vacuum… I must trust someone, and like it or not, you have that honor," Devon says with a smile, pushing the envelope to see if his back is covered. Alone, he cannot pull off his plans.

Taligarr and Janick keep their own company, thinking themselves above the common soldiers of the group, including Captain Pirus.

While the squad gives the people of Ariet… and themselves… a breather before approaching, a tiny sphere zips into the clearing and straight into Taligarr's hands. He glances around and observes that no one seems to have noticed the capsule's arrival.

Taligarr signals Janick and they walk further into the forest before opening the sphere. He presumes it comes in response to his message regarding Devon's solo excursion a few days back. Taligarr twists open the pod. He withdraws a single small slip of paper.

It reads: *"The boy's powers serve me... If need be, his head will serve me as well... Take no action till I command."*

He hands the slip to his brother with a satisfied smile.

Topolina loves the loose-fitting ceremonial robe that was left for her to wear; it's as colorful as her bird self.

Peter and Jarium pull at their own garments.

"No idea why I have to wear this frock," Jarium grumbles.

"On this, we agree. I feel like a Technicolor monk," says Peter. "No matter which way I pull it, it still feels odd." Glancing at Jarium, he adds, "At least yours isn't as bright."

Jarium admits, "Actually it's rather comfortable, but feels stupid."

They don't get much sympathy from Topolina, who admires hers in the mirror. She laughs at them, saying, "You two are starting to sound like an old married couple." She adds, "This is their land and we are guests... get over it."

Jarium hates letting her have the last word. He mumbles, "Maybe they're so bright to make us better targets."

Topolina just shakes her head as they wait for an escort to the feast.

"How long do you think we should wait before approaching?" Devon asks Pirus. The team has held its ground outside Ariet for a couple of hours now.

"Hard to tell. If I had eight men senselessly killed, there wouldn't be a time limit... but I'm not from here," says Pirus.

"If they're approachable, they'll send someone... if they don't, then we have to send a darker message."

Just then, in the distance, they see a lone man coming over the bridge leading from the city. Pirus and Devon get up. Taligarr and Janick quickly join them; the remaining men grab their weapons.

"No hostile action without my orders," Captain Pirus warns.

All nod their understanding, but hold their weapons tight... just in case.

Reaching the team, the emissary observes silently for a few long moments. Not in an angry or a frightened way... more like he is trying to size the group up. Both sides seem to be waiting for the other to speak first.

Finally, "My name is Marr. I represent Chief Adair of Acculas. It was wise of you to have initially remained at a distance, many of our troops itch for retribution." Marr pauses to hear a response, probably trying to gauge hostility.

"Have your chief... Adair, I think you said, come out and talk with me. I am the son of Lord Kildemar, ruler of the land of Goreipor," Taligarr says, with a clearly exaggerated tone of self-importance.

Marr muffles his amusement. Then he says, "That will not happen. You are in our land... an audience is ours to grant."

Diplomacy is new territory for Taligarr; he thinks on this a few seconds. "Then we demand entrance into your city, and to speak with your chief," Taligarr spouts arrogantly.

Marr, as if looking through Taligarr, looks over the group and says, "Which of you used magic?"

Before Devon can say anything, Taligarr takes a step toward Marr. "The one who used magic serves me. If you wish to address him, you will talk with me."

Having recently resolved to play more to Lord Kildemar's heirs, Devon lets Taligarr take the lead... unless he totally begins to screw things up. He stands his ground and says nothing.

"My chief will only allow the one with the magic into our village," Marr says with conviction.

"And I am the son of our chief, Lord Kildemar. If anyone should be invited into your village, it is I." With a slight pause, Taligarr adds, "I will meet with your chief and bring my witch with me... That is what I offer."

Taligarr attempts to sound statesmanlike though he would prefer simply to make demands. He tries to think of how his father would handle things. He also has no interest in entering the village alone without the protection Devon can offer... of course, that is not something he wants known.

Marr continues to scan the group. His eyes settle on Devon, as if he knows who has the magic. It's not that far of a leap since Devon doesn't have the same leathery completion as the rest. He looks back to Taligarr and says, "This is acceptable."

Then Marr turns and steps a short distance away, knowing the group will probably have things to say to each other. He stands near the edge of the bridge and waits.

Janick rushes up to his brother, "You sure you want to go in there alone?"

"We're here to make our demands known and with eight men I don't think we'll be able to storm the place," says Taligarr, knowing he would rather not be exposed, but he's not sure how else to play it.

Glancing over at Devon, Janick whispers a bit too loud, "You trust him?"

"If you whisper, the idea is to whisper," says Devon with a mischievous smile. "As Taligarr said, I serve him... and your father. He will be safe in my hands,"

Captain Pirus pulls Devon off to the side. He actually does whisper, "I don't like this... you go and allow Kildemar's son to get killed and it's my ass."

"Then... I'll try to get him killed," Devon responds.

"Try not to let him threaten to kill everyone... it would greatly increase the chances of your returning alive," says Pirus glibly.

Chapter Thirty-One

R amie is busy being Ramie. He's off exploring the fortress, just as Witch Racinda advised him not to do. All the dark passages and ominous aura of intrigue fascinate him. Being one of the only three people in Goreipor with magical powers also inflames his confidence, regardless of Devon's warnings.

As Ramie runs down a dark torch-lit passage, he races around a corner and straight into Lord Kildemar. The impact is hard enough to bounce Ramie back on his rump. He jumps to his feet, realizes whom he has slammed into and freezes.

"Boy, your name is Ramie, I think... is that not correct?" Kildemar says in a decidedly less intimidating tone than usual.

Ramie tries his best not to have the fear he feels show in his voice. His words still stumble as he says, "Yeah... I mean, yes, sir... you're not wrong. I mean... my name is Ramie."

"Settle down, boy, I mean Ramie... I don't eat kids."

Kildemar is not used to trying to sound friendly. He does his best, because unknown to Ramie, this encounter is not entirely accidental. He hasn't been stalking him, but Kildemar has been prepared to run into him sooner rather than later.

Ramie still appears uneasy, but his muscles relax a bit.

"How are your powers progressing?" Kildemar asks.

This sets Ramie back on edge, and it's visible.

Kildemar notices this and tries to soften down a bit more. "I know you have powers, like everyone else in your land... it's completely OK. I didn't mean to frighten you... just checking on your training."

Ramie's not sure how to respond to this; he thought his training was taking place in secret. He telegraphs his thoughts much more than he is aware.

"Do you think anything in my land is beyond my knowing?" Kildemar says without sounding intimidating.

"I... I guess not," Ramie stammers.

"Witch Racinda is...," Kildemar starts to say.

"She's not a witch," Ramie blurts out. Trying to back-pedal, "I mean... she's a sorceress... sir."

Actually Kildemar likes the hint of tenacity the boy shows. For the sake of his goals, he is willing to sound more lax than he truly is.

"I stand corrected... my sorceress. My father called her a witch for so long that the name stuck."

It's working to some degree since Ramies knees aren't knocking as much as before. Perhaps Ramie becomes too much at ease; to his own surprise, he blurts out, "Why aren't you letting me go home?"

Kildemar pauses, struggling to hold his composure while trying to appear like he's contemplating the question. Not many dare question him.

Finally he says, "You should consider yourself more an emissary from a neighboring land than a prisoner." He adds, "We have met with your leaders and pose your people no threat... They understand you're staying here for a while to help us."

"But... you're going to let me go home?" Ramie asks.

"Of course... eventually, but for now you are needed here, for the sake of both our lands," says Kildemar, lying through his teeth.

Ramie suspects this is all bull, but he likes the term 'emissary', though he's not quite sure what it means. He starts to say something more confidently, but Kildemar holds up his hand... He stops.

"We can discuss how you might be of help at another time, Ramie, but I am late for a meeting now."

After Kildemar says this, he strains a bit to pat Ramie's head, then abruptly turns and leaves... too much of being a '*nice guy*' is getting to him. The initial contact has been made... there will be sufficient time to put this naive boy to use.

Armed warriors fall in behind Taligarr and Devon, led by Marr, as soon as they cross the bridge. Taligarr keeps glancing over his shoulder at the added escort, while Devon doesn't seem to be disturbed in the least. Marr keeps moving forward, unconcerned over how the two perceive it.

Marr finally glances back, "I wouldn't eyeball them too much; some of the men that were killed were their friends."

"I didn't kill anyone... and those men dared to take us prisoner," says Taligarr in his defense. He doesn't realize how irresponsible this answer is.

"And you're their leader?" is all Marr says, not actually expecting an answer.

As they walk through the intricate web of the tree city, Devon and Taligarr are treated to a very different experience than Peter received; they are viewed with fear and mistrust. They sense little warmth from the multitudes they pass, and probably avoid outright hostility only because they are in the charge of Marr.

When Devon and Taligarr are led into the Big House... a festival does not greet them. They find a big empty room except for a number of stern-looking chieftains sitting at its far end and armed guards around the interior perimeter... it is as far from festive as a setting can get.

All Devon is grateful for is that they are not being led in bound, even though he could easily overcome that. Taligarr is irritated they are not encountering people who bow to him.

Marr turns and gestures for them to go no further when they reach a safe distance from the council of chieftains.

Chief Adair slowly stands and carefully looks the two up and down. After a long inspection, he says, "I see the resemblance... Your brother paid us a visit recently."

Taligarr is aware that Devon's brother could be exploring the lands as well, but until this point it has not been a certainty. Devon has been certain, both from knowing his brother and from the visions that have struck him.

"Was he treated with this disrespect?" blusters Taligarr.

"He killed no one," Chief Adair responds to Taligarr, with an equal intensity. Then he looks directly at Devon, "I was told you have magical powers, as your brother has. Is this true... are you as powerful as Peter?"

Trying to retain his authority, Taligarr interrupts with, "The boy serves me... and my father, Lord Kildemar."

Adair waves his hand to silence Taligarr, "I did not put the question to you."

"You would be wise to let me speak for the forces of my land, which are many," Taligarr replies arrogantly.

"Let me choose my own wisdom... Again, I asked you a question, young man."

Adair has little respect for Taligarr, but his view of Devon is still unclear.

Tiring of being the *lackey*, Devon speaks up, "It's true that my brother has powers, as I do... mine may be stronger, I don't truly know. The difference that should concern you is that my powers are much more aggressive."

"Did you use that aggression against my men?" Adair asks bluntly.

"The team I'm part of attacked and killed your men, but only in reaction to their hostility towards us... I am partly to blame," answers Devon with equal bluntness. He adds, "If I had chosen, many more of your men would have been casualties in our second encounter... but they are not. Do you require a further display of my abilities?"

Devon knows what Taligarr does not... that not to take responsibility for the squad's actions is an insult to the chieftains. He also wants to gently make his threat clear.

Chief Adair sits down among the chieftains. After a few seconds, he says, "And what do you come to my land to ask?"

Taligarr is not about to allow someone who serves his father to be the voice for Goreipor. He steps forward, ahead of Devon and announces, "In arriving in your... *village*, I saw some who might loosely be described as a military and many civilians. In my land of Goreipor, all are hardened soldiers. What we ask, or should I say, demand of your people is support when the walls between the lands come down."

"You sound very certain the walls will topple... when they've stood through many generations," says Chief Adair, realizing he can't ignore Taligarr completely.

"And no one has been able to cross the walls in many generations... Things change. Keep that in mind if you wish to protect your people. The land of Spirin offers little; they are a weak people. You would be advised to keep in mind what my land can offer... for or against your people," Taligarr replies, almost as a demand.

Chief Lorid, who sits at Chief Adair's side, speaks, "You have but one man who has magic. The rest of your men, by our accounts, are men as we are... maybe less."

Devon remains quiet, waiting to see how Taligarr answers this one.

"To each team, we assign one servant with magic power... which is very different than just one servant," Taligarr responds, lying through his teeth. He knows Devon wouldn't dare contradict him on this.

Concerned mumbles resound amongst the Chieftains. Adair holds out his hands in both directions to quiet the council.

Then he says to Taligarr and Devon, "We will consider what you've said in council. Upon your visiting our land again we will give you an answer. There is much for us to think about." He adds, "If there is any more aggression against my people, it will weigh heavily in our thoughts."

Devon sees this as reasonable progress, but when he senses that Taligarr is about to push further, he clears his throat... hoping this will be understood. Taligarr far from appreciates this action... he has to have the last word, even if unwise.

"I advise you to think hard and well on your answer before I return... the consequences could be dire," Taligarr says.

Chief Adair recognizes the bluster of one not actually in power and chooses not to dignify it with a response.

Devon thinks, *'How stupid the lord's son's final remark is.'* He keeps this thought to himself, even though he feels that Chief Adair can hear it... Maybe that's a good thing.

Chapter Thirty-Two

Another land... another feast.

The setting for this feast is in yet another very large common room somewhat as in Acculas, colorful and loud, but in its own style. The Big House in Acculas feels like a cross between a South Pacific and an Indian tribal gathering, while the giant room in Capulia's castle seems more like a cross between a pirate and a Viking gathering. One commonality is loud laughter.

The one big difference is the Capulians' love of their weapons... broadswords and axes worn by all the men, and half the women.

When Captain Varner brings Peter, Jarium and Topolina into the hall, a general roar of applause welcomes them.

Peter is a bit dismayed by how easily the population greets the first beings to ever cross their walls, at least in a good number of generations. Perhaps it's by decree of their leaders, but it feels more like a complete lack of fear. With this many weapons present the people can't be alien to conflict... but there's something else to it that he can't put his finger on.

For all that is rushing through Peter's head, Jarium's observation is simple, "Why are we the only ones wearing these stupid colorful frocks?"

Topolina shakes her head in dismay at her husband's relentless singlemindedness.

"Because the clothing is reserved for guests," Varner says.

Pulling this and that way on his robe, Jarium grumbles quietly, "Because nobody else would wear them."

Two humungous main tables sit in the foreground, flanking the king's throne. Each table has a row of what Peter guesses are nobles, seated in high-back chairs along the viewing side. The King sits on his throne with his Queen at his side.

Peter, not knowing the proper etiquette, assumes he should wait until they are introduced. His patience seems to bring a smile to the king's face.

Captain Varner steps forward and says, "I present to you King Crustivor and Queen Tania."

The King remains seated, eyeing the three visitors; his look is more of amusement than threat. Finally he stands, steps forward and announces in the manner kings seem to do, "We've waited a long time to meet someone from beyond a wall... and now we meet people from beyond two of our walls. It's a time for rejoicing... if you come with open hands."

"You have not asked why we come," Peter ventures to say.

"The whys will come later... now is time to feast," King Crustivor proclaims in a booming voice. He grabs a horn of wine from the table and raises it high. All in the hall follow suit. He yells, "To new friends!"

Serving wenches bring goblets to Peter and his friends.

"More drinking," Peter mumbles quietly.

Jarium elbows him and laughs, "The only way you'll learn to drink is to practice."

Everyone toasts... and the feast is on!

Marr and a couple more level-headed soldiers who won't seek revenge escort Devon and Taligarr over the bridge. Some distance from Pirus' men they turn back with no farewell. Devon and Taligarr walk the last distance alone.

"They dare to question our authority, our power," Taligarr grumbles as they go.

"If they questioned our power, we would have not come back intact. It was a win, Commander Taligarr... see it for what it is," Devon says, hoping to avoid further actions. He truly believes they accomplished as much as they could, given the handicap of bloody hands they came with.

Captain Pirus greets them with, "I'm amazed... you two came back without getting killed... and, I assume, without killing anyone."

"Nice to see you, too," says Devon.

Passing by Pirus, Taligarr says, "Prepare to move on."

That's fine with Pirus... he's not comfortable with such a small force within range of such a large one.

A short while later the team is pulling together their gear to move out. As they often are, Taligarr and Janick are off in the distance on their own.

All of a sudden a speedy little gnat of a sphere zips towards Taligarr but, unlike before, the message sphere whips through the group to find him. Taligarr self-consciously catches it and quickly stuffs the sphere in his pocket... as if he were getting away with hiding it... He's not.

Keeping up the façade, Taligarr turns away from the group and, as stealthily as he can, brings out the sphere. He opens it and quickly reads the tiny note.

Pirus, standing off at a distance, watches this laughable attempt at spy craft. He half expects to see Taligarr do something absurd like eating the paper.

Tto cut through it all, Captain Pirus walks directly to Taligarr and his brother, "What does your father have to say?"

Caught like a cat with a bird in his mouth, Taligarr says, "This is a private communication."

"If they regard our movements, they are not. Unless he's sending you a birthday card, I...," Pirus starts to say.

Cutting him off, Taligarr blurts out, "Lord Kildemar demands our return immediately." It's clear by his tone that no reason has been given and he is somewhat distraught by the orders.

"So your daddy wants you to come home," says Pirus, knowing it will irk Taligarr no end.

In truth, such an order coming from Kildemar, without explanation should cause all to be concerned... It could mean anyone's... or everyone's... head. Pirus has no time to worry over such matters.

The grand hall in Capulia is akin to the one in Acculas in yet another way... the people are fond of their loud games. Here it reminds Peter of films about Vikings he had seen as a youth. Most of the games have something to do with their weapons. Over to one side, two heavy-set men hurl broad axes at a wooden slab target to the whoops and hollers of the crowd. King Crustivor and his family are among the revelers.

With the throwing match over, a somewhat drunken bearded man in the crowd yells out, "Laasper, how about a rematch... if you're not too drunk?"

A blond-haired man of about thirty who sits behind the main table uses his chair as a step-stool to climb atop the table. He yells back, "Yar... I'll meet you anytime, drunk or sober."

Once standing on the long table, Laasper unsheathes his broadsword and the crowd cheers. A bit drunk as well, Laasper bows to the crowd with a big smile and jumps down in front of the table.

Leaning into Peter and his friends, Captain Varner says, loud enough to be heard over the crowd, "That's Laasper, the King's oldest."

Topolina finds she has to yell to be heard, "Are they really going to fight?"

"No... They're just playing. Sometimes they get nipped, but it's all just good fun," says Varner, as he watches them get ready for the match.

By the nature of the *good fun* the people of Capulia indulge in, Peter surmises that they are not strangers to warfare. Whether they embrace it is another matter.

As the swords clang in the good-hearted fight, Varner leans in again and gestures towards two other people a little farther down the main table, "That's King Crustivor's other two children, Obarr and Lonny."

Obarr is a husky young man of twenty-two and Lonny's an attractive woman who looks about twenty.

Topolina laughs, "She's not going to be challenged to a fight, is she?"

"Not many would dare... she's as good with a sword as she's pretty. I should know, I taught her," Captain Varner responds.

The bout continues with amazing agility considering the size of the swords the men wield... and how drunk the contestants are. Peter has no doubt that these men of Capulia, though appearing to be quick with a laugh, would be scary adversaries to face on a battlefield. But, so are the men of Goreipor.

It also dawns on Peter that, even though he doesn't see their behavior as fake, this display of their prowess with weapons might be put on to make a point for him and his friends. Maybe the old King wants this point made before discussing the reason Peter is in his land. He cringes at the thought that too much of Devon's suspicious nature has rubbed off on him.

The current fight ends when a humble Laasper, who's clearly winning, calls the match a draw... probably before his friend Yar gets hurt... or loses face. Yar is happy to call it a draw.

Festivities have gone on for hours, and, even though Peter has tried to talk of substance with King Crustivor, he has been brushed off every time. There's always another match to watch or toast to make. Peter has had to turn down the advances of a few attractive wenches, and Topolina has successfully shooed a few away from Jarium.

What Peter figured would eventually come happens when Obarr jumps out on the floor and challenges him to a friendly fight. Peter is way too drunk for such a match.

"Thank you for the honor of a challenge, but I surrender to your skills with a sword... truth is, I don't think I could even lift one right now." Peter says this knowing it may not be sufficient to satisfy honor, but he has no interest in getting his head bashed in either.

"I hear you have other talents," says King Crustivor. The other Capulians applaud the idea of seeing Peter try to entertain them.

Peter suspects that the king knows exactly what he's doing. But he's not as prone as Devon to demonstrate his powers, especially in front of those he's not sure would be amiable to an alliance.

Jarium can sense what's rushing through Peter's head and decides to get the boy off the hook. He jumps over the table and takes a stance in front of Obarr.

"If you'll allow me, I will take his challenge."

Topolina doesn't look pleased be her husband's choice, but would never shame him by publicly protesting it. She also knows Jarium would fare much better in the ring than Peter.

She senses Peter doesn't want to expose his powers yet, so someone has to represent the group.

"My honor," Obarr says with a smile and a taunting bow.

The bout goes on for a good ten minutes of serious sword clanging, both men holding their own, and neither taking more than a few small nicks.

Getting a stealthy look from his father, Obarr finally holds his broadsword out in both hands and places it on the floor before Jarium. This is the sign of a draw and respect to his opponent. Ten minutes with a broadsword would test the strongest man's stamina. Jarium is fairly worn out and more than happy to call it a draw.

The rest of the crowd, including King Crustivor and Topolina, stand and applaud both men.

Before leaving the ring, Jarium gives a wink to Peter that seems to be understood. At least Peter thinks he understands it. Jarium nods for him to proceed.

"If you please, your highness, my friend has another skill that is as magnificent as his bravery," Peter tells the King.

With this, Jarium waves people to clear an area around him. Once there is enough space, Jarium spins around and transforms from his man-self to his saber-tooth tiger self. The crowded room is struck silent and all back away a step, until King Crustivor stands and applauds. The crowd's cheers start small, but grow to a deafening roar as Jarium reverses the process and becomes a man again. He takes a bow... and gives Peter a wink.

Peter knows this is exactly what was needed, and is more than grateful that Prince Jarium knows it as well.

The feast continues well into the night and becomes something of a blur to Peter.

Except for the snores of the many passed out revelers, the hall is quiet. Peter is one of those passed out. He feels a foot push on his shoulder a few times and gradually manages to open his eyes. Staring down at him are King Crustivor, Laasper, Jarium and Topolina. Jarium splashes a few drops of wine at Peter's face to get him more focused and offers him some hair of the dog... Peter refuses, more than willing not to see another *dog* in his life.

"Now, young Peter, it's quiet and time to talk of the *why* of your visit to my land," says King Crustivor quietly as he gestures for him to follow.

Peter sits up and shakes the sleep away. He sees the others head across the room towards a set of doors, careful not to step on any sleeping bodies. He gets up and follows, wishing it could have waited till the next day... but he has been pushing to talk all night; now how can he refuse. If this is the King's negotiating strategy, it's a sneaky one... and damn good.

Chapter Thirty-Three

Gran-D stands on the bluff overlooking Shan's training grounds. Her forces have continued to grow and there are quite a few older kids down in the ravine working out. *Kids* is quickly becoming the wrong term since most are at least in their late teen years, but more importantly... what they're studying is aging them beyond childhood. Gran-D should be smiling at the progress, but he's not; what he sees, disturbs him. They are taking too well to aggression.

At one end of the ravine, he sees kids practicing defensive spells derived from old spells Carringer has come up with. This doesn't bother Gran-D as much as what he sees at the other end of the ravine... kids practicing one-on-one combat. Some engage in hand-to-hand fighting, others wield sticks representing swords and spears. This is the harshest, rawest form of violence he's ever seen... and his granddaughter is in the middle of them... teaching them how to do it.

The old man, once convinced that paving the way for what he sees as an inevitable prophecy is best for Spirin, now questions his wisdom... the problem with such questioning is that the time to change course has long passed.

Taking a break from training, Shan heads up to join Gran-D.

As she comes up on the bluff, Gran-D sees something even more disturbing taking place down in the ravine.

A sword match between Yadar and another boy is getting overly aggressive. Roland, who has been given some authority over the trainees, blows a whistle to stop the match. The boy breaks off his attack, but Yadar strikes another blow after the whistle, sending his opponent sprawling to the ground.

Roland jumps in and catches the length of Yadar's wooden sword as he's taking another swing at the downed kid. Roland wrenches the sword from Yadar's hands but Yadar charges forward at him. The two exchange aggressive pushes back and forth. Finally Yadar slugs Roland, in the same way Peter had long ago slugged him.

Up on the bluff, Shan turns to see what concerns Gran-D. Before the fight below progresses any further, she levels the lance she now often carries and an energy ball fires from its end. It explodes close enough to get the boy's attention, but far enough away not to harm him.

Down in the ravine the two boys break it off. It's clear that Roland takes the warning of the blast as Shan intended; he nods to Yadar that it's over. Yadar takes it as the last straw.

He yells up at Shan, "You are teaching us to kill, and I don't stop till my enemy is down. I've had enough of this half training, half nice guy stuff. Fighting is not about fair play."

Yadar slaps his hands together in a way of saying enough, turns and storms away. As he goes, Creb, Kyra and a few more kids turn and follow him, clearly showing that lines have been drawn.

All Shan can do is watch; attacking the kids who are leaving would serve no purpose. Roland looks up at her and shrugs.

She turns to Gran-D, "I'll get them back after tempers settle down."

"You sure about that? Child, I'm here because of complaints the members of the Council have been getting from parents about their kids acting differently... some kids not even coming home at all," Gran-D says.

Shan doesn't look like this is news to her; she just looks frustrated. Trying to avoid what's rushing through her head, she attempts to address at least part of what he says, "Some of the older kids have set up a camp beyond the ridge, but I told them they have to keep checking in at home regularly... I guess they haven't been doing it."

Gran-D sees there's much more bothering her, "Shan, you know I can see you... what's really on your mind?"

Finally she blurts out, "Gran-D, I don't know what I'm doing out here. I'm introducing them to a side they've never seen in themselves. I'm not just introducing them to violence... I'm drilling it into them. They each react differently to it."

She starts to stomp away, but turns. Pointing at the exiting kids, "Yadar is right! You can't be half-willing to kill! How do I bring them back from where I'm taking them?"

Shan breaks down crying. Gran-D takes her in his arms.

"Devon and Peter are night and day over the idea of power. You can't always control what comes out. All you can do is your best," says Gran-D. After a few moments he adds, "We did such a good job of training violence out of them that we thought it didn't exist anymore. Maybe it was just buried and now we've opened the door... because it's needed. Shan, all you can do is try to guide them when they come through that door."

Shan knows his words are meant to ease her mind... but they don't manage to ease her conscience.

Gran-D sees the torment, but can't soothe it.

"We were wise to do all this in secrecy, I'm not sure if the people of Spirin would understand yet... no matter how important it is."

"I'm not sure I do," Shan says as she wipes her eyes.

A spy globe floats in a room of dark wood and rows of books. The room has a lawyerly feel. Within the globe is an image from high above of the ravine where Shan's recruits train. The image zooms in, not on Shan and Gran-D, but on the small group of kids who have left with Yadar.

Master Sashaw sits back in his desk chair as he continues to watch the spy globe. Lying on the desk before him are two tiny message spheres... one is split open and a small slip of paper rests next to it. Sashaw reaches out, picks up the slip and silently reads it again. He glances back up at the globe with a face that seems torn with conflict.

The team falls out of the door near the Goreiporian camp by the wall. They're greeted by dark skies, cracking thunder and a drenching rain. Through the storm they can barely see the encampment. Each finger of lightning is amplified when reflected by the mirror wall.

"To the camp before we drown," yells Pirus.

Devon glances up at the angry sky and wonders how high the walls must go... they have just left a land with crystal clear skies. The other thing crossing his mind is that the pendant, in the hands of Taligarr, seems to drop them roughly close to where they left. He has a gut feeling that, in his hands, he could better control its targeting... but it's only a gut feeling for now. He keeps his feelings to himself.

As they make their way down towards the encampment, Devon conjures a half-shield that floats over his head, keeping the rain at bay. The shield infuriates the soaked Taligarr and Janick... Devon knows it.

Once in the camp they pass a corral with many more horses than the number of men in the camp. Pirus suspects they haven't seen the last of the rain. Before they even get to a tent, a soldier comes out to meet them.

"Captain, Lord Kildemar sent horses for you to set out immediately for the fortress," the soldier says, with a bit of apology in his voice.

Pirus sees the urgency is playing on his men's fears.

The Captain pushes by him with, "Lord Kildemar can wait till my men are fed." After all, they're a good night's ride from the fortress.

Peter can hear Jarium and Topolina enter the room but the idea of opening his eyes to the overly bright sunlight is not a welcome thought. Sledgehammers already dance in his head.

With one eye slightly open, he says, "Promise me that whatever land we visit next... no matter how great an army they have, if anyone even mentions a festival... we run."

Topolina lets out a laugh a little too loud for Peter and he grabs his head in pain.

There's a booming knock on the door.

"Shoot whoever that is," Peter moans.

Jarium goes and opens the door. Laasper comes in, takes one look at Peter and laughs.

"Our young wizard is new to the drink, I take it?" he says. "No matter... it's time to rise, young Peter, my father has thought on what you said last night and requires your presence." He then glances at Jarium and Topolina, "The presence of all is requested in the throne room when the sun is high."

Jarium glances out of the window and sees the sun is almost there. They have allowed Peter to sleep a long spell this morning. He nods to Laasper that they will be ready.

Laasper leaves with one last laugh at the ailing Peter.

"What did I say last night?" Peter moans.

                     STEVE GRAZIANI

Topolina smiles, "Actually you were quite eloquent and passionate about your cause... for being so... impaired."

"I think his timing was on purpose," Peter grumbles as he manages to sit up and finally open both his eyes.

"Of course it was; he's a crafty one... your words came out true... " Jarium says in support of both sides. Being uncommitted, though, he adds, "from your point of view."

When Peter, Jarium and Topolina arrive in the throne room, they find King Crustivor, his three children and Captain Varner standing around a map on the table. Absent from the family gathering is the Queen.

Crustivor laughs, "My wife is busy fuming. She's upset with me over trapping you like I did last night... I hope you forgive me. At times I like to hear tongues that are... let's say, that are not well rehearsed."

"Did I make any sense?" Peter asks.

"You stood well for yourself... all things considered," King Crustivor assures him. "I especially liked the show of your wizardry."

Puzzled, Peter glances over to Jarium.

"You became invisible... once... or twice... I don't remember," Jarium says with a guilty smile.

Topolina slyly holds up two fingers.

"Enough of niceties... To the matter at hand," King Crustivor says as he takes a seat on his throne, now donning the look of authority. "My people are not new to war; for that matter, we enjoy a good war. But that is warring among the people of Capulia. Once the war is done, we mend fences... and eventually drink together."

This doesn't make any sense to Peter; it shows on his face.

"It clears out the bad blood, and reminds us to enjoy peace... to enjoy the moment... till next we fight. No one owns anyone at the end of a conflict... just a few more ships or a little more land," Crustivor says, not really expecting Peter to understand. "What you talked of last night is a darkness our gods warned would come... it is a different kind of war. It's a kind of war where we risk all we have. The gods have foretold us of victors and slaves... they haven't told us who is what."

"We have a Prophecy...," Peter starts to say.

The King cuts him off, "You spoke of it last night... and you spoke of not knowing the outcome either. To my people, fighting comes natural... slavery does not. It would go against all our gods."

Peter can't mount any argument yet because, in truth, he has no idea what he said to the King last night... and he senses the King is not finished.

"I've held counsel with my family and commanders and there are strong arguments to keep out of your affairs," says King Crustivor. From Peter's face, he sees his words are not setting well with him. "But, I am the King and sometimes I have to act against counsel. Burying our heads is a poor defense. That said... I am committing nothing to your cause other than an open mind."

Peter's youth gets in his way; his mind screams for simple, straightforward answers. Perhaps he's just too anxious to find a simple solution for a complicated problem... and he needs to exercise a little patience. Then, perhaps he's too caught up in his own side of things to be willing to hear answers from other perspectives... another handicap of youth he rarely sees.

"My son has urged me to follow the example of Prince Jarium's father and attach a representative to your exploration to get a better feel of things. I suspect this comes more from his desire for adventure than statesmanship but, regardless, there's a grain of wisdom to it," says King Crustivor.

Jarium makes no remark, but he totally understands. He is on this quest more for the excitement of visiting lands long denied him than to bring his people into a war. In truth, he is not sure such a war is inevitable... or that the walls can be brought down.

"To that goal Laasper, my eldest, will accompany you for a time," the king says.

Princess Lonny clears her throat rather loudly.

An irritated look washes over King Crustivor's face. "And... I've been bullied into allowing my daughter, Lonny, to accompany you as well."

It's clear from Peter's expression that he welcomes the addition of Laasper to his quest, but is troubled by the inclusion of the king's daughter. He doesn't want to be responsible for her safety.

The king probably sees this concern on his face, but Peter expresses it anyway, "Your Highness, I have no idea what we will encounter in the other lands... they may not be as gracious as you have been."

"I've already lost the argument with her and her mother. Do you think I'm going to lose face by allowing you to win? The matter is settled," he says, but he adds, "This does not mean that I do not place their safety in your hands."

At this moment, Peter has a choice: He can refuse to take on the responsibility and lose all connection with Capulia, or he can shoulder the extra weight. He's also a bit surprised that Captain Varner has not been included.

Finally he says, "I accept you decision and will do my best to protect your family."

King Crustivor tries not to let it show, but there's a hint in his eyes that he has almost wished that Peter would refuse.

Laasper and Lonny both appear happy about their forthcoming adventure. Unfortunately, the king's younger son, Obarr, is not happy about being excluded. The king can hardly send all his heirs off on an adventure. Captain Varner looks a bit disappointed as well.

As for Peter's current companions, Jarium shows his dislike of the situation, while Topolina seems supportive of having another woman along. After all, Captain Varner has noted that she is a competent warrior in her own right.

"Your Highness, may I ask you of another matter?" Peter says. At the king's nod, he says, "You spoke of something your gods warned of... Was this oral folklore or was it written anywhere?"

"There is much folklore in my land... even more if you take into account all the people of Capulia... very little is in writing," King Crustivor answers.

Peter holds out the pendant that hangs from his neck, "Have you ever seen anything like this?"

"The tool you use to cross the walls... no. What are you seeking?" he asks.

"Probably nothing, but there is something I'd like to explore before leaving your land. Would it be possible for Captain Varner to assist me for a day?" Peter asks.

"As you wish... as long as you share with me what you discover... if anything," Crustivor responds.

Peter nods his agreement even though, if his suspicions are correct, he may not be willing share the outcome... at least not for the present. He knows that if he discovers something and doesn't share the knowledge, he must not be caught. Perhaps it was a mistake requesting Captain Varner's help. It crosses his mind that Devon would not have made such a blunder.

Chapter Thirty-Four

Captain Pirus and Devon have been summoned to the war room. Both are tired from the night's ride but as they stand there alone, without Pirus' squad, they feel all's well... or at least heads aren't going to roll. If Kildemar were going to mete out punishment, he would want an audience... that's more his style. Now the big question is, what is the urgency to return?

The doors leading from Kildemar's quarters open and Lord Kildemar enters, followed by Taligarr and Janick.

Devon doesn't care for the satisfied smirks on the Lord's two son's faces. He has to remind himself that in a planned, short-term confrontation with a small group of Goreiporians, his powers would prevail... but he's far from invincible.

The one person conspicuously absent is Witch Racinda. As best Devon can recall, he's rarely met with Kildemar without her presence; he's assumed she is Kildemar's protection against his powers. Either the Witch is no more, or matters she is not privy to are about to be discussed. Either way, he figures this ups his stack of chips in the game.

"My sons have disclosed to me much information... some is of some use... other things show their weakness," says Kildemar.

The smirks on Taligarr and Janick's faces disappear.

"Problem is these things show our weakness as well. Unfortunately, this comes as no surprise to me," says Kildemar.

Devon wonders if he's going to have to go on the offensive or not. Pirus doesn't seem phased by it; words are words... he'll know when action is needed and, hopefully, know whom to take it against.

"Unlike Spirin, the other lands you have visited thus far have warriors as we are. I have no doubt we could vanquish them, but in warfare I don't believe in gambling. Two men with swords on equal ground... either could win, especially if both are experienced soldiers. I plan on giving ourselves an overwhelming advantage." He says this with a slight glint in his eyes, something Kildemar rarely has.

He looks directly at Devon, "In your case, I suspect you had a dark side before you had powers... The funny thing about getting power... it will often grow a dark side of its own."

Now Devon is completely lost as to what is going on.

"I own a person on Spirin's almighty Council who I can exploit... Soon you and my witch will not be the only ones with powers who serve me," Lord Kildemar announces.

Devon would love to question this but realizes he will get no answers before Kildemar chooses, and the dark lord's style tells him that is not now. If this is true, he knows that this could be a major game changer.

Peter watches the horizon as Captain Varner's ship slips out of the port. Topolina steps beside him and whispers, "What are we really looking for?"

"Like I said, I don't know yet," Peter responds. Her look says that will not do. He glances around to see no one is close and then he holds the pendant away from his neck slightly. "Another one of these."

Peter knows he can't be secretive with everyone if he expects support.

Jarium was more than happy to pass on this outing since he did not take well to the last sea voyage. Even when Peter told him they would not be going far, he politely declined.

On the other hand, Varner was not willing to leave port without Laasper on board. Peter well knows the king's son is there to watch him. That's fair enough, but Peter has no interest in bringing Laasper into his confidence yet... especially regarding something valuable Peter intends to steal from the land of Capulia.

Peter feels a pair of eyes burning into the back of his head. Turning around, he sees those eyes belong to Laasper who approaches with Captain Varner at his side.

"We've about cleared the port. I need to know to where I'm setting sail, more than just to follow the tack we sailed in on." Varner clearly doesn't appreciate Peter's vagueness about this mission.

"When we approached the island, we passed a point where I sensed something, I'm not sure what. I can't tell you the exact point till we are aligned with the landmarks," says Peter. This is truthful, without giving away too much.

The Captain takes a puff from his pipe, trying to decide what Peter is not saying. Laasper's glare is even less trusting.

Varner turns and tells Master Mate Yarlick, "Keep her under quarter sail." He yells to the helmsman, "Steer west by southwest." After setting the course he glances back at Peter, "OK, we're slow on the course. You yell out when you think you see your landmarks."

Peter nods his appreciation that he is not pushing for more information... yet, but he knows that will not remain so. With that settled for the moment, Peter heads for the bow of the ship to make out the landmarks in the reverse direction of how he saw them on their approach to the island.

He's still aware of Laasper with his eyes glued on him. Peter liked Laasper better when they were all drunk at the feast.

The masts of the ships in the port disappear as they round the point and Peter knows they are getting close. He alternates his view between the points on the land and the pendant in his hand, trying to remember everything as he saw it several days ago.

He finally sees the distinctive rock on the hillside that is one of his markers. Glancing around to the right, he looks for the stand of trees. There it is. Now the two have to come to a right angle. Before they completely align, Topolina taps his arm and points at his chest... the jewel in the center of the pendant glows faintly.

"Captain Varner, we are very close," Peter yells.

"Master Mate, drop the wind," Varner yells out.

Peter pretends he's only judging by physical landmarks when he yells again, "We are on the spot." In truth, the glow of the jewel is at its brightest. Having been spoken to by the pendant, he now slips it back under his shirt.

"Drop anchor," Varner yells out. Considering they are only under quarter sail, which has already emptied its wind, the ship smoothly comes to with the anchor's bite.

"What now, lad?" Captain Varner asks Peter.

The water in which they lie is as clear blue as the Caribbean... with proper perspective, it could be read like an open book. Peter conjures up a spy globe that forms over the middeck. Sailors back away from it in fear but, fascinated by the phenomenon, Laasper stands his ground.

Within the globe appears a bird's eye view from about a hundred feet above, down towards the sea below them.

"I'm jealous... I thought that was my special gift," whispers Topolina.

"Your way of doing it is probably more fun," Peter replies.

Peter could have simply disappeared and flown up for the view, but it is a good opportunity to accomplish two tasks: First to get the view, and second to impress Laasper. He wants the young prince who is joining his team to know there is more to him than meets the eye... becoming invisible doesn't quite do that... besides he apparently already did that the other night.

The image floating in the globe is not new to Capulian sailors. From the crow's nest, many have been able to see the sea's floor with a fair amount of distortion. From high cliffs along the sea's edge, they've seen a different kind of distortion. But... from a hundred feet up, peering straight down, they can now see a painting, where before they only saw sketches.

Captain Varner steps up beside Peter. "What are you looking for down there? We've all seen the bones and ghosts of dead ships off this point. Not a man sailing these seas doesn't have a tale of this treacherous stretch of water when it's angered."

Peter points up at the spy globe as the image within it climbs higher. Distinctly articulated rectangular patterns mix with other patterns below; all radiating out from what appears to be a roughly drawn circle. With a little imagination it looks like the roadmap of a city... but one has to be looking for it.

"So what are we looking at?" asks Varner.

"Do you not have tales of an ancient city around here?" Peter asks in return.

Captain Varner points at the cliffs off to the right, "Agula. Everyone from Capulia knows the ancient tales of the city of Agula... yet few know much about the city. The ruins are atop that hill."

"Are there any writings from this Agula?" Peter asks.

"The royal family has some old scrolls. Some are readable; others are in a language they don't recognize. Are you in search of the prophecy you asked the king about?" he responds.

Peter has set in motion what he wants. He points back up at the spy globe, "I think the ruins of a temple of Agula are in the waters below us."

Varner, now joined by Laasper, peers closely at the globe that floats well above the middeck.

"Even if Agula wasn't much larger than your history remembers, it could be that a temple was outside the main city," Peter offers as an explanation.

Laasper pays token homage to the past, like most in Capulia, but being a young warrior, can really only deal with what is present and directly in front of him... abstractions are for older men like his father.

He glances over the ship's rail and turns to Peter, "All right, maybe there's a temple down there. That doesn't tell me why we are here. Why are old ruins important?"

Captain Varner is older, and brother-in-law to Laasper's father, so he does see more abstractions. He glances back and forth between the globe and the water, and then says, "Because young Peter here is looking for a parallel prophecy left by the ancients... is that not so?"

Peter smiles in agreement, even though that is not what he's looking for at all. It does cross his mind, though, that it would be interesting to find such an item... but he's actually more like Laasper, only concerned with what he can use at the moment... another pendant.

These academic pursuits bore Laasper; he wants to be done with them. "So in addition to being a wizard, you can breathe under water? If not, why are we here?"

"I haven't actually tried it out, but I think so. And we're here because I think it's important," says Peter.

This is not a lie... he's not sure it will work. If he were to actually say what he's after, he would probably lose Capulia. He also says this to set some ground rules; if Laasper is going to join Peter's adventure, Peter doesn't want every decision he makes questioned. This doesn't guarantee that Laasper won't question him... but it might establish some protocol.

A few minutes later Peter stands near an opening in the ship's railing, Topolina close at his side. He has a rope around his waist, from which hang some heavy chain links... and there's a cannonball near his feet. To reinforce the pretense of what he's after, he has a thin tie line that he will supposedly attach to any ancient tablets he might find on his dive. Peter has already told them that if he tugs on the line to pull it up.

"You sure about this?" Topolina asks.

"Not really," Peter says with a hint of nervousness in his voice. He has kept on his shirt to hide the pendant resting against his chest. Peter figures the only way he will find the other pendant before he drowns is with the guidance of the one he already has.

Seeing the concern in Topolina's eyes, he adds, "The weight belt has a slipknot; if I get into trouble I'll drop the weights and come up."

Before he loses his nerve, Peter bends down, grabs the cannonball and jumps off the side of the boat. As he hits the water, Topolina sees Peter has generated a large invisible protective globe around his upper body, no doubt to be his air supply... if it will be enough is an unknown, but now she sees the reason for all the weight.

With Peter gone, so is the spy globe. Topolina knows how foolhardy her husband can get in trying to accomplish a goal, and senses Peter could be just as bad. Not willing to just wait and hope he makes it back up, and not caring who sees it, she transforms into her bird self. She flies up and begins circling the sky above the dive site.

Half enveloped in his air bubble, Peter still quickly descends to the sea's floor. As he's about to touch down, he releases the cannonball and he lands softly. His estimate of the amount of weight tied to his waist to counter the buoyancy of the air pocket is pretty accurate... he finds he can both breathe and move with relative ease. Peter can almost imagine what walking on the moon would feel like... his steps float.

Peter pulls his pendant out, hoping it will serve as a divining rod to the pendant he believes rests here amongst the relics of an ancient time. As his eyes get used to the wavering images of the water, Peter sees collapsed marble columns and soft edged stairs, reclaimed by coral almost into obscurity.

It crosses his mind that his pendant is already glowing brightly... how can he determine if he's getting closer to another one? As if the pendant has heard Peter's thoughts, the center jewel dims slightly. It dims even further as Peter sets off in one specific direction... he now has a guide.

Peter shifts directions and the jewel encourages him by brightening. Directly ahead of him in the distance is a lone arch that has escaped collapse; the building it once led into has not fared as well. The novelty of moonwalking underwater wears off as Peter reminds himself that his globe only contains so much air... he only has so much time.

High above, Topolina continues to circle and observe. Her eyesight is much sharper as a bird than as a human. She vaguely discerns the movement of a non-aquatic being about fifty feet deep that she suspects is Peter... she finds herself silently urging him to get his tail end moving.

Peter passes through the lone arch far too slowly. His only encouragement is the jewel getting brighter... his time is running out. Suddenly the jewel goes dark and panic strikes Peter, but it brightens again. The jewel now pulses.

Topolina, becoming more anxious, sees Peter's bubble getting larger, meaning he's rising... she hopes. The distorted circle keeps rising and she's sure he's out of trouble. Suddenly the bubble bursts, erupting a massive burp of remaining air, or carbon dioxide, to the surface.

In the depths of the water, Peter has gone limp; he begins to drift downward, his arms and legs dangling in the current.

Topolina is not a fish-diving bird, which she's grateful for since she doesn't even like the taste of fish. Nonetheless, she arches her wings back to streamline herself and rockets down into the sea's surface.

Propelling herself as deep as she can, Topolina swoops under the limp Peter. The turbulence formed by her large bird body causes his body to swirl upward. Transforming back into her human form, Topolina grabs Peter by his shirt collar and strokes hard for the surface.

Breaking out of the water, Topolina waves frantically towards those on the ship, doing her best to keep Peter's head above water.

Chapter Thirty-Five

A bunch of the maverick kids like Yadar, Creb and Kyra, being sorcerers, have created a tent city that's slightly more than an actual tent city. They've conjured up all kinds of imaginative small structures ranging from mini-pyramids to floating bubbles to live in. Some of the kids have permanently moved out of their family homes, while others play hooky from home as much as their parents will tolerate it.

The kids still come to Shan's gatherings, but the frictions continue to grow. Their chief reason for coming is they don't want to miss out on any of the new defensive spells Master Carringer introduces... at least until Shan decides to no longer invite them.

While most gather to head to training, Yadar kicks back, clearly not planning on going anywhere.

Kyra storms up to him, as if it was part of an ongoing argument between them, and demands, "You giving up?"

From his smile she can tell something else is going on, but Yadar offers no explanation beyond, "Maybe I'll catch up later."

She shakes her head and leaves without him.

A couple of minutes after she's gone, a wisp of smoke comes down to join Yadar left alone in the maverick camp. The wisp turns into Master Sashaw.

"So what's a big shot Master like you want with me?" Yadar says irreverently.

Ramie turns a corner in the halls of the fortress and sees Devon walking along with Captain Pirus. He picks up speed to catch them, his enthusiasm building as he nears them. Pirus turns in time to see Ramie rushing forward.

"Have other business to get to," says Pirus, splitting off.

Devon is surprised by the suddenness of this until he sees the reason for Pirus' departure heading straight for him.

Pirus' exit is not unwelcome to Ramie since the man truly scares him. Ramie picks up steam.

As a preemptive strike, Devon spins around, "You're bubbling over with energy... in the next few feet, bring it down a bit."

Ramie freezes in his tracks... but only for a second. Then he barges forward again, talking as he goes, "Some of my friends are coming."

Now he has Devon's attention.

"What do you mean... your friends are coming?"

"Well... they're not really all my friends... but, other kids from home," Ramie says, trying to clarify. Then his energy perks up again, "And I'm going to be in charge of them... or, at least, partly in charge."

He pulls a lieutenant's military patch out of his pocket and waves it at Devon.

"I don't have a uniform yet but when I do, I'll be a lieutenant," Ramie blusters.

The day is full of surprises.

Devon isn't sure what Witch Racinda or Lord Kildemar did to the kid, but he's definitely singing a new, and very different, tune. For the moment, there's not a hint of desire to go home in his words or tone.

"Now settle down and tell me exactly what you're talking about... and where you heard this nonsense," Devon demands.

"Actually... I don't know exactly how it's happening... and the king told me," Ramie responds.

"King? You mean Kildemar?" Devon asks.

"Yeah... him. He said others with powers are going to come and help... and they'll need a friendly face to greet them... that's me," Ramie says enthusiastically.

"I guess... congratulations, kid."

Devon turns to walk away, a bit dumbfounded. At this point there's little more he can get from Ramie, but much he needs to think about.

Ramie's a little disappointed, but shakes it off, looks at his new patch and heads the other direction.

Now Devon has a slight idea of what Kildemar was talking about so vaguely, and it is a game-changer. How... and who... could he get to come from Spirin voluntarily? He suspects Kildemar might be planning a mass kidnapping, but what good would a bunch of kidnapped kids be?

If there's any truth to this, Devon has to face what is really bothering him... others with powers will dilute his importance. Maybe Kildemar was just giving Ramie something to keep him quiet. But that doesn't make sense; if Ramie were being that much of a bother, Kildemar would just remove his head. Besides, it confirms what Kildemar all but said the other night.

If this is true... somebody in Spirin has to be working with Goreipor... The big question is... Who?

As Devon wanders, pondering the weight of what he heard from Ramie, Pirus rejoins him.

"We're shipping out again," Pirus says with little emotion.

That's the life of a soldier, short breaks and shipping out again... nothing changes. Actually, to Pirus, being in the field is preferable to the land mines of being in the court.

Devon takes a chance, "You hear anything about gathering kids from Spirin?"

"Lord Kildemar didn't say anything about it, but maybe that's why we are going out with Janick only. Taligarr is remaining in Goreipor this trip," says Pirus. "If it's true, you may not be the only wizard on the block."

"Sorcerer! I'm a sorcerer... I've never been a wizard... or witch," Devon snaps in irritation, but he is well aware of what Pirus means... and somewhat unhappy about it.

Before he leaves to prepare for the mission, Pirus says, "The other thing you should know is that our orders are to go in hot."

"What's that mean?" asks Devon.

"It means we won't show any weakness again... it means things are probably going to get bloody to get our point across," Captain Pirus says matter-of-factly. For him, it's simply an order, not a debate. He turns and heads away.

"How you feeling?" Topolina asks as soon as she enters Peter's room. "You were pretty out of it on the sail back."

In answer, Peter pulls the second pendant out of his pocket and holds it up with a smile. "By the way, thanks for saving my life," he says.

Topolina knows how valuable the extra pendant is so she doesn't bother giving him a hard time over risking his life in the first place.

"My pleasure," she says, but she can't resist adding, "No more water... I don't like fish."

There's a knock on the door and Peter quickly stashes the pendant... just in time before Jarium enters, followed by Laasper and Lonny.

"You look to be doing better," Laasper says. "Sorry you didn't find the legend in the deep."

"It might have once been down there but all the carvings are too worn away," Peter tells him, glad that his ruse seemed to have worked.

Perhaps once he gets to know these two better he may tell them what he was truly after. Then he thinks, probably not, since he's taking the artifact from their land. They wouldn't have known to look for it in the first place... but there's no use rubbing their nose in it.

Peter knows the advantage of having a second pendant will be invaluable in the long run. And now he is also sure that there are more pendants out there to be gathered... that is, if Devon hasn't figured out the same thing.

"What were you hoping to find in the legend?" Laasper asks.

"Information... I don't know," Peter says with a shrug. "Any extra candle in the darkness helps."

"My grandmother used to say, '*The more stars we make friends with, the easier our way*,'" says Lonny. "That's why she shoved my head into books and scrolls when all I wanted to practice the use of my sword."

"She managed to master both," Laasper says with a laugh.

"Are we setting out in the morning?" asks Lonny.

Both Jarium and Topolina look to Peter.

"As generous as your father has been, it's time to get back to exploring," says Peter. He knows Jarium longs to get going.

"The sooner the better, I'm so anxious to see beyond the walls... it's gonna be great!" Lonny bubbles over.

"Then it's time we prepare," says Laasper. He heads towards the door, gesturing for Lonny to come with him.

Before they leave, Jarium points out, "You know... they might try to kill us beyond the wall."

"Let'em try," chirps Lonny. Before she says anything more, Laasper gently pushes her ahead of him through the door.

"She's going to be perky every morning... isn't she?" says Topolina, clearly not a fan of *perky*.

Chapter Thirty-Six

Janick has a renewed puffed up sense of importance now that he alone represents his father on the expedition. Not having to play second fiddle to his brother is a welcome relief. That it's due to his more liberal taste for bloodletting doesn't bother him in the slightest.

The team now consists of Janick, Pirus, Devon and eight soldiers. Captain Pirus is still in charge of his men, but Janick is somewhat in charge of mission goals... how that actually plays out is still to be seen.

The team arrives in the now not so small encampment near the wall. With all this wall-jumping, the camp has been growing into a semi-permanent installation with more soldiers and more tents. It looks like they are preparing for something more than just occasional jumps. If so, it's being kept very quiet.

Pirus' men ready their equipment, though they don't know when the jump will take place... meanwhile, Devon wanders off near the wall.

He stares for the longest time at his reflection, going over events that have led to this point... reflections often cause that. Devon truly believes that he is meant to lead, to change worlds... but it's cost so much.

Back in the quarantine zone on Earth, Devon had learned to let conscience take a back seat to survival. At a young age, it became clear to him that was the nature of war. It's always bewildered him that Peter doesn't understand this reality... maybe someday.

As if his reaching to see the future provokes it, another uncontrolled vision of Peter hits Devon. He reels back as an image of his brother looking out from a castle onto a harbor floods his head... Devon now knows Peter is in Capulia.

The vision disappears as quickly as it has come, and, just like before, it leaves Devon disoriented. It takes both hands to catch him self as he staggers up against the wall.

As if in a haze, Devon hears from behind him, "What was that all about?" Devon turns to see Captain Pirus.

Devon is too drained to be surprised. Once he composes himself, he simply says, "Nothing." He considers Pirus a valuable ally, maybe even a friend, but he's not about to confide everything... especially uncontrolled visions.

"It's not the first time that's happened, is it?" Pirus says... knowing Devon is hiding something.

Regaining his composure, Devon says, "Like I said, it's nothing important." He sees Janick approaching from behind Pirus and adds, "And it's not something we should be talking about now."

Pirus reads this well and turns as Janick arrives.

"I've been thinking about what would serve my father best... I think we should take out your brother before we go to this other land," Janick announces as if it's the final word.

"Chasing someone, even if we know where he is, is not the mission your father is sending my troops on," Pirus says. He's aware that mission parameters are flexible; he simply doesn't like last minute changes, especially from a youngster. "We have few enough men to accomplish our goal in Capulia as it is. I don't plan on losing any of them on a wild goose chase."

Devon remains quiet. For once he's hoping Janick wins out because he knows Peter is exactly where they are going. If things shift to chasing his brother, he can simply misdirect the group. For the moment, he has no interest in having the inevitable confrontation with Peter, but he can't appear to be avoiding it.

After a couple of moments thinking on what Pirus has said, Janick concedes, "Very well, Captain, we can deal with his brother later." Glaring at Devon, he adds, "But we will deal with your brother in the end."

"OK, now that we're back on track, I suggest that I jump alone to scout things out," says Devon. He hopes to redirect events in some way, as he often tries to.

"I thought my father made it clear that you were not to separate from the team... the answer is no!" Janick snaps.

"You want to land in the water again? And lose more men?" Devon responds, knowing this argument will play on Janick's part in the last fiasco.

Janick glares at him. If it would not displease his father, he would be more than happy to take off this boy's head.

Pirus steps between them and announces, "Devon will scout the drop with one of my guards."

"Hope it's one who swims well," says Devon, with a nervous laugh. He wasn't hopeful about getting away on his own but he figures having only one guard is better than going through in force. Perhaps he can still shape things.

"Very well, but if you leave the man in your wake you'll answer for it." Janick is an angry young man, but he's not a total fool wanting to land like they did last time... or, at least, not be blamed for it.

"If we land badly, I can transport one man to a better location and then reopen the door," Devon assures them.

"If you think I'm going to give you the pendant, you're dead wrong!" spouts Janick.

Captain Pirus' gaze settles on Janick. As much as Devon doesn't want to, he also stares at Janick, knowing it's the only solution... a lousy solution, but the only one. From Janick's look, he regrets it even more than Devon.

Devon and Janick are spit out of the swirling door into the water. This jump ends up a bit better; they splash down much closer to the safety of an island than before. Both quickly swim for the sand.

Once they're out of the surf and on solid footing, Janick appears relieved for only a split second before he snaps, "We didn't need this test jump after all. Sure you weren't just trying to get off on your own?"

"By the way, you're welcome," is all Devon says. Appearing like he's getting a read on the location, Devon walks a few yards towards the island's jungle.

"You didn't do anything," Janick says from behind him.

Without looking back at Janick, Devon says, "We didn't land in the ocean... how do you know I didn't do that?"

"Doesn't matter... it's time to bring my team," responds Janick.

Devon's not actually paying attention to Janick. He knows that the unplanned visions have been crossing walls but, now in the same land where last he saw his brother, he hopes to be able to sense Peter with more control. More importantly... he hopes Peter will do the same in reverse, if he's still in Capulia.

Not liking being ignored, Janick demands, "Did you hear me? We have a safe spot to land and I'm opening the door to bring the team through."

Devon doesn't want to appear to be doing something other than the task at hand, even if he is.

"The reason for the trip is to pick a better landing location... not just a non-wet one. We don't need to be island- hopping if you allow me to explore a bit."

Before Janick can protest the idea of Devon *exploring*, Devon generates a spy globe. A few seconds after it's created, an image races across the seas, passing one small island after another.

Even Janick can't hide his fascination with this spell. He holds off saying anything till he sees what Devon is up to.

Devon carefully directs the vision to find where his senses perceive Peter without actually finding him so that Janick would be aware of it. The image flies towards a mainland island; as it proceeds, Devon slows it down.

Devon's sure Peter is somewhere there. The castle he had seen in his unbidden vision means Peter is not only there, but is meeting with whoever controls this land. Devon thinks, "*Well done, Peter.*" Then he sincerely hopes Peter is as aware of his presence and sees it as time to move on.

Having gotten close enough, Devon pops the globe.

"So, what now?" Janick asks, oblivious to all the wheels turning in Devon's head.

"Now, we get the team... if that's your wish," Devon says.

If Peter is still here when they return, so be it. He knows they will eventually have to run into each other, and he mustn't appear too weak to do so.

Peter and his new team, now four strong, stand in the courtyard of the castle. The yard is filled with citizens of Capulia, celebrating like it is the beginning of yet another festival. Instead, it's a turn out to see the group off.

King Crustivor is reluctantly saying his farewells to his daughter, Lonny, up on the castle steps.

Peter appears to be distant... distracted by something unseen... something weighing heavily on him.

"Where are you?" Topolina whispers in his ear.

Snapping out of it, Peter smiles and says, "Sorry, just thinking of... something." Truth is, he sensed, for a brief instant, Devon's presence. He looks about, a little confused over what to do with this new revelation.

Topolina steps away and quietly talks with Jarium.

After a couple of moments, Jarium comes over, "What's your call... we staying or going?" The way he says it sounds like he has some insight on what's going on in Peter's mind. He adds, "These people can handle themselves."

Peter stares at Jarium, now almost sure he can read minds. Then again, maybe he's not that good at masking his thoughts, especially from Topolina. He can't function as Devon does, in a total void... trusting no one.

Finally Peter says, "My brother is close, not here, but he's coming soon. I'm not sure what to do."

"You learn to lead," Jarium says. "What serves this mission better, confronting your brother or finishing surveying the lands? You make your decision... and then live with it."

"What would you do?" asks Peter.

Jarium thinks for a second, then, "It's not my war... I'm just here to watch you." He knows Peter is looking for more, and in truth, he's glad he doesn't see someone who thinks he knows all the answers. He adds, "I would want to plan where I meet my enemy... and do exactly what I have set out to do first, find my allies."

Peter knows his brother has dangerous powers, but he still doesn't see him as bloodthirsty. After all, Devon's trying to do the same thing jumping from land to land as he's doing... trying to line up people... it wouldn't serve for him to be too heavy-handed. All Peter can hope for is that Devon's nature speaks for itself. The people of the lands will have to use their own wisdom to see what's truly being offered.

"We move on without provoking anything yet," Peter finally says. He prays this is a right decision.

A booming voice comes from the castle steps, "Enough of the long faces down there, come join me, Peter," yells King Crustivor. The old man clearly has good timing.

Peter joins the King on the steps. Crustivor slaps him on the shoulder and says, "As you leave, have your friend do his little trick for my people... just to give those that didn't see it a thrill."

Peter smiles and walks down the steps towards Jarium. Before he reaches him, Jarium says, "I have cat's ears, I heard his request."

"I think he has his reasons," Peter says quietly.

"You're not the one putting on the show," he responds.

Topolina steps up to the two before they start bickering again, "Then let's put on a good show."

Jarium smiles, nods and turns into the massive saber toothed tiger he is. Topolina transforms into her bird self and flies upwards.

Peter joins in by disappearing into a wisp of smoke that swirls in the air before lightly coming down and reappearing on Jarium's back. Now sitting on the tiger, Peter reaches down and takes Lonny's hand and hoists her up behind him.

The crowd goes crazy with applause... Peter is now sure the old King has his reasons... he's a sly old leader.

Peter's new team, including Laasper, marches out the castle gates with the fanfare of Capulia in their ears.

Chapter Thirty-Seven

"**T**here's a world of difference between you and your brother, yet both of you are born of my loins," Lord Kildemar says sitting in a chair at the head of his war room table.

Taligarr, who's not real happy to have been excluded from the scouting expedition, stares at the lands on the map engraved in the top of the table. Kildemar has demanded Taligarr remain behind but has yet to tell him the reason... everything has to be at his timing.

Lord Kildemar scratches his chin with his steel-clawed hand. "You're upset over being kept here, aren't you?"

"With new lands to be seen out there, of course I am... but I serve you, father," Taligarr responds. He tries to keep his tone as neutral as possible since he has seen how harsh his father can be, even with those of *his loins*.

"Though it hasn't come fully to the surface yet, Janick inherited the bloody side of my ruthlessness," Kildemar utters '*ruthlessness*' with no apology in his voice, more with a tone of pride. "You inherited the cunning side of it."

Taligarr looks up, sensing this is some form of compliment.

"You tried to win the approval of the land you visited... all I want is their fear," his father says.

"My brother slaughtered sleeping men... is that what passes for bravery?" Taligarr spouts, losing concern over tone.

"Who said anything about bravery? All soldiers are brave, including theirs. I'm not interested in showing bravery... I'm interested in showing hard, cold resolve," Kildemar snaps as he stands abruptly, his voice rising. Bringing it back down, "What he did is slaughter the enemy, asleep or awake makes little difference to me. It sent a message. What you should have done is slaughter the next group that appeared to reinforce it."

Taligarr knows not to push the blame off on Devon, it would be seen as a sign of weakness by his father.

Lord Kildemar eases back down in his chair. "Your brother is like a ferocious dog... I can train dogs. Your skills serve me better in the harder side of strategy... deceit and manipulation of an enemy. Leave the bloodletting to Janick for now." He decides to throw his eldest son a carrot, "It's your strengths that I can use in running a land if you know when... and how... to use your brother's."

Taligarr now sees this conversation in a different light... it leads him to believe remaining in Goreipor is in his favor.

Lord Kildemar sweetens the pot, "I need someone I can trust to do a different kind of exploring... someone I can trust with my only remaining pendant."

As a result of Devon's scout with Janick the team has a target area. To insure it would work, the two traveled to the target area before jumping back for the team... thus, the door should reopen where it last was. Devon has yet to explore the idea of being able to mentally direct landing zones. He plans on doing so, but not till he regains a pendant of his own.

The team begins landing exactly where Devon planned... on a bluff over the port of Realia. As each man comes through the door he scrambles to clear himself away from the swirling door to avoid being landed on by the next man through.

Off in the distance is the city, most of which is surrounded by Realia's defensive walls. Its harbor is filled with moored sailing vessels of all sizes and shapes. Some appear to be war vessels with massive crossbows and catapults on deck, while many others are clearly fishing craft with large nets hanging from booms.

As with Peter, the stone walls that surround much of the adjacent city tell Devon that the people of Capulia have at one time or another had enemies. The arrow slots reinforce that, even if no military presence can be openly seen.

Pirus doesn't necessarily need to see what to expect. He's used to reading the setting and estimating his enemy. Naturally more details would be of use, considering their situation. They never made contact with those living in Capulia before retreating... now the mandate is to bring them to heel with only eleven men... one being a sorcerer.

Devon knows exactly how to impress the people of Capulia while limiting the loss of life, but he holds his tongue for the moment. He wants to be asked, or to at least hear the commander's plans, before stepping forward. One of his short suits is thinking he's the only one with ideas, but it would be hard to convince him of this fact.

"It's time we stir up some fear," says Janick arrogantly.

"All eleven of us," remarks Pirus.

Before Janick can react self-righteously to Pirus' remark, Devon steps up and points down at the harbor, "I have spells that can easily set those ships on fire. That will make our point at a distance."

"That's a start," says Janick dryly.

Captain Pirus gives Devon the go ahead with a nod. He's not used to warfare from a distance, and, in truth, is not sure of its impact, but given the size of their force it's worth a try.

Devon levels his lance at one of the larger war ships in the harbor. A fiery globe about six inches in diameter shoots from its end but, as it travels towards the ship below, it enlarges dramatically. By the time it reaches the unsuspecting ship, it's six feet in diameter.

It explodes on deck like Greek fire, instantly spreading over the entire deck and climbing the masts. Men not immediately caught by the fire dive overboard. Others, less fortunate but who can still run, are quick to follow. Barrels of oil on the deck, presumably used for lighting and soaking projectiles, explode and spill into the sea. It gives the water a fiery skin that's hard for sailors to escape.

Even from this far away, screams can be heard.

From behind him, Devon hears Janick say, "Again."

Devon glances over at Pirus.

"You heard him," Pirus says, nodding at the harbor. His tone is that of following orders with a lack of enthusiasm.

Once again Devon lowers the lance at another of the larger ships but, seeing a full crew on deck, he discreetly shifts his aim to one with a skeleton crew. The ball fires up and expands as before with the same results.

Explosions and the close proximity of the ships lead to the deadly flames jumping from ship to ship.

Many men on the surrounding ships are frantically lowering longboats to rescue their fellow sailors struggling in the water. Others, having seen the second fiery globe, point up at the Goreipor team on the bluff. At this distance, there's little more they can do than see their enemy; they're too far off to even try using any of their weapons.

"Do a few more for good measure," demands Janick.

Devon can't appear weak; all he can do is be choosy, picking ships that seem to have most of their crews on shore. He has shown powers that surely demonstrate a superior force, why kill needlessly?

Even Pirus looks uncomfortable with repetitious attacks.

By now, men line the city walls, staring out in disbelief at the carnage in their port.

Devon hits two more ships. The men on many of the remaining vessels abandon ship in any way possible before the next barrage can come from the bluff.

Just inside the open gates of the city, men can be seen chaotically scrambling to mount horses in preparation to launch a counterattack. As the first wave of soldiers comes out of the gates, Devon sends another globe that explodes well ahead of them as a warning. The explosion scatters the troops.

Janick glares at him, apparently preferring hitting the enemy to warning them.

"Cease fire," Pirus orders. "They've gotten the point."

"No, Captain, they haven't," Janick snarls.

But instead of ordering another volley, Janick calmly tells Devon, "Enough of your toys. Your powers are a novelty... What these people need to know is the fierceness of the Goreiporian warrior." He looks back at the castle, "Let the next wave of their men come forth." Then he says, "Captain, we'll stand our ground on the ridge to teach them what a Goreiporian soldier truly is."

To Devon's surprise, Captain Pirus yells, "Sergeant, to arms! We have thirty to be to the ready."

What Pirus, and even Janick, know is the only way to earn the fear of an enemy is to strike it into them on the battlefield... mere superiority of equipment will not have the same effect. Combining the two, advanced weaponry and superior soldiers, weighs heavily. They have shown the former... now they must show the latter.

Even Janick takes up his arms.

Devon thinks, '*They're only eleven strong.*' This is absurd, but he is left with little choice. "Captain, let me... "

Pirus cuts him off, "No spells." He adds, "If you wish, use what you need to protect yourself." He smiles, as if he knows something Devon doesn't.

Peter's team stands speechless, looking out on Cretorn.

Finally Laasper says, "That door of yours works both ways, doesn't it?"

Peter can hardly blame him for the remark. What stands before them would unnerve the staunchest of explorers. There's absolutely nothing inviting in the blood red jungle they look upon. Between the orange-ish steam rising through the trees and the stifling humidity, it feels as if the whole landscape is coming to a boil.

Far away there are jagged red rock cliffs erupting from the jungle. Over cleared paths they must be at least a day's hard march away; in the denseness of trees and vines, it is probably more like three days afield... three difficult days.

"I think I'm going to do a fly over," Topolina says.

"You don't have to, I can create a spy globe," says Peter, trying to save her the trouble.

Before transforming she says, "Keep your toys. I'm doing it to get out of this stench... something's rotting here. Maybe it's better from the sky." Without waiting for a response, she turns into her bird self and launches up towards the sky.

Topolina and Jarium have heightened senses of smell from their animal nature, but it doesn't take those gifts to tell she's right... there's an odor of death that permeates the land.

All can sense it.

Chapter Thirty-Eight

The gates of Realia, closed after Devon's last blast, slowly open again. From the Goreiporians' position on the bluff, Devon estimates about forty soldiers in the column that emerges. About a third are mounted on horseback; the remainder is infantry. Being an unplanned action, they have no equipment heavier than catapults that he can see. The defensive equipment atop the walls of Realia is geared for forces rushing on the city, and Pirus' men are far out of range.

The number of Capulian soldiers doesn't seem to faze Captain Pirus or his troops. They stand ready on a ridge looking out on a narrow road the enemy will have to use to approach them... a bottleneck that will serve them well.

Devon suspects that the small number of Goreiporians doesn't appear to present a threat to the larger force being sent out, even if Pirus' men have the high ground. He suspects Pirus sees his men's advantage as opposite to the Capulians' assumption.

"Archer... set two hundred," orders Pirus.

One of his archers steps out and releases an arrow into the air. It strikes ground to serve as a marker about two hundred yards out.

Captain Pirus sees Devon nervously watching the prelude to battle with a mixture of doubt and curiosity. He points to the opposing forces.

"We are testing for the range of their bows. If they advance to that marker before deploying archers, I have them," says Pirus. "But part of the fight will have to be hand-to-hand. We'll cut them down to size first."

"And if they stop before that mark?" asks Devon.

"I can tell the capability of their bows from here. The cleared land in front of the walls gives them away," Pirus assures him.

He turns back to his men. There is no time for lessons; Devon will simply have to watch and learn.

The Capulian forces continue to advance... inside four hundred yards... inside three hundred yards... ever moving forward. They have not yet split off their cavalry to flank them for two reasons: They still approach the narrow section of the road and they are still safely out of range... so they think.

Pirus has estimated the range of their bows correctly as the troops keep moving towards the two hundred yard marker. At about two hundred and forty yards out, they begin to slow.

Devon looks over and realizes Pirus has stationed a line of a few soldiers to mask the archers prepared to fire.

As the Capulians march into the bottleneck, before their cavalry gets to where they can split off, Captain Pirus yells, "Archers, release!"

The first volley of arrows flies through the air. The range marker was a ruse... the Goreiporian archers' range is closer to three hundred yards.

The first to fall are the horseback riders.

With their hand played, all of Pirus' men take to longbows. Their next volley topples all but a few of the mounted soldiers. The third wave concentrates on the ground troops moving forward to get within their own bow range. Before the enemy is close enough to launch a single arrow, their forces have been cut in half.

When the Capuliands reach a distance to return fire, Pirus' men, with precision timing, form what is akin to a Roman turtle. Only one man takes an arrow in the arm; a couple others receive scratches. The turtle opens and the Goreiporians let loose another eight arrows. The approaching soldiers are easy targets and a few more fall.

The only options the Capulians have are to retreat or to charge into close combat range. Since they still outnumber Pirus' soldier, retreat is unthinkable... They charge forward.

In a solid position, the Goreiporian archers fell another four Capulians as they charge across the remaining fifty-yard distance.

"To steel!" yells Pirus.

His men swiftly form a wedge to repel the last fifteen attackers. When the two forces slam into each other, it's clear which is the superior. The men of Capulia are able warriors who have seen no serious war in years; they're a poor match for hardened troops.

Pirus' men cut a brutal path through the Capulians. Even the less experienced Janick more than holds his own.

After a brief clash of swords and lances, the few Capulian soldiers left standing attempt to retreat. As they run Janick orders, "No survivors."

The men glance at Pirus and he nods for them to follow orders. A couple of archers bring down the handful of fleeing soldiers.

Pirus has lost two men and two are wounded... The Capulians have lost at least forty, not to mention many ships... A message has been sent in Janick's brutal way of speaking.

Devon can't believe these are the same sort of soldiers that he, Peter and Shan had fought on the plateau some time back. How could the three have survived that encounter?

Pirus, out of breath and spattered with blood, walks up beside Devon and, as if he knows what's going through his mind, says, "Boy, you only encountered palace guards."

With a wave of his hand, he proudly says, "Now... you've seen true Goreiporian warriors... my soldiers."

"I stand corrected," says Devon. "What now?"

Janick steps up, "Now we go in like before, but this time we don't ask... we tell."

"And then we leave quickly before they can figure out what hit them. Fear and rumors will take over from there," says Pirus, with confidence in their strategy.

Devon thinks it was overly bloody but is wise enough to keep this to himself. Whether they make allies through fear or enemies out of hatred is up in the air.

The land of Cretorn is hardly what Laasper and Lonny have hoped for when they anticipated seeing the fascinating wonders beyond the walls that have imprisoned them through the ages. Meeting Peter, Topolina and Jarium has shown them that more wonders exist out there... but that's not here.

After a brief and limited scouting flight, Topolina comes back and sets the group on a hike-able direction. Then she quickly goes back aloft.

Peter already feels that if they don't find anyone soon, this land may be a wash. Judging from the ambience of this place, though, they may not want to meet anyone.

As a precaution, Jarium has transformed into a tiger and takes the point as they struggle their way through the jungle. The other three trudge along at a distance behind him, watching every eerie shadow that moves. Progress is painfully slow and, apart from creepy crawling bugs, they have seen no forms of life.

After hours of sweaty struggle through the jungle, they break out into an open clearing. It's the first they've seen of the sky in a while because of the dense canopy covering the few long miles. Beyond the clearing is a wall of more jungle.

Topolina comes down. She flares her wings as she lands and becomes a woman. From the look on her face and the shake of her head, she's not bringing optimistic news.

Jarium rejoins the group, becoming human in the last few feet as he nears them. He glances at Topolina, "See anything ahead... like water?"

She appears almost sad to have to tell them, "There are people... somewhere... some kind. I saw a suspension bridge over a deep canyon that's at least a day north of here... as dense as this jungle is."

"Maybe we oughta just skip this land," Peter admits.

Jarium looks around, not happy to be here either, but he says, "Would your brother skip it?"

Peter thinks on it a moment... he tries to see it as a chessboard as he knows Devon would.

"I don't think so. He looks at everything before he makes a move."

Peter knows Devon looks not only for strengths, but also weaknesses that can be exploited. If anyone lives in Cretorn, they must be primitive... and if so, they are people his brother could put to use. Also, leaving a blind spot is not a smart strategy.

It dawns on Peter that he might be able to use his powers to jump the entire group, but a voice inside says that exposing all his powers at this point wouldn't be wise. After all, his companions haven't committed their lands yet. There's also a difference between him and his brother: Peter is more cautious about pushing to the limits of his powers. Over his two years in Spirin, he has discovered his powers have their limits.

He's saved from the dilemma by Jarium saying, "Then we stay the course."

Jarium knows this answer does not please Topolina, but if their land gets drawn into a fight he too needs to know what's behind *all* the walls.

"We should make camp here," Laasper tells them.

Having given those behind the walls of Capulia a little time to absorb the lesson dealt out by his troops, Janick is ready to approach the gates. Following such a total defeat, he's counting on brashness, to be his calling card. This is something Devon understands; he used the same strategy in Goreipor... though he didn't kill so many.

Janick, Devon and Captain Pirus approach just within archer's range of the wall and stop. Seeing no arrows fired at them, they move closer, to within hailing range.

Janick yells out, "We demand an audience with the leader of this land."

Janick may scoff at Devon's *toys*, but one of his invisible shields now protects the three. There's a certain amount of bravado needed for this presentation, but none of them are total fools.

"If the gate doesn't open, I want you to let loose one of your spells and breach it," Janick tells Devon.

Devon would prefer waiting for them to send an emissary out, but Janick speaks for Lord Kildemar for now. Perhaps he's even right.

After a very long pause, the main gates creak open. A scarred man, clearly an old soldier, comes out and approaches the trio.

"I am Commander Keel. You have earned the right to be heard. Are you willing to meet our king unarmed?" he asks.

"I have thousands of troops at my command... I will enter as I please," Janick says with a sufficient amount of arrogance.

"Why not?" Pirus proclaims with an unconcerned smile.

He figures if you're going to bluff, you might as well play it to the hilt. He unsheathes his sword and drives it deliberately into the ground.

"When I leave, I expect that to be right here."

Devon stifles his smile. This is either going to work... or they will be dead within the hour. Either way, he likes the level of the game being played.

Janick and Devon go along and do the same with their weapons, being equally deliberate about sticking them in the ground next to Pirus' sword.

Commander Keel nods and turns to lead the way in. The three follow as if with no fear whatsoever. Devon makes sure the invisible shield stays with them longer... just in case.

The two Goreiporians don't seem to notice, but Devon finds the sound of the gates closing behind them a little unnerving. Of course, he doesn't let it show.

As they move towards the castle, people in the square recoil from them. All three men can smell the fear their brutal show has brought out in these people... it will only grow as the day's deeds are retold.

Chapter Thirty-Nine

Gran-D watches the people of the village as he and Master Carringer casually walk through the square. There's something in the air that he has never seen before... mistrust... uncertainty... fear. Carringer can feel it as well.

People gather in small groups and whisper after the two pass by. Rumors run rampant. There's no use in the two trying to address the people, especially since half of what they would say would be only lies meant to ease their fears.

They see Master Sashaw approaching. Gran-D shakes his head and quietly says to Carringer, "That's all we need now, more accusations."

In spite of their emitting a vibe of '*not now,*' Sashaw keeps coming directly for them.

The first thing out of his mouth is, "See what Peter set in motion... everyone is scared. It isn't helping that you two are letting Shan stir things up with that absurd training camp."

"Nice to see you too, Sashaw," says Gran-D.

"You didn't think we knew Shan has ramped up her antics? Half the kids of the village are out there every day... and some don't even come home," spouts Sashaw, as if a prosecutor.

Trying to keep his voice down, Gran-D leans in to Sashaw, "You're not helping things with your rant."

He knows this is not news to Sashaw... the man just loves having an audience. Sashaw is on a roll and he doesn't care who hears him.

"We agreed to stay out of Goreiporian business, and they agreed to leave us be. What do you think will happen when they discover Peter is out there stirring up things... or when they find out Shan is building an army of kids to fight?"

The crowd in the village square steadily grows. They remain at a distance from the feuding Masters but they hang on every word. Gran-D glances around at the people.

"There's a time and place for this... and, Sashaw, it's not here."

One of the men from the village yells out in anger... a tone unusual for Spirin, "Why not here? My son hasn't been home in a week... I deserve to know why."

Some others in the crowd nod their agreement.

"They want to know what you're up to... and so do I," Sashaw says with the same anger.

He stares at Gran-D, but the old man seems to be looking past him. "Did you hear me?" Sashaw insists.

Gran-D appears not to be listening as he looks beyond Sashaw. In a slightly distant voice he says, "Not now."

Puzzled by Gran-D's distracted attention, Sashaw glances back over his shoulder. Taligarr and two Goreiporian guards stand quietly at the outer edge of the square.

Small groups of people in the village constellate together and back away to the distant side of the square. The leathery appearance of the Goreiporian strangers heightens their instinct for fear... An instinct so very alien in Spirin that it itself compounds the fear.

Gran-D puts on his best Grand Master Dar face and walks towards Taligarr. As he gets closer, the two guards grasp their weapons, but he keeps coming. Taligarr subtly signals for them to stand down.

"I thought you agreed to make your communications only to the Council," says Gran-D without a hint of anxiety in his voice.

Taligarr glances slowly around at the many people gathered in the village. After a couple of seconds he says, "Would that be because you haven't told your people of our existence?"

Before Gran-D can answer, Taligarr takes a step forward and raises his voice, addressing all clearly, "We are from the land of Goreipor, just beyond your western wall. We don't mean you any harm... as long as you understand a few simple rules."

From the looks on faces around the square, his tone does not help set people at ease. Still, no one dares say a thing.

Yadar and a few of his disgruntled friends can now be seen near the back of the crowd. Unlike the rest, they appear more interested in the new visitors than afraid.

"I insist that this is a matter best discussed with the Council," Gran-D asserts.

"You insist?" responds Taligarr with a glare, clearly not interested in being told what he should or shouldn't do. Then he softens his look, trying to remember his father's advice.

"If you truly lead your people, then I'm sure you are not in the game of hiding the truth." This seems an odd argument for one of Lord Kildemar's sons, but he's not handicapped by having to be honest... or sincere.

He turns back to the crowd, "We come simply to ask for your help with a few small matters and, if we receive it, we offer to protect you from threats from beyond the other walls."

A buzz of mumbles arises over the idea of a threat from not only one wall... but from all of the walls. It doesn't matter what is behind them... multiple unknowns are enough to spread the panic.

Normally the people of Spirin would rely on the Council, but that reliance appears to be breaking down. The man who spoke before before braves speaking out again. His words are shaky, "What do you want of us?"

"Volunteers... volunteers to join my people in defending yours... that's all," Taligarr says this like it's the most common of requests.

Gran-D knows the cat's out of the bag and there's no way of putting it back. All he can do now is try to stall in order to inform his people in a more controlled manner later.

"We will think on your request. How do we reach you?"

Not used to being questioned in any manner, Taligarr exercises restraint. He gives the old man a strained smile. "We will get back to you... that is, unless you have a pendant hidden up your sleeve somewhere."

It's now crystal clear to Gran-D that Taligarr knows that the people of Spirin have a pendant. He probably knows that Peter is out exploring other lands. Calling him on this would serve no purpose... they already see the lies in each other's eyes.

Gran-D simply shrugs as if he doesn't know what Taligarr is talking about.

"Very well... we'll get back to you... soon."

With this, Taligarr nods farewell... but before he turns to leave he gives Sashaw a brief, slight glance.

As abruptly as Taligarr has shown up, he and his men are gone.

Janick leads the way as the team of three is escorted before King Crustivor. Their swagger is not of men being granted an audience... but of men who demanded one. Guards all around the hall have their weapons at the ready but this doesn't seem to faze the three... the act has to be played out in full.

They stop in front of King Crustivor.

"Where do you and your men come from?" Crustivor asks.

"I am Janick, son of Lord Kildemar, from the land of Gor-eipor... beyond your walls," says Janick in an unapologetic and commanding tone.

Devon can't help but notice that the King keeps glancing at him as Janick speaks... He's pretty sure he knows why.

"Impossible... The walls cannot be crossed," declares King Crustivor... but again he glances at Devon.

To Devon it's clear that the King is lying. Peter was here; he sensed his presence days ago and he knows he's now gone. The big question is why he's lying so?

Coming to the point, Janick says, "Nevertheless, we are here. Have you ever seen men like mine? More important, have you ever seen men who fight like mine?"

"You've killed my soldiers and set fire to my...," Crustivor starts to say.

Janick cuts him off with, "...With only eleven warriors."

"Why should I not send out more men to kill those eleven soldiers? Eight, if I strike you three down," says King Crustivor defiantly.

Unintimidated, Janick steps forward... the guards tense.

"Because you will lose many more of your men today... and all of your people, when my father learns of our sacrifice." Al-lowing a second for that to sink in, Janick adds, "Are you willing to gamble your land and people against the fifty thousand sol-diers my father can unleash upon you?"

King Crustivor's silence in response is all the answer Janick needs.

"We ask little of you," says Janick, sure of what will come.

With a hint of defeat in his voice, King Crustivor says, "What is it you ask?"

"Your neutrality... simply your neutrality when the walls fall. This is a small price to pay for the safety of your people," says Janick, trying now not to sound intimidating. It doesn't matter what Goreipor eventually demands of these people... a simple concession is the doorway to bigger ones.

Clearly uncomfortable with this decision, but trying to sound statesmanlike, the King says, "As far as I know you could be from one of our distant islands... it's a big ocean. I do not believe the walls will fall. But, in the spirit of avoiding further unnecessary deaths, on both our sides... neutrality is a reasonable request. We do not wish to be in anyone's war."

The king is not prepared to buckle, but he has to take the care of his people to heart. Peter has not honestly explained the degree of the threat... and Crustivor has to keep his options open.

Janick smiles, not for the concession... but for the win.

Obarr strains to step forward to speak, but his father gestures for him to hold his peace.

"Very well... we're of an accord. Remember it," Janick says, and turns to leave.

Pirus follows, but before Devon turns, Obarr says curtly, "You look familiar, boy."

"Leave it be," his father orders.

"Never mind, the other was of more noble blood," notes Obarr.

Chapter Forty

"It surprised me that my father came through the wall on his own... I guess the old man still has some moves."

Taligarr's words startle Master Sashaw, who has been waiting in a gully not far from the western wall.

Regaining his composure, Sashaw declares, "You shouldn't sneak up on people like that."

"It's not I who has to be sneaky," says Taligarr with a smile, knowing he already has the upper hand.

"Your father said nothing about you showing up at the village... let alone addressing the people."

Sashaw is clearly nervous about this meeting; he's not accustomed to this cloak and dagger stuff.

"Take it easy... we're just asking you to help your people, even if they don't know they need your help," says Taligarr. He's wise enough to lead this traitor on slowly; to push hard would spook him.

In truth, Sashaw sees himself keeping options open for his people... a far sight from being a traitor. But then again, he's the one hiding in a gully... He's not opposed to keeping things open for himself as well.

Seeing Sashaw's turmoil, Taligarr says, "Trust me, we're not nearly the threat that some of those we've seen beyond the other walls are. It's time for us to set our differences aside."

"What sort of things have you seen?" Master Sashaw asks. He wants to be convinced so that the weight of his guilt will be eased.

"Beings that eat their own, for one."

Taligarr figures a half-truth plays better than an outright lie, and that does describe those he encountered in Cretorn.

With a very concerned look, he says, "The problem is, I don't think your council is as willing to listen as you are... at least that's what my father said. Your Council does not believe the threats I speak of... do they?"

"What are you suggesting?" asks Sashaw, knowing Taligarr is getting at something and he'd just as soon have him get to it.

"Someone on your Council has to step up because we need your support... again, to defend both our lands." Seeing Sashaw still listening, he goes on. "You spoke of young warriors not content to stand by... I think I saw some of them at the edge of the village."

Sashaw wonders how Taligarr could possibly tell that. What he doesn't know is that restlessness radiates its own aura... Taligarr, being from a land of discontent, can see these things.

Taligarr continues, "If you could convince some of them to aid us in Goreipor, we could become the first line of defense against any impending threat."

"So you're asking me to intervene with these kids on your behalf?" Sashaw knows what is being asked of him, but he wishes to shift the responsibility for what he does onto Taligarr.

"Your Council doesn't have the willingness to make this decision... it takes a leader to step up," says Taligarr, dancing around the sticking point.

"And, in the future, what kind of protection would that leader receive, personally... and for his people, of course?" Getting down to the nitty-gritty, Sashaw figures it's time to negotiate.

In his defense, Sashaw truly believes that if the walls fall, or even just the one wall falls... the people of Goreipor will overwhelm those of Spirin... someone has to establish some kind of leverage for them.

"He would be well protected... in case any friction develops between our lands," says Taligarr, fully realizing that neither land could ever trust such a person again; but he's learned from his father how to set the hook... before tugging too hard.

Though he's probably already made up his mind, Master Sashaw appears to think on it, and says, "Naturally, these kids you speak of would have to be willing to join you... and, of course, they would need to know they could come home."

"Of course... Master Sashaw, I suspect you have a mighty power of persuasion when you set your mind to it," says Taligarr, oiling the Master on.

Sashaw pauses again, as if giving the matter serious thought before committing.

Finally he says, "If I can provide you with the information and support you need, do I use one of those spheres your father gave me?"

Pulling out a few of the spheres, Taligarr hands them to Master Sashaw, "Here are some extras... just toss one in the air and your note will come directly to me."

"Where did you discover such a tool?" asks Sashaw.

The workings of such a sphere are no mystery to Sashaw... but he hasn't figured out how it has come to a land supposedly without powers. This further helps him to convince himself that his betrayal is less than traitorous in nature.

Taligarr knows that if his father wanted this traitor to know, he would have told him. "We have a few tricks," is all he says.

Trudging through the jungles of Cretorn, Peter and his group fight for every yard gained in this dense funereal version of nature. They've been at it for a day and half and figure they must be getting close to the suspension bridge. Topolina keeps them on track... but the track is so slow-going.

As they move on, Peter often takes a look at the pendant around his neck to see if it's speaking to him again. He knows there is probably another pendant hiding somewhere in this land. The question is whether Devon has already found it. Till the walls fall, if they can, every pendant gives greater mobility. Though not as acquainted with warfare as his brother, Peter knows that's a major tactical advantage. Unfortunately, the pendant has yet to speak to him.

Through the few sporadic holes in the jungle's canopy, they catch glimpses of Topolina circling high above. This is one of the few times Jarium would happily trade animal natures with his wife.

Jarium comes back to the group and transforms from tiger to man. He tells them, "The canyon is just up ahead."

"Finally... Any more of this and home will start to look pretty good," admits Lonny.

In an ominous tone, Jarium adds, "It still might."

Peter thinks what could be worse than the hell they've been slogging through but, from Jarium's grimace, he knows there must be something even darker ahead. Jarium doesn't offer an explanation; he just turns and leads the way... the rest can see for themselves.

The jungle dumps out onto a ledge, only a dozen feet wide, at the edge of a deep canyon. The canyon is about fifty feet wide with sheer drops straight down on both sides. How far down is hard to tell since the bottom is shrouded in a deep layer of orange fog churning softly. On the other side of the canyon is... more jungle. In the distance beyond are high red rock cliffs extending up to low hanging clouds... none of which appear inviting.

"There's your suspension bridge," says Jarium pointing about a quarter mile off to the west. "It definitely says something human lives here... what kind of something, I don't quite know."

Topolina flares and lands by the group now that they're in the open. She looks like she's a little tired of flying anyway.

As they get closer to the bridge, Peter sees the reason for Jarium's ominous tone. It's a narrow rope suspension bridge that has long ago seen its best years. Rickety would be a generous description, but that's not what catches everyone's attention. Dozens of skulls, apparently human, hang from the cross anchor poles at both ends of the bridge. Warning, decoration, ritual trophy, or all three... is uncertain.

The closer they get, the more precarious it appears. The walking slats are old, some broken, some missing altogether. The slight breeze makes the bridge sing with constant creaks. They can only imagine what it will sing when they step out on it.

Peter feels obligated to ask, "Do you still want to keep going? We can still skip this world altogether."

"After chopping our way half way through this ridiculous place, we might as well find out what lives here," says Lonny.

The others in the party find it hard to disagree in the face of her tenacity... they all reluctantly nod their agreement.

Peter is well aware he could fly across the canyon but that wouldn't set the right example for his companions. At least if he goes first and the bridge breaks, he can fly his way out of trouble.

As Peter walks directly up to the bridge, he stumbles over one of the anchor poles. Suddenly disoriented, he staggers around. Lonny grabs him before his reeling takes him over the edge into the canyon.

As if in a convulsion, Peter's eyes roll up in their sockets. Another vision has struck him. He sees Devon walking, silhouetted against some sort of fire. This vision is more abstract than usual, with no distinct landmarks. He knows Devon has visited Capulia, but that was days ago. Like blanking out a bad memory, Peter denies what the fires might mean. Then... all of a sudden, Devon looks directly at him, as if he sees into Peter's dream... Everything goes black!

Peter comes out of the blackness drained. Everyone is leaning over him, looking down intently with worried eyes.

"I've seen you go through this before and didn't ask, but now we all need to know what it's all about," says Jarium, with a mixture of concern and accusation in his voice.

Peter realizes that if this were to happen in the middle of a fight, or some other critical moment, he would be jeopardizing his friends. A fair question deserves a straight answer... at least as straight as he can be about something he's unsure of himself.

"I don't know where it comes from. It's not from powers I know of... but I'm being hit by visions of my brother. There's never any sound and they're vague," Peter says. He's trying to be as clear as he can be, but they're still a mystery to him. "I have no control over when they happen and they're a huge strain. That's why you've seen me weakened."

"Can you tell where he is in these visions?" Jarium asks.

"Is he in my land?" asks Laasper anxiously, clearly concerned about the welfare of his people.

"It's... it's more like hints of where he is... and sometimes of who he's with... but it's so vague," Peter admits.

Still, having been in some of the lands now, the visions seem to give Peter an idea of location. He wonders if he's intentionally vague for fear the group will break up.

Perhaps, but this last vision is a truly a mystery... maybe not, if he delves into his worst suspicions. Peter decides it serves no purpose to worry his friends with mere guesses... Then he wonders if he's becoming too much like Devon.

"If you see a vision of him in one of our lands, will you tell us the truth?" asks Lonny.

"When they happen again, I will," he says. "I've been honest about my brother exploring the lands and the dark men he travels with... if you feel you must go home, I'll use the pendant to send you."

He'll have to live with keeping his previous guesses on his conscience for now... Peter hopes he won't regret that decision.

The members of Peter's expedition glance at each other. After a few silent nods, Jarium speaks for all, "We knew this was a possibility and, even though no one is making any long- term commitments, it's best for all our lands to keep going."

Others nod their agreement.

"Very well... and thank you," says Peter. He'll have to live with wondering if their decision would be the same if he were totally forthcoming.

Helping Peter to his feet, Jarium says, "Maybe someone else should cross the bridge first; you're still wobbly."

"No, I'm fine," Peter insists.

He steps up to the pole anchor leading onto the bridge, carefully avoiding the hanging skulls.

The second he steps on the rickety bridge the whole structure creaks loudly. He can feel the aged boards under his feet bend as if they could snap at any second. After a moment, Peter takes another step.

By the fourth step, his movement starts making the bridge sway. The swaying in turn causes the hanging skulls to tap against each other, creating a hollow rattle like a human wind chime. Each step makes all the sounds grow louder... maybe it's just Peter's imagination.

Far below, the fog swirls more quickly, as if it knows someone is challenging the bridge above it.

After a few cracked boards and some harrowing swings of the rope bridge, Peter makes it to the far side, once again ducking under hanging skulls. He waves back to the group.

Topolina has gone aloft again, just in case she's needed.

The group has decided that Jarium, being the heaviest, would bring up the drag.

Lonny is next. Her lighter weight causes less swinging, but each step still brings moans from the structure. About halfway across, a sudden hot gust of northern wind shoots down the canyon, causing the bridge to shudder. Lonny crouches down and holds tight.

Circling high above, Topolina has become extra alert because of the swaying motion, but nothing prepares her for what comes next. Dramatically, the hot wind stirs the deep layer of fog on the canyon floor, whipping it around enough to virtually cleara away. Human bones fill the floor of the gorge ... wall to wall. They can only imagine how deep the pile of bones goes... or how many people it took to make such a gruesome carpet.

As the gust of wind dies down, the layer of fog swirls back to cover its secrets.

Getting over the shock of what lies below, Lonny gets back to her feet and continues forward on the bridge.

At the far end, Peter silently roots for her. With no warning, an arrow breaks the silence as it thuds into one of the bridge's cross supports next to him, partially cutting a key rope. The rope starts fraying.

Two more arrows find their mark, slicing more ropes. Peter can't see where the arrows come from... just from somewhere in the jungle on his side of the bridge.

Like a breaking rubber band, the right handrail of the bridge snaps. Along with it the footing planks drop to a forty-degree slant. Lonny grabs the left rail and hangs tight. With every second, another strand or rope snaps, bringing the bridge closer to complete collapse.

Topolina dives towards Lonny. As she gets close, she flares her wings back and extends her massive claws out front. The final support rope breaks with a deafening snap. As if in slow motion, the far end of the suspension bridge breaks loose and the horizontal spans start plummeting down in a wave.

As the bridge gives way under Lonny, Topolina's claws grab her shoulders. The remaining length of bridge pivots, descending into the orange fog. Reaching the foggy layer below, it slaps up an orange puffy cloud high above the gorge's lips.

Lonny's weight drags Topolina down into the canyon and the two disappear in the cloud for excruciating moments. Suddenly they break upwards out of the cloud. Before losing her grip, Topolina drops Lonny on the side of the now unbridged canyon where Jarium and Laasper still stand.

Lonny lands hard.

Immediately Peter uses his powers to transport himself as smoke across the ravine, completely forgetting the arrows and where they come from... they've ceased anyway.

Lonny lies unconscious; her brother leans over her.

Jarium steps up to the materialized Peter and says, "Her arm's broken in a couple of places. It's going to be hard to set."

"We have to get her back home... now," insists Laasper.

After thinking for a second, Peter says, "We'll take her to Spirin. We have a Healer who can fix it quickly, before there's any other complications."

He knows this may be seen to be an insult to the medical abilities of Capulia, but he knows that the powers of sorcery in the right hands outweigh traditional methods. His concern is for Lonny, not etiquette.

Laasper thinks on it and nods his agreement.

Peter glances down at the pendant hanging from his neck... it still hasn't spoken to him. He's pretty sure there's a pendant here, but he's not so sure that Devon hasn't or won't find it. No matter... the pendant has to wait. Lonny's care is the first priority.

Who fired the arrows also has to remain a mystery.

Chapter Forty-One

Gran-D joins Shan on the bluff over the training ravine. After Taligarr's visit to the village the word has spread quickly; her training activities aren't exactly a secret any longer. The Council has yet to take action against her, but the turnout has substantially dwindled already.

"You come to tell me to stop?" Shan asks the old man.

Looking down upon the dozen or so remaining recruits, he says, "Looks like their, or their parents' fears are doing a pretty good job of that. I'm sorry, child."

Shan shakes her head, "No, something else is going on. I expected a drop off, but I had almost eighty kids here. Yadar and his crew of misfits come and go, pending on Master Carringer coming up with new spells... but even with them playing hooky today, there should be more than twelve down there."

The absence of her usual easy-going style tells Gran-D she's truly worried.

"I'll do a little digging around. I'm already in hot water with everyone from the Council to your father... how could it get any worse?"

Gran-D's not one to take things too seriously, even now, but occasionally he does miss the calmer days before Peter and Devon arrived from Earth... even if he has had a hand in orchestrating a lot of what's transpired since.

Devon is off by himself. The team is readying to move on in Capulia. Upon leaving the castle, they found their weapons in the ground outside Realia where they had stuck them. The three retreated from the city past the raging fires in the harbor, without any further incident... except in Devon's mind.

Devon's now lost in thought, bewildered how, in front of the inferno of the ships, he came to be injected into Peter's vision. Just like one of his own visions, it came out of nowhere, but this time he could tell the vision was not his... somehow he was conscious of a vision Peter was having... and just for a second, he looked into it. It's hard for Devon to fathom these visions... and what's worse, not knowing what controls them.

He knows Peter now is in that horrible land of Cretorn. Devon is sure Peter won't find anything he wants there. It crosses his mind, '*Hopefully he'll make it out alive*,' and then the thought is replaced by, '*Of course he will*.'

Devon knows that if anything were to happen to Peter, it will be between the two of them... if Peter must be brought down, it will be at his hands, no others'.

"You going to join us any time soon?" says Captain Pirus, surprising Devon slightly.

Devon quickly sets aside his thoughts. "So, is the grand prince ready to trek on to another location?"

"He's demanding that we divert back to Goreipor," says Captain Pirus. "Supposedly he's received a message to that effect... I wonder."

"He offer any reason?" asks Devon.

Devon knows protest would serve no purpose, but the plan was to seed more locations in Capulia... they have gotten the impression there are other large islands and other tribes. Actually, as bloody as this visit has been, Devon almost prefers calling it quits. He knows he can probably manipulate things to explore at another time on his own.

"Doesn't matter, I'd just as soon go home and wash the blood from my hands," Devon says.

And, to speak of the devil, Janick approaches Devon and Pirus.

Janick says, "We need to get ready for the jump home." Thinking he sees a hint of objection in Devon's eyes, even when it's not there, he adds, "We've seen all the lands... there's only one other thing I could think of doing here."

"What might that be?" Devon says, even though he senses he's being baited.

"Killing your brother," says Janick with a perverse smile.

Devon doesn't want to touch that out of fear he will touch it a bit hard. Finally, all he says is, "Perhaps... another day," and offers an equally perverse smile.

Captain Pirus lets out a booming laugh.

A small gathering of kids mill about near the wall, not that far away from the cave Devon once blasted out of a rock overhang. In the center of the group stands Yadar. They're clearly waiting on something... or someone.

Master Sashaw abruptly appears out of nowhere.

"Even old sorcerers can still do tricks," laughs Yadar.

"Youngster, I can not only disappear... I can make you do the same," Sashaw responds in a less friendly tone.

Yadar gets the point and leaves off the banter. Sounding more impatient, "OK, where are these people you have us here waiting on?"

Suddenly a swirl of light appears near the wall. Reaching full size, Taligarr jumps out of it. He's followed by two of his soldiers.

It's clear from Yadar and the other kids' faces they are more than sufficiently impressed. There is also a touch of fear... for a teenager this equals adrenaline, their favorite drug. And why not, at that age they're invincible... in their own minds.

Taligarr sees all of this and fully plans to play on it, at least till he gets what he wants. Carefully studying the dozen kids gathered, he announces, "Welcome... young adventurers all."

These words immediately pump up every kid in the group. After all, Spirin is not a land ripe with adventure. The idea of the unknown is a lot more exciting than daily classes... and the known. The thought of this being an act of betrayal doesn't even cross their minds.

The slightest hint of doubt has already been erased by Master Sashaw's sales pitch. For Yadar and his friends, this adventure is also offered as a chance of being of service to Spirin... few actually care if this is true... *it's an adventure.*

Not wanting to complicate things with details, Taligarr uses the pendant to generate another Sorcerer's Door. Once the swirling portal is formed, he simply says, "If you follow me through, you'll be treated well... but you will serve Goreipor."

Knowing they will follow, Taligarr steps through the door. Taligarr's guards wait... In case the kids don't, the soldiers will strongly encourage them to do so.

Master Sashaw remains silent, hiding his guilt even from himself. When a few of the kids glance at him with concern in their eyes, he simply nods towards the door with a strained smile.

The call of the unknown and excitement is simply too much for the kids... all but one of them dives eagerly through the door. Without a word, the two guards walk forward and sweep the single hesitant boy through the portal with them... he doesn't have time to protest.

The swirl disappears, leaving Master Sashaw standing alone by the wall. He glances all about, making sure no one is watching, and slithers away. All that's missing is the presence of dark shadows.

The log near the Graveyard of Spells has often welcomed Peter's return... now it welcomes Peter and his new friends. With all five through the door, Peter immediately tugs for the Healer.

Then, without a word, he walks over to the log that bears the scars of Devon's razor discs. He wonders how it's all come to this... racing around a world looking for people to send to a war... a war between two brothers.

Laasper snaps Peter instantly back to the present, yelling, "My sister's arm needs the mending you promised." He stands there in front of him with Lonny in his arms.

Conjuring a hoverboard, Peter says, "Give her to me, I'll get her to the Healer and come back for the rest of you."

He sees right away this idea doesn't set well with the others... whether from not fully trusting him yet or from simple concern for Lonny. He has to remember this new land is as alien to them as their lands were to him.

Peter makes the hoverboard larger.

"Laasper, I'll carry your sister and you ride behind me. Topolina and Jarium, I'm sure you'll know how to keep up."

The Acculasians both smile and turn into their animal selves.

The group swoops over the peaceful blue hills of Spirin... Peter rides the board with Lonny and Laasper, Jarium bounding along as a saber toothed tiger and Topolina flying high above.

On the bluff above the Dees' home, Peter stops to take in the welcome view for a second... Before Topolina and Jarium can become more presentable, a familiar sight emerges.

Atta Dee comes out the front door and storms up the hill towards them, a mixture of love and anger in her eyes. Peter suspects it's going to be embarrassing getting yelled at by his adopted mother... and is overjoyed at the prospect.

Atta pauses a split second at the sight of a giant tiger and an equally large beautiful bird, yet she proceeds forward. All she gives Peter is a scowl before she gently brushes the hair back from the unconscious Lonny in his arms.

Atta's arm shoots out pointing towards the house. She snaps, "The Healer is here... get the poor girl inside."

Peter smiles... he's home.

Kalish Dee holds the front door open for Peter and points up the stairs where the Healer stands. As Peter rushes the girl up to the Healer, Kalish curtly says, "I refuse to adopt any more kids!"

Chapter Forty-Two

Half asleep, Lord Kildemar is draped on his throne. The main hall is strewn with courtiers in various degrees of slumber or hangover. The day is not yet awake.

The massive door to the hall bursts open with a wave of Witch Racinda's hand and she storms in. Normally Racinda is more guarded with her opinions but today she's beside herself... and a bit out of control.

She yells, "What have you done!"

When a witch yells in a stone hall the sound of her voice echoes as if it is amplified... it gets the attention of everyone who isn't dead... and would raise the dead if there were any.

Kildemar, holding his head, tries to focus on whoever dares kick up such a ruckus in his fortress. With his hangover, the sooner he can figure out who it is, the sooner he can figure out whom to kill!

But when his eyes focus enough to see it's his witch, he yells, "Everyone out... Everyone out now!" Then he adds, "Except you... witch!"

His command is not questioned... everyone, drunk, hung over or sober, scrambles to get out of the hall. With the racket of scrambling subsided, an awkward silence hangs over the room.

"Now, witch... how dare you come in my hall and yell at me. Have you lost your mind?" demands Kildemar.

Witch Racinda comes back with equal volume, "You dare to kidnap children from my land? Don't deny it... young Ramie told me as much, though I don't know why he should know of it."

Lord Kildemar would normally strike down anyone challenging him in such a way, even his witch... but he knows his action conflicts with the long-term arrangement his father made with Racinda. That consideration alone would not stop his wrath, but he still has use of her... and now, even a new use.

Trying his best at composure, he says, "Young Ramie will be working with them... They were all volunteers, at least according to my son... and I did not use your skills to procure them, so I did not break my father's word." He adds, "Be careful of what next comes from your lips next... You are no longer the only one with powers in this land."

"Then why should I care what you do with me?" The outrage and arrogance has not left her voice.

"Because you might be able to protect our new arrivals," he says. "For some reason I still trust your loyalty, but if I were to think your kind can't be trusted... who knows what I might do with others from your land." Kildemar has never been subtle with his threats.

Before going through the wall to Spirin, Taligarr had expanded the encampment used for door departures even more. He had impressed on his men that once he brings the kids back, they must make the new arrivals feel important... at least for the time being. He knows now is not the time for a heavy hand.

Taligarr finds his new practice of deception to be to his liking... it's more intriguing than just drawing blood.

As a well-orchestrated touch prepared for the kids' arrival, a troop of soldiers sweep into the encampment... with Ramie in a Lieutenant's uniform riding at the head of the column.

Lacking the demeanor of a hardened soldier, when Ramie sees the Spirinese kids, he waves energetically with a big smile spread across his face.

Taligarr shakes his head in dismay... Ramie is his father's idea, not his.

As Shan and Gran-D walk home, Shan suddenly perks up. Her concern over the missing students is replaced by a smile.

"I heard the tug. Careful, don't rush to him so quickly... he'll take you for granted," Gran-D says with a slight laugh.

"With all due respect, bite your tongue, grandfather. My Peter knows who has his back... this he doesn't take for granted," says Shan, picking up the pace. Seeing Gran-D is not keeping up, she says, "See you at home."

She conjures up her hoverboard and takes off.

If Janick would allow Devon to adjust the pendant, they could jump back into Goreipor a little closer to the fortress... but mistrust guides all of Janick's decisions.

The team, less two men they buried in Capulia, drops in at the base camp they departed from. They notice that the camp is much expanded... for what reasons, they don't know. All that crosses Devon's mind is that it's still a good night's ride to the fortress and a warm bed.

This abruptly changes when Devon sees Ramie run out of a large tent in the distance. That in itself is a surprise... the fact that he's in a uniform is completely bewildering. Then Yadar, another kid he recognizes from Spirin, comes out of the same tent and follows Ramie.

Having a limited number of players with powers in Goreipor has been part of Devon's game plan; he suddenly realizes something is in the wind that is not in his playbook. Seeing Taligarr turn the corner of that tent, he knows this is what Kildemar was hinting at... and who's behind it.

Ramie turns towards Yadar but, all of a sudden, sees Devon watching from the distance. He drops everything and runs towards him, apparently less displeased with his original kidnapper than before.

With a flourish, Ramie gestures towards his duds, "How do you like my new uniform?"

"I noticed... just trying to figure out why you're wearing it... you're not quite the army type," says Devon. Seeing that his remark wounds Ramie's ego, he adds, "But it wears well on you. Now... you want to tell me why?"

Taligarr walks up, "Because young Ramie here is helping me break in some new volunteers from Spirin." From his air, and glare, it's clear that he wants no details about the matter discussed... at least not in front of Ramie.

Knowing he'll weed though it later, Devon nods to Taligarr, and then to Ramie, "Congratulations on your new job, whatever it might be."

Over Taligarr's shoulder, Devon sees more Spirinese kids emerge from the tent. He wonders how many are here... and how he is going to have any control over them?

While Devon's head is churning, Janick walks up behind him and quietly says, "Looks like you're not the only talented kid on the block anymore."

Devon would love to put Kildemar's son in his place, but that doesn't play to his plans yet.

As Devon walks off, Captain Pirus joins him.

"I'm glad I only hedged my bets and didn't go all in." He says this in a matter-of-fact tone... not to taunt.

"You're a professional warrior... you should know the battlefield is always fluid," responds Devon.

"Lord Kildemar does a good job at that. Trust me, this has his signature, not the sons'," Pirus warns.

"Do I look a fool? Of course it is," says Devon.

Shan bursts in the front door, immediately looking around for Peter. When she sees him in the living room, she rushes to throw her arms around him... but stops abruptly when she beholds the attractive Topolina by his side. After a second, she also sees Jarium, but her focus remains on Topolina.

Topolina gives an understanding smile, "Come hug your man."

Relieved, Shan does just that.

After a moment, she glances back at the two strangers, "Sorry, I forget my manners."

"This is Jarium, my husband, and my name is Topolina," she answers before being asked. "We come from the land of Acculas."

Peter adds, "There are two other new friends upstairs... Laasper and Lonny from the land of Capulia."

"Upstairs?" Shan says with concern. She's well aware of what *upstairs* too often means, having nursed Peter there.

"Lonny got hurt... the Healer is with her," says Peter.

"Our Healer is good at what she does, though she tends to have a contrary temperament," Shan reassures Topolina.

Standing off to the side, Kalish grumbles, "She's a temperamental, headstrong nut case."

Atta comes in from the kitchen with a tray of snacks. Noticing Shan, "I see you've all met." She glances around, "Any idea where the absent joker, my father is... the pub perhaps?"

Materializing in the room, Gran-D says, "Daughter, you'll give these visitors the wrong impression."

"How many times have I told you not to do that in the house... and when we have guests, no less," Atta admonishes her father. From his innocent shrug, the guests see this as ongoing, friendly banter... though Atta doesn't see it that way.

"Don't let us keep you and your boyfriend from going out for a long awaited walk," Topolina tells Shan with a smile.

Shan knows she's going to like this new friend.

Atta smiles and nods her agreement. "You can meet the others later at dinner."

A little while later Shan and Peter sit in the soft grass leaning against their favorite log. They silently stare out at Spirin's peaceful landscape. It's been a while since Peter could simply relax.

Shan finally says, "If you go off again, I'll be by your side... This teaching is for the birds."

"You know how necessary it is," says Peter, trying to bolster her.

"You mean... while you have all the fun? Never mind... in your vernacular, our cover is blown... the training is no longer a secret. Gran-D or Master Carringer can wipe snotty noses. Besides, I even have students who can teach now," says Shan defiantly.

Peter laughs, "You hear yourself... how did you get students who can teach now if you weren't good at training them in the first place?"

"I'm so good that some of my students have up and disappeared," she snaps. "Magic at its worst!"

Maybe because Peter's been on the road, often thinking about Devon's strategy, and maybe believing less and less in coincidences, but this strikes him as odd. "What do you mean by *disappeared?*"

"Not long after that soldier from beyond the wall... I think his name was Taligarr... showed up, a number of my more maverick students stopped coming to classes. They were only catching classes part of the time anyway," she explains.

"Maverick?" The term confuses him.

"Teaching offensive skills seems to bring out the darker side in some of the kids. They tend to get more aggressive, some downright dark... sort of like your brother."

Peter thinks back on Earth. If there weren't eighteen year olds to train, there would be fewer wars... and now he's part of training them. He reflects on how survival turned Devon.

As if she reads his mind, Shan puts a hand on his knee, "It's not your fault that we have to get ready."

Back to the moment, Peter asks, "How long since you've seen these kids?"

Shan suddenly knows what he's getting at, "You think they might be beyond the wall... with Ramie?"

Peter thinks on it a moment.

"If they are, it wouldn't have been Devon's doing; I'm sure he prefers having the advantage of being the only one with powers over there... Also, I was hit a number of times with visions of Devon. He's been out there doing exactly what I was doing... looking for an army. How many times did this Taligarr show up?"

"Only once that I know of," she answers.

"Only once," Peter ponders... and then, "Maybe someone from over there took them, but somebody here had to set it up."

Peter realizes the implication of what he's saying... so does Shan.

They both long for the time when their biggest concern was what to do with a peaceful day.

"Enough thinking," Shan says as she snuggles next to Peter.

Chapter Forty-Three

"Contrary to my son's report, Captain Pirus stands behind you and observes that you've been of vital importance to the operations of the exploration missions," Lord Kildemar tells Devon. He thinks on Janick for a second, "I'm not surprised by the discrepancy."

Devon is wise enough to simply listen, keeping his opinion of Janick to himself... unless he's asked. Even so, he would probably temper it.

"The violent nature of Janick has his uses, but I gather you prefer diplomacy," Kildemar continues.

Devon glances about the war room; he finds it a bit unnerving to be having a private audience with Kildemar. From the trophies adorning Kildemar's walls, he can't imagine diplomacy being one of the dark lord's preferred methods. Devon hopes his head is not being sized up for a basket... he would hate to have to strike Kildemar down so early in the game.

"Well... say something, boy," Kildemar snaps at him.

Devon suspects being timid is just setting himself up as a target... if he's going to be a target, it might as well be for having an opinion.

"Using force should be a case by case decision. Your son and I don't see eye to eye on that... but I'm not here to serve your son, am I?"

"As long as it serves me, you are," Kildemar says, aware that Devon gets his meaning.

"In a primitive land like Cretorn, fear is the only currency but, in lands versed in war, a lighter hand may avoid creating an enemy at your flank."

Devon feels this is as far as he should push. He knows that Kildemar is constantly on the lookout for anyone who hints at desiring power... to squash them before they become an issue. Lord Kildemar stares at Devon for a few moments, sizing up his ambition. After the long pause he breaks his glare.

Changing the subject, he points up towards the ceiling and says, "You know what those are?"

Devon glances up to see slots high in the ceiling, somewhat like the ones in the main hall. He suspects what they are but doesn't want to take the wind from Kildemar's sail. He shrugs.

Kildemar, with his hand still raised, closes his fist. An arrow shoots out from one of the slots and crisply embeds in the war table inches away from Devon. The arrow quivers from the impact.

"They're called killing slots. I have them manned by soldiers who I've had struck deaf, so they cannot hear what takes place below... but they're very useful to me in their way," Kildemar says.

He watches Devon's reaction carefully and adds, "I know whom you serve... as long as you remember... You're dismissed." Kildemar turns and walks away, with a swagger that says he has no need to watch his back.

Devon likes to consider himself brave but, he has to admit, he breathes a sigh of relief. All the magic in the world won't protect him from being caught off guard.

The Dees have a full house for dinner, to the degree that Atta and Kalish have to use a bit of sorcery to stretch out the dining table. Atta is bubbling over at the large attendance, while Kalish pretends to be grumpy about it.

Actually the house has been a little lonely for both of them, with Ramie stolen, Peter off to who knows where and Shan out all hours with the training she ineffectively pretends not to be doing.

"How do you keep your fur so nice?" Atta asks Jarium.

Topolina muffles a slight laugh while Jarium, as politely as he can, says, "She makes me do it."

Jarium doesn't mind a silly question because he knows how alien being half-human, half-animal must seem to her... and, she's being so politely motherly about the silly questions.

Master Carringer leans in to Laasper, "How's your sister?"

"She's resting. Your healer did a much quicker job with her magic than ours could have done," says Laasper, almost whispering.

He's more used to loud festivals around the grand hall than tamer dinner parties. Laasper would be more at home with a mug of grog than the sweet tea Atta serves, but *'when in Spirin'*... he and the other visitors do their best to fit in... After all, Peter did his best to keep up with the drinking and the brawling in their lands.

Dishes of food magically fly in and out of the dining room, keeping all well fed. This alone is fascinating enough to the three dinner guests to make their visit well worth it.

As dinner winds down, Kalish knows there will be other things discussed and he chooses to help Atta in the kitchen. The rest gather in the living room. Gran-D glances around to be sure Atta is out of the room... and then he brings out a jug. To his guests, "Perhaps I can offer you more than sweet tea."

With all their teacups refilled, Gran-D offers a toast, "To a peace that we would all prefer happening."

After the toast Jarium says, "But peace is not what Peter has been warning us will come."

"Hope for one... prepare for the other," responds Gran-D. "Has Peter been able to convince your lands to lean one way or another... if the latter comes about?"

Peter immediately appears uncomfortable with such a direct question, but he has never dictated what Gran-D says or thinks.

Jarium takes a breath and says, "Peter's a fine lad, but I'm simply traveling with him to see the people of the other lands and take what I see back to my council of chieftains. I cannot answer such a weighty question for my people."

Laasper's nod suggests his answer would be the same. He looks out towards the entry where they all have hung their weapons at Atta's request. "For people who warn of a prophe-sized war, I have seen no weapons of any sort."

"We may not have weapons as yours, but tomorrow perhaps we can show you something from our imagination," says Carringer with a glint in his eye.

Peter doesn't want to step on Carringer's enthusiasm, but he can only imagine what's going through Laasper's mind... *'toys don't make warriors.'*

Lord Kildemar's court can hardly be described as filled with gaiety, but it can be loud in a roughly jovial way, granted that Lord Kildemar is not out of sorts.

The only two who appear put out tonight are Taligarr and Janick. They take exception to Devon and Captain Pirus having been allowed to sit at the main table, but aren't about to challenge their father over it.

Witch Racinda doesn't look too happy either, but she rarely does. Her anger has less to do with who sits at the table as it does with who sits in the encampment near the wall. Thus far she's not learned the plans Kildemar has in store for the kids who have supposedly come here '*of their own free will.*'

"I was telling our hotshot wizard here... is that wizard, or witch... that is, if there is such a thing as a male witch...," expounds Janick half drunk.

"Sorcerer," Devon dryly answers. He knows Janick's realizes the difference and is only baiting him.

"Get to the point," snaps Kildemar.

"He's not the only hotshot now," is Janick's slurry finish.

Taligarr shakes his head at his brother's drunkenness.

Lord Kildemar coldly says, "Things will change less than you think. I'm not foolish enough to invite more into the fortress with powers. Once those kids learn who's in charge, one will be assigned to each of my companies... they're simply weapons,"

Witch Racinda stares the other way, clearly displeased.

"We've seen the other lands and my guess is we have at least two out of three. Combining these kids' powers with our armies, we're invincible if the walls do fall," says Taligarr. Not everyone in Goreipor truly believes the walls will fall.

"And what of Ramie?" Devon chances to ask.

"From sources beyond the wall, I've discovered the boy is important to some... we'll keep him close at hand... useful, if possible, but at our hand either way," Kildemar says in an even icier tone.

"What to do about your brother should be the question at hand... he is more of an immediate threat," Taligarr suggests. There's a silence as many at the table look towards Devon.

"On this matter, I must agree with my sons... your brother wandering about out there presents a problem that should be dealt with," says Kildemar. He waits, clearly expecting a reaction from Devon.

Devon knows he can't hesitate too long.

"I agree... as soon as I have a sense of where he is, I will disclose it... I will even do the deed myself."

He would actually like to put forward an argument in favor of using Peter, but Devon's well aware this is not the setting for doing so.

"I think not. This is where Janick's skills come in best... and I wouldn't want you to have to kill your own blood," says Kildemar in a manner not open to debate.

Master Carringer points down at a high wall of stones he's magically fabricated across the ravine. Like a stage magician, he dramatically sets up his presentation with flourishes and gestures. One would almost expect him to yell, '*Voilà!*' as he conjures a horizontal, black cyclone that worms its way to the wall and penetrates through to the other side.

At Carringer's signal, a number of kids run through the dark spot in the wall and emerge beyond it. Then, at Carringer's command, the dark hole disappears as quickly as it formed.

Carringer turns to the visitors, except Lonny who's still healing, and nods just shy of taking a bow. "That's what I call '*Cave of Darkness*.'"

To his surprise, they don't look impressed.

"But can those kids fight?" Laasper asks dryly.

Master Carringer is taken aback for a second by the question, clearly disappointed that all can't see the strategic value of his spells.

"Frantically flailing around with a piece of sharp metal is not the only way to win," he says in an insulted tone.

To prove his point, Carringer revs up to present another of his inventions, but Peter steps in and gestures for him to hold off. He's aware that conjured up spells don't tell the visitors anything about the people of Spirin... about their willingness to stand the line and defend their land.

Shan senses what Peter is thinking and she flies down to the kids in the ravine. After a few moments of talking to them, she flies back up and says, "This is new to us but my kids are trying."

She signals her recruits.

A half dozen kids below pair off with wooden sticks. They go against each other, but it comes off as very rigid, classroom-style combat. The heart is there but the technique is more like a tournament for show.

Frustrated with this display, Laasper jumps off the ridge and scurries down the embankment. Indelicately shoving aside one of the kids and taking his wooden weapon, the Capulian confronts Roland to take his stance. Roland glances up at Shan and she gestures for him to proceed.

Roland sets his stance formally and then attacks. Laasper quickly kicks dirt into Roland's face, knocks the feet out from under him and deals a mock deathblow... as if it had been for real. It's not pretty... but it is what it's truly about!

As if that is not enough of a demonstration, he proceeds to informally take out five other kids... with little effort.

"I think what he's saying is that you are in no way prepared to partner in war... it's not a playground exercise," Jarium tells Shan. "From what I see, they have no idea of the cost of losing a fight. It's dirty, it's bloody... and if you fall, the man next to you might, as well."

"The woman you're speaking to saved my life in a heads up fight... and she has two kills," says Peter angrily. "None of us know what it's like until we have to be in it."

By this time, Laasper has made it back up to the ridge. "True enough... but I have no interest in gambling my life on how they *might* stand the line. All I see down there are a few kids out of all your land. You speak of an alliance and show us nothing tested to ally with."

"But we have the skills of sorcery," insists Carringer.

Topolina, ever the most balanced of the group, steps up, "You have to see it from our side. What it sounds like is that if we put the flesh and bones on the line to defend your world, you'll add a few wizards to help give us extra weapons... but it's still flesh and bones that are being wagered... ours."

Laasper makes the most direct point, "I don't stand beside troops that haven't been bloodied. And I doubt my father would commit my people to do so either." After this, he turns and walks away.

Shan looks to Peter, in pure frustration.

Gran-D, who's been there the whole time, but unusually quiet... steps up and ushers Peter to the side.

"Despite your travels, if the walls fall we may have to prove ourselves before anyone will stand with us... you know what that means, don't you?"

"That we have to bleed," Peter says sadly. With no more enthusiasm, he adds, "Or they will have to bleed enough to accept any help offered."

Peter hates how coldly that came out.

"Or they simply join Goreipor to protect their people," says Gran-D, as a third, even less attractive outcome. He knows the implications of this... will Spirin surrender and be subjugated without a fight? Will the prophecy come true... only opposite to what he thought it would be?

Peter glances over Gran-D's shoulder at Jarium and Topolina. Jarium gives him a silent look that tells Peter Gran-D may very well be right.

Chapter Forty-Four

Rupert serves Witch Racinda a cup of tea. He's more than happy that Ramie is occupied with the Spirinese kids at the camp by the wall... word travels fast at the fortress. He's back, temporarily at least, to being her number one assistant... That is, when she's at the fortress.

There's a knock on the door.

Rupert goes to open it and finds Devon standing there.

"May I speak with Madame Racinda?" Devon says as politely as possible since their relationship hasn't been on an even keel. Devon has viewed her abilities as a threat to his future plans but, now with others in Goreipor with sorcerers' abilities, he has to rethink things. Perhaps consolidating and protecting those with talents is a wiser approach... and, besides, he needs some help at the moment.

Rupert looks to Racinda and she gestures to let Devon in; then a second gesture tells the assistant to leave. Rupert, concerned over her safety, hesitates.

"It's all right... I'm sure the young sorcerer isn't here to bring harm... he's more devious than that," says Racinda, resting her chin on her hands and turning to stare at Devon.

Rupert reluctantly leaves, closing the door behind him.

"I don't see you as a social person... so why am I graced with your visit," says Racinda, and to get her point across, she adds, "What do you want?"

"An alliance... we share a common interest," says Devon.

"And what might that be?" Racinda asks suspiciously.

"The children who were brought here from Spirin... though hardly children since none are under sixteen and, from what I gather, they are not at all innocent," explains Devon.

"This is an odd concern from the one who kidnapped Ramie." Racinda has no doubt Devon has ulterior motives.

"I never wanted Ramie harmed, and I'm pleased he's under your protection... but, do you think these others will be so lucky? Once they realize they're being used, if any choose to run away... will Kildemar hold back his wrath?" Devon asks.

She glares at him a second. "Though I seriously doubt the motives for your concern, I can assure you they have little chance of running away."

"I heard... You've conjured a spell that restricts our kind... that right?" He's getting down to the crux of it.

Racinda has no interest in dancing and suspects his true interests. "Careful how you use the words, '*our kind*'... What do you want with the spell?"

Devon actually prefers getting back to straight talk... it's simpler. "I will not use it in Spirin, you have my word. But yes, I do have a use for such a spell... and, I'm willing to trade for it." He figures, given time, he could create the spell on his own... but he doesn't have that time.

Although Racinda regards Devon's word as meaningless, she is curious as to what he offers other than a hollow word.

"What do you suggest trading?"

"I'm gaining influence with Lord Kildemar... granted slowly... and even though you doubt my word, I give it anyway... I will do all in my power to protect every kid he brought here," says Devon, trying to sound sincere. "I also have friends in the military... friends in the units where these kids will be assigned... the same military that has little regard for you."

She thinks this walks a fine line between offer and threat. "As for your word about the spell's use, it's unimportant since the spell can't be used within the borders of Spirin. It was another of my husband's crazy inventions that I immediately modified to present less of a threat when I was commanded to create a barrier. Does it still interest you?"

Assuming he is lying about not using it in Spirin, Racinda thinks this revelation will change his mind.

"It can't be changed... if you're still interested, I will hold you to your word about the children." She adds, "And by the way... the military may have little regard for me, but they fear me... That has equal weight."

"I am and I understand. You know... there may come a time when all of us with powers will need to work together," says Devon.

Witch Racinda views this suggestion as simply and inevitably trading one tyrant for another. She doesn't see Devon in charge of Goreipor's war machine as being much better than Kildemar.

Now that her arm healed enough for travel, Lonny is up and about. All together in the living room, she, her brother, Jarium and Topolina look forward to the prospect of going home. It's been quite an adventure but they long to see family and friends.

Atta is being her motherly self, making sure her guests have no shortage of tea and cookies.

Gran-D is being pleasant, attempting not to press them on issues regarding the Prophecy and alliances... even if both weigh heavily on his mind. He has to believe that these seemingly good neighbors can see through the differences between what Peter and Devon have to offer. Truth is, they have not encountered Devon or anyone from Goreipor, though their fathers probably have y now.

Peter enters the front door and asks if anyone has seen Shan.

After sufficient strong-arming, Shan has convinced him to take her along when he returns their visitors to their homes. Peter doesn't like the idea of the two best equipped to defend Spirin being out on the road together and thus doubly vulnerable to attack... but he has had little luck in convincing her of the danger involved.

Atta suddenly looks concerned, "I gave her a tug, nothing." Her concern is amplified by the loss of her other child.

Peter hasn't been worried since Shan is always late to things, but he sends out a tug... Nothing.

Gran-D does the same, with the same result.

Without another word Peter heads out the front door and streams away into smoke.

Peter materializes at the log by the Graveyard; his travel is too urgent to use a hoverboard. He immediately sees what he fears he might find, a note pinned to the shade tree with a razor disc... Devon's calling card.

Taking the note from the tree, Peter gives Gran-D a tug. The last thing Peter wants to do is announce its contents in front of Atta without warning. Perhaps the old man can ease the news... and Peter could use his counsel.

Gran-D materializes near Peter seconds later. Without a word Peter hands him the note.

"In your travels have you been to this land?" Gran-D asks. He only knows the Portal from the maps he's seen and that it's the only exceptionally small segment of the Sphere. He suspects that no people reside there... that it must have some other significance. Why would Devon have kidnapped his grand-daughter to that place instead of Goreipor?

"Lonny's broken arm cut our travels short before we got there," answers Peter. "He demands I come alone."

"Do you think there's any chance he'll be alone?" asks Gran-D.

Letting out a sigh, Peter says, "Doesn't really matter." With the next breath, he tries to make a plan, "I'll give Master Car-ringer the other pendant I found and he can take the others home. He can plead our case in my stead."

Gran-D chuckles, "That ought to be interesting... an orange lizard presenting what he thinks is a logical argument. I can come to stand at your side against Devon... I'm not that old."

"I appreciate the offer, and I know you're more powerful than either of us, but you'll be needed here," Peter says. He knows the old man has good intentions, but outside of theory, he has no idea what it means to fight.

Shan paces... or rather stomps, back and forth near one of the marble buildings at the temple on the mount of the Portal. Two guards patiently watch her. She has quickly discovered that powers of sorcery don't work here... otherwise she would have zapped Devon over and over again... twenty-fold.

Devon sports a bright red left cheek sore from her fury... probably the reason he's standing a fair distance away from her. Captain Pirus is at his side. Pirus holds back his smirk over the girl's tenacious attack on Devon.

"It's not going to take long before we're missed from Gor-eipor... you know that?" Pirus warns. "By the way, how did you get your hands on a pendant... I know neither Janick nor Kilde-mar would have released one."

Devon has to keep someone in his confidence, if only for nothing more than to foster loyalty. In truth, he also needs someone to bounce off of... going it totally alone doesn't feed his ego. Still, he knows to be judicious about what information he shares.

"I disappeared during the night when we were in Cretorn... and I found a worthwhile reward. I didn't see any reason to bring it up," Devon says with a sly smile. "If we're missed, it will not be assumed we are beyond the walls."

Satisfied, Pirus asks, "So there are other pendants out there?"

"I think there's one for each land, but probably better hidden than this one was... the savages had no idea what they had, so it was proudly or superstitiously displayed atop that pyramid... for all to see." At least Devon hopes the remaining ones are well hidden.

"So what's our play?" Captain Pirus asks. By *'our play'*, he's referring to the four personal guards he brought along on this mission. He figures Devon already knows what he wants from this move.

Devon thinks a second, as if he had not already decided. "Peter's as powerful as I am... and I fully plan to use that power in our future. This means he's not to be killed... If anyone comes with him and chooses to stand by his side... they are expendable."

"Including the girl?" Pirus asks.

With a glance over at Shan, "It would be much better not to have her harmed... but if necessary, including the girl."

Now that Lonny has vacated the space, Peter rummages thought a chest of his belongings up in the loft. After a couple of seconds he pulls out a rag-wrapped item. He carefully unwraps a 9mm and one clip.

It's the 9mm he brought from Earth when he rescued Devon from the quarantined zone... the 9mm that, when he tried to throw it into the Graveyard, the green mist spat back to him as though it knew he would need it someday. Slipping in the clip, he puts the gun in his belt and makes sure his shirt covers it.

He sits down on the bed to think about what's to come.

Shan carefully watches the two guards who have been assigned to her. The instant both glance the other direction at the same time, she makes a break for the edge of the temple mount.

One guard raises his crossbow but is waved down by Pirus.

Devon, without any sense of urgency, steps to the edge of the ridge. He holds up two small rock slabs hinged together like an open book. He closes the slabs together as if closing the book.

A short while later, Shan scrambles down the narrow path on the sheer side of the mountain and she finds her progress halted by a flat glowing plane extended out before her, like an Elizabethan collar placed around the top half of the mountain. It's just below the level where spells cease to work.

She comes up short and stares at the apparent barrier. Shan picks up a stone and throws it at the glow... the stone sparks.

Shan hears Devon's voice yell down from high above, "Shan, you can't leave. Should I send men down to fetch you or are you going to come back on your own?"

She thinks for a second, and then kicks the stones at her feet, and starts heading back up. She's not about to give him the satisfaction of seeing her manhandled back up to him.

As Peter comes down the stairs the mood in the Dees' house is far from jovial. Kalish is off to one side trying to console

Atta. He would prefer her angry mumbling rants to this depression she's now suffers... she has yet to adjust to Ramie's absence.

Carringer is over talking to Gran-D. He came at Peter's request, and would have showed up regardless, to offer his hand in any manner Peter might need since he knew this was the day Peter was returning the visitors.

Laasper is off in yet another corner arguing with Lonny... what it's about, Peter can't hear.

Jarium steps up to Peter at the bottom of the stairs. "When are we heading out to get that girl of yours?"

"I appreciate it, but we are not. Master Carringer is going to use my other pendant to help you get home. This is something I have to do alone," Peter says, trying not to sound insulting.

"Nonsense," Topolina declares. "From the impression I've gotten, this brother of yours is not going to be alone... and neither are you. This is not a matter of discussion."

Jarium smiles, "You heard the lady."

In the midst of their own arguing... Laasper trying to force Lonny to keep her arm in the healer's sling while she insists on pulling it out... the Capulians overhear their friends' dispute. Not to be left out, Laasper comes over, followed by a steaming Lonny.

Laasper takes a second to look away from her, "I'm in."

"So am I," demands Lonny.

"No... You're not!" Laasper declares.

She bristles. The hand of her uninjured left arm grabs at the handle of her sword. Her teeth can almost be heard grinding.

Laasper laughs, "You're not a lefty, sis. What use would you be in a fight, flailing a blade around with your left hand?"

Before Peter has a chance to present an argument to them, Carringer steps up, "I should be going as well."

Breaking away from Kalish, Atta surprises them all and storms over to the group at the bottom of the stairs.

"Enough! Peter, you're going to get my daughter, and your friends are going with you to help... all but Lonny, who is staying here till her arm heals. I don't trust that brother of yours... and I will not tolerate you getting killed... And, Carringer, you wouldn't know how to fight your way out of a bag... so you stay."

Everyone steps back, stunned.

Kalish and Gran-D simply break out laughing.

Chapter Forty-Five

The swirl of the Sorcerer's Door once again appears in the air and Peter, Jarium, Topolina and Laasper jump out at the base of the Portal's mountain. All are armed, though Peter has yet to expose the gun he carries in his belt.

This is the first Peter has seen of this land and its central mountain. He glances around and sees that it appears to be bounded, at roughly the same distance, by the outer walls. He immediately realizes that what's important in this land lies at the peak of the mountain and instantly senses that Devon is up there, too.

To get the lay of the land Peter generates a spy globe. The image within it follows the steep cliffs only about half way up before it goes blind... This puzzles Peter.

"Don't go using any of your tricks to go up on your own," warns Jarium in a friendly manner.

Peter reluctantly nods that he understands. He knows to do any different would offend the warriors who have chosen to stand at his side. He hates the responsibility... he wonders how he would handle the responsibility for a war if it were to come?

Resolved that they all go together, all start up the narrow mountain path.

Atop the mountain Devon glances over the edge, well aware of Peter's approach. He opens the small stone tablets, breaking the glowing barrier well before Peter comes upon it. It was never meant to keep Peter out.

Shan sits in the background, well-guarded and with a gag over her mouth. Apparently Devon has grown tired of her insults. All she longs for now is a sword in her hands.

Seeing movement below, Captain Pirus gestures for his men to come to the ready. Regardless of what Devon says, he doubts that Peter will come alone.

Remaining near the edge, Devon waits to see that Peter, and whoever might be with him, reach the upper half of the mountain... then he closes the barrier spell. Once this is done, Devon backs into the center of the temple's altar stone.

Pirus' men fan out. The soldier with a tight hold on Shan stays near Devon there in the center. His greater bulk only barely contains Shan's constant and strenuous squirming.

Peter comes over the edge of the mountain followed by his three friends. Once on the ridge, he immediately sees Shan... and Devon, and his support team.

Although outnumbered, Jarium, Topolina and Laasper fan out to cover their counterparts....

"I thought I said come alone," Devon says loudly.

Peter waves his hand at the four men backing Devon's play.

"I didn't say I would," quips Devon.

It falls on deaf ears.

Peter says, "I'm not here to play your game... I came to get Shan, plain and simple."

"There's nothing plain and simple about any of this. You're trying to rally the lands to stand against me," says Devon, nodding towards the three backing Peter.

"And you're not doing the same?" responds Peter.

While this banter goes on it's clear that the combatants on both sides are getting antsy with tension.

"And tell me you didn't set this up to kill me... and Shan," adds Peter.

"No, big brother, I don't want to kill ya... Maybe I did at one point... but now all I want to do is control you. I want to keep you safe till you see things my way," says Devon, believing his own bull. "I don't even want to kill Shan... though I suspect the feeling is not mutual."

The air is thick with tension; while these two stand around yammering and the rest stare each other down... it's like a gunfight with no count to the draw. Who's going to blink first?

Devon glances at Jarium and back to Peter, "You don't even know what they're doing out there... Did he tell you that Acculas has a whole other population that your friends have forced into prison camps?" Then he looks at Laasper, "And his land has caved to us at the first threat."

"Enough!" yells Laasper.

Though Laasper has not raised his weapon, his loud outburst is enough to ignite the tension already poised on a fragile hair trigger.

Bows are leveled; swords are drawn... Chaos ensues...

One of Pirus' soldiers lets fly the first arrow at Topolina. She sidesteps it...

Shan slams her heel down on the instep of the soldier holding her. As he falters, she grabs a stone with lightning, non-magic speed, spins and strikes his head with it. He topples and she grabs the sword from his belt...

Jarium sends a lance flying at the man who shot at Topolina... the soldier jolts back violently as the lance strikes home...

Everyone jerks and dashes in and around the temple in a heated frenzy...

Out of nowhere an arrow plunges into Jarium's side. He stumbles back against a rock...

Devon releases his first blow, but not at Peter. He shoots a razor disc flying at Laasper, striking him down...

It's out of his hands now; Peter has no choice but to fight. He reaches into his belt and withdraws the 9mm...

Topolina slings a knife at Devon, but only nicks his shoulder...

Peter has a bead on Devon, but he hesitates. Suddenly seeing a soldier level his bow towards Topolina, he pivots his aim and fires... the round slams the soldier back...

More comfortable with close combat, Pirus draws his sword, charging Jarium who has regained his footing...

Topolina moves to intervene but an arrow strikes her in the leg...

With his sword in her hands, Shan parries against the lance of the soldier she has taken it from. She musters a valiant defense but she's driven back by his repeated and skilled swings...

Peter once again sights Devon when Shan screams... he swivels his handgun towards her attacker and fires a second round...

It creases the soldier's cheek and the man breaks off his attack on Shan to charge Peter... who fires again and misses completely...

While Pirus and Jarium match swords, blow for blow... the man charging Peter knocks the 9mm to the ground with his lance.

Just as he's about to thrust the tip of his lance into Peter, Devon spins and unleashes another razor disc... it strikes down his own man...

Pirus roundhouses a swing that cuts into Jarium's arm... Suddenly a grappling talon jerks Pirus's shoulder back... It's the flying bird Topolina...

Releasing Pirus, Topolina withdraws and dives in again. She snatches the wounded Jarium up in her claws and swoops with him into the air...

A soldier releases a bolt that misses her as she struggles to fly while carrying Jarium over the side of the mountain...

Peter frantically glances around for his gun... seeing nothing, he unsheathes his sword and charges Pirus...

"Enough!" yells Devon.

Peter looks over to see Devon kneeling over Shan with the tip of his knife at her neck. A trickle of blood drips down on her blouse.

Breaking off his charge, Peter stoops over, out of breath... He drops his sword... it clangs against the stony ground. He lifts his head and surveys the carnage.

Laasper lies motionless with a razor disc in his chest. Topolina and Jarium are nowhere to be seen... perhaps they have met their fate on the rocks far below.

Peter's alone... and defeated.

Sure that Peter is done, Devon takes his blade away from Shan's neck.

Captain Pirus rubs at the bloody claw marks on his shoulder. He pans around... two of his four soldiers lie dead, and the other two are wounded. He walks over and kicks Peter's sword away, lest he change his mind.

At Devon's gesture, the more lightly wounded soldier comes over to hold a sword on Shan.

Devon then gets up and walks towards Peter. On his way he notices the gun in a crevice and reaches down to pick it up.

Waving it triumphantly, he says, "This is the one you wouldn't allow me to bring from Earth... I had no idea. I guess it's come full circle back to my hand... where it belongs."

Peter's still a bit out of breath from the skirmish... perhaps more from losing it.

He finally lifts his head, "Now what, little brother?"

"Now nothing... you're alive, as I wanted... and you will stay alive, safely stashed here."

Devon points to one of the five buildings surrounding the large center altar. "Within that structure are supplies enough to sustain you and your girlfriend for some time."

"You're just going to abandon us here?" Peter asks.

Devon leans down to Peter and snatches the pendant from around his neck.

"The alternative my Lordship had in mind was somewhat more permanent." Stepping away, he adds, "You can thank me later."

"For my friends' deaths?" Peter says with anger mounting.

"That's on you. You're friends died because they followed you... not because of me," Devon crows self-righteously.

Peter doesn't respond... as he sits there he knows Devon is partially right. Devon clearly has no intention to kill him... if Peter had held his ground and come alone, three others would still be alive.

Devon quickly tires of seeing Peter beating himself up... it's time to move on.

"The next time you see me will be when I bring down the walls... by then our forces will either occupy the lands or be perched ready to take over. By that point, I trust you'll be prepared to join me."

He gestures for Pirus to gather up their men, alive and dead.

He turns back to Peter, "As you've guessed, your powers are of no use up here, so don't waste your time. Enjoy it... I'm leaving you with a girl... and a temple."

"You can't do this!" protests Shan.

"Quiet or I'll just leave him with a temple," says Devon.

Again turning back to Peter, "Just thought you oughta know... there's a barrier half way down the mountain. Even if you could get to the bottom, without this," holding out the pendant, "you aren't going anywhere... and I'd prefer you don't set up any surprises below."

Pirus, his wounded men and their fallen comrades are already near the edge, prepared to leave the mountain.

With one last look at Peter, Devon simply says, "Take care, big brother... till we meet again." He joins his team.

Shan jumps up and runs to Peter... but she can't help glancing down at the dead Laasper as she goes past him.

Before Devon and Pirus head over the edge, Pirus glances at the 9mm in Devon's belt and asks, "What's this strange weapon?"

Glancing down, and quickly covering the gun with his shirt, Devon answers, "Oh... just another one of those spells we have in Spirin... sorcerer stuff."

Captain Pirus knows he's lying.

About a half hour later, Peter and Shan sit on a stone looking around at the temple where they have been marooned. Surprised, they hear stones tumbling beyond the edge of the mount. Though neither has much fight left in them, they grab for the few weapons overlooked and left behind by Devon's team.

They ready themselves for a second bout.

Limping, Topolina helps Jarium up to the plateau. Both are injured, but alive. Peter and Shan rush to help them.

"I thought we lost you," Peter says with some relief.

"Almost," grumbles Jarium with some strain. He bleeds from his arm and another deep wound in his side.

Topolina glances all around, "Laasper?"

"He didn't make it," Shan quietly says, nodding towards his body.

"It's my fault," mumbles Peter.

"That's not your blade in his chest... we don't have time for your whining about field decisions," Jarium snaps.

"Time is what we have... they took Peter's pendant," Shan whispers.

Wishing to change the subject, Topolina looks out on the temple, "What is this this place anyway? It looks like a gigantic version of that pendant."

Peter has not paid much attention to the Portal with all that has taken place since arriving. Jarium is right; there's no use wasting time whining... he stands up and takes a good long look at their new home.

She's right... it does appear to be a fifty foot diameter stone version of the pendant. He thinks, '*If only it could be dialed,*' but clearly it's not meant to do so. He notices that, unlike the working pendants, there is only one ring of symbols and a small pedestal at the head of each just outside the ring. What the significance of the five marble buildings around the altar stone is a mystery.

Shan has slipped away while the others ponder this.

A short while later, she emerges from one of the buildings carrying a pitcher of water and some fabric.

Approaching the others, Shan says, "Solve the mysteries of the world some other time... now's time for dressing wounds."

Chapter Forty-Six

S ince they have plenty of time on their hands, Peter uses part of it to explore the five buildings to try and make some sense of the Portal's significance.

Clearly it means something to the Sphere... and to Devon. Somehow he knows it's the key to lowering the walls. He also knows Devon isn't sharing that information with the people in Goreipor... at least not yet. He remembers Devon's words, *'Next time you see me will be when I bring down the walls,'* and knows this must be where the walls start theira fall.

So far Peter has recognized that there is one marble building for each of the inhabited lands on the Sphere. This has been easy since, once he brushed the muck accumulated by age on the arches over the doors, he found a symbol for each land. That's where the easy part ends.

Inside each building, the walls are etched with writing Peter can't decipher. He has gotten used to both vocabulary and writings being magically universal in the other lands... no such case exists here. Even with auto-translation, the characters do not resemble any he has seen in the other lands. He wonders if he could decipher this with the aid of the green mist in the Graveyard of Spells. It doesn't matter; the green mist is in Spirin... and he's not.

Besides the writings on the walls, there's nothing else of possible importance in the buildings other than a round pedestal in the center of each. He detects no seams in the pedestals so they don't appear to house any further secrets... Across the universe, though, he's come to accept that appearances can be deceiving.

Peter comes out of the last building, no closer to solving the riddle than he was going into the first.

From the blankets, bread baskets and water jugs strewn around the temple area it's clear that the Goreiporians had been there for at least one night before they came. The weather in the land of the Portal is temperate and Peter sees that camping will only be a strain to the nerves.

Laasper's body had been put in one of the buildings.

The wounds Topolina and Jarium suffered are dressed and healing as well as possible.

Shan has gathered up all the weapons left from the battle, in case they might be needed.

Time is now their biggest foe, but Peter doesn't seem too upset by this.

Suddenly the sounds of tumbling rocks arise from somewhere down below. Shan and Topolina scramble to arm themselves.

"Should I try and fly out?" Topolina whispers.

"No need," Peter assures her. He walks towards the edge of the plateau.

Shan and Topolina huddle by Jarium... all are armed and ready. Peter waves for them to stand down.

More rocks are kicked loose by whatever or whomever is coming.

Finally, Master Carringer stumbles up and over the edge, tripping at least twice in the last few steps. He's clearly not a mountaineer. Being more agile, Lonny follows him, no doubt to steady him when necessary during the climb.

"Hi all, sorry it took me so long to get here," Carringer says with a big smile on his face. His smile fades when he sees the bloodied clothes and bandages on Topolina and Jarium.

Peter greets them, "Not to worry... I hoped you'd make it."

Shan drops her weapon and runs to Master Carringer... she gives him a big hug. She turns to Peter, angrily saying, "Why didn't you tell us?"

"Because I wasn't sure he could get up the mountain... we might have had to come up with our own solution," he responds. Realizing that he is becoming just as manipulative as Gran-D, he adds, "I'm sorry."

Lonny stares at the group, as though she knows what's coming. Before says a thing, she asks, "Where is he?"

Peter steps forward, ready to bear the weight on his shoulders, but Shan steps past him and says, "I'll take you to him."

She leads off towards one of the buildings... Lonny follows her silently.

Topolina watches them walk. She's glad they had removed the disc from his chest and cleaned the blood away as best they could... but no decoration can hide death.

All remain silent.

After a couple of minutes, Lonny and Shan emerge from the building in which Laasper lies.

Lonny shows little emotion as she comes to Peter.

Peter doesn't know what to say other than, "He died fighting at our side. We all owe him... and I owe you."

With no warning, Lonny slaps Peter across the face.

"He died for you and your imaginary war... you've done enough." She storms off towards the edge of the mountain.

Peter starts to follow her but Shan grabs his arm. "Leave her be for now... excuses can come later."

Everyone takes a deep breath, knowing Shan is right. Everyone needs to deal with loss in his or her own way, and now Lonny needs silence. She has no need for explanations of the *bigger picture*.

Peter will have to live with his guilt... he will get no absolution from her nor does he expect any.

Coming back to the immediate situation, Peter turns to Carringer and sees the pendant he found in Capulia hanging around the Master's neck.

Also knowing to keep moving forward, Shan asks Carringer, "How did you get beyond the barrier Devon placed around the mountain?" Having explored the full circumference of the mountain, hoping to find a break, she found none.

As if it's nothing at all, Carringer says, "Oh... I recognized my father's signature on the spell... once I knew its origin, it was easy enough for me to manipulate it... but I wonder how my father's mark got on it?"

Peter keeps throwing concerned glances over towards Lonny until Topolina comes to his side, "She's a warrior, not a jumper... I know her as I know myself. The best you can do is focus on the problems at hand so his life will not have been wasted... that's how you work off the guilt."

"Welcome to just a fraction of what a war will be like. A war you think you want," says Jarium.

If anything causes Peter to question the Prophecy that Gran-D regards as inevitable, this moment does. Shan steps up beside him and takes his hand.

Chapter Forty-Seven

Epilogue

Devon stands on a rocky ridge overlooking the growing encampment established not far from the wall. He watches the dozen young people from Spirin being trained by the military far below... or it's perhaps the other way around. He doesn't bother turning when he hears footsteps behind him.

"Those kids are downright spooky," Captain Pirus states as he steps beside Devon. "They're coming up with ways to use your hocus-pocus that even I find scary. Maybe I'm just an old soldier who only understands a straight up fight."

"Times are changing," is all Devon says.

They both stand there quietly watching a possible future.

Down below, in the encampment, Yadar yells to the soldiers who stand behind him, "Close on me."

About fifty yards ahead of Yadar, a platoon of soldiers serves as the training opposition. Yadar marches forward, raising his hands in front of him and then spreading them apart as he walks. A translucent double-wall wedge forms in front of him and his men, like a snowplow but much higher.

The opposing soldiers fire-blunted arrows all ricochet off the protective barrier moving forward with Yadar.

Above, Pirus comments, "Almost takes the fun out of the fighting."

"So far they're only willing to support the fighting... none of their spells go in for the kill," says Devon. He glances over at Pirus, "Your fun is not yet at jeopardy."

"I'm sure Lord Kildemar will train that out of them," Pirus responds.

Witch Racinda comes out of a tent in the camp, followed by Ramie. From Devon's vantage point, it's clear she's trying to oversee the training... as much as Taligarr allows.

Pirus says, "I got the impression she was against the use of these kids."

"She developed a bad case of mother-hen syndrome... that may be why the kids are holding back. She may have to go," Devon says with the coldness that has been steadily growing in him.

"Think your brother is still on that mountain?" Pirus asks.

Devon glances at him, "I hope so, but he has a nasty knack of surprising me... at least I'm trying to keep him alive."

"By the way, with all these new wizards, if you've figured out how to lower the walls, I'd keep it to yourself... for a while," Captain Pirus advises.

Irritated, Devon mutters, "For the last time... I'm a sorcerer, not a wizard... and thanks."

The encampment by the wall is not the only sign of expansion that can be seen in Goreipor. Larger camps have been formed just outside Lord Kildemar's fortress to accommodate the companies of soldiers he's called in from the field.

Looking out on his growing army, Kildemar stands with Taligarr and Janick on the fortress battlement. For a scarred, claw-handed warrior of old like Kildemar, it's a warm sight. He has vanquished most of his internal enemies and welcomes the possibility of Devon collapsing the walls. He plans to deploy even if the walls don't fall... if need be, they will go in waves through the door.

Taligarr welcomes the challenge of leading, while his brother, Janick, just looks forward to the thrill of letting his violent side go unbridled. Father and sons all relish the prospect of war.

After this silence in which each sees what he looks for, Taligarr says, "The boy, Devon, sees himself with power... he could become a problem."

"Then... once he brings the walls down, Janick might have to take his head... We now have other little witches," says Lord Kildemar without taking his gaze off his troops.

Janick smiles. He has never taken to Devon.

The green mist confined in the Graveyard of Spells is especially active tonight... it bubbles as if boiling.

Gran-D says, "It seems to sense the turmoil we face."

Peter reaches his hand over to the ornate fence and a finger of mist comes up to touch him.

"I wish I spoke the mist's language, it seems to have answers... but it only speaks when it wants to."

"Now that your friends are almost healed, I think Carringer... or I should escort them home," says Gran-D.

He doesn't have much hope Peter will listen, but Laasper's death weighs heavily on the boy's soul and he could use a respite.

"What friends? I've managed to alienate two lands," Peter says morosely. Still caressing the finger of mist and looking off into the Graveyard, Peter says, "You know I have to take them... I have to answer for what came down."

"What you have to do is win them back," Gran-D tells him.

After giving that a second to sink in, he says, "I'm going to head back home... you coming?"

"Nah, I'm going to stay here for a while… maybe this damn mist will have something to say," Peter quips. He doubts it, but facing Lonny has become increasingly uncomfortable.

A couple of seconds after Gran-D disappears Shan materializes next to Peter.

"I thought he would never leave. He out here trying to have you let Carringer take them home?"

"Yep… Told him I had to do it," answers Peter.

"We have to do it. Remember, it was my tail that was being saved… it's part on me," she says with determination.

Peter glances at her.

"The training's no longer a secret… some hate it, some don't… Carringer can work with the ones who still want it. You need someone to have your back again, so it's not a request," says Shan. She knows that even if he doesn't need a fighting partner, he does need an emotional one.

"We lost the support of those lands you're so anxious to visit," Peter warns her.

"We'll win them back," is all she says in response.

Peter has learned when it's a waste of time to argue with her and he peers back into the Graveyard.

He says distantly, "That's what Gran-D said… I don't know if he's trying to protect us, or his precious Prophecy… I'm not sure we deserve to win them back."

Storm clouds form high above the temple in the middle of the Portal, very odd for that land of temperate weather. The clouds open up and a beam of white light shoots down and strikes the enlarged jewel in the center of the gigantic pendant-like altar stone.

Instead of being a solid beam, though, the energy itself that somehow forms the beam is broken down. Sputtering like

Morse code, the beam strives to remain congealed and whole, but it can't. Maybe it comes from too far away... or too long ago.

During one of the beam's longer dashes, a faint light is emitted from each of the doorways of the five small marble buildings. The lights are accompanied by wisps of green mist barely drifting out.

The beam sputters again... then dies completely. The beam, the jewel and the doorways go dark.

THE END

9 780099 613753 9